Di Morrissey is Australia's leading lady of fiction. She planned on writing books from age seven, growing up at Pittwater in Sydney. She quickly realised you don't leave school and become a novelist. Di trained as a journalist, worked as a women's editor in Fleet Street, London, married a US diplomat and in between travelling to diplomatic posts and raising daughter Gabrielle and son Nicolas, she worked as an advertising copywriter, TV presenter, radio broadcaster and appeared on TV and stage. She returned to Australia to work in television and published her first novel, *Heart of the Dreaming*, in 1991. *The Reef* is her thirteenth novel.

Di lives in Byron Bay, New South Wales, Australia, when not travelling to research her novels, which are all inspired by a specific landscape.

Di Morrissey can be visited at her website:
www.dimorrissey.com

THE
REEF

DI MORRISSEY

PAN
Pan Macmillan Australia

First published 2004 in Macmillan by Pan Macmillan Australia Pty Limited
This Pan edition published 2005 by Pan Macmillan Australia Pty Ltd
1 Market Street, Sydney

Reprinted 2006, 2007

National Library of Australia
cataloguing-in-publication data:

Morrissey, Di.
The reef.

ISBN 978 0 330 42215 4.

1. Great Barrier Reef (Qld.) – Fiction. I. Title.

A823.3

Typeset in 11/13pt Sabon by Post Pre-press Group
Printed in Australia by McPherson's Printing Group

Internal illustrations: Ron Revitt and Pauline Jonoch

Papers used by Pan Macmillan Australia Pty Ltd are natural, recyclable
products made from wood grown in sustainable forests. The manufacturing
processes conform to the environmental regulations of the country of origin.

To all those who work to save the sea

Acknowledgments

For all the women in my family, my women friends and mentors over the years – thank you. I hope I lived up to expectations.

And special love to my mother Kay and my own bella daughter Gabrielle. You're both an inspiration!

To darling Boris, whose love and support makes my life easier and happier. (And we share the delight of Bunya.)

My son Nick for his love, wisdom and gentle humour.

And for everyone at Pan Macmillan, including my publisher the intrepid James Fraser, my editor the gorgeous Nikki Christer, and good road buddy and publicist, the indomitable Jane Novak.

Thank you Ian Robertson for being the sweet old-fashioned lawyer (!) and good mate that you are.

For Rosemary and Jim Revitt. Jim continues to be my biggest mentor since I was a little girl.

Thanks Ron Revitt for the drawings and for being more big brother than Uncle.

A huge thank you to Southern Cross University – especially Professor Peter Harrison, Director Marine Studies and Director SCU Whale Research Centre, for all he taught me on Heron Island and his patient corrections. And David Lloyd, School of Environmental Science and Executive Officer SCU Whale Research Centre (of which I'm proud to be Patron). Also thank you Dr David Miller for medical and nautical advice while we played tennis. And special thanks to Liz Adams for being a great sounding board!

DM

I

Country Victoria, 1980

The Seventh Wave

JENNIFER WATCHED HER MOTHER stow their holiday necessities in the small caravan, making sure her favourite doll, colouring book and pencils were put in the box with her brother's fishing rod, books and the snap cards.

Christina Campbell pushed the box under the bench seat alongside the dropside table. 'There, now you know where your and Teddy's things are kept.'

'Can I have Daisy back now? It's dark in there.'

Christina smiled at her anxious five-year-old daughter. 'She'll be fine, she's asleep. Daddy wants everything we're taking packed in the caravan by tonight. You don't want to leave Daisy doll behind, do you?'

'Where's my bucket and spade?'

'It's in, darling, we won't forget anything.' Christina hoped she was right. The caravan, though old and travel-weary, was a new acquisition for the family and this would be their first real camping holiday. Most important of all, they were going to the seaside. A first. It would be a welcome diversion from their daily struggle on the farm, battling drought and low stock prices with the bank manager hovering. Christina thought again how her husband Roger had surprised them all with the caravan.

He'd towed it home one afternoon after being away for two days trying to placate the bank manager, going to the cattle sales and talking to other farmers in the same boat as they were. She worried about him spending money on something as unnecessary as a caravan, never believing they'd take it away for a proper holiday. But, for the first time in many months, Roger looked cheerful.

'Rolly Blake was practically giving it away. Now his wife's gone and the kids want to sell up he figured they'd have no use for it. And you know what, love, things could get a bloody sight worse than they are now judging from what I heard in town. So I reckon we should give the kids, all of us, a bit of a break. God knows when we'll be able to go again.'

Or when we last did, Christina thought, but

she merely opened the door to see what the van was like inside. The kids had come running, and jumped around in delight at the little house on wheels. And Christina had to admit it looked very practical; indeed, well laid out. A woman's hand was evident in the interior. She glanced back at her beaming husband. 'It's very serviceable. Where would we take it? Surely not far?'

'I've figured it out. Bernie Allen next door is going to come in and mind the farm so I reckon if we sell that old bull we'll have enough to go right across to the coast.'

Their seven-year-old son Teddy yelped at this. 'You mean the seaside, Dad? We can go fishing!'

'You bet. No more trying to find a yellow belly in our dam. We'll fish for the big ones in the ocean.'

Driving to the coast was an adventure, for they got to spend two nights in the caravan. The children wanted to travel in the caravan as they drove but had to content themselves with bouncing in the back seat of the car, pestering their father.

'Are we nearly there yet?'

'How much longer?'

'I want my bucket an' spade.'

The caravan park faced the strip of beach through shady she-oaks. The headland on the south jutted into the ocean and white-tipped waves crashed on rocks at its base. A tidy light-house sat on top. At the northern end of the beach flat rocks were exposed at low tide, filled with rock pools and small channels. Waves lapped over the edge of the rocks and high dunes rose beyond the sand.

The Campbell family were welcomed into the tight-knit caravan community. Most were old hands who went there every year, so the family were quickly initiated into the customs and methods of caravaning. The children had playmates, the men drank beer and yarned, while the women discussed shortcuts in preparing meals and daily chores. Christina, 'Call me Tina, Roger does', had been shy at first. Most of the women in the park were from city suburbs or small towns and not an isolated farm. It made Christina realise how starved she was of female company.

The family tended to keep to themselves for most of the day, coming back to the caravan with its awning over the table for lunch. Christina indulged in the rare pleasure of an afternoon nap while Roger took the children to the beach for several hours. Evenings were sociable times with games and occasional meals shared with neighbouring campers.

Teddy and Jennifer loved the beach, although they didn't venture into the sea. Jennifer couldn't swim at all and Teddy had only had a couple of sessions at the community pool in town. And town was too far away for regular lessons.

There was a small pool in the grounds of the

motel next door to the caravan park and one of the parents in a neighbouring caravan offered to teach Teddy to swim 'in no time flat'.

Teddy wanted to catch a big fish. His father had put a new reel on his old rod and now knew the best kind of bait to use. Several of the men had brought back fish they'd caught off the beach and there had been a big communal fry-up of whiting fillets. Teddy wanted he and his dad to catch a bigger fish, like a blackfish or a cod, and so Roger promised to take him to the rock ledge at low tide the following afternoon.

'Coming, luv? Sit under the umbrella and watch us bring in a big one for dinner?'

Christina shook her head. She looked forward to the luxury of lying on the plastic lounge with a paperback Deadwood Dick while Roger entertained the children. 'Jenny . . . put your sunhat on. You too, Teddy.'

'Aw Mum, I've got zinc on my nose. That's enough. My hat'll blow off or something.'

'He'll be right. Now, you got your bucket and spade, Jennifer? You got the bait, Teddy? Then we're all set. See you later, Tina.'

'Have a good time. You be a good girl, Jennifer. Don't you wander off. Keep an eye on her, Roger.'

'Tina, she's happy as can be making castles and emptying the rock pools into her bucket. You have a nice relax.'

'You sure you don't mind?' said Christina. Roger had offered to take her lounge chair down onto the sand with the beach umbrella, but Christina found it too hot and glary. She liked the time on her own outside the caravan where she could get a cool drink or make a cup of tea. Sometimes she had a cigarette and a pot of tea with the woman in the next caravan. In the heat of the afternoon it was quiet around the park and Christina enjoyed having time to herself for once, with no pressing jobs at the house or farm, or children demanding attention. She wanted to make the most of this two-week respite before returning to . . . she hated to think.

She sighed and dropped her book in her lap and closed her eyes. Why was her life so damned hard? She was so naive when she got married. God, if she'd known this was how her life would be . . . Her mother's pursed lips and disapproving expression flashed into her mind. Roger Campbell hadn't been deemed 'good enough'. But who was her mother to have airs and graces? Christina's father was a hardworking, heavy-drinking panel beater barely able to provide more than the basic wage for his family.

Christina didn't want to marry any of the sons of her father's friends or those in their small suburban social network. A chance meeting with a boy from the bush seemed like an escape route. Little did she know. Still, eventually she and Roger had managed to scrape together enough to buy their own small property.

She'd make damned sure her daughter did better. She wanted Jennifer to have a good job, something she could fall back on if she needed. Like teaching, nursing, working in a bank. Christina didn't trust, or like, men much. They couldn't be relied on to live up to their promises. She'd watched her father wear her mother down, so many women friends had talked about their disappointments in marriages, and Roger hadn't turned out to be the success she'd hoped. Maybe she wanted too much. Roger did accuse her of never being satisfied with her lot. If she had a career, a job of some kind, maybe things would be different. But what could she do? She had two young kids and was a farmer's wife on a dying farm.

Tina stubbed out her cigarette. Well, she'd have to make the best of it for now. Once the kids were older and when the farm had, hopefully, come good, then her life might change for the better.

To Roger the coast was a world free of cares. Free from the endless round of jobs to be done, the gut-wrenching sight of thin cattle, scrappy feed and near-empty dams. Of constantly feeling tired and depressed but putting on a brave show for his cheerful and eager children while a weary Christina wore a tight, unhappy face.

Here he felt like a kid again. He and Teddy talked at length about rigging their lines, casting, and how they'd land their big catch. He kept glan cing back to Jennifer, who was totally absorbed in paddling and peering into the rock pools, finding small shells, seaweed and pretty rocks to put in her bucket of water. She was an independent little thing, he thought, fondly. She'll be all right in this world. He just hoped Tina wouldn't lay all her ambitions on Jennifer and try to live the life she never had through their daughter.

He knew they were having a tough time financially, and it had drained them both of all feelings. They went through the motions, but the closeness, the affection, the friendship, weren't there. Had they ever been, he wondered with a flash of insight. He knew how Tina felt and it made him feel more inadequate and sad. She'd known what he was, what he'd aspired to do – own and run his own farm – and he'd done that. His mother had told him to marry a girl off the land, they knew what they were in for. A girl from the outer suburbs of a big city wouldn't last when they hit the inevitable tough times that were part of country life. Well, at least Tina was sticking by him.

He tried not to listen to a niggling voice in the back of his head that questioned their staying together. Maybe they'd be better off going their own ways. If it wasn't for the kids. They were the glue that held them together. And Roger adored his kids – the thought of not being with them every day was anathema to him. As his mum said, for better or worse, you made your bed, you sleep in it.

His musings had distracted him and he glanced at his son concentrating and fiddling with his reel before he turned to check on Jennifer. She wasn't there.

He felt the bile rise in his throat and he took a step back and then saw her small figure, her sun-hat blown off and caught at the back of her head by the elastic band, as she crouched over the pool at the edge of the rocks. She'd obviously followed the small channel to the edge of the sea, fascinated by the life in the flowing underwater highway. But she was too close to where the waves came onto the rock ledge.

He turned away and shouted past Teddy, 'Jennifer! Jennifer . . . go back to the beach. You're too close to the . . .'

Teddy turned and looked at where Jennifer was crouched, so none of them saw the looming large and unexpected wave.

They say it's every seventh wave. But who was counting. This swollen wall of water must have been waiting, gathering the ocean volume into its breast so that it was full, robust and consuming. In a charged rush it flushed itself up and over the rocks in a release of foaming energy that swept all before it. Roger was bowled over and staggered backwards, helplessly reaching, grasping, straining towards the disappearing figure of his son. Both were swirled beneath the churning white water and bumped off the ledge.

Jennifer hadn't seen it coming either. She'd lifted her head at the sound of her father's voice, then her world was turned upside down. She didn't understand what had happened. She closed her eyes in fright as she felt herself being tumbled off-balance, felt something hard against her leg, a roaring in her ears.

Was she floating? Flying? She opened her eyes. All was silent and calm around her. She was suspended in a blue void. Was that sunlight ahead? A small bright red and green shape buzzed past her. She turned her head. It was a beautiful little fish. A very busy fish that darted down to where a lacy pink and purple carpet was spread. Slowly she saw other movement: the gentle sway of a long necklace of green seaweed, the pulsing dance of a cluster of translucent lavender anemones hiding a hovering tiny orange and black fish. Bubbles floated past.

'I'm under the water,' thought Jennifer. 'I'm in the city of the sea!' She'd been imagining the channel in the rocks as being like a busy road leading to some magic place – and here it was. She moved an arm, kicked a leg and found she could move effortlessly in this strange world. She stretched out her arms and felt herself moving upward. The blue shimmered with golden arcs like wheat fields.

But then a great black shape shot in front of her and lunged at her in a hiss of bubbles and she felt herself grabbed and forced up towards the light. In a panic she tried to fight off whatever was holding her, but suddenly she was thrust out of the beautiful world to crash through the surface of the ocean. There was a watery, wavy image on the rock ledge, a man waving and shouting something. Was it Dad?

She turned and saw she was being propelled forward by a strange man dressed all in black rubber from his head to his big flippers. Only his frightened white face showed. He was saying something. All she could hear was the ocean surging against the rocks. Then hands pulled her out onto the rocks and the strange sea man clambered after her, stumbling in his big, flippered feet.

'We got her!' And she was lifted and the man who had been standing on the rocks began carrying her back to the beach in staggering slipping haste.

Jennifer struggled, the enormity of what had happened slowly dawning. 'Where's my daddy? Where's Teddy? I want Teddy!'

There were people all around now but the man wouldn't let her go as he clutched her face to his shirt, shouting towards the beach, 'Is he all right? Where's the boy?' And then her father was lying in the sand, sodden without his hat or his sandals. But he turned and sat up, coughing and rubbing his face. The stranger lowered her to the sand and she ran to her father.

'Daddy . . .'

He clutched her, making strange crying noises Jennifer had never heard before.

She rubbed her hand over his wet hair. 'Don't cry, Daddy.' He held on to her, clinging to her as people stood around staring at them. Awkwardly, she turned around, calling, 'Teddy . . . Teddy . . . where's Teddy?'

People were grabbing at her again, pulling her away from her father, helping him to stand, leading him away from the beach. Jennifer wrenched her hand from the stranger's grasp and ran back towards the rocks calling, 'Teddy . . . Where are you, Teddy?'

They caught and forcibly carried her away as she kicked her legs and began howling, 'I want Teddy.'

'It's her brother,' she heard someone say.

And then there was a siren and more people and she was put in a car.

They were in a doctor's room. Jennifer was sitting on the edge of a flat hard bed, a lady dabbing at scratches along her legs. She had tears running down her cheeks and Jennifer wondered why she was crying. It was *her* scratched legs that stung.

She was led outside and was shocked to see her mother slumped in a chair, her arms wrapped around her body, her head bowed, her shoulders heaving from the sobs that racked her body. Her father was standing beside her, a blanket over his damp shoulders. His face looked grey and ill. Jennifer ran to him but he moved her away. 'Go to your mother.'

Jennifer was frightened to see her mother like this. 'Is Mummy sick?'

Her mother reached out, her eyes squeezed shut, an arm blindly pawing the air as if to retrieve the hour before when her family was intact. 'Jennifer . . .' Her voice was harsh, hoarse, and Jennifer took a step backwards, fearful she had done something wrong.

'The mother's had an injection, better give a sedative to the father. The people next door have offered to keep the girl till . . . they find him,' someone said.

A great pain shot through Jennifer, burning the soles of her feet as it roared all the way up her small body to the top of her head, and she heard again the raging cry of the ocean on the rocks. She knew Teddy was still out there, wrenched from her. 'Teddy!' she screamed.

They held her flailing limbs as she fought to get away. 'I want to go . . . I want to go with Teddy.' The thought he was in that beautiful blue world beneath the sea broke her heart. They'd always done everything together.

The nurse knelt beside her. 'Your brother, Teddy, he's gone to heaven, sweetie. He's with the angels . . .' she said, her face still wet from crying.

Jennifer stared at the woman, her shouts subsiding and replaced with a hard disdainful expression. 'Teddy isn't with the angels. He's with the fish.'

She was bustled away. They went back home. Days blurred. Her mother stayed in bed and if she was awake she cried or lay there staring at the wall, saying nothing. Her father was a shadow.

Aunty Vi, Christina's sister-in-law, who had arrived from Sydney, cooked and cleaned, and strangers came and went. Her father stayed out on the farm from daylight until after dark, when he ate and slept in the sleep-out on the verandah. But Jennifer knew he wasn't working on the farm. She saw him wandering aimlessly, or just sitting, or leaning on a fence.

Eventually Aunty Vi's husband Don, Christina's brother, joined them and talked to her father.

Then they were alone. Just the three of them. Her mother moved around the house and yard doing what she'd always done. But her steps were slow, her movements lethargic, her face drawn and sad. She rarely looked anyone in the eye, avoiding contact. Especially with her father. She brushed Jennifer's hair, put meals on the table and washed clothes, but she didn't read her a story and didn't tuck her into bed. Jennifer quietly slipped between the sheets and hugged Teddy's favourite knitted turtle and pushed her face into the pillows so no one heard her sobs of loneliness.

One afternoon she came unexpectedly into the kitchen and found her father standing by the stove, his hat on the floor, his arms hanging by his sides, his head thrown back, his eyes closed. Her mother was pummelling him, swinging her clenched fists at his chest as he stood and made no move to avoid her wild attack. There was a look of pain on his face, but it was not from the blows flung by his desperate wife.

Christina was shrieking, 'Damn you to hell! You killed him! You killed him! You took my boy from me. I hate you, hate you, hate you . . .'

Jennifer wanted to stop her mother hitting her father like that, but she turned and ran and ran until her legs wouldn't hold her up any more. Then she lay on the ground and hit the earth like she'd seen her mother flail at her father. She wanted her brother Teddy back. She wanted everything to be as it had been before.

That night her father came and sat in the dark on the edge of her bed. He smoothed her hair and brushed his hand along her cheek. 'Don't cry, Jen . . . if I could change it all I would. I will never forgive myself. But you mustn't be so sad. You will grow up and be a beautiful princess and live in a castle and be happy.'

'With Teddy?' she sniffed.

'No, Jennifer, you won't see Teddy for a long, long time.'

'Will you and Mummy come to my castle?'

'No. I'm going away, Jen . . . I mightn't see you for a long time. So you must be a good girl . . .' His voice made a funny noise in his throat and he stopped speaking.

They stayed silent in the quiet dark for a few minutes. 'Are you going to see Teddy?' whispered Jennifer. She knew there was something secret, to be kept from her mother, in this talk.

Her father squeezed her hand, lightly touched

her hair, then bent and kissed her cheek. 'Sweet dreams, little princess.'

She didn't see her father again. She was never completely sure what happened. When she was a teenager she found a tightly folded newspaper article in the back of her mother's photo album that she kept in a drawer in her bedroom. It was not a big article, but it recounted the facts in a dry and impersonal voice. A small aluminium dinghy had been found floating, abandoned off a beach. A fisherman was missing. Conditions had been calm that night. Police were investigating as the man's clothes were found neatly folded on the shore. There was no evidence of foul play. Eighteen months before, the man's son had drowned off the same beach.

She replaced the newspaper cutting, instinctively knowing she could not discuss this with her mother. Christina refused to talk about her father or her brother. If Jennifer mentioned them, her mother's face tightened in pain and she turned away. But Jennifer longed to talk about her brother and her father. It made them seem close and she was frightened she might forget them if she didn't. So she chatted to her brother as if he were playing beside her, and put her father first in her prayers.

Christina had agonised over selling the farm after what became known as 'the accident' but, after struggling for a year with neighbours' help to run it, she could see it was not going to be a viable financial proposition. The place was lonely, filled with family memories. She had only Jennifer as company. The local men who helped out were tired, preoccupied with tractor breakdowns, lack of rain or cattle feed. Their wives had full and busy lives. Christina didn't drive and a trip to town on the bus or a lift with neighbours was a rare treat. Conversation with her daughter centred around Jennifer's interests. During the day the radio programs only made Christina realise how out of touch she was. Evenings passed in the company of American TV sitcoms.

Jennifer would always recall that year on the farm after the accident as one of freedom. Her mother told her she'd have to entertain herself. So the little girl's world expanded into one of self-discovery and adventure. There was no Daddy or big brother to protect her, but neither was there anyone to divert her attention to activities they thought she should be doing. Instead, her eyes and enquiring mind found all manner of fascinating things: plants, small creatures, birds and the unexplored bush 'out there'. She would squat, oblivious to anything around her, unaware of time passing, as she watched a procession of ants carry their load home to the nest, a caterpillar scallop the edge of a leaf in silent bites, or a bird feed her young.

It was a time that opened her eyes to a different world. A world that existed within hers, yet was separate. The world of nature; of plants and animals, their dependence on their environment, their survival tactics, their devotion to protecting and propagating their species. Gradually she didn't feel so alone. As well as the cattle, the dogs, the big paddocks and the distant dam, there was another world teeming with life at her back door.

It was on one of her expeditions where she walked or sat with eyes focused on the ground that she found the shell. A bandicoot had dug a hole around the roots of a tree and she glimpsed something pale stuck in the soil. She pulled out what she thought was a rock but as she turned it over in her hand she saw the unmistakable shape of a shell. It was so embedded in the rock that it was part of the limestone. She traced the ridges of the shell with a fingertip, and there in the heat of the paddock, beneath a chortling magpie in a gum tree, she heard, faintly, then in an engulfing wave, the sound of the sea. She closed her eyes, clenching the fossil in her fist as she remembered the smell of salt air, the clean breeze on her cheek and the rhythm of the ocean came back to her. She took the shell home, washed it and put it in the shoe box that held her special treasures.

When Jennifer drifted out of the house and was gone for hours her mother thought she was wasting time and shirking chores and schoolwork. When she came back and was asked what she'd been doing, she answered vaguely, 'Nuffing.'

She was forbidden from going near the dam, though it was so low and muddy it would not have reached her shoulders. She heard in her mother's voice and saw in her eyes an implied fear and danger associated with any stretch of water.

And then one night as Jennifer stood at the sink doing the washing up, her mother came and picked up a tea towel and began to dry the dishes, which were normally left to drain.

'I have something to tell you.' She pushed a fistful of cloth into a glass and twisted it. 'Ever since . . . the accident . . . it's been very hard to run this farm on my own.'

'I help! And Mr Allen next door comes in and does things for you, Mum.'

'I know. But it's not enough. I have to think about the future. So, Jennifer, I've sold this place –'

'But this is *our* farm. *Our* home . . .' Tears welled in her eyes and she turned a stricken face to her mother, her hands grasping a plate in the soapy water.

Her mother kept her eyes down, concentrating on polishing the glass. 'It's for the best,' she said meekly. She knew this would shock her daughter. This farm was all she'd ever known.

'Where will we go?' Jennifer burst into tears.

Her mother put the glass and tea towel to one side and smoothed a strand of pale blonde hair back from her young daughter's teary cheek. 'Come and sit down. I'll make you a glass of Milo. We're moving into town. You'll like it. You'll have friends close by, be able to go to the pictures, walk to school.'

'I don't want to leave here.'

'Well, we're going and that's all there is to it.'

Christina was finding the whole idea difficult enough and she'd hoped Jennifer would see this as a big adventure. 'I have to think about our future. Your father left us without anything to fall back on, the farm isn't doing well . . .'

'Dad loved our farm. He wouldn't take me away.'

'Well he's not here, is he.' Her mother's patience snapped. 'I have to go out and get a job, for God's sake! A paying job. Heaven knows what. I'll probably end up cleaning people's houses or work in a shop. Just to put you through school.'

'I don't want to go to school. I want to stay here!' Jennifer ran to her room and slammed the door shut.

'Don't make this more difficult than it is,' Christina called after her.

The subject wasn't discussed again. Numbly, Jennifer watched as her mother packed up their possessions and walked around with the auctioneer, who was selling off items not included in the sale of the farm. She remained withdrawn and sad as events began to move more quickly. It wasn't until their neighbour Mr Allen appeared with his truck and tied her father's dogs in the back that Jennifer let out an anguished cry and ran at him and pulled his shirt sleeve, jumping up to reach the dogs.

'No, Mr Allen. Bluey and Charlie have to stay with us. They're Daddy's.'

'Jenny, love, you can't take dogs to live in town. Not where your mum is going. Besides, they're working dogs. They need lots of space. Mrs A and I will look after them real good.' Jennifer looked wildly around at the piles of boxes filled with clothes and kitchen utensils, the empty shed, the farm equipment and household items spread around to be auctioned. It seemed to the young girl that her whole life was being packed up, taken away, given away or sold.

The old farmer bent down and patted her head. 'They'll be all right, pet. You can come and visit them. Come and see Mrs A and me.'

She looked at his unhappy face and knew this would never happen. She couldn't even look at the dogs that had followed her dad everywhere, riding on his old motorbike, one in front and one behind. She nodded, and without a backward glance walked slowly towards the house. Bernie Allen stood and jammed his hat back on his head, thinking what a bloody shame it had come to this. Roger had been a damned fool to go rock fishing when he knew bugger all about the sea, fishing or swimming. Christina Campbell was a tough woman but she'd never get over this and he felt sorry for her little girl.

Christina and Jennifer moved into a small house on the edge of town. Jennifer's world closed in. Gone were the garden, the animals around the wood pile, the hens and ducks in their pen, the cows in the paddock at the back, the small creek beyond the fence. Gone were the small and large creatures, the plants, and the closeness and awareness of nature that had been their environment. Now she lived in a small country town that was trying to keep up with city advances and she had to adjust her observations to suit.

Jennifer struggled at her new school. There were so many other children around. They were fast and noisy and charged around the asphalt grounds playing silly games. After three years Jennifer tried to remember what it had been like back home. The paddocks, the trees and gentle cows. The fresh air. The still quietness. Her father doing something to a fence, his blue shirt rolled high up his arms, his bush hat pulled low. The smell of her mother's baking in the kitchen. Washing flapping on a clothes line propped up by a forked stick. She missed Teddy.

Her mother went to work now. She had a job in the local library. 'Someone has to look after you,' she sighed to Jennifer. 'You're all I have in this world.'

Jennifer bit her lip. 'I'll look after you, Mum. When I grow up I'll get a really good job and you can stay home.'

Her mother shrugged and looked away from her daughter, giving her usual answer, 'We'll see.'

Christina had to learn the library filing system as she pushed the cart of books and returned them to the shelves. To make extra money, she cleaned the library after hours. After eighteen months she asked if she could do other tasks as well.

The head librarian was firm, 'Only if you learn to type.' Christina complained to Jennifer about what a dragon the head librarian was and how she kept putting her down because she didn't have 'office skills'.

It was Jennifer's suggestion that her mother go to TAFE and learn to type and do basic office work. Her mother was initially resistant and it occurred to Jennifer that her mother was uncomfortable, indeed, resentful that her daughter knew more than she did about how to get ahead. When Christina began to mumble about finding a better job, maybe at the pub, Jennifer tackled the issue differently.

'Mum, I just know the basics really, I'm sure you'll learn it much quicker than I did. Then you can brush up on the finer points and show me.'

Jennifer was aware she had a responsibility to her mother; that she had to fill the space left by her father and brother. She didn't like school but she sensed working hard at her studies would be some kind of escape. Teachers gave her the idea that learning had one objective – to get a job. The enjoyment of study and exploring subjects that had little relevance to employment were dismissed as being distractions. Jennifer became aware of implied and subtle pressure nosing her towards acceptable jobs like teaching, nursing, bookkeeping. Other girls wanted jobs where they would make friends and save money until the day they 'settled down'.

The only times Jennifer was dragged from the mundane world of small-town jealousies and limited prospects were nights when the dream came. Once more she was floating in the strangely beautiful world peopled by incredible creatures. They lived amongst the sculptured architecture of coloured rocks and fantastic gardens. And all around was the great blue space of invisible sea.

2

Country Victoria, 1992

Ripples and Whirlpools

FOR CHRISTINA AND JENNIFER this hot Christmas holiday was spent as was the norm now: sweltering in their small house listening to neighbours splashing in their plastic pool, or kids across the road squealing under the hose on the brown front grass. Another strange man sat next to her mother at the dinner table but by now Jennifer had stopped bothering to be nice to these gentlemen callers. She was polite but not encouraging. And they soon ceased trying to chat to the withdrawn seventeen-year-old girl.

Jennifer had learned her lesson a few years back when, to her surprise, a man had 'dropped in' for a cup of tea. A few days later he drove Christina home from work. At fourteen, Jennifer had been thrilled to think her mother had a boyfriend. The next time he came to take Christina to dinner at the Bowling Club, Jennifer had dressed nicely, brushed her hair, put on a pale pink lipstick and some blush on her cheeks, and painted her nails the same pale pink. She was animated as she chatted to Mr Teddich.

Rather than looking pleased, Christina's face was tight, flushed and angry. 'You're not coming out with us, you know,' she hissed at Jennifer in the kitchen.

'I know. I have my homework to do and you've left dinner on the bench for me,' she said in surprise.

Her mother pointed at Jennifer's flowery 'best' dress. 'And you can get out of that little number, quick smart. I know what you're up to. Go to your room, change and wash that muck off your face. Don't come out until I've gone.'

'But I have to say goodbye to Mr Teddich.'

'You've said quite enough, my girl.' Her mother flounced out, firmly closing the door.

Jennifer was hurt and went over and over the conversation with her mother's friend, trying to think what on earth she'd said or done to make her mother so angry. The subject was never raised again and Mr Teddich never reappeared. But then he was a salesman so maybe he had just been passing through town. Jennifer was sad and vowed she'd try to be much nicer and more careful next time her mother brought a friend home.

Shortly afterwards, Jennifer heard Christina talking to Vi on the phone, saying she would never marry again. No man was worth changing her life for. 'God helps those who help themselves,' Christina told her sister-in-law. The inference was clear – don't rely on others, especially men.

All Jennifer wanted was a father. She envied her schoolfriends who had fathers who took them out or were, simply, there. Memories of her own father stirred and made her weep. The more she puzzled over her mother's rejection of male companions the more she began to fret it was her fault. Then she had a horrible and shocking thought. Could it be that because she'd tried to look and be nice, Mr Teddich thought she was flirting with him? That she was being precocious and provocative? Surely not. But that could well be how her mother saw her behaviour. Jennifer cringed at the thought, guilt stricken that she'd ruined her mother's chances to remarry.

Jennifer didn't need to be pushed by Christina to get an after-school job. She was very aware of their strained financial circumstances, so she took a casual job with the National Parks doing general office work. She also assisted the two rangers compiling survey materials, questionnaires and reports. She found the information intriguing and she gradually came to learn a lot more about her hometown, the operation of the parklands around it, and the conflicts with farmers, developers and people concerned with animal welfare and the preservation of bushland.

Christina had little interest in the stories Jennifer gleaned from the taciturn head ranger and she continued to encourage her daughter to join the local dramatic society. 'Just help out backstage like I do. I know you're not the sort to get up on stage and perform in public, but you have to learn to mix with people, Jennifer. You're such a wallflower.'

'That's okay, Mum, you're the star in the family.'

Christina missed the sardonic note in Jennifer's voice. 'Someone at work said the other day I should be on the stage,' she smiled. 'You have to speak up in this world, Jennifer. The squeaky wheel gets the oil. No one else is going to help you. I'd hate to see you turn into a doormat.'

'I'll be all right, Mum. People are always kind and helpful to me.'

'That's because you're still young and innocent. Such a softie. You'll have to toughen up when you're dealing with a roomful of yelling, obnoxious brats.'

Jennifer sighed and turned away. Her mother was determined that she become a primary school teacher. There had never been any discussion. Her mother had raised the idea as a job with good prospects, talked at some length about what she'd been told by one of the teachers who frequented the library, and convinced herself this was Jennifer's calling. Her daughter hadn't been consulted. Jennifer's careers adviser at school had agreed that a teaching career would be desirable. So Jennifer went to see her adviser about university degrees in education. After looking at Jennifer's high scores, and knowing her mother's financial situation, he helped her fill out an application for a bursary.

It wasn't till Jennifer and her mother were walking home after her high school graduation ceremony, where Christina had basked in her daughter's good results, that Jennifer announced she wanted to apply to Sydney University.

Her mother shook her head in sad resignation. 'That's all very well and good, but there's no way I can afford to keep you there. And why bother? You can get a teaching degree at the local regional university.'

'With my marks, I have a scholarship, Mum. A bursary and my government allowance will pay for accommodation and extras. And if I get a part-time job I can live cheaply on campus and pay my way. With a degree I can get a much better paying job.' She took a breath to make her next announcement as casual as possible. 'I've been considering my options and what I'm really interested in is nature and the land . . . and in Sydney I can study Environmental Science.'

Her mother stared at her tall, pretty daughter as if seeing her for the first time in years. Her expression was that of someone who had eaten something bad. 'And what good is that? What sort of job will that get you?' she asked.

Jennifer was faintly bemused at her mother's attitude. 'Something really interesting. I could share a house off campus, but I thought a college that was close to the library, classes and the cafeteria would be easier.'

'You would move away from home?' Jennifer didn't answer. 'You've looked into this and made up your mind without asking me?' asked her mother in a slow, even voice that presaged trouble.

Jennifer ploughed on, her heart sinking. 'I just thought I'd find out everything first, that's all.'

'Well, you've wasted your time. It's out of the question.' Her mother's mouth snapped closed, her lips thinning.

'Mum, do you want to see the program, the handbook, the classes I can take?'

Her mother's pace picked up. 'I do not. Who do you think you are, anyway? University! It's just an excuse to get away and play up.'

'Maybe Aunty Vi and Uncle Don could help out a bit. They don't have any kids. They always said I was like a daughter to them . . .'

Her mother stopped and turned to Jennifer, hissing through clenched teeth so as not to make a scene in public. 'That will do. What have they ever done for us? For you? They'd think we were just using them. I couldn't hold my head up.'

'Mum! They always asked me to go down and spend holidays with them in Sydney. Or offered to take me places. You never let me!' A deep and long-suppressed anger exploded, causing Jennifer's chest to tighten, making her breathless. 'We never went anywhere! We've stayed in this town for ten years. I hate it!'

'I work hard. I never had money to let you go on holiday jaunts. I never had a holiday either!' Christina snapped back.

'You could have let me go with my friends. Their parents said it wouldn't cost anything to go camping with them. Uncle Don offered to send the train fare.'

'I will not have you conniving behind my back and I will not be beholden to anyone. There's only one way to get on in this world and that's to pay your own way.'

'Why don't you trust people, Mum?' asked Jennifer quietly. 'You think the whole world is against you. Everyone is out to do you down.' Jennifer's anger dissipated and she sounded more bewildered than upset.

Her mother strode ahead. 'You'll learn. The hard way. And one day you'll thank me. You think being sweet and nice and playing up to people is going to help you? People use you, Jennifer. Men can't be trusted and women are always jealous. You stand on your own two feet and do it yourself.'

Jennifer lengthened her steps to keep up with her mother. She was sad that her mother felt like this. She didn't see the world or people in this way. And beneath her mother's steam and fury she saw a frightened and insecure woman who was getting

31

by in life on bluster and artificial self-confidence. Jennifer had seen the reality of her mother behind closed doors and it was very different. For the remainder of the walk home each kept silent with nothing resolved and little said about how they felt or what they really meant.

Jennifer's pleasure and pride about finishing school with flying colours evaporated. She'd failed her mother again. And she'd worked so hard through high school. All she knew was that she desperately wanted to get away from this town. And her mother. Now Christina knew it too.

It was a visit from the school principal later that shocked Christina into agreeing to allow Jennifer to apply to Sydney University.

Christina was more angry about, as she put it, 'That man turning up unannounced when we hadn't tidied or cleared the table. Making me feel like a fool who didn't know anything. Didn't care about your future . . . when I've sacrificed every-thing for you.'

'Mum, please. They're trying to be helpful. Get the best deal for me. Help you –'

'I don't need any help. You seem to have taken matters into your own hands. It's on your head, Jennifer. You know I can't afford to bail you out of trouble.'

'What trouble, Mum? I'm not getting into anything I can't manage. I just have to watch my money and not be frivolous. When I'm settled in and seen what my workload is like, maybe I can find a job for some extra cash.'

'You've got it all figured out, haven't you?' She paused. 'And if, just if, you get into this big deal uni in Sydney, I suppose you're planning to see Vi and Don? Are they in on this?'

'Mum, there's no secret about this. I haven't mentioned it to them. Just in case it doesn't come off.' Jennifer turned her face away, hating the swift look of satisfaction that slid across her mother's features.

'Well, let's not count our chickens then.'

Her mother sat at the kitchen table watching Jennifer take a small tub of ice cream from the freezer. Christina lit a cigarette and slowly blew a jet of smoke towards the ceiling. As Jennifer put tall frothy glasses of Milo milkshake on the table Christina reached out and touched her hand. 'Don't aim too high and get your hopes set on something people like us don't deserve, Jennifer. There're a lot of opportunities around here.'

Jennifer didn't answer. But inside she was yelling, *Why don't we deserve good things in life? Why shouldn't I set my sights as high as I can see?*

Her mother was feeling cheerful and in control again. Jennifer's aberration of going to Sydney University would be put to rest.

Jennifer washed their glasses and went to her room. If only she had someone she could confide in, ask advice, someone who had no agenda but guiding her in the best possible direction. She started to change out of her school uniform.

Maybe her mother was right – you were all alone in this world and had to manage your life yourself. She stared at herself in the mirror and saw a young girl on the verge of womanhood: fine pale skin, curves that were still filling out her body, shining golden hair that she cut herself, clear blue eyes and a mouth that was soft and sad. 'I don't want to be alone,' she thought.

How she missed her father, her big brother. There were no photos of them in the house though she knew about her mother's photo album in the bottom of a drawer in her bedroom. Jennifer closed her eyes, remembering a laughing boy who'd held her hand, tousled her hair and whispered stories to her when she stole into his bed.

Sometimes scenes of the sea, that day on the beach, the image of her mother hitting her father in the kitchen, flashed into her mind like a blinking light, but she pushed them aside. It had taken a while but she'd taught herself to make her mind go blank when these uninvited images darted across her interior vision. She swiftly thought of a black night sky. Then small specks of light hovered and she replaced these specks with snapshots that made her happy – brightly coloured fish in pink seaweed, the soft silvery skin of a gum tree beneath peeling bark, a butterfly perched on a leaf about to flutter into sunlight. Then she'd open her eyes and, sighing, return to the moment.

Jennifer sat on a warm wooden bench at the edge of the university quadrangle gazing at students strolling or sitting on the emerald lawn. Idly, she wondered who else had sat on this old seat contemplating the mellow stone archways and high windows glinting in the sunlight. Much as she loved her university classes and the freedom of being on her own, halfway through her first year at Sydney University she still felt she didn't belong here.

Her mother's belief that she had stepped beyond their boundaries had taken root in some deep place within her. It coloured how she approached everything in this new life. She never felt she wore the right clothes, or knew the same places and people and fads as other students. She felt she had to do her best and get good marks. That she had something to prove not only to herself, but also to her mother. There was a constant pang of guilt over her mother's living alone in an isolated Victorian country town, even though she knew friends and neighbours were popping by, inviting her mother out as much for Jennifer's sake as for Christina's.

Jennifer's own social life was uneventful. She sometimes joined a group of friends from uni who went to cafes and bars nearby. Every second Sunday she was invited to Uncle Don and Aunty Vi's for lunch and she found she enjoyed being with them. Sometimes they went out for an afternoon drive or to see a movie. She would stay the night in the downstairs guest bedroom, which was comfortable and spacious. A sliding door opened onto a small patio and the neat back garden where Uncle Don bred birds.

The compact brick house was almost identical to its neighbour, and, while pleasant enough, it was to Jennifer's mind a suburban lifestyle that she wasn't interested in. If she couldn't have the open space of the country she'd rather have the vibrancy of inner city life. Especially the energy of the students and interesting characters who frequented the blocks around the university campus.

It was a train ride and a bit of a walk or a long bus trip from Vi and Don's house to her room at uni, so Jennifer chose to get up and leave early on a Monday morning rather than travel at night on public transport. Her aunt and uncle wanted her to think of the spare room as her own and leave some of her belongings there, but she was reluctant. She enjoyed having the family contact and knew her visits, where she talked about all she was doing, brought them great pleasure. Jennifer found, however, that she had to downplay these visits when she spoke to her mother. Christina's resentment, or was it plain jealousy, crackled down the phone line.

'And what did you talk about? Must be nice for them to get all the little details you never have time to tell me. At least you're getting a good meal when you see them. I suppose Vi still does the big baked lunch. Goodness, I can't remember when I last had a slice of roast lamb.' And on it went.

Jennifer didn't have the heart to tell her that Vi only occasionally did a traditional meal. She was experimenting with ethnic dishes and once a month they went to various restaurants scattered around Sydney – Greek, Vietnamese, Lebanese or Chinese cuisines. She knew her mother wouldn't approve of 'foreign' food. But worse, in her mother's eyes, was the fact that Jennifer was gadding about enjoying herself with Vi and Don.

Jennifer's favourite place to eat near uni was a small cafe called 'Crush' that specialised in inno-vative natural foods and juices. There were tables with umbrellas outside; inside, long bars with stools ringed the walls, and one large wooden table dominated the room. Everyone shared the space and it was a good way to meet people. A selection of newspapers was always on hand and a bulletin board was smothered in notices of events, trade or sale items, people looking for a ride out of town and almost anything else of interest to a university crowd.

Jennifer enjoyed sitting outside and lingering over a smoothie or her salad while she read notes or a book with the background chatter and laugh-ter of other students. You were never hurried along and she liked the friendly young staff. She had thought of asking for a job there but was a bit intimidated by all the organic foods, many she hadn't seen before like wheat-grass juice, pome-granates, and a variety of Asian vegetables. Instead, she was working in the university library – which pleased her mother – but she was hoping to find another part-time job.

A salad with roast beetroot stuffed with

bocconcini and topped with roasted pine nuts and fresh coriander was put in front of her. She was surprised to see one of the chefs serving.

'Is this one of your specialities?'

'All my own work. Hope you like it.'

'How come you're serving as well as cooking?'

'One of the girls is running late, had to see her tutor. I said I'd cover for her.'

'That's nice of you. Are you at uni, too?'

'No. I've just finished my course in hospitality at TAFE. I'm doing this for experience and to save some money. I want to go to one of the big hotels overseas.'

He was medium height and build with pleasant features and unruly curly dark hair. Jennifer thought he looked like a nice person. 'To work as a chef?'

'Actually no. I'm more interested in hotel management. I've been doing a bit of everything. Oops, better go, the other guy in the kitchen will have the next order ready.'

He came back to her table several times to top up her water, take away her plate and persuade her to try the fruit flan. When she left he gave her a wave. 'Enjoy the meal?'

'I certainly did. And the service was great.'

Jennifer began to visit Crush more frequently and she and Blair – as she now knew the young chef's name to be – exchanged friendly banter and carefully dropped bits of information that gave each other clues about their families, future plans and the things they liked.

A few weeks later after they ran into each other at the Sunday farmers' market in the city, they strolled around the stalls as Blair bought fruit and vegetables. Jennifer had an armful of flowers, some homemade chutney and jam, and two ripe mangoes, a fruit she'd just discovered.

'Are you buying for Crush or yourself?' she asked.

'Today myself. I'm tired of eating at the restaurant or taking home leftovers. I thought I'd rustle up a decent lunch.' He glanced at her pretty face lightly touched with just the right amount of make-up, her pale gold hair that looked like she'd just washed it and let it dry. It fell around her face to her shoulders and, with her blue eyes and pale skin, the exotic and brightly coloured flowers in her arms contrasted with her translucent colouring. There was a faint sweet perfume around her from the flowers or her hair, he wasn't sure which, and he suddenly wanted to lean closer and breathe in the fragrance. He realised he was staring at her. 'Look, would you like to come over and share lunch? I live in Glebe, not far. I do sort of feel we know each other.'

'Me too.' She felt ridiculously pleased.

The lunch was delightful. She loved his little terrace house and the way he was so comfortable about pouring her a glass of wine as she perched on a stool and watched him casually throw together an informal meal, which they ate off big, brightly coloured square plates on his tiny patio. She felt very cosmopolitan and tried not to show

how impressed she was. She couldn't imagine any of the boys she knew back home, or any of her mother's friends, entertaining like this. She insisted on helping him clear up and then as the lazy, empty afternoon loomed, she was overcome with anxiety and made excuses about having to leave to see her aunt and uncle.

'It's been really lovely. I'm sorry I can't reciprocate. I'm living on campus.' Then she had an idea. 'How about a picnic one day? I'll do the food. When you have time, of course.' She had no idea where they'd go but she'd research that one.

'I'll definitely make time for that. Here, I'll give you my phone number.' He reached for a pen and a slip of paper on the kitchen bench.

'I'll probably see you at Crush anyway?' she asked.

'I hope so. Can I drive you anywhere?'

'No, I'm fine. I'll grab a taxi.' She picked up her shopping and hurried to the door in case he offered to phone for a cab. She had no intention of spending money on such a luxury. She'd walk. 'Thanks so much, Blair . . . talk to you soon.'

'Bye, Jennifer.' He was already planning to phone a couple of mates to go down to the pub to watch the footy.

Jennifer sat in the library and began to read the course notes her adviser had given her about directing her study focus. Teaching science was beginning to look less attractive to her and she didn't believe she had a forceful enough personality to dominate a classroom. Research, investigation, winnowing out information and fitting pieces of a puzzle together – especially in the field of nature – fascinated her far more.

She read the summary of one of the courses: 'Conservation biology examines the ecological theory behind genetic, species, and ecosystem conservation. A range of techniques for reserve selection, planning and management is examined, and supported by case studies of Australian protected areas.'

There were so many new – to her – subjects available for study. Big-picture topics right down to very specific and narrow subjects which were nonetheless important in the grand scheme of how humans could coexist more sustainably with nature and the planet.

Jennifer thought back to the routine she remembered of her childhood on the farm. The predictable rotation of seasons and weather, animals that were born, fattened, slaughtered or sold. Wallabies with young joeys in their pouch, the birds that returned to nest each year, the paddocks that flourished again after harvest. It was only later, when she and her mother were alone on the farm, that she listened to men complain about how everything was changing. That things were not how they used to be. Or should be. And she remembered how the men shook their heads and made dire predictions. And no one could tell her why.

Answers. That's what intrigued her. If she could

examine the phenomena of cause and effect in the environment, maybe solutions would become apparent.

Over a coffee at Crush with Blair she raised the subject of switching the focus of her degree from teaching to research, but he only shrugged.

'Sorry, Jenny, out of my field. Can't you just get the teaching degree thingy and decide what to teach later?'

'Actually, teaching is looking less attractive. I'd like to get into the research area. I think I should take more science subjects.'

'Yeah, well. Hands-on is best, I reckon.' He grinned. 'Look at me.' He waved a white napkin draped over his arm and pointed at the kitchen. 'Waiter, front-of-house, chef, staff co-ordinator, computer jock. And on Monday morning I'm helping repaint the front. Never know what you're going to be asked to do. Jack of all trades. I'd get the broadest, easiest degree that gives you the most choices.'

Jennifer nodded, thinking how different their attitudes were. She recalled the second part of being a jack of all trades – *master of none*. Well, she was a bit more particular, or maybe had a more narrow focus. Though he was right in that having a flexible degree would give her more options. Well, she'd just get on with it. Take the courses that would help her in the research field. Her mother would be none the wiser. A degree, in her eyes, would be a degree. As long as Jennifer could get a job, her mother would be satisfied, even if it wasn't as a primary school teacher.

Jennifer's routine changed little in the next few months. She and Blair saw each other on a regular basis, but it was still casual and friendly, and each had their own set of friends and activities. Blair liked to spend time with his mates – watching sport, going to the pub or 'hanging out'. Jennifer felt there were girls involved some of these times, but she never asked and he seemed to prefer to keep her separate from his 'guys' gigs'.

They hadn't slept together, because Blair sensed her reluctance and reticence, so both agreed to pull back when things looked like getting out of hand when they kissed. Privately Jennifer was disappointed. She realised he thought she was holding back, but she didn't want to be the one to make the move, especially as it was her first time. She had made up her mind that if she was going to lose her virginity it would be with Blair. But he muttered about 'respecting her' and 'not wanting to push her into something they might regret'.

Jennifer's life swung between her studies and Blair. Then one day Blair announced he had been offered two positions. One was as a junior manager at a top hotel in Lausanne, Switzerland. The other was in Sydney at a new international hotel, where he would be assistant general manager.

As he explained to Jennifer, 'One gives me

international references, but, frankly, I wouldn't be learning all that much – I reckon I'd be doing a lot of the dirty work as a junior. There are dozens of hopeful European hotel staff doing the same job. But here in Sydney I think I could get ahead quicker.'

'It's an international hotel chain. Surely that will open other doors down the track?' said Jennifer, hoping he wouldn't move overseas.

'That's what I thought,' said Blair, grasping her arm and squeezing it. 'So that's what I'm going to do. I reckon if I do well, I can go to their hotels in other parts of the world or look for opportunities in Europe.'

'You're on your way, Blair. Just what you wanted. Good on you,' said Jennifer warmly. She meant it, but she could see Blair's star soaring out of her little hemisphere.

He sensed her mood. 'Listen, this is good for other reasons. We can still see each other. You're nearly done with your degree . . . who knows what opportunities might come your way?'

She gave a brief smile. 'Yeah. Who knows. But I don't think Europe is interested in what I'm doing. I'm looking at Aussie issues first . . .' she paused. 'What happens here is just as important, even more so in some ways, as we can be a leader in conservation for the rest of the world. In some countries it's already too late.'

Blair nodded encouragingly but Jennifer knew he didn't really grasp what she was on about. He was into tourism, trendsetting lifestyles, food,

getting ahead to make money. Jennifer was beginning to sense that Blair's ambitions were in total
conflict with her own studies. Their conversations
about biodiversity, sustainability, conservation, the
environment, disintegrated before they got heated as
he wasn't interested and Jennifer felt she didn't
know enough to convince him that tourism, development and a slash and burn approach to land and
sea care were not viable in the long term.

He would laugh and tug her hair or tweak her
nose. 'You're sweet, a dreamer, an idealist too.
Enjoy life, Jenny, that's my motto.'

Despite their ideological differences, they
shared a good social life, a continuing physical
attraction and, slowly, their personal histories.
Blair was sympathetic about her childhood trauma
of the loss of her father and brother. So he agreed
to accompany Jennifer to Sunday lunch at Aunty
Vi and Uncle Don's. To Jennifer, and to her aunt
and uncle, Blair's willingness to step into her family circle represented a major shift in their
relationship. That first lunch was couched as a
casual social occasion, and, to Jennifer's surprise,
Blair seemed genuinely to enjoy Don and Vi's company. He found Vi a bundle of laughs and loved the
fact she was so interested in different cuisines.

Blair came with Jennifer on several more visits
and also took them to various restaurants that Vi
found stimulating. In fact, Vi and Blair bonded
over the food, restaurants and cooking, leaving
Jennifer and Don to talk about bird breeding, her
studies and anything else that came to mind.

Jennifer was amused at Vi and Blair, their delving into the pantry or Vi's old cookbooks, only too happy that Blair was accepted. And she liked the idea of them being recognised as a couple.

Jennifer also talked to Blair about her mother living in Victoria. Blair's family was fractured and scattered, too, and he seemed to have little contact with them, although they all got on well when they did see each other, he told her. Blair liked the connection with Vi and Don. It held no obligations but gave him feedback from a different generation and class.

'They're good people,' he told Jennifer. 'Salt of the earth.'

Their relationship took a different turn when Blair started working at the hotel. He put in long hours and was distracted and fretted over incidents and people at work. They seemed trivial issues to Jennifer but she listened, and made comforting and understanding noises. Gradually he would let work go and enjoy himself.

They now had a regular group of friends, some living together, some married, and Jennifer felt life was settling into a routine that she quite liked, although she rarely mentioned her study and university work, and then only in passing. She still had the part-time job in the university library that gave her a little extra money.

Christmas came and they both decided to visit their families. Jennifer's train pulled into the station and she recognised most of the people getting off the train or waiting on the platform. As she retrieved her bag, her mother came hurrying up to her.

'Sorry, sorry. Damn bus was late. Was going to get a ride with a friend to the station but at the last minute her car wouldn't start. Hopeless, she is.' Christina embraced her daughter and took Jennifer's handbag so she could manage her small suitcase. Jennifer knew that as her mother chatted about changes around town, what neighbours were doing, what had happened in the past year, what they might do together, she was also taking in every minuscule detail of Jennifer's appearance: her new shoulder-length haircut, her professional but natural-looking make-up, her casual but smart clothes and expensive-looking shoes, and her chunky silver jewellery. The hesitant, pale girl had been replaced by a poised, capable and attractive young woman.

They caught a taxi home and her mother fingered Jennifer's handbag. 'This is nice. Real leather, is it? Must have cost you a bit. I hope you're not frittering your money away, Jennifer. Do you save anything?'

'Oh Mum, I don't fritter. I save up and get one good thing at a time at the sales or discount places. There are lots of bargains in a big city,' she laughed.

'Yes, I suppose there are a lot of things in Sydney you can't get here in this little town. But it is your home, remember, Jennifer.'

'Of course, Mum. Well, home is where you grow up, really. I think of the old farm as home. And that's not far from here anyway, is it?' added

Jennifer quickly, seeing her mother's mouth tighten at the mention of the farm.

The holidays dragged for Jennifer. It was a strain listening to the minutiae of her mother's life – the people she worked with who, in her mother's view, all seemed to be incompetent. The dreaded head librarian was still extremely difficult; the young girls were silly giggling twits or thought they knew everything and tried to boss her around now that they had computers.

'Mum, do a computer course, it's the new way to go. Everyone is using them,' said Jennifer.

'I suppose you have them at your university?'

'Well, yes, in the library. I don't have a personal one, of course.' She didn't add that Uncle Don was planning to get one to organise his bird breeding program and had offered to let Jennifer use it too.

'You'd be very surprised at who comes in to use ours,' confided her mother. 'I can't imagine what some of the old ducks are doing. They sit there pecking away like . . .'

'Old hens!' laughed Jennifer. 'Maybe they're writing their life stories.'

'Tosh. None of them has had an interesting life.' This launched her mother into stories of the health, family upheavals and financial doings of half the town. Jennifer winced. Christina had become the town gossip and seemed to know what everyone was up to. She also had the awful feeling that her mother probably passed on in minute detail every aspect of Jennifer's life.

Thank goodness she was judicious in what she told her. But what disturbed her most was her mother's negativity. She didn't seem to have anything nice to say about anyone or anything. Jennifer ignored her mother's barbed enquiries about her personal life, her friends and her future.

But after a week, she was burnt out. There was no reprieve from the onslaught of her mother's attentions. Christina had also taken holidays so they were together from first thing in the morning when her mother brought her a cup of tea far too early. Jennifer now drank coffee, Blair's influence, but suffered through her mother's breakfast, which she insisted on making with all the works, from the ironed tablecloth and serviettes, to the best plates, to the cereal, Vegemite, raspberry jam and butter dish all set out the night before. Sleepily, Jennifer confronted the array on the table as her mother bustled in the kitchen.

'Here's some toast, butter it before it gets cold while I do the eggs. I bet you don't get food like this down there at that university canteen.'

Jennifer lifted the lid on the butter dish to find an oily liquid that had melted during the hot night. 'No, that's for sure,' she thought to herself. She had fresh fruit, cafe au lait and a croissant, or else sprinted down to Crush for a delicate omelette, frittata or fruit concoction.

Her mother sat opposite her with a mug of tea and a cigarette. 'Come on, eat up.'

'Where's yours, Mum?'

'Oh, I don't eat a big breakfast. A piece of toast does me.'

'Then I wish you wouldn't go to all this trouble . . .'

'Nonsense! I enjoy having my girl home. Now, what are we doing today?' asked her mother brightly.

Jennifer glanced at the kitchen clock and wished she was still in bed. 'I don't know. It's too early to think about it.'

'Goodness me, you can't waste time sleeping in.'

'I *am* on holidays, Mum,' said Jennifer, more snappily than she meant to. 'I don't know, do you have any plans?'

'I never do anything, so what would I know? I never go out much. I work, come home and clean up. It's pretty quiet around here.' *Not like smart Sydney and all the fun things you get to do . . .* hung in the air unsaid.

'I thought you told me you went to the club, and the pictures with Elaine. And what happened to the Bridge group?'

Her mother stubbed out her cigarette and gathered her dressing gown around her. 'One time. That's all, Jennifer. And I don't go to the club very often. I can't afford it. And that Bridge group was very snippy. Complained about every bid and every card I played. I wasn't going to be treated like that.' She carried the ashtray and tea mug to the sink.

Jennifer spoke cautiously. 'I thought I might

have a day out on my own today. Hire a bike, maybe head out to the old place, say hello to Mr Allen.'

'What on earth for? Well, if you'd prefer to spend time with people you hardly knew when you were a child . . .' Christina flounced back into the bedroom.

Jennifer put her head in her hands. She'd take her mother to the pictures, then they wouldn't have to talk. Somehow she'd break the news that she had to go back to Sydney early. She'd think of a reason for cutting her holiday short.

Her mother stood beside her on the railway platform, radiating hurt and martyrdom. Jennifer glanced at her watch. Four minutes to go.

'Won't you be lonely back up there? Surely everyone will still be away enjoying their holidays until classes start?'

'No, Mum, there're always heaps of students around. Many can't afford to leave, or they get summer jobs. I'm hoping Blair can help me get a job in the local cafe, I'll make a lot more than in the library.' *Hell! It had just slipped out. Would her mother pick up on it?*

Christina pounced, turning wide, interested eyes to Jennifer. 'Blair? Who's Blair? Have you mentioned him before? A friend, is he? Or is he the owner of the cafe? Frankly, I don't think waitressing is a very ladylike job, Jennifer.'

'It's a cutesy place that's very popular with the

uni crowd. You don't get a lot of tips as most people there are also poor students. But it's considered a good job.'

'And this Blair, he works there?'

'He was a chef, he's now assistant to the manager at a new hotel.'

'I see. A cook. A good friend, is he?'

'Ah yes, kind of. I have a lot of friends.' *Where's the damn train?*

'That's nice for you. But he's a special friend, I take it?' Her eyes hadn't left Jennifer's face, noting her discomfort.

'Kind of. Well, yes. We go out a bit.'

'So my daughter has a boyfriend. Well. I hope he's a nice boy, Jennifer, you know what I mean? From a nice family that teaches their son to respect girls.'

'He's very nice. Don and Vi like him a lot.' *Oh hell!*

'They do, do they? They've met this boy and I've never even been told he exists. By my own daughter, or my brother and his wife.' There was a pitiful catch in her voice.

'Mum, here comes the train. Look, don't be like that. No one thought to mention it because it's no big deal, there's nothing serious. I go out with lots of different people,' she lied quickly.

'I suppose you want to go back early so you can see this person?'

She hugged her mother. 'No, he's away with his family. Thanks for a wonderful time. I'll phone you tomorrow night. I'll try to come again at Easter.

Bye, Mum.' She grabbed her suitcase and bundled it into the carriage.

As Jennifer sank into her seat the train moved forward, passing the figure of her mother with shoulders slumped, head down, as she trudged, so sadly, along the platform. Furiously Jennifer slammed her handbag under her seat.

Blair wasn't due back for another week. Despite what Jennifer had told her mother, all her usual haunts were half empty or filled with tourists. She decided to go down to Circular Quay for brunch. Blair had told her of a little outdoor place near the hotel where he worked.

When she got there she was shocked to see Blair sitting at a table under an umbrella with a girl and two other men. She stopped, embarrassed, but it was too late to turn away. He leapt to his feet.

'Jenny! Hey! Come here.'

Shyly, she joined the group and was surprised when Blair hugged her effusively. 'Why didn't you tell me you were coming back early?'

'You told me you'd be up north for another week or more,' she said lightly.

'Touché, Blair . . . you'd better confess,' laughed one of the boys.

Blair looked sheepish. 'Pranged my brother's motorbike, had a row with my dad and my mother threatened to walk out, so I was stuck with cooking for fifteen people. Bugger that. I had an urgent call to come back to work,' he laughed. 'And these are some of my work mates. This is Jennifer who I was telling you about.' He pulled her down next to him. 'Let's order a bottle of wine to celebrate.' He kissed her cheek. 'How come you're back early too?'

Jennifer couldn't help laughing. 'Couldn't take the mothering any longer.'

The brunch lingered into the early afternoon. They caught a taxi back to Blair's place and Jennifer felt flushed and tipsy.

'Too hot to do much. Do you want to go for a swim?' asked Blair, as he flung open doors and windows.

'The beach will be hot and crowded. I might go home and have a nap.'

'You can rest here. I'll watch the cricket on the sofa. We can go out when it cools down.'

'Sounds good,' sighed Jennifer. Blair kissed her and led her to the cool, dark bedroom.

They kissed again and fell back on the bed. 'On second thoughts, the cricket can wait. Can I stay with you?' He ran his hand along her cheek and down her throat, kissing the top of a breast.

'Oh, yes, do,' sighed Jennifer and drew his body close to hers.

Three weeks later Jennifer moved in with Blair.

She was in Blair's den where they'd set up her desk and bookcase when Aunty Vi rang.

'Jenny, dear, I think you and Blair better know – your mother has sold her house. She's moving up here. Staying with us. To be near to you. Shall you speak to her or shall I? I don't know why she didn't want me to tell you. Wanted it to be a surprise. Don thinks she should have consulted you.'

Jennifer rubbed her eyes. 'No, she wouldn't do that in case I tried to talk her out of it. She doesn't want to surprise me, she wants to make a scene and mess up my life.'

'Oh, Jen, that's a bit harsh. She's lonely and misses you. She can stay here as long as she wants.'

'Aunty Vi, that's nice of you, but I wouldn't actually say that to her.' Jennifer slowly replaced the phone. 'Well,' she thought, 'this is going to test the strength of the bond between me and Blair.'

3

Sydney, 1997

Sea Borne

THE MARRIAGE OF BLAIR and Jennifer was a modest occasion, though the weeks leading to the day had been occasionally stressful and frustrating. Now as Jennifer walked down the aisle of the small church in Lavender Bay, her arm linked through Blair's, she was only peripherally aware of the blur of smiling faces from the pews. The church was cool and shadowy in the late afternoon light, but what beckoned, drew her forward, was the bright sunlight glaring through the stained glass window. To her it represented the future. A step into a new life with Blair, and, as much as she hated to admit it, an escape from the oppressive presence of her mother.

What an emotional roller-coaster the year had been since Christina had moved to Sydney. She had entrenched herself in the downstairs bedroom and ensuite at Vi and Don's and spread out onto the patio, so she had small but comfortable private quarters. Her brother always had an escape to his bird pens in the backyard while Vi had struggled with the adjustment of a domineering woman in the household. There were occasional upsets.

'I was only trying to be helpful, Vi. If you'd rather I sat back like Lady Muck and let you do *all* the washing, cooking and cleaning, then fine. I'm just trying to pull my weight.'

'I appreciate that, Tina. But you know how it is, you have your own system and routine for these things . . .' *Small laugh.* 'I'm a bit set in my ways after all these years, and I've figured out the most hassle-free way to get the jobs done.' *Unlike you, Tina. You have a knack of turning any task into a drama.*

'Well, as my mother always said, if you're going to do anything, do it properly. I just feel helping out is the least I can do as you've both taken me in.' *Sniff.* 'Seeing how my own daughter has rejected me.'

'Now Tina, stop that silliness. Jenny is a young woman at university, she shouldn't be living with her mother in some small uncomfortable place.

You're much better off here with us. There's plenty of room.'

'I could buy a little place . . .'

Vi's patience was running out, her voice was firm. 'Now, we've been through that one. Don is right, you save your money until you decide what you want to do. Let's all support Jenny and be here for her as family and when she graduates then let's see what the future holds. Maybe you could take a trip.'

'That'd be nice. Jennifer and I sailing to Europe . . .'

Vi hoped Tina wouldn't suggest that to poor Jenny. 'Heavens, Tina, I was thinking you should see Australia. Go north, or over to the west, the outback. You never know who you'll meet.'

'Oh, I couldn't possibly travel on my own.'

Vi suddenly remembered the ill-fated caravan trip to the coast. 'I was thinking of groups, go with people your own age, who have the same interests.' She saw Christina's lips tighten and her face set in dismay. 'Anyway, no point in talking about it now. So, what are your plans today?' She bustled past Tina, feeling the need for fresh air. 'I'll just pop down and see what Don wants for tea tonight.'

'I suppose I'll just have to drag myself out to work . . .'

Vi pretended not to hear. They'd been down that track before too. She and Don had encouraged Christina to look for a job, part-time, casual, anything to give her an interest and get her out of

58

the house. Money wasn't a major problem, though Christina was understandably cautious with her spending. She had finally landed a job in a real estate office answering the phone for the agents, pinning up ads and updating flyers.

Over dinner she regaled Don and Vi with examples of what and who were selling. Most places, according to Christina, were, 'Outrageously overpriced . . . dumps! You should see how they pretty-up the photos. And the descriptions! It's a joke. I wouldn't pay that sort of money.'

'It's what you have to pay these days, Tina. The housing market has changed in Sydney. It's not like rural Victoria,' said Don.

'Well, you might call our town a backwater, but I had a very nice cottage and every amenity was right on hand. I could walk everywhere.' Tina didn't drive, which was an irritant to Vi and Don, who had to juggle trips to include Tina. Fortunately they lived on the bus route to the real estate agency.

'Tina, I'm not saying you lived in a backwater,' said Don in a resigned voice, ignoring the eye signal from Vi, *Don't get into this*. 'Sydney is really the metropolitan capital of Australia. Everyone wants to be here. Look at all the young kids starting to move into the inner city.'

'I wouldn't live in those slums. It's bad enough Jennifer spends time hanging around that university area.'

Vi got up and cleared the plates. 'Well, you'll

be in a good position to hear about a little flat or townhouse when Jennifer is ready to buy something of her own,' said Vi.

Christina reacted in surprise, then dismissed Vi's remark. 'That will be a fine day. She's a long way from getting a proper job that will earn her enough money to buy even a car. All this research business and environmental studies nonsense. What good is that?'

Don carried the teapot to the sink and nudged Vi. 'Maybe she'll marry some rich bloke.'

Christina's short laugh had the brittle tinkle Vi knew held no mirth. 'Those kind of boys won't look at a country mouse like Jennifer. Anyway, she's not remotely thinking of any such thing. Heavens, Don, she's still so immature.'

Vi and Don exchanged a glance. Christina had met Blair but refused to acknowledge him if his name came up or if Jennifer mentioned they'd been somewhere together. She appeared to operate on the principle that if she ignored his existence he would disappear. Jennifer and Blair sometimes met Vi for lunch in town or in a suburb known for some speciality restaurant. Jennifer had the excuse that her mother was working so was unable to join them.

After Christina and Blair's initial meeting at a Sunday lunch at Vi and Don's, where Christina virtually ignored Blair, Jennifer and Vi decided things would run more smoothly if they kept Christina out of the loop. Privately Vi thought it best so, in case Jennifer and Blair's relationship floundered,

Christina wouldn't be able to say to Jennifer, I told you so, men can't be trusted . . . and so forth. Though from what Vi had observed, she thought Jennifer and Blair were quite serious about each other, and she told Don.

'Jeez, I hope not, luv. He's a nice enough young fella, but Jen needs to get out in the world a bit. You know, live a little.'

'I wish she could afford to go overseas when she graduates,' sighed Vi. 'The trouble is, Tina would want to go too.'

'Ain't that the truth,' agreed Don. 'I'd offer to throw a bit in the kitty if Jen did want a trip. But not if her mum tags along. Maybe she wouldn't be able to get time off work,' he added.

'Don, Tina would simply chuck in the job if it meant travelling with Jenny.'

'You're right, luv . . . Do you want to come and see my two new peach faces?'

Jennifer was the happiest she could remember. Her relationship with Blair had steadied and grown. They spent most weekends together in a comfortable domestic routine. She was glad her mother was no longer lonely and seemed stimulated by her job, even if the stimulus came from being critical of housing prices, agents' tactics and the rest of the staff. Jennifer made frequent flying visits to see Christina at Vi and Don's. To assuage her guilt at meeting Vi (sometimes Don came along too) and Blair for their epicurean lunches, she'd treat her mother to a lunch or a dinner.

Christina spent most of the meal tut-tutting over the prices. 'You shouldn't spend this money on me. My goodness, how can they charge these prices for that amount of food?'

But what was especially fulfilling to Jennifer was her own work. She loved her courses and was taking an extra course in ecology. Her part-time job with the National Parks had escalated. Her connection from her after-school job had proved useful, and now she was spending time in the field with several of the rangers. She travelled to areas fringing Sydney's north and south and was captivated by the inland waterways, wetlands and bushland. Standing on the headland at West Head, Jennifer thought she'd never seen such a magnificent location in all her life. She gazed across at the Palm Beach peninsula with its blunted tip of Barrenjoey Headland; Lion Island faced the swell of the Pacific Ocean at the mouth of Pittwater and Broken Bay; and she had the sweep of Ku-ring-gai National Park behind her. Here there were animals, plants and Aboriginal rock carvings that had existed centuries before Captain Cook ventured past this coastline.

Jennifer took deep breaths to steady herself. She had a sudden desire to fall forward, over the headland, and, as if in slow motion, fly. She could feel exactly the sensation of swooping, gliding, drifting on currents of air, soaring from a great height to skim across the surface of the water.

There would be a feeling of being supported in the air as if underwater. She smiled to herself. How joyful she felt when she was surrounded by the beauty of nature. From the silvery grey lichen on the log beside her, the smudges of colour on the smooth and pitted surface of the rock on which she stood, the old gums and twisted banksias with their knobbly trunks and gargoyle seed pods, to the slick of blue sea and sky divided by the finger of land, the silent caress of wind on her face. The stillness almost overwhelmed her.

But when she closed her eyes she heard the calls of birds, the rustling of leaves, and in her mind she could see the busyness of ants and insects, gliding snakes, the quietness of sleeping night creatures curled and furled into the crevices of trees and roots and rocks. She knew there were yachts and boats and homes and shops across the stretch of water, but they were just temporary brushstrokes on God's great canvas.

She fervently hoped this place would never change and she was glad she was involved with dedicated, admirable people who worked to protect areas such as this.

She enjoyed sharing her observations and thoughts about these issues with the rangers as it wasn't a subject she could discuss with Blair. She knew he wasn't thinking about what she'd do when she got her degree because he was concentrating on his own career.

And Blair's future was looking bright. He'd made a big impression in the year he'd been at the hotel as assistant to the manager. He'd been given more responsibility as they recognised he had a flair for controlling staff and keeping them on-side and motivated. His youth was seen as an advantage and he had solid marketing and admin-istrative skills plus experience in hands-on hotel work from the kitchen to the front desk. Everyone predicted he'd achieve success in whatever direc-tion he chose to direct his energies.

'Jenny . . . I've been thinking about your birthday.'

'Why Blair? It's not till next week.'

'I was trying to make it a surprise but you'd better get time off over the weekend. I thought we'd go away.'

'Really? That'd be nice. Where? How long?'

'I could only get three days away at the moment, but there's a fabulous boutique hotel up in the Hunter Valley. I can get a great deal through our hotel. How about it? All those wineries, nice restaurants, romantic suite . . .'

'How cool!' She hugged him, trying not to let him see that her eyes were suddenly filled with tears.

Jennifer's announcement of her birthday plans was not well received by her mother.

'You're going away for your birthday? With somebody?' Christina's expression was a marked contrast to Vi and Don's beaming faces.

'Not somebody, Mum. Blair. We've been together for nearly a year now. He's made the arrangements. It all sounds lovely. We're going to the opera in the vineyards!'

'Since when have you been interested in opera? Be careful, Jennifer, I don't want to see you get hurt by this fellow. He obviously comes from a better background than you and like sticks with like, you know.'

'There's nothing wrong with Jennifer's upbringing or family,' said Vi smartly. 'And how else are you going to grow and learn about things if you don't experience them?'

'Well, I hope she appreciates these opportunities to *experience* things,' sighed Christina. 'It wasn't done in our day, Vi. Going away for a dirty weekend with a man – and bragging about it!'

'Would you rather I sneaked off and said I was going with a girlfriend?' asked Jennifer quietly. She was hurt, her mother had sullied the shine of the whole idea now. She looked at Don, hoping he'd step in and deflect her mother's anger. She knew he wouldn't tackle Christina by criticising her but he could diffuse the tension that was building among Vi, Christina and Jennifer.

'What say we have a little pre-birthday party? Go somewhere nice for dinner. Maybe do something a bit different . . . have a picnic?'

'That's a lovely idea, Don,' Vi jumped in.

'We *are* being spoiled this year,' said Christina with a thin smile. 'Whatever you want to do, Jennifer.'

'A picnic sounds lovely. Thursday night.' Jennifer was relieved.

'Oh. Thursday.' Christina looked around. 'Is there a calendar somewhere?'

What now? Vi and Jennifer exchanged an amused glance, both ready to explode in laughter.

Christina turned her back to them as she flicked pages of the calendar on the kitchen wall. 'Oh dear.' She turned a stricken face to them. 'Well, I'll just have to cancel.'

'You have something on?' asked Vi with a raised eyebrow.

'Nothing important.' *Pause*. 'I've been taking tennis lessons for the past six months. We have our first little comp on Thursday night.'

They all stared at Christina who looked genuinely distressed. As she looked at the three stunned faces she became aware of the effect of her words.

'What's so shocking? I'm not senile, you know.'

Jennifer looked at her mother, really looked at her dispassionately, for the first time in years. She saw a slim, wiry thin, but fit and tanned woman in her early fifties. She'd coloured her hair. Jennifer had never noticed. Christina used to have a few grey hairs, now they'd gone and her nails were painted red. 'Mum! That's fantastic! Why didn't you tell us?'

'What! And have the lot of you down on me for starting something like this at my age? Telling me I'd injure myself?' Nonetheless she was looking a little pleased at their reaction. 'Actually, I'm not bad. Should have done this years ago.'

A nerve twitched in Jennifer. An instinct that told her Christina no doubt blamed her late father for the lost opportunity.

Don slapped his sister on the back. 'That's bloody beaut. Good for you. No wonder you're looking so trim. Play with ladies do you? Or are there a few blokes at the club?' he winked at Vi and Jennifer.

'Where, when have you been doing this?' asked Vi.

'With some people from work. We go at lunch times. Thursday is our first social outing.'

'Well, you can't miss that,' said Don.

'What say we all go?' said Vi.

'Yes, Mum, we'll come and be your cheer squad.'

'Oh, I'd be so embarrassed. I mean, I'm still learning . . .'

'Don't go all coy, Tina. We'll be there. What do you say, Jen? We'll take your birthday cake and some champers to share.'

'And celebrate your big win,' smiled Jennifer. She knew her birthday would be downplayed and they'd all pay lots of attention to Christina. That was fine by her. The break away with Blair would more than make up for it. And besides, she was keen to see her mother in this new light. *I bet Vi thinks she has a bloke. Well, I hope she does.*

67

To everyone's surprise it turned out to be a fun evening. Christina was a different person around other people. Vivacious, laughing, teasing her partner on the court, and she played well enough to help win the match. There were several men in the group but Christina didn't pay attention to anyone in particular. 'She plays to the gallery,' thought Jennifer. When Don broke out the champagne, one of the women laughed.

'Hey Tina, you came prepared to win. You had the game won before we started.'

'Here's to a rematch!' Christina raised her glass.

'And happy birthday, Jenny,' added Vi and Don.

'Oh, we didn't know. Happy Birthday, Jennifer,' chorused the group. Vi was furious. Why wouldn't Christina have mentioned it was her daughter's birthday? Darling Jen, so good natured. She hoped Blair would make it up to her.

And he did. Whether by good fortune, smooth management, or sheer luck, every moment of the three days was blissful for Jenny. The weather was perfect: cool fresh early mornings when they walked along the river watching wisps of mist drift across the gardens; warm balmy days as they explored the country around the vineyard towns, ate lunch in stylish and quaint restaurants, swam in the bathwater-warm pool at their elegant hotel; then lazy afternoons in their luxurious suite making love, sipping wine, before dressing to go out for dinner or staying in and being pampered on the terrace by candlelight. The Saturday night opera under the stars in one of the major vineyards had Jennifer clutching Blair's hand as she wept at the sheer beauty of the evening.

'Oh Blair, the night, the stars, those amazing voices, the music went right into me. I couldn't believe it was me sitting with a glass of champagne with all those smart people . . .'

'The midnight feast in the marquee, was that a triumph of catering or what?' Blair had paid great attention to the details, the flowers, the candles, the table settings, how they'd got power into the huge marquee to keep the food warm, or ice cold, and provide just enough amplification for the chamber quartet. 'Great setting for a wedding, or any convention function. Brilliant. I was talking to one of the organisers who told me how they managed in wet weather.'

Jenny smiled, knowing Blair was filing all this away should the day ever come when he could do something similar.

Blair rolled over in bed and reached for her hand. 'Had a nice birthday?'

Jennifer hugged him. 'The best ever. Thank you, thank you.'

'Jenny . . .' He was about to say something else but his words were stopped by Jennifer's flood of kisses.

The next morning Blair met Jeff, the manager of the hotel, for morning coffee. Meanwhile

Jennifer and Jeff's wife Trudy headed to the river to share a kayak and paddle down to a spot where Blair and Jeff would meet them and they'd all go to lunch.

Jeff and Trudy were in their thirties and had been managing the hotel for two years. 'It's been gorgeous because we've had a house here. Last job we had to stay in the hotel. But we'll be moving on at the end of the year. Down to the snow. I learned to kayak and did a wine appreciation course while we've been here. Suppose I'll be taking skiing lessons next!' laughed Trudy.

'Sounds like a good life,' said Jennifer. Though she thought living in quarters in a hotel or having to be on call and close by all the time would be a bit claustrophobic. She didn't ask what they'd do if they had children. Vi had made her aware that childless couples might be trying desperately to have a baby. But Jeff and Trudy seemed such an ambitious couple, children didn't seem part of their immediate plans.

'Are you and Blair serious?' Trudy asked Jennifer suddenly.

'Depends what you mean. We've been together a year but I've still got to finish my degree. And then think about finding work.'

Trudy didn't answer as they concentrated on dipping their paddles into the smooth water. As they glided forward Trudy pointed. 'Look, there're the guys. I'm ready to eat.'

Jennifer thought back to that afternoon several months later and wondered if Blair had talked about his future with Jeff. Jeff had promised to let Blair know of any job opportunities he heard of along the grapevine.

Two weeks later Jennifer came home late on Saturday afternoon, after staying much longer with the rangers than she'd planned, and found Blair pacing around the patio.

'Hey! I was getting worried. You said you'd be back after lunch,' he grumbled.

'Oh, did I? Blair, it was so fascinating, we were with this professor who's been studying the disappearance of several species of frogs from Sydney. It's all to do with the pollutants in the water, it's shocking what people put down stormwater drains –'

'We're supposed to be going over to the Harrisons' for drinks.'

'Oops, is it that late? I'll be ready in a flash.' Jennifer dashed into the bathroom, peeling off her clothes.

Standing under the shower she felt cross that Blair wasn't the least bit interested in what she'd been doing all afternoon. Admittedly, threatened amphibians mightn't interest Blair, even if it was ringing alarm bells in environmental circles, but he could at least listen to her for ten minutes or so. Jennifer sighed as she towelled herself dry and wondered what to wear. The Harrisons were important to Blair, and she'd never met the general manager of the hotel and his wife before.

Blair eyed Jennifer as she emerged from the bedroom in a simple beige silk shift caught at the shoulders with tiny gold buckles. Her legs were bare and she wore sand-coloured Italian sandals and simple but tasteful gold jewellery. Her damp hair was brushed smooth, falling to her shoulders and caught to one side with a comb. She was wearing lip gloss and eyeliner which made her blue eyes stand out. It was a dramatic change from the young girl who'd dashed in in khaki shorts and an old T-shirt shortly before.

'Do I look okay? My hair will dry by the time we get there.' She still felt insecure about looking and behaving appropriately with Blair's friends and colleagues. Not to mention the big boss. God, what would she talk about? Not frogs, that was for sure.

'You scrub up very well,' said Blair gruffly and he picked up the car keys. Jennifer followed, feeling chastened, unsure of Blair's mood.

When they returned home Blair seemed elated. Maybe it was the wine, though the company had been stimulating and, although the other couples were older, Jennifer had enjoyed herself too.

Blair made love to her with passion, murmuring endearments. As Jennifer was about to fall asleep in his arms he asked, 'What did you and old man Harrison talk about for so long?'

'Umm, sailing. Fishing . . . lots of things.'

'You don't sail or fish. Anyway, he liked you. So did Mrs H. She thought you were lovely and natural.'

'That's good. How else could I be?'

Blair tightened his arms and started to say something but Jennifer had fallen asleep.

The following Thursday night Blair and Jennifer were cleaning up after a home-cooked dinner. Jennifer was scrubbing the pan the bolognaise sauce had been cooked in. She was in shorts, a tank top, her hair scrunched back, her face scrubbed clean. Blair thought she looked about fifteen. How sweet and unaffected she was.

'So I think I'll go back to the library tonight. I want to go through my lecture notes and get ready for Dr Mylan's class tomorrow morning.' Jennifer pulled a yellow rubber glove off with a snap.

Blair stepped behind her, wrapping his arms around her, pinning her against the sink. 'Don't go, Jenny.' He kissed her ear.

Jennifer reached around to pat his head. 'I won't get any work done if I stay home tonight.'

Blair's grip tightened. 'Marry me, Jenny.'

They both froze. Blair stepped back allowing Jennifer to turn and face him, a stunned expression on her face.

'Will you, Jenny? Marry me?'

Jennifer shook her head as if to clear it and, looking at Blair's hesitant nervous expression, she exploded in laughter and flung her arms around him. 'Yes, yes. Oh Blair. Are you sure?'

'Are *you*?' He kissed her long and hard then drew back. 'Phew, I've been trying to get that out since your birthday. I thought that would be such a romantic place to do it, and, I don't know, I kept getting nervous waiting for exactly the right moment and something always happened. Tonight, it just popped out. Sorry. But I do have a ring.' He fumbled in his pocket and produced a small velvet box.

Jennifer reached for it, then realised her left hand was still encased in the rubber glove. Laughing, they pulled off the glove and Blair opened the box and took out a sparkling sapphire surrounded by tiny glittering diamonds. He slipped it on her finger and kissed her.

'Now you can't go back to study. You can stop worrying about those lectures.'

Jennifer was swept up in his embrace before she could protest. Never mind, she thought, he'd have to realise that much as she loved him, and this new idea of getting married, she was not giving up her studies.

Jennifer broke the news on the phone to Vi and Don, asking their advice on the best way to tell her mother. Neither had a concrete suggestion.

'Just don't let her know we knew first. Maybe arrive and wave your left hand around. Is it a pretty ring?'

'Oh Vi, it is pretty.' *If you like sapphires*, thought Jennifer, then scolded herself for being ungrateful. 'It's a circle stone. But it wasn't the world's most romantic proposal. I'll be telling my grandkids about it, that's for sure,' she laughed.

Privately Vi was horrified that Blair had proposed while Jennifer was scrubbing a pot at the kitchen sink. That was not the role she saw for her niece.

Jennifer dropped by Vi and Don's on a casual surprise visit and made a pot of tea and chatted to her mother while Vi and Don disappeared into the garden to clean out the cage that held Don's bleeding heart pigeons. She waved her hand with the ring in front of her, held it under her chin, pretended to wave away a fly and did everything but push it under Christina's nose.

Jennifer gave up. 'Mum, Blair and I want to take you out, or do something together . . . have a talk . . .'

'Who? Oh, that boy. I don't have anything to say to him, Jennifer. Why don't we go out for a meal, seems ages since we had a little tete-a-tete.'

'Mum, I want you to see Blair, talk to him.' *Deep breath*. 'We're engaged.'

Light laugh. 'Whatever are you talking about, engaged? That's ridiculous. At your age.'

Silently Jennifer held up her hand, dangling the ring before her. Christina's expression darkened, then looked tortured. 'You can't be serious. Jennifer, you're so young, you don't know what you're doing. You can't rush off with the first fellow who's smitten –'

'Mum, listen to me. Blair and I have been together for over a year. We're very committed to each other, he's proposed and I can see a good future with him.'

'Rubbish. What would you know about staying together? You haven't done anything in your life. Why throw it away on some man?' She looked genuinely concerned.

Jennifer was hurt, but she wasn't angry with her mother. Some instinct recognised the rationale behind her mother's objections and she saw that her mother's protective flare was ignited.

'Mum, it'll be all right. He's a decent guy, he has a good job, big prospects. What don't you like?'

'Jennifer, what do you know about him, really? His family. What are they like?'

'I've just met them, they seem nice. But Mum, we've got lots of time. We're not rushing into anything. We haven't even set a date.'

Blair had made noises about getting married in six months' time. Jennifer wanted to delay the big day, though she hadn't told Blair that it was because of her studies. Nor had Blair told Jennifer that Jeff, the hotel manager in the Hunter, had advised him that having a wife made his chances of promotion much better. 'They like couples, mate,' he'd said. 'A wife can be an asset if you're posted away, it also takes away the temptation to eye-off guests or staff.'

Christina had another thought. 'And how much is all this going to cost? I can't afford to pay for some fancy wedding.'

'I'm sure Vi and Don will help out,' said Jennifer quickly. 'I just want to keep it simple.'

As the weeks passed, Christina took over the wedding planning with an enthusiasm bordering on obsession. She called Jennifer constantly to check small details until Jennifer asked wearily if she could save up all her questions till they met on

Saturday morning. This was when Jennifer and her mother met for coffee, ran through Christina's inevitable list and then made a foray through fabric shops, gift shops, homeware places, and talked to photographers, florists and bridal stores.

'Now, isn't that lovely? That's just the sort of dress we want. Let's try it on,' enthused Christina, eyeing a frothy confection of lace and tulle.

Jennifer shuddered. 'Mum, that's not my style. Too fussy.'

'Oh Jennifer, you like such plain things. Surely your wedding dress could be a bit more . . . showy.'

'I like simple, uncluttered lines, and it's far too expensive anyway. I'd much rather Vi's friend the dressmaker make me something. You have to find your outfit, don't forget.'

The mother of the bride outfit diverted Christina's attention long enough for Jennifer to pick the fabric and pattern she wanted and have Vi's friend start sewing. Nevertheless Christina insisted on buying and presenting Jennifer with her 'trousseau outfit'.

Jennifer showed Vi the nylon shortie and matching robe, both embroidered with lace flowers and small beads, all in pale baby-doll pink.

Vi giggled. 'What'll Blair make of you appearing in that on your wedding night?'

'Probably throw up or call me cupcake. I can't hurt Mum's feelings, but we do have such different tastes. I'm a white cotton girl, which she hates.'

'I don't think she had any frills when she

married your dad, so go along with all this, Jen. Soon enough you'll have control of your own life.'

Jennifer looked at Vi. 'Do you think so? I just worry Mum will be over to the house redecorating. Blair has everything the way he wants it. He won't want her interfering.'

'Darling, it's your home too now. You make sure you put your stamp on it even if he owns it. You and Blair need to move somewhere else, start out fresh together.'

Jennifer nodded. Vi was right of course. But she didn't like to mention moving because she knew Blair could be offered a job anywhere, even overseas. And while they considered themselves equal partners in the relationship, Blair was older, made more money and had a definite career path. Jennifer's rambling studies of biology, biodiversity and natural history as part of her environmental science course were not exactly pointing to a clear career choice. Teaching was a possibility but it didn't excite her. After studying the work of early and renowned ecologists and biologists she wanted to research, explore and examine something that would add to the knowledge and preservation of the natural world.

Eight months later they were married. The wedding had escalated from Jennifer's original idea of keeping it simple, but she went with the flow of organisation that had zapped between the two families. Neither Blair nor Jennifer had a strong church affiliation but Jennifer's desire to be married outdoors 'in nature's cathedral' was brushed aside. They chose the small church in Lavender Bay and had their reception at Kirribilli Yacht Squadron, which Blair's parents arranged and paid for. For their honeymoon they planned to fly to a lodge in New Zealand famed for its food and fishing as Blair wanted to 'check it out'. And they got a discount.

Their honeymoon was Jennifer's first time out of Australia and her mood and spirits lifted higher than the plane as they left the east coast behind them. They toasted each other with a glass of champagne and Jennifer felt the stress of the wedding finally disappear.

As Jennifer's wedding day had drawn closer Christina had become withdrawn and distracted. She was quick to explode and everyone tiptoed around her.

'What's wrong with her, Vi?' asked Jennifer.

'Don and I have been thinking that maybe it's hit her that her little girl is leaving home and making a life without her.'

'Well, that's not really the case, is it?' sighed Jennifer. 'A ten-day honeymoon and I'll be back in the same city and see her as before.'

'She's probably thinking of your dad . . . not being there to give you away.'

'Uncle Don is like a dad,' said Jennifer and impulsively hugged Vi. 'You guys are so cool. With Mum, me . . . everything.'

'We love you, Jen. You know you can always count on us.'

Everything had gone as smoothly as possible on the day until they were about to leave for the church. Jennifer came out of a bedroom dressed in her gown – a straight cream slub silk with a square neckline and three-quarter sleeves. It was softened by a very low back with a slight train falling from the point of the V back. A plain tulle veil hung like a mist over her head and face and to the floor at the back. She carried a bouquet of wildflowers and native orchids and wore a strand of pearls Blair had given her.

Her mother hadn't seen the entire bridal outfit on and she stopped dead in her tracks as Jennifer came out of the bedroom. Here she was ready to step from a mother's reach into a realm where the mother–daughter relationship was now one of equal rights. Custom required Christina to relinquish her role of authority and it struck her like a sudden injury. A wound that was raw and, she felt, one that would never heal. There would always be a scar, a scab, that she'd pick at till it festered and bled. And it was that blood that united them, through distance, through silences, through moments of forgiveness and love. And loss.

Seeing the shock on Christina's face, Vi quickly bustled around exclaiming how utterly beautiful Jennifer looked. Don wiped a tear away.

Jennifer smiled at her mother. 'You're a knock-out, Mum, you look fantastic. I'll throw the bouquet to you.'

They all agreed Christina did look very glamorous in her cyclamen silk suit, a wisp of a matching bow and feather perched on the side of her head. She had matching brilliant lipstick and nails. But suddenly Christina clutched her chest and staggered forward, gasping for breath.

'God, Tina, what's wrong?' Vi rushed forward as Christina looked like she was going to faint.

'Mum!'

They helped her into a chair and Don rushed for a shot of brandy. He poured one for himself as well. 'Here, luv, have this.'

'Don, do you think it's her heart?' asked Vi.

Christina waved an arm as Jennifer crouched beside the chair. 'Don't crush your gown . . . I'm all right.'

'Should we get a doctor?' Don glanced at his watch.

Christina gulped the brandy and mopped her forehead. 'I'll be fine . . .'

She rallied and, apart from looking pale and saying little, she got into the car with Vi while Don and Jennifer waited for the bridal car. They later assumed it was stress that hit Christina but Vi was irritated when they arrived at the church and Christina stepped from the car smiling and greeting guests 'like a queen', Vi told Don later.

Christina wasn't to be seen when Jennifer finally threw her bouquet, but when she and Blair were leaving the reception for their hotel Don took Jennifer aside.

'You'd better see your mother. Say goodbye. She's upset.'

Blair rolled his eyes and turned back to his friends who wanted to chauffeur the newlyweds in a wildly decorated car. Jennifer had refused and asked for a taxi.

Christina was at a table in the empty restaurant, sobbing into a tissue, Vi's arm around her shoulders.

Jennifer went and touched her arm. 'Mum, what is it? Please don't spoil my day.' Jennifer was tired, it had been a long, exciting, draining and stressful day. They had stayed too long at the reception and she wanted desperately to be alone with Blair to savour all the moments of their wedding.

'Spoil? Jennifer, I've tried so hard to make this a wonderful day for you. I've only ever wanted to make everything nice for you. How can you say that?' Christina was sobbing.

'She didn't mean it like that, Tina. Jen hates seeing you upset. It's been a wonderful, wonderful wedding,' said Vi.

'It has, thank you so much, Mum. I mean it. What's upset you so much?'

Christina lifted her tear-stained face. 'How can you ask that?'

Jennifer looked despairingly at Vi.

'She feels she's losing you. Her little girl is leaving the nest. It's just hit her.'

'I'll be so lonely without you, Jennifer. You're all I've got in this world.'

'Mum, don't be silly. Nothing is going to change, you'll see us just as often. And you have Vi and Don and all your friends. Come on . . . cheer up.' Jennifer spoke brightly, determined not to get into a maudlin discussion.

Vi spotted Don waving at the doorway. 'Jenny, your taxi is ready. Better not keep your husband – and all the guests – waiting,' Vi said with relief as she got to her feet.

Christina's head snapped up. 'Taxi? We paid for a bridal car.'

'Mum, you should see what the boys have done to it. It's embarrassing. I'm not about to arrive at the hotel trailing tin cans and rude slogans all over the car.'

Christina smoothed her skirt. 'Honestly, Jennifer, sometimes you can be such a stick in the mud. Why wouldn't you want everyone to know you just got married? It's nothing to be ashamed of, after all.' Christina was on her feet, leading the way out of the room. 'Come on, Don, let's go throw roses, rice, whatever we're allowed . . .'

Vi's shoulders sagged and she squeezed Jennifer's hand as they headed for the taxi that would drive Jennifer and Blair to their new life.

4

Sydney, 2004

Adrift

THE FIRST YEARS OF Jennifer's marriage to Blair had blurred. They'd slipped into a comfortable routine and it seemed to Jennifer that not a lot had changed after she signed the marriage certificate. She'd imagined there would be heart-stopping moments and a great sense of freedom. Being Mrs Blair Towse gave her an identity that meant tradespeople asked for her husband, bills came addressed to him and, increasingly, Blair made decisions about what items they could afford to buy for the house or where they'd go for dinner. If she suggested a restaurant he generally shook his head, 'No I want to try this other place, see what the chef is doing, check out the decor. It's getting good write-ups.'

'Why don't you go for lunch? Then we can go out on a weekend for fun, with friends.'

'Jennifer, I don't have time for lunches. I eat in the hotel. You don't seem to realise the kind of pace I work at, what's involved. I have to be on the case, on top of everything. We've got a lot of important people in the hotel, a convention, so I have to be around.'

'That's fine, Blair. Just give me a clue about the dress code for Saturday night.' She'd been caught out a couple of times, dressing too casually for a five-star restaurant then overdressing the following week for a new French brasserie that was yuppily casual. 'I'm off to class. I might stay late and talk to some of the students about their papers.'

He nodded, his attention on the computer screen. Jennifer had lost her small workspace in the terrace house and Blair refused to consider buying anything bigger.

'This place is very rentable and the mortgage is reasonable. Why should I sell when we're sure to be moved when my promotion comes through?'

Jennifer hadn't argued. The house had been bought by Blair and stayed in his name. She kept her salary for her personal purchases, running her little secondhand car and buying some household things as well as paying half of the weekly food bill. She thought they could have economised more on the food end but Blair liked the best quality organic produce, expensive cheeses and good wine.

Jennifer had invested in a sophisticated laptop through the university which helped her work-load. When she had to work at home on assignments for her undergraduate degree the lap-top was compact and easy to set up on the kitchen table as Blair generally had the TV on. He kept it on whether he watched it or not. When he wasn't there Jennifer rejoiced in playing her CDs.

Their life revolved primarily around Blair's career. He earned more money, he held their future in his hands, while her job was considered an inter-esting side bar. And one that no one apart from Vi and Don took any interest in. Her mother was more concerned with their domestic arrangements. Their friends had corporate or sales jobs and couldn't relate to an 'academic'. Though Jennifer felt flattered to be considered 'an intellectual', she was still fumbling her way in her quest to find a proper role and direction within the fields that interested her. She had a bread and butter job, but she was still seeking a way to move in a direction that would allow her to research, to exchange ideas, to make her own mark somehow. The pro-fessors and PhD students in the school of environmental sciences were accommodating, sharing information, letting her read papers, and answering her questions. But they were frequently absent on research and study excursions and when they came back they went to the pub and talked about places and experiences she couldn't share.

Jennifer wondered where she would find a particular niche in her life that was hers alone.

She touched lightly on the subject with Vi who told her, 'Sweetie, it's all well and good, interesting to you, and maybe in some small way it's valuable, but that's not your life. Your future is linked with Blair's. The fella is the breadwinner, I can't see a lot's changed even with all this gender equality and women's lib.' She saw Jennifer's face close up. She was thinking Vi was out of touch. 'Mark my words, you'd better accept that it is the woman who always has to compromise. So keep your hand on the tiller and your toe in the door, but be ready to change everything if Blair gets a job in Vienna, Paris, Bangkok, wherever.'

Jennifer and Blair were snuggled close in bed. Blair, satisfied after lovemaking, was sinking into sleep. Jennifer stroked his arm.

'Sweetie, what do you think about children?'

'What about them?'

'Well, when, I mean, maybe we should try . . .'

Blair opened his eyes. 'What do you mean? You don't mean now, do you?'

'Why not?'

'Jennifer, don't be crazy. How can you ask that? A kid would complicate our life, my job prospects, no end.' Blair was wide awake.

Jennifer felt his arm stiffen. She took her hand away. 'What about my job prospects?'

'C'mon, if you're thinking of a family you

can't be serious about full-time work. And a kid would cost heaps. There's plenty of time.' He paused. 'Are you bored?'

'Not at all.' She rolled away from him. 'I thought I could juggle motherhood and uni, plenty of women do.'

He heard the resentment in her voice. 'Jennifer, if you had a baby you'd have to do most of the looking after it. You know what my work schedule is like. Unless you want your mother here all the time.'

'If *we* have a baby. It's a joint effort.'

'Let's discuss this another time. Don't spoil a nice evening.'

It's all right for you, you've had a great meal, the house is clean and tidy, you're sexually satisfied, you don't want to think about anything that might mean you have to put yourself out. 'Forget I mentioned it.'

Blair decided that would be best. He turned on his side and was swiftly asleep. Jennifer lay awake for some time thinking about her future. Their future.

'Look at this. What a disaster!' Jennifer was eating a piece of toast, watching the early-morning TV news. The news helicopter was flying along the southern coastline of Sydney where a sludgy brown slick was covering several kilometres of the normally pristine ocean.

'What is it?' Blair glanced up from the newspaper.

'A sewage leak. That's raw crap floating out there. It's a disgrace.'

'Better swim at the northern beaches.' He returned to the paper.

'Blair! That's not the point. Haven't you heard about the contamination around sewerage outfalls? Now they're finding that fish are changing sex or not developing their reproductive organs properly as a result of the estrogens in contraceptive pills flushed down toilets through the drains and out to sea.'

Blair gave a slight smile. 'Sure. One of the chefs says some of the fish they serve are known as shitties 'cause they feed where the sewage goes into the ocean.'

'That's disgusting. The sea isn't a waste dump. All that the government and councils worry about is making sure that shit doesn't land on the sand.' Jennifer dropped her bowl in the sink. 'I'm going to uni.'

In the staff room in the environmental sciences block there was heated debate stemming from the morning news on the issue of the outfalls and the health of ocean ecosystems.

One of the staff summed up, 'Damage to marine biodiversity is a major issue that isn't recognised or funded enough.'

'Big field of study, too. There's a PhD in that for you, Jennifer,' added another.

'Oh, I hadn't thought that far ahead,' she said. 'I've got too many areas of interest.' But she was thinking of Blair, his career, his plans, his reluctance for her to get too involved in interests outside the home. Even in the home, like having a baby.

'Professor Matt Dawn is looking for a grad student to work with him on his study of the EAC. You could apply,' suggested one of the lecturers.

As she looked blank, he explained, 'The East Australian Current. It's the biggest ocean current around the coastline of Australia. It starts in the Coral Sea and shifts a surface stream of warm water, tens of metres deep, along the boundary of the Coral and Tasman seas.'

Another professor added, 'Scientists have been studying it for a century but only in the last decade have they realised how important it is to our lifestyle and livelihood. Not to mention aquatic plant and animal life.'

'Sounds interesting. I think I'd rather do a study on land though. I'm a country girl.' Jennifer got to her feet, glancing at her watch. 'I'd better go, I'm late for my class.' She was helping her professor with occasional classes, organising lectures, dealing with students and doing a lot of what was considered 'grunt' work for the senior professor in her department. She was considered a good writer, combining academic material with a poetic and sensitive flair, and she was often asked to edit dry factual papers to make them more accessible to students.

They watched her leave. A woman member of staff said quietly, 'Jennifer is not comfortable with oceanic studies. Her father and brother drowned.'

There was a muttering of sympathy but attention swiftly moved to their own commitments.

Several weeks later Jennifer tapped the newspaper Blair was reading. For the past three weeks breakfast had been their only time together. Blair was working a night manager's shift and on weekends he slept at the hotel. 'Hello. Anyone home?'

'Umm . . . yeah?'

'Blair, I'm working on a book.' She grinned.

'Like, writing?'

'Of course. I'm quite excited about it.'

He looked puzzled, not fully understanding her flushed and expectant face. 'What is it, a romance? The Great Australian Novel?'

'No. Don't be silly. It's an academic book. On pollution. I'm helping with writing up Professor Dawn's studies.'

'Oh.' *Is that all* seemed to drift above his head. 'So what's that mean? More money, I hope.'

'Maybe.' She then burst out, 'It mightn't sound interesting, but Professor Dawn hopes it could be groundbreaking and important. Like, you know, *Silent Spring*, or something. I'm helping with interpreting his research. One day I'll do my own study.'

Blair folded the newspaper, rattled at the intensity in her voice. 'Listen, Jennifer, you're not making a full-time career of this stuff. It's just a job . . . for now.'

There was something in his voice that made

her uncomfortable. Why were they always talking at cross purposes, never really communicating? 'What do you mean? I'm just filling in time before we have babies? Of course it's a *proper* job.'

'I hope you can continue this book project long distance.' He got up from the table and gave her a strained smile. 'I was keeping my news for a surprise. I was going to tell you over a bottle of champagne.'

'Tell me what?'

'I've got a promotion. Assistant manager. At a resort hotel.' He opened his arms. 'Aren't you pleased? It's a big step up. Thanks to Trudy and Jeff who we saw in the Hunter.'

Jennifer felt her head start to spin. 'The couple who ran that hotel? What's that got to do with us? What do you mean by resort? Where is it?'

'It's a tropical paradise. An island. On the Great Barrier Reef. How about that?' His smile faded as Jennifer stood staring at him in shock.

'An *island*?' She could hardly choke out the words. She couldn't imagine anything worse. Somehow she'd imagined their first move, when it eventually happened, would be somewhere overseas. She'd imagined boulevards, cafes, antique markets. An island resort was the last place she'd imagined, not even Asia or the South Pacific, and not this soon.

'It'll be great. I'll have a lot of responsibility, really be able to make my mark in the boutique hotel line.'

'What about me? And what about uni? My book project?'

'Listen, sweetheart, you knew this was on the cards, what our plans were. You're not on contract, and can't you do the book thing by email?'

'But what'll I do?' Jennifer sounded on the verge of tears. This had come as a shock. 'I didn't even know you were thinking of applying for this job!'

Blair became defensive. 'You could get a job at the resort.'

'What, making beds?'

'C'mon. I'm sorry if this has come as a surprise. I thought you'd be pleased. Let's talk about it tonight. I'll bring all the brochures, pictures, CD-ROM . . . you'll love it. I'll let you know where we're going for dinner. I got the night off.'

'Why can't you tell me now? I might have to go there straight from my meeting with Matt Dawn. God, I don't know how I'm going to tell him about this.'

Blair yawned, and headed to the bedroom. 'I thought we might eat later with the two corporate managers. Then you can hear about it firsthand.'

Jennifer just stared at him. 'And I won't be able to complain or say I don't want to go there and embarrass you.'

'Don't you want to go?'

'Do I have a choice?' Jennifer turned her back. 'Just let me get used to the idea, Blair.'

Later in the week Jennifer had lunch with a girl-friend who worked in the admin department of the university and Trisha, her friend from university. Trisha thought the resort and the island sounded stunning.

'Jenny, it's right on the Barrier Reef – one of the wonders of the world!'

'God, I can see myself sitting by that pool with a pina colada watching the waves crash on the reef outside the lagoon,' added the other girl.

'For a week or two, then what do I do?' sighed Jennifer.

'Can't you work on your laptop and email?' asked Trisha.

'Or commute? How far away is the mainland? What town do you go from?'

Jennifer could see they were not seeing this from her perspective. Neither was married and they had office jobs, not academic positions. 'From Headland Bay. There's a catamaran service that takes a couple of hours. Or an expensive heli-copter trip. It's a really small place.'

'How romantic.'

'Yeah. You have to go to the mainland for shopping, entertainment, everything. I'll probably get seasick.' The girls laughed but Jennifer was concerned. The more she heard about the place from Blair and Reg Holding and Joe Fanzio, the corporate managers representing the resort own-ers, the more depressed she became.

She rang Vi and asked to meet her for a coffee, telling her the basic news. 'But don't say anything to Mum yet. I'll tell her when I can come to terms with this whole idea.'

'It doesn't sound like what you'd hoped Blair would do. What about your book? Could you stay on the mainland and visit Blair on the island?'

'That's not a silly idea, Vi,' said Jennifer. 'Remember what you told me, the woman always has to compromise. It doesn't seem fair.'

'If you love him, that's the trade-off, sweetie.'

Jennifer got on the internet and trawled through sites that covered Australia's magnificent Great Barrier Reef. There were a few mentions of Branch Island and she spent time looking at the resort's website trying to imagine how she would spend her days. Tears of frustration sprang to her eyes and she wondered what she'd done to deserve this place, of all locations, as her home for the next eighteen months – at least. And home meant a suite in the resort. Not even separate quarters.

Blair cuddled her tightly curled body, trying to ignore her weepy voice as he held her during the night. 'It's going to be fine, trust me. I know you're not a beachy person, but this is a big move for me. Just support me, hang in there for this first gig and then we'll get a post in Europe. Somewhere nice. I know it.'

Jennifer felt mean and selfish. And sorry for herself. The conversation with Professor Dawn about her move and the future of their collaboration had been traumatic. The arrogant and austere professor was relying on Jennifer more than she knew to turn his work of important, but dry, facts

95

about the dangers of world pollution into a polished and emotive book. He had reluctantly agreed – 'as I have little alternative' – to work long-distance by email and exchange drafts of hard copy by post. Jennifer tried to be as accommodating and positive as she could because she saw this as the only intellectually stimulating diversion she'd have on the island and the only means of continuing and promoting her career.

Vi and Don invited several of their friends to Sunday lunch, knowing Jennifer was going to break the news of the move to Christina. Blair was working so they thought their friends would act as a buffer. Vi had suggested Christina invite any friends from work or the tennis club.

'Now, Vi, why would I want to do that? I thought this was a family luncheon. I see little enough of my daughter as it is. She's always in a rush, I don't want strangers monopolising her.'

'Well, our dear friends Harry and Joan are going to be here, they like Jennifer such a lot, I just thought . . .'

'Of course, I'd forgotten Jennifer must know all your friends seeing she spent so much time here while I was on my own. I so wanted to show her off when she came to visit but she never had time to socialise with any of my friends down south.'

Jennifer had told Vi of her mother's life in the claustrophobic town, how Christina had kept close tabs on the activities of people in the area through gossip in shops, the street, the library and the club without developing any close friendships or ever visiting people in their homes. Yet when Harry, a bird fancier like Don, and Joan, who played bowls with Vi, arrived, it was Christina who turned on the charm and personality, swamping them with anecdotes and feigning tremendous interest in their life while almost ignoring Jennifer.

In the kitchen Jennifer whispered to Vi. 'How am I going to tell her? Maybe I should wait till after lunch. Or after everyone has gone, when it's just the two of us. But she'll go on and on and be negative. And I'm not wildly positive myself, so I don't want her to see that. If she finds out in front of other people she can't shoot the idea down so much.'

'I'll prompt Joan to ask you about your plans,' suggested Vi. 'Play it by ear, Jen.'

And so in an apparently light-hearted, off-the-cuff response, Jennifer prefaced her announcement before turning to Christina, 'Well now, funny you ask. That's the big surprise I have for my mother.'

'I don't like surprises,' said Christina.

'Blair has a great promotion. He's going to be running a resort on the Barrier Reef. Very exclusive, very beautiful. We're so excited.' *Oh God, I deserve an Oscar.*

'An island? You'll live there? What are you going to do?' asked Christina. 'When are you supposed to go there?'

'Well, it's all a bit sudden, someone got sick, had to retire early so it's a great opportunity for Blair.'

'A tropical paradise, I could take a bit of that,' smiled Harry.

'What do you mean this person got sick? Is the water safe to drink? I suppose they have to send food over so it must go off,' remarked Christina.

'You can always live on fresh fish,' said Harry.

'It sounds pretty expensive, I think they have very flash food. Probably a top chef there, eh Jennifer?' Don smiled encouragingly.

'How do you get there? It doesn't sound like a promotion to me,' sniffed Christina. 'What about cyclones?'

Jennifer ignored the cyclones. 'I'll show you pictures. It's going to be a bit of a change of lifestyle, that's for sure. And we have to be up there by the end of the month.'

'So soon! How are you going to manage that?' Christina was visibly shocked.

'Well, it could have been Europe,' said Jennifer, gently trying to remind her mother that she was only a few hours up the coast and not on the other side of the world.

There was a hasty removal of plates and passing of fruit salad and showing around of photos and brochures. Christina was very quiet.

As arranged, Blair arrived late in the afternoon to collect Jennifer and over a beer, at Don's insistence, accepted the congratulations and answered a barrage of questions. Christina busied herself in the kitchen, ignoring the group still gathered around the dining table.

Jennifer closed the dishwasher. 'Come on,

Mum, let's join the others. We have to go soon. Lots to do at home. And I have to get ready for uni tomorrow.'

'Well, I suppose you can forget all about that now.'

Jennifer winced. 'Oh no, Professor Dawn has been great. I'll be able to get a lot done on the book on the island without distractions and classes.'

'And how long will you be at this place? I don't imagine the likes of us will be able to afford to come and visit.'

'I'm sure Blair can arrange a family rate. Unfortunately we won't have our own place. Just a suite with its own garden area but it looks lovely.'

'You'll live in two rooms? What about all your things? Your place here?' Christina was aghast.

Yeah, tell me about it. 'Storage, Mum. We'll rent Blair's house. We plan on saving as much as we can.'

'It's your house, too, don't forget, Jennifer. You won't be earning any money. Does he give you housekeeping money?' she asked suddenly.

'Oh Mum, that's so old fashioned. I might be able to get a job in the resort or on the island.' *Fat chance. Blair is management and that puts paid to hiring family.*

'Do you have a phone in your room? When are we going to see you? It all sounds very odd.' Christina's voice trembled.

Jennifer gave her a swift hug. 'Come on, Mum,

it's not so bad. Just think of it as one long holiday. People pay a fortune, come from all over the world to visit the reef. We'll get you over there or meet you on the mainland in Queensland for a visit.'

Christina brightened visibly. 'I suppose I could take holiday leave. What's this island called again? Not that I plan on going. But a visit up the coast would be nice.'

'Mum, let me get settled in first! It's Branch Island. Off Headland Bay. Way up north. Come on, let's join the others.' She took her mother's hand and drew her outside, catching Vi's eye who gave her a 'Well done' nod.

Blair went ahead to Branch Island to 'settle in', leaving Jennifer to drive Blair's car, crammed with belongings, to Headland Bay. She'd sold her old car and put the money in her personal account. It would take her two days to drive, but Jennifer enjoyed being in her own space after the hectic weeks of packing up, rounds of farewells and reorganisation of their life. Without Blair around she had packed two big cartons of books, despite his repeating that they should take as little as possible.

'You don't need many clothes. It's all very laid-back. Just something nice to wear to drinks with guests occasionally. If you have any questions call Rosie, she'll tell you what not to bring.'

'Who's Rosie?'

'The manager, on the island. The bosses are in Sydney, you met them.'

'So she's your boss. On the island.' Why was she pleased to know Blair would be answering to a woman boss?

'I have my instructions from corporate head-quarters. She's been there for yonks. Probably a bit out of touch, though she has good local knowl-edge, I suppose. She's not circulating through the hotel chain like I will be.'

'Let's hope!'

'Listen, Jenny, this is a kind of trial. The big boys have their eye on me. I'll be doing a bit of everything at the resort, to get the feel of how these boutique places work. It's different from a big international hotel where you hardly get to meet three-quarters of the staff. I'll be putting in long hours.'

'And I'll be working on my tan,' she said flip-pantly, but he chose to ignore it.

The packing process brought home to Jennifer how few possessions were hers. Apart from her clothes, books, a couple of paintings, her laptop, CD player, work materials and the juicer she'd bought, the house and everything in it, from fur-niture to placemats and bedsheets, had been bought by Blair. She'd walked into a ready-made marital home. She had added pots of flowers and herbs to the tiny terrace patio and she handed these over to Vi and Christina, 'in case the renters don't water the garden'.

She imagined her mother had also pared back her life in the move from the farm to the house in town and then to a couple of rooms downstairs at her brother's house. But to Jennifer's surprise when she went to see her, her mother had pointed at a battered shoe box sitting on the kitchen bench.

'Had that tucked away, don't know if you want it.' She put it in a carry bag. 'Take it with you – I've got enough clutter in my room. When I get a place of my own I'll spread around the stuff I have stored.' Christina busied herself elsewhere. This was sensitive emotional territory.

At home Jennifer took out the box, her childish writing on the lid, and she felt a catch in her throat. It held her treasures, gathered lovingly from the farm, which she'd kept under her bed in the house in town to remind her of the childhood home she'd lost. She gently separated the dried leaves and flowers, a silkworm cocoon, a dried-up stick insect, a butterfly whose wings had lost their powdery beauty, some drawings and the fossilised shell.

She turned the shell over in her hand, wondering at its life span, the millennia it had taken to create this slice of earthly evolution. She put it with the jewellery she was taking with her, conferring on the ancient limestone a sense of value, of being somehow precious.

As she drove, Jennifer thought about what she had packed for herself: the books waiting to be read, the notes and tapes from Professor Dawn, her collection of CDs to enjoy and the tennis racquet her mother had given her, 'To fill in time. Get someone to teach you how to play, then we can have a game when you come to visit.' She didn't want to leave the racquet behind as her mother would notice, but Christina probably didn't realise how hot it was going to be. Jennifer assumed there'd be air conditioning and a nice pool. She kept blotting out the knowledge of the sea that surrounded this supposedly idyllic island. Much to her relief Blair had told her their room didn't face the ocean, that was for the high-paying guests.

Don had wanted to give her one of his masked lovebirds in a small cage but Vi had talked him out of it.

'I don't think you can take animals onto the island because it's mostly National Park,' said Jennifer. 'Besides, the place is teeming with birds, but thanks for the thought.'

'You will send us emails and tell us all about it?' said Vi.

'Of course. And you two must come and visit.'

'Well, until we get up there and see for ourselves, we got you a present,' said Don. He handed her a small satellite radio.

Jennifer was touched. 'Don! Vi! You shouldn't have. This is so great!'

'We know Blair has a digital camera. You can send us photos on the email,' said Vi. 'I'm having lessons on the computer. And it'll make your mum happy too. Don thought the radio reception might be sketchy and he knows you like the news.'

Jennifer wondered what she would photograph after the first week or so with the island being so small and there being so few people, but she was glad she'd be able to keep in touch with civilisation and thanked them profusely. 'You've been so good to me. And Mum. I hope it won't be too much of a strain with me not being around.'

'Don't you worry, pet. She'll be fine. You get on with your life.'

Jennifer had been surprised that the farewell with her mother wasn't the emotional battleground she'd expected. In retrospect that would have been easier. Seeing her mother vulnerable and teary, defenceless almost, upset Jennifer. Christina clung to her.

'I'm not going far away, Mum. Not like overseas or anything. We'll get you up for a visit in a couple of months.'

'You're my girl, you remember that, Jen-Jen.'

The mention of the pet name her brother Teddy had called her brought tears to her eyes and she couldn't speak.

'Off you go. And please be careful. Call me when you get up there. I hate you doing that long drive.' Christina tried a brave smile.

'I'll be fine. It will all be an adventure. I'll call along the way when I stop. Love you, Mum.'

Christina nodded, too choked up or just unable to utter the words that meant so much to Jennifer.

The terminal at Headland Bay where the Reef Cat was berthed was crowded and chaotic even at this early morning hour. Jennifer stood in the middle of the swirling sea of holidaymakers, tourists and a class of excited schoolchildren. The staff, dressed in crisp white shorts and T-shirts emblazoned with a red sail on one shoulder, remained calm and smiling. One woman, noting all the boxes and bags piled on the luggage cart next to Jennifer, took her aside.

'Hi there, you moving to the island? A new staffie?'

'Ah, sort of. My husband is the new assistant manager.'

'Ah, Mr Towse. Checked him in over a week ago. Left you with all the packing and baggage, eh?' She grinned. 'I'm Vera. Tell you what, we're a bit full with these kids – going over on a school excursion. So how about we throw all your gear on the cat, you grab your handbag and I'll put you on the chopper. There's a spare seat.'

'Oh, how much is that?'

'Don't worry about it. You're staff, take it as a welcome to Branch gesture. You can store your car here too, if you like. The chopper has to make the trip anyway, and it's only forty-five minutes. The cat takes over two hours.'

'I was scared I'd get seasick. The helicopter would be fantastic.' Jennifer hadn't ever been in one before but she'd have walked on water if she could save herself the sea trip.

The other passenger waiting with the pilot was a tall man with a short beard, greying hair pulled back in a pony tail and granny glasses. He wore a faded Hawaiian shirt and navy shorts. He carried a computer bag and a briefcase, which contrasted with his outfit.

The pilot shook Jennifer's hand. 'Bob Ford. You're Jennifer Towse. Good to have you guys on board. Blair's settling right in to island life.' He smiled. 'This is Professor Macdonald Masters.'

Jennifer and the professor nodded to each other as the pilot stowed their laptops behind the seats.

'I hope I'm going to enjoy Branch Island as much as my husband does,' Jennifer said to Bob. 'This is my first time up here.' She was suddenly nervous. The helicopter was so small.

'Hey, there's plenty to do . . . snorkelling, fishing, exploring the reef, sailing, bird-watching. Soon be turtle time too, hey prof?'

'Another month.' The older man got into the rear seat. 'If it's your first visit to the reef you should be in front.'

Bob ran through the safety procedures and showed Jennifer how to put on the headphones with their attached microphone. He offered to give her a bit of a running commentary.

She nodded, swallowing hard as the rotor whirred and lifted them off the ground so gently she was barely aware of it until they lurched sideways as Bob angled the chopper out over the marina and across the bay towards the open sea. Jennifer closed her eyes, hoping she wasn't going to be sick.

Gradually the sensation in her stomach and throat settled and she began to relax. Encapsulated in the plastic bubble of the cockpit she felt as if she were in the all-encompassing eye of a bumble bee. Blue sky met blue sea, its surface occasionally stirred by white frills where a boat ploughed or a bird swooped. The water began to change colour, becoming more aqua and turquoise as if lit from below by a blazing torch.

'Just like the tourist brochures, eh?' Bob's voice crackled in her earphones. 'You'll start to see the reef soon. Well, bits of it.'

She smiled at him. 'How long is it? Is it all islands or is it joined together?'

'Almost as big as Texas! Bigger than Great Britain! It's nearly three thousand individual reefs that extend off the Queensland coast from the Gulf of Papua to just beyond the Tropic of Capricorn. Truly one of the great wonders of the world. And one of the few major reef systems left that haven't been totally devastated. You have to go underwater to really appreciate its beauty.'

'Not me. I'm no diver. I don't even snorkel.'

The pilot gave her a quizzical look. 'Well, you can always explore the edge of the reef at low tide. Look at that.'

It was breathtaking. Beneath the surrounding clear turquoise water, she could see the shadowy patches and ribbons of reef and, above the surface, small coral cays, some edged with patches of gold or ripples of white. It was like a giant creature lazily hovering just below the surface of the sea, bits of its scaly, horny back protruding into the sunshine.

'Branch is one of only three coral islands that are on the actual spine of the main reef. The other resorts are on outcrops of reef, which means you have to get on a boat or a chopper to get to it for diving or fishing or whatever. We're lucky. On Branch you can roll out of bed into the sea and you're there.'

Jennifer nodded. She was overwhelmed by the scope of the stunning beauty below her. And frightened at being at its mercy. As Branch Island loomed it looked so small, a tiny green dot surrounded by a narrow white strip. It seemed to her that billions of grains of sand clinging together were all that protected her from being swallowed should that peaceful sleeping sea change its mood.

The helicopter began to descend. She was landing on an alien planet adrift in wet blue, turquoise and gold. She saw the thin lace of vegetation and prayed she would find a sanctuary hidden from the sea amongst the spindly windswept trees.

5

Branch Island, 2004

Storm at Sea

THE ISLAND LOOKED BIGGER and busier as they skimmed over the deep indigo water outside the reef and across the pale turquoise lagoon to where the sandy beach met the broad expanse of coral that formed the island. The fringe of reef looked like sepia crochet, clumps of coral linked by small pools and patches of white sand. The tide was halfway across the shoreline reef, rivulets and channels rushing towards the sand where, come moonrise, the aqua coverlet would turn back upon itself again.

Jennifer saw the rusted skeletal remains of an iron boat jammed into the reef; it jarred the pristine scene. Further away on the horizon was a smudge that Bob pointed out to her.

'That's Sooty. A tiny private islet the resort leases from the owner. It's got the more rustic eco accommodation. Y'know, mozzies, safari tents, campfire, barbies and skinny dipping. Upmarket roughing it.'

'Sooty is a strange name. Was it a volcano?'

'The Great Barrier Reef is millions of years old. Nah, it's named after the sooty-headed terns that roost all over it.'

Spread over several kilometres of ocean were dive and fishing boats; closer in, windsurfers and kayaks. An extended jetty had tourist boats tied to its spindly legs. Floating bodies of splayed snorkellers drifted face down, peering at the mottled sea bottom. Figures lazed around the flash of vivid blue swimming pool beneath leaning palms. Jennifer glimpsed the marked-out circle of cement at the edge of the sand where three people waited. And then with a scratchy bump they were on the ground.

Bob helped her down and she felt the heat whack her in the face, hot and moist. She squinted in the glare looking for Blair. A woman in big sunglasses came towards her.

'You must be Jennifer. Welcome to Branch. I'm Rosie Jordan. Blair is over at Sooty, he thought you were coming on the cat.'

'It was a fantastic trip. Thank you, Bob. And nice to meet you, Professor Masters.' Jennifer took her laptop, which he held out to her. 'I'm glad I was in the front.'

'Welcome back, Mac, be seeing you round.'

'Sure thing, Rosie.' The professor pulled on his cotton hat and smiled at Jennifer. 'I'm sure we'll meet again. The island can be a small place.'

'Come on, Jennifer, I'll take you to your quarters and then show you around if you'd like. It might seem a small world but staff get off the island for a break every two weeks. In fact I'm leaving this afternoon on the cat as I haven't been off the island for a month.' She looked at Jennifer who was glancing around. 'Blair has told me how excited you are about this move. He's already settled in and making his mark.'

As Jennifer walked beside the manager across the blinding hot white sand she thought she heard a hint of irony in her voice. Typical of Blair to indicate everything was one hundred per cent hunky dory. 'It will be different, that's for sure. Although I've lived in Sydney for ages, I'm really a country girl.'

'Me too, actually. But I love it here. I was in Prague before this. Give me the sun and a resort over the formal city any day.'

It was Jennifer's turn to be surprised. She had the impression from Blair that the woman manager was not very experienced or efficient. Rosie, big boned, tall, a mass of dark curls tinted a rather outrageous red, radiated strength and confidence. She was also very warm and friendly. Jennifer liked her immediately.

A wooden pathway led from the beach into the resort area. It was a small village of gleaming white-sand pathways winding past clusters of double-storey villas that faced the sea. The central area was like the hub of a wheel with the rooms, villas and separate cottages radiating from it all surrounded by small trees. In the hub was the main reception area with comfortable cane chairs, a computer with expensive internet access and an information desk. Next to reception was a games room and bar. Opposite it Jennifer noticed a small boutique and the dive headquarters crammed with wetsuits and underwater paraphernalia. Guests wandered past in swimwear or very casual clothes. To a new arrival wearing town clothes they looked to be part of a colourful semi-naked tribe.

'We'll skirt off to the back track,' said Rosie, leading her onto a sandy path shaded by squat stunted dark-leafed trees. Jennifer slowed as she noticed the white gluey patches over the leaves and the ground and did a double take as she came face to face with a dozen birds' nests along the branch in front of her.

Side by side, so close they could peck each other, the birds sat atop scrappy leaf beds spattered with the white guano that glued them together. Along the branch and wherever there was a fork of fragile twigs a nest had been constructed. Each was occupied by a stoic black noddy tern whose partners hovered close by or swished around the tree and to the ground taking no notice of humans. The tree shivered and rustled with squabbles and movement, shrieks and jostlings. Airborne they swooped on silent wings that Jennifer found unnerving.

'There must be hundreds of them!' exclaimed Jennifer.

'We get over a hundred thousand in the breeding season. You can't put a pin between them in the trees,' laughed Rosie. 'Branch Island is famous for birds. Those are pisonia trees. The leaves are handy for their nest building.'

'They're not the least bit afraid of us.' Jennifer leaned over and put her face centimetres away from a bird that turned its head with a disdainful, bored expression.

'Rule number one on the island: this is a National Park, nature comes first.' They continued walking. 'It can be difficult not to pick up a bird fallen from a nest, or a tern with sticky pisonia fruit glued to it, or help a stranded baby turtle, or take a pretty shell or coral.' Rosie paused, then said almost to herself, 'It can be an interesting rule when applied to the humans on the island, too. You'll find sometimes people overreact, or behave differently than on the mainland. Some call it island fever. Only natural when a lot of different personalities are thrown together in a small isolated community.'

'That will make Blair's job interesting,' commented Jennifer.

'Blair was selected because he has good people skills. And being young is an advantage,' said Rosie.

Jennifer wondered how Blair would cope in

this island hothouse. She knew at the outset she was going to find it a challenge.

After walking through a tunnel of thickly clustered trees, they came to an open sandy clearing circled by staff quarters – simple, airy duplex units with small verandahs festooned with wetsuits and flippers, and towels flung out to dry in the communal spaces. There was an outdoor barbecue area with tables and chairs, and it had the air of a holiday camp. Jennifer's heart sank, she was hoping this wouldn't be where she and Blair were to be living.

Maybe Rosie read her mind. 'The admin staff are scattered further away amongst the trees. Though occasionally the staffies' music gets a bit loud. That's why they're as far away as possible from the guests.'

They came to two adjoining bungalows that faced tangled trees. Each had a simple wooden balcony with two chairs and a small table. A privacy divider separated the balconies but every word would be overheard.

'Who's next door?' Jennifer asked, trying to think of something positive to say. 'It's rather sweet, a bit like a cubby house.'

'Next door is reserved for people who come occasionally to do business. The accountant, inspectors, all kinds of people. The head office managers stay in the hotel suites.' Jennifer detected a slightly disdainful note in Rosie's voice. 'Look inside. It's comfortable, not flash. Only a small kitchenette as you and Blair will eat in the dining room.'

Jennifer glanced around the open-plan dining area, kitchenette, lounge room. 'Do we have to eat in the resort dining room all the time?' The idea depressed her.

'Of course not. I find I want to get away and eat in my suite as often as I can. Blair and I are supposed to be out there, keeping an eye on things, socialising with the guests. You can do what you want. There's a big bedroom and ensuite that is air conditioned. But this is it. As management, you can use the hotel pool and drink in the bar, staffies can't. But they entertain themselves very well back in their area.'

Jennifer pushed the sliding glass door open and walked inside. Her world, for a year or more, had shrunk to this turquoise and white fern-patterned hideaway. She hoped Rosie wasn't expecting a gushing reaction.

Rosie put her head inside. 'I'll leave you to freshen up. I was going to say have a swim but of course your bag isn't here yet. Come over to my office through reception and we can have morning tea if you'd like. I'll show you the resort side of things. I live in a suite over there so I can be on the spot if there's a drama.'

'Thank you, Rosie.' Jennifer felt oddly disoriented, she wished Blair had been here. She dropped her handbag on the bed and took off her sunglasses. The cabin, cottage, unit, she couldn't think how to describe it, was impersonal and certainly compact. Fine for a holiday, but as her home for a year? Where could she make her space? The bathroom was big with a bath and a shower. Blair's shaving kit and toothbrush were spread on his side of the vanity. The room was obviously serviced as it was spotless with carefully folded fresh towels. Blair was casual about dropping his wet towels on the bathroom floor.

In the bedroom she opened the closet to see Blair's clothes hanging to one side. She slid the door closed and the room returned to the impersonal. A ceiling fan slowly turned above the bed. There was a framed photo of a turtle on the wall.

In the living room were two prints of underwater scenes of coral and colourful fish. Jennifer wished she'd brought a couple of her favourite pictures of rural Australia. Where would she put her books, set up her laptop and work area? Depressed, she decided to have a shower. Whenever she was confused, unhappy, trying to clear her head or find inspiration, she stood under the hot sharp needles of water. But this time there was no benefit or improvement in her attitude to the place. And suddenly she found herself crying as she held her face up to the shower head, her tears mingling with the cascading rainwater.

By the time she arrived in reception to meet Rosie she felt better, emotionally cleansed if not more positive. She was introduced to a cheerful young man and an attractive young woman behind the desk. They wore the staff uniform of white shorts and printed shirts with a choice of fish, coral, turtles or flowers in white on a turquoise background. She felt overdressed in her linen slacks and shirt jacket. And unhealthy. Everyone was brown, sunburnt or artificially tanned, and looked relaxed and jovial.

Rosie showed her the bar and games room, and the terrace bar that faced an emerald lawn ending in a low rock wall and frangipani trees. Attractive cane furniture was dotted around the terrace, wooden lounges were set around the lawn.

'Great place to watch the sunset. Also a favourite place for wedding photos,' Rosie said.

'Do many people get married here?'

'Quite a few. A lot from overseas who want a romantic, low-key, small wedding. Often it's just the bride and groom. We arrange everything.'

'That's nice. We almost eloped at one stage. Weddings can get stressful.'

'Sometimes they've had the big family party, or they have a reception when they get home. I thought it seemed a bit sad at first but often they're saving money having a slap-up honeymoon and wedding all in one.'

They walked past the luxurious pool and wet bar towards the dining room. Jennifer was impressed with the understated classy style of the decor, which suited the island setting. Within the entertainment area of the resort the grounds were landscaped and looked lush, tropical and highly maintained in contrast to the casual naturalness of the accommodation and staff areas.

'Everything looks so open, airy and cool. What happens when it rains? Does it get cold at all?'

'They're all cyclone-proof structures and you'd be surprised how everything unfolds and folds up in bad weather. Cold? Occasionally in the wet season, but a light sweater is all you need.'

'How often does a cyclone come in?' asked Jennifer warily.

'Not very often. Big storms, but I've been here four years with never a cyclone,' Rosie said reassuringly.

They went through the large dining room that looked very Balinese with its big wood columns, carvings and bamboo blinds. It was screened from birds and insects, with tropical plants in pots dividing various areas. In the centre was a huge serving area where the lavish food was laid out. Another self-serve bar was at the far end.

'Food is included in the tariff, though there's a big choice, of course, including house wine. Spirits or other wines you pay for. Dinner in the evening is a choice of à la carte or buffet; breakfast and lunch are buffet style. But you can also order hampers and picnic baskets,' she added. 'The chef is good, I hate to think how many kilos I've gained since I've been here.' They sat in a small cafe across from the dining room that served snacks and drinks during the day.

'How did you get into hospitality, Rosie?' asked Jennifer.

'My mum and dad ran a pub,' she laughed. 'An old-fashioned country pub in southern New South Wales. Then they started one of the first B and Bs. After I'd travelled around Europe as a backpacker I knew looking after people, making their holidays comfortable and interesting, was what I wanted to do. I did a business degree. Unlike Blair, I've never been a chef.'

'Do I hear my name being bandied about?' Blair came to the table as Jennifer pushed her coffee to one side and started to stand up. 'Hey, princess, welcome to the island.' Awkwardly, they kissed quickly, Jennifer half out of her seat and Blair pulling out a chair. He grinned at her. 'I hear you conned yourself a ride over on the chopper.'

'It hadn't occurred to me. Vera at reception arranged it. I was glad I did. I was afraid I was going to be seasick.'

'The cat is very stable, it travels above the water, no pitching, it's really quite comfortable,' said Rosie. 'Well, I'll let you two catch up. Welcome again, Jennifer. If you need anything, any questions – that Blair can't answer – give me a holler. If I don't see you later I'll be back in a week.'

Jennifer wondered if she was reading more into Rosie's smile than a simple welcome. There seemed a subtle hint that we girls need to help each other.

'Thanks for showing me around, Rosie.' Jennifer watched Rosie pause to greet a couple a few tables away. 'You're lucky to have such a pleasant boss. She's not what I thought she'd be at all.' *You made her sound an inefficient bitch.*

'She handles the admin stuff okay. I've been brought in to jazz up the menu and liaise with the staff. There are always problems but they're magnified because they live here for their shifts. So, everything okay?'

Jennifer was ready to collapse in his arms. 'I'm exhausted, Blair, packing up, moving out, the goodbyes, then driving up the coast to goodness knows what, I feel a bit fragile.'

'Rubbish. Look where you are! Don't you think it's great? People pay a fortune to be here. The time will whiz by and then I'll be off to somewhere bigger, hopefully OS.'

'I hope the time will whiz for me too,' said Jennifer in a small voice. Thank heavens she had something to keep her somewhat occupied. 'I'm wondering where I can work. The accommodation is nice but compact, don't you think?'

Blair got up. 'Jeez, Jenny, don't start whingeing. You're not even unpacked. Give it a chance. Come on, let's go, the cat's arrived, your stuff will be in the room by now. The boys were running it up from the jetty.'

Jennifer had seen the small electric carts that ran around the resort delivering luggage, laundry and supplies. 'Great. Maybe I can try out the pool,' she said, trying to make amends and please Blair.

'You do that. Get settled and I'll meet you in the dining room at twelve-fifteen for lunch.'

'You're not coming for a swim? Help me unpack?'

'Jenny! I'm working, remember?' He gave her a quick kiss. 'I'll walk you back over to our place.

I'm counting on you to make it nice and homey. And, tonight, I'm off duty, so I'll make it up to you then, okay?' He squeezed her round the waist.

It was romantic. Over a creamy cocktail with a slice of pineapple in it, they watched the brilliant sunset from the terrace bar. The water was gilded with soft gold and rose tones. A cluster of clouds backlit by the setting sun made the scene spectacular. 'Just like the travel brochures,' thought Jennifer. Flashes from cameras captured the moment.

'There go those terns back to their nests. It's amazing how unconcerned they are at all the people around them,' said Jennifer.

'Place is overrun with birds. Wait till the turtles come in to lay their eggs and later, when they hatch, it's quite an attraction,' said Blair. 'Personally, I can think of better things to do in the middle of the night or at dawn than crawl around the beach with a flashlight.' He squeezed her leg. 'Now, after dinner, we're going round to the staffie party. I want to show you off to all the kids.'

'Kids? Most of them aren't much younger than us. But do we have to? On our first night here?'

'C'mon, Jenny, you can't be that tired. It'll be fun, and it'll be good for you to get to know the girls. If they can't talk to me about certain problems they can go to you.'

'Why not Rosie? She's very approachable. I'm not employed here.'

'What's got into you? You're being such a downer. Don't be a pain, Jenny, you're supposed to be here to support me.'

'Sorry. I just feel like a fish out of water.' She glanced at the sea, so close to where they sat, and shuddered. 'Let me get used to all this. You've been here a week.'

'All right. But I loved it from the minute I stepped ashore. Come on, let's go and eat.'

They passed a noisy group at the bar inside and Jennifer recognised Dougie Wilson, known as Willsy, a presenter from a TV show. 'That's the guy from that crazy reality show. Used to be a singer, didn't he?'

'Tried to be. Before that he was a third-rate boxer, then he got into the personal fitness business. He's got a big following now.'

'When all else fails, find fame as a TV host. Then what?' asked Jennifer dryly, looking at the hangers-on around the trendy TV personality who was featured frequently in the gossip magazines.

'You can't blame him for making hay while the TV spotlight is on him,' said Blair. 'I'm hoping he might get one of the travel shows to do a segment on us.'

'This place doesn't need it,' said Jennifer.

They reached the dining room and Blair led her to a table for two in a quiet section of the screened verandah. On the table was a bottle of champagne in an ice bucket and a candle surrounded by frangipani flowers.

'I know you like flowers, but these and a few hibiscuses around the resort are all there is, I'm afraid. Mostly it's all prickly native crap.'

'Oh Blair, thanks for thinking. And the champagne, lovely.'

A pretty waitress immediately came to their table and poured the champagne. 'Welcome, Mrs Towse. Do you want the à la carte menu or the buffet?' She gestured to the centre of the room where guests were milling around the lavish spread of food.

Before Jennifer could answer, Blair thanked the waitress. 'We'll go for the works. It's seafood night.'

'Blair, I'm not all that hungry.'

'You'll love it. Doesn't come any fresher than this. Well, we tell the guests the fish were swimming this morning, but a lot of it is chilled, brought in from the mainland,' he confided with a grin.

Jennifer walked around the buffet holding an empty plate. She couldn't bring herself to heap her plate with seafood like everyone else. Two glasses of champagne seemed to have gone to her head. She felt dazed, as if she was observing everything from an out-of-body experience. The glassy-eyed dead crayfish and prawns didn't tempt her. The huge fish whose eyes and expression seemed to indicate it had died a slow and lingering death lay there as flesh was hacked from its body. Oysters, on their bed of mushy ice, looked like woeful eyes dismembered from some strange beast. The ravenous, grasping, fat and sun-red guests circled the prey and pounced in a feeding frenzy. To Jennifer the people looked like what they were eating: bulbous red arms with diamond-decked claw fingers dived into second helpings. A tall thin man waving tongs looked like a boiled shrimp. She felt like she was in an aquarium of weird marine people.

'Jenny? Can't make up your mind?' Blair was smiling at her, holding a plate overflowing with fleshy white fish laid out on lettuce.

A scene from a movie in a morgue filled with bodies under green sheets flashed into her mind. 'I think I'm going to be sick. Excuse me.' She fled to the ladies' room.

She struggled through dinner, pushing food around on her plate and only half listening to Blair's potted life histories of the key staff.

'As far as I can figure, there are a couple of really bright and ambitious kids. The rest are just here filling in time, trying to save a bit of cash, or they think it's a cushy job at an island resort. A few of them could be encouraged to see a future for themselves in hospitality,' said Blair as they walked hand-in-hand along the path leading from the dining room. 'Tell me what you think of them. See if you can pick the bright sparks.'

'You mean now? Are we really going to this staff party? I'm a bit tired, Blair. It is my first day here, after all.'

'We won't stay long. You tell me when

you're ready to leave. I promised we'd put in an appearance.'

They walked in silence along the sandy path lit by an occasional small light at ground level. They heard the laughter and music as they approached the staff accommodation. Coloured lights were strung up and several tables spread with food and plates were pushed together. Young men were turning sizzling chops and sausages at the barbecue. Now they were out of their staff shirts their individuality was more apparent.

Blair took Jennifer over to a tall, thin young man in a red shirt that hung partially open revealing a pale, hairless chest. He was pouring margaritas.

'Doyley, this is my wife Jennifer. This is Kevin Doyle, he manages the bar and supervises in the dining room. He's also the resident funnyman.'

'Hello Kevin, pleased to meet you.' Jennifer shook hands, liking his open friendly face. He had a hooked nose and lank hair and she supposed he was one of the not-so-handsome guys who used humour instead of looks to charm people.

'It's Doyley, you know those little lace things your mother sticks around on tables and things,' Blair corrected her. 'He won't answer to Kevin.'

'Bit how's your father, though it's not as bad as Bruce,' Doyley said, pointing to an exceedingly handsome blond surfie-looking spunk who was obviously called Bruce. 'So, what do you fancy? A couple of snags or a chop?'

'We've eaten, thanks. What's to drink? I'll have

something sent over from the bar,' said Blair eyeing the cartons of wine.

'There're plenty of these.' He held up the pitcher of margaritas. He reached for a glass with a salted rim, filled it and handed it to Jennifer.

'I'll get a beer.' Blair headed to the table holding the drinks.

'How long have you been here?' asked Jennifer, gingerly sipping the potent cocktail. Kevin, Doyley, was the one person she'd seen who wasn't tanned.

'Long enough to know to keep out of the sun. It's bloody hot. Keep plenty of blockout on. These northern Europeans all want to go home looking like natives.'

'I intend to keep out of the sun as much as possible,' said Jennifer.

Blair joined her with two pretty girls in tow. Both were very brown. Jennifer grinned at Doyley. 'Meet Sheree and Rhonda, currently in housekeeping,' said Blair.

Jennifer smiled and asked how long they'd been on the island.

'I'm a Brit, travelling round Australia, this is such a gorgeous place I haven't got past Queensland and Sydney yet,' said Sheree.

'Sadly, I'm coming to the end of my time,' said Rhonda in a soft Irish lilt. 'Over a year in Oz, six months here on Branch.'

They swirled around her, as Jennifer was introduced to the two dozen staffies. Most seemed to be about her and Blair's age though Blair, despite his jovial, casual manner, still had an air of being

126

the boss. Even though the staffies had been drinking, Jennifer could tell they were being careful in front of him. She joined a group that was sitting to one side and discovered the girls were talking about the resident 'perv'.

'He's always watching you. His name is Patch 'cause of the patch on his eye. He's probably more harmless than Methuselah,' laughed one of the girls.

'Methuselah is a two-hundred-and-fifty-kilo grouper that has lived around the wreck and the wharf for years,' explained Rhonda as she sat next to Jennifer. 'Patch is an old bloke who works here repairing machinery. He's just unnerving, you turn around and he's there. He walked in on one of the girls cleaning a bathroom once.'

'Why hasn't he been warned by management?' asked Jennifer. Surely Rosie wouldn't tolerate such behaviour.

'He's very old and he's worked here since it opened, when it was just a casual holiday place,' explained Rhonda. 'He's a harmless old bugger. He nearly had a heart attack the other day. He caught one of the girls sunbaking topless out the back of her room and when she spotted him perving she jumped up and held her boobs out to him and yelled, "Come on, come and have a feel!" He nearly dropped his teeth and fled.'

They all laughed but Jennifer didn't find it funny. She sipped her margarita and watched them, listening to the chatter and the bursts of laughter, sensing the under-currents of flirting and the prickly relationships. She wondered how often the tensions flared during their two weeks on the island before they had their one-week break back on the mainland.

She excused herself and edged around to Blair, standing close to him and signalling she wanted to leave.

'Hey missus, want another wine?'

'Since when have I been the missus?' she asked lightly, but her voice carried an edge Blair knew meant she was annoyed. 'It's late, could we leave the gang to party on?'

'Sure, sure.' He turned back to finish his story and Doyley topped up his own drink, giving Jennifer a wink. She put her hand over her empty glass and shook her head. Doyley nodded and moved on, pausing to speak to Rhonda.

While Blair continued talking, Rhonda touched Jennifer on the arm. 'I'm heading back to the resort, would you like to walk with me? We can swing by your place on the way. It can be confusing at night when you've just arrived,' she said softly.

Relieved, Jennifer nudged Blair. 'Excuse me, darling, Rhonda is heading off and I might walk with her and get settled. I'll see you later, okay?' She hoped Blair would get the message, put his drink down and go with her.

'Great, fine. Thanks, Rhonda. I won't be long. We'll have a nightcap and watch the moon rise over the ocean, right?'

'Right.' *In your dreams, even if we had an*

ocean view. 'Goodnight, everyone,' she nodded to the group and moved quickly away.

'Thanks, Rhonda, I'm so tired. I hope I'm not dragging you away.'

'Not at all. I want to use the phone outside reception anyway. Thank Doyley, he figured you were looking a trifle weary. Being your first day and all.'

They left the party and walked quietly, their footsteps muffled on the sandy path.

'Do you feel safe here?' asked Jennifer. 'That lecherous old man sounds a bit of a worry.' She glanced around at the shadowy trees, the poorly lit path. She heard rustling in the trees from the birds, and the occasional scratchy sound in the dried leaves and undergrowth.

'It took me a while. But then I'm not used to living so up-close-and-personal with the wildlife,' said Rhonda. 'I'm from Dublin. It takes a while to adjust to the fact that you can't run far.'

'What do you mean?'

'Being on an island. No trains, buses, or winding roads. A boat twice a day. A helicopter in an emergency.' She shrugged. 'When I first came I was worried about accidents, being cut off, stuck with the same people, all that sort of thing.'

'I think I'm going through that. And this is only my first day,' said Jennifer rather ruefully.

'You get over it. I like the relaxed, away-from-it-all atmosphere now. And the birds, the turtles, the whole nature thing. I'll miss it.'

'When are you leaving?'

'In two weeks. Family things back home. Sheree is staying though. Well, there's the track to your place that way. Just a hundred metres through the trees. I'm going to the main area. You'll be all right?'

'Of course, it's not far. But it is dark.'

'Leave a light on outside your cabin at night.'

'I will. Thank you, Rhonda.'

'Goodnight. Sleep well.'

'I certainly will.' Jennifer hurried, nervous at the quietness around her. Everyone was either in bed or out somewhere. Their cabin was tucked away from it all. She now wished they had neighbours in residence. She tripped as she hurried up the step onto the small deck and reached for the sliding door. Maybe they shouldn't leave the place unlocked. She fumbled for the light switch and as the pale glow lit the main room, she slid the door shut and pulled the curtain across it, glad that the ceiling fan was whirring gently. The light was dim, the power was not strong, probably from a generator. She turned on all the lights and, tired as she was, for once she longed for a TV set to keep her company. Then she remembered Vi and Don's satellite radio. She decided to have a shower, get into bed and see if she could tune it to whatever band reached Branch Island, a dot in the Coral Sea on the edge of the Pacific Ocean.

The sheets were crisp, smooth and cool. Jennifer gave up trying to tune the radio and lay back enjoying the light whoosh of air across her body from the ceiling fan. She left the bedside light on, thinking she'd read a magazine, but her eyes closed and she drifted to sleep.

She didn't hear Blair come in and slip into bed beside her. He tried not to wake her and in seconds he was in a deep sleep too.

Later, Jennifer thought it must have been around two in the morning, she was jolted awake. Was she dreaming or had she really heard a terrible wail? A baby in unspeakable pain? Someone strangling a cat? She stumbled from bed, crashing into the bedside table in the dark. She found the sliding door handle and wrenched the door open to the small balcony as Blair stirred.

The air was warm. All was silent. Then it came, close, so close she jumped in fright. A guttural agonised wail. Another. And another.

'What the hell is it? Who's there?'

'It's the mutton birds. I forgot to tell you. It's all right. Come back to bed.' Blair's voice was thick and sleepy.

Jennifer was running her hands along the wall, groping for the light switch. 'Mutton birds? What's happening to them?'

'That's the sound they make. They nest on the ground. Probably right outside the door.'

The light on the little verandah came on and Jennifer stepped outside. The ground was faintly illuminated. Several black blobs were squatting close to her. One of the birds stood up, one flapped its wings. They didn't move away but the hoarse groan was picked up and passed from bird to bird in a painful chorus.

'That's horrible. Are they going to do that all night?'

'You'll get used to it.'

'Can't we move them?'

'Against the rules. Besides, the bastards have sharp beaks. I'll deal with them in the morning when they go back to their nests.'

'In the trees?'

'No, underground. They dig holes so be careful you don't trip down one.'

'Oh, God. This is all I need.' She flipped off the light and in the darkness they resumed their activity with more wails. But above the squawks, squabbles and moans of the mutton birds she heard in the distance another shriek, a cry, a scream.

Jennifer sat up. 'That wasn't a bird. Was it?'

'Put the air conditioning on, then you won't hear anything.' Blair rolled over and flung an arm around her hips. 'Want a cuddle? Make you sleep. I've missed you.' He kissed her belly.

'Blair, can you check outside? I just have this funny feeling –'

'Jenny, I'm not going outside to trip over those bloody birds. Unless you want to skinny dip. There's no one around here . . .'

Jennifer got out of bed, pulled the curtain and stepped outside. She looked at the sky. It was dark, clouds covered the moon. She stepped onto the sandy path and recoiled, losing her balance as her foot tripped on a soft squashy bird that grunted and pecked at her foot with a sharp beak that drew blood. 'Ouch, yuk.'

She leapt back onto the decking and there was a flurry of shadowy creatures around the cabin and nearby trees. She couldn't see them properly. They didn't seem like birds, just fat grey blobs like some underground creatures that had erupted from deep in the earth. They gave her the creeps. Her foot was hurting, she turned to go inside. Then she heard it. A throat-catching sobbing, a being hurrying, crashing amongst the trees, someone in a heedless flight.

'Who's there? What is it?' she called in alarm, fumbling for the light switch by the sliding doors. 'Blair, come out here, quickly . . .'

In his underpants Blair flicked the switch and the outside light snapped on.

At the perimeter of the pale yellow arc a figure was hunched, swaying, then it dropped to the ground, rolling into a ball. A young woman was choking on hoarse sobs and cries.

'Oh my God, what's happened?' Jennifer couldn't move.

Blair rushed forward and stooped over the woman, trying to lift her to her feet. 'Jesus, what happened to you? Jennifer, quick, help me. It's Rhonda.'

'Rhonda?' She recognised the auburn hair but as Blair lifted her she saw the bruised and bleeding face, the ripped T-shirt and torn pants. She could barely equate this shattered girl with the bright young woman she'd left only a few hours before.

'Get her inside. It's all right, Rhonda, come on, try to walk.'

Supporting her on either side they half dragged

her inside. Blair pulled the curtain shut and switched on the inside light, turning off the outside one. 'Get her some water. No, better, there's a small bottle of brandy in the mini bar.'

Jennifer's hands were shaking as she handed Rhonda the glass with four fingers of brandy in the bottom. 'Here, drink this. Take deep breaths.'

Sitting up and shivering, Rhonda gagged on the drink. Jennifer suddenly realised that Rhonda's underpants as well as her T-shirt were ripped and she had only one shoe.

'What the hell happened?' asked Blair. His voice was edgy.

'Blair, be gentle, let her get her breath,' admonished Jennifer, sitting beside the frightened girl, taking her hand and stroking it.

'He attacked me. Tried to rape me. When I wouldn't, and started to fight him, he just . . . beat me. He ripped my pants off and then when he started to pull his trousers off I kicked him and ran. I thought I was going to die,' said Rhonda, her Irish accent thick with fear.

'Who? Who did this to you? Blair, call the police, someone. Do you want a doctor?'

'Jennifer! Calm down. Let me handle this,' snapped Blair. 'There are no police here and no doctor. Just a nurse.' Jennifer was shocked into silence. He took Rhonda's other hand. 'Are you hurt, injured? I mean, cut, any wounds other than this?' He lightly touched her gashed cheek and she winced.

'Of course she's hurt. Shouldn't we get some help?' hissed Jennifer.

'Let's find out the details first. Are you sure he was trying to rape you?'

Rhonda gave a look that silenced Blair.

Jennifer pressed Rhonda's hand. 'What happened after you left me?'

Rhonda drew a shaky breath. 'I was on the phone outside reception and a group came out of the bar and said they were having drinks by the pool, to join them. I know I'm not supposed to mix with the guests but . . . well, it was late, no one else was around and they were laughing and having a lot of fun. Willsy was with them . . .' Her face screwed up and she took a moment to compose herself before going on. 'There was one other girl but she left with one of the guys. After one drink I said I should go. They were going to continue partying in one of their suites. Willsy was drunk and trying to kiss and grope me and so I left. I decided to walk around the beach to my room and when I cut into the dunes . . . I was grabbed.'

'It's all right, Rhonda.' Jennifer was going to say she didn't have to go into painful details, but one look at Blair's tight face told her to keep quiet.

Rhonda shuddered and her voice was a whisper. 'He grabbed me from behind, put his hand around my neck and mouth so I couldn't scream and pushed me down onto the ground. I hit my face on a rock and I think I was a bit dazed. When I tried to stop him he started swearing and just whammed into me.' Tears began running down her face.

Jennifer went to get the box of tissues from the

bathroom. She felt sick to her stomach. She heard Blair's low, insistent voice.

'You're sure who it was? It's dark, he came from behind . . .'

Rhonda's head came up. 'Oh yes, it was Willsy. But . . . he said if I said anything to anyone he'd deny it and the guys would say he was with them.'

'Well, we can disprove that, surely,' said Jennifer. 'I mean, did you scratch him or anything?'

'Leave it, Jennifer. Rhonda, you're sure you didn't do anything to lead him on, you know, why'd he get so mad? Are you absolutely sure he was going to rape you?'

'Blair! Even if she was flirting, or led him on, nobody deserves a beating like this!'

'He was drunk. He kept mumbling something while he was hitting me,' whimpered Rhonda. 'Can I have a shower, please? All I want is to forget this ever happened. Please, please, don't tell anyone.' She began to cry again. 'I just want to go to sleep, curl up in a ball and make it all go away. My face hurts so.'

Blair stood up. 'Go and have a shower, Rhonda, we'll look after you. You can stay here tonight.'

Jennifer was still holding Rhonda's hand. 'You don't think we should report this?'

Rhonda tightened her grip on Jennifer's hand. 'I'm not reporting this. I beg you not to say anything. I don't want people to think that I was raped. No one will believe he just beat me up. I want to forget this ever happened. Please don't tell Rosie. Don't tell anyone. Ever.'

'Of course. This will never go outside this room,' said Blair in a soothing tone. 'Jennifer, help her. I'll get the first-aid kit from reception and clean up those scratches.'

Scratches! Her face looks like she had rocks thrown at it. Why do you want to keep this quiet? 'Okay, Blair, whatever you say. Come on, Rhonda, you'll feel better after a hot shower. I'll make us some tea.'

Rhonda was still under the shower when Blair hurried back with the small first-aid box. 'Good, she's still in there.'

'She's just standing under the water like she's trying to wash the whole thing out of her head and body,' said Jennifer. 'God, this is awful. The poor thing.'

Blair took Jennifer's arm and turned her to face him, speaking in a low urgent voice. 'Listen, Jennifer. We have to keep this quiet. Very quiet. No one is to know. It will be a disaster for the resort. If she comes out and accuses a well-known TV person he'll deny it and he has the backing of a powerful TV station and a whole raft of important people. They'll crucify her, and this place. I'm not going to let that happen.'

'She doesn't want to tell anyone. But it doesn't seem right. That man shouldn't be allowed to get away with it.'

'It's probably happened before, and probably will again,' said Blair.

'That's criminal!' exclaimed Jennifer.

'Would you want to go through the public

humiliation of a trial, have people think you were raped, that you led him on? You know what people are like, always want to think the worst. Where there's smoke . . .'

People like you, thought Jennifer miserably.

'It is terrible, but she'll get over it and get on with her life. She's an Irish Catholic, for God's sake, think how that would go down back home if it hit the newspapers here and, innocent or not, her reputation would suffer.'

'I don't see how you can keep this quiet.' Jennifer was shocked. Shocked at herself for starting to accept Blair's viewpoint. She was already rationalising things to herself. Nothing happened. Rhonda wasn't raped or killed. Blair would be in the firing line, trouble in his first job like this didn't look like he had a firm hand.

'We'll fly her out tomorrow morning,' he continued. 'Say she had an accident, too many drinks, walking back she fell on the rocks, the sea wall, something. She's due to leave anyway, she can leave now with all her stuff and entitlements. She'll agree with that, I bet.'

The shower finally stopped.

'What would Rosie say?'

'She's off the island so I'm in charge. She's not to know about this. Rhonda fell, end of story. It's what she wants, too.'

Jennifer was numb. 'I'll get her some clean clothes.'

They cleaned Rhonda's wounds, gave her painkillers and made a bed for her on the sofa for what was left of the night. They left a light on and locked the doors. She lay there clutching the sheet around herself, eyes squeezed shut, tears still shining in her lashes.

In the bedroom, Jennifer curled beside Blair, her arms encircling him. She was too tense to sleep and felt deeply disturbed. It had been a hard first day and now this horrific event. She was having difficulty coping with it all. She kept imagining how it must have felt, to suddenly be grabbed, thrown to the ground . . . Jennifer tried to still her mind, not think about what had happened to Rhonda. But it only confirmed the sense of foreboding she had about being marooned on this island. Beautiful it may be, but beneath its still waters she felt there was a malevolent presence. Would she ever adjust to living here?

6

The Beachcomber

JENNIFER HEARD BLAIR OPEN the curtain near the bed. She stretched. Pale washed-blue sky. The top of a tree. In the courtyard at the base of the outside shower – a simple arrangement of a showerhead on a pole above a square of tiles – there was a large clamshell full of water. A grey heron was gracefully dipping its beak into the shell, throwing back its head, shaking sparkling droplets. She smiled and rolled over, wondering why she felt so tired.

Then she remembered. She sat up, the calm morning sullied. 'What time is it? How's Rhonda?'

Blair, in casual shorts, was pulling on a T-shirt.

'Not sure. We have to get her up and packed. I've called the chopper and said she'd had a bit of a fall . . . nothing madly urgent. Didn't want to set off alarm bells.'

Jennifer grabbed a sarong, wrapped it around her and tiptoed into the shadowy dim lounge room. Trying to be as quiet as possible she found the electric kettle and was carrying it into the bathroom to fill when Rhonda spoke calmly.

'I'm awake. Make as much noise as you want.'

'Did you sleep?'

'Not really. It's better being awake. I kept dreaming . . . nightmares . . . I heard Blair on the phone. I'm being picked up at eight?'

'I guess so. I'll help you pack up your things.'

'That's all right. I can manage. I just hope my roomies and Sheree don't think it's all a bit . . . odd.'

'Say it's Blair's idea. He's being overcautious. In case you have any severe concussion or something. Are you owed any holiday leave? Say you're using that up.'

'Makes sense. Are you making coffee?'

'I am. Shall I get you some breakfast? I could bring it over here,' offered Jennifer, knowing Rhonda wouldn't want to be seen with a gashed face and bruises.

'I'm not hungry. Just coffee.' She swung her legs over the edge of the sofa and rested her chin in her hands. 'This isn't how I saw leaving the island for good.'

Jennifer bit her lip as she emptied sachets of

coffee into cups. 'Could you come back for a farewell party? Or have one over on the mainland? When are you going back home to Ireland?'

'My ticket is booked. I leave in ten days. A family wedding. I'm a bridesmaid.' She touched her face. 'Damn him to hell.' She was angry.

'You'll look fine by then, really you will,' said Jennifer, thinking to herself, *The bastard. He'll go on like nothing happened. At least Rhonda is mad rather than sorry for herself.*

Blair came out of the bathroom and smiled at Rhonda. 'I've had an idea. We know a really nice lodge down in the Hunter Valley. Would you like to chill out there for a week before you leave? Recuperate. I'll arrange a special deal for you.'

Rhonda brightened slightly. 'If it's not too expensive, I'd like that. I just want to go away by myself. Lick my wounds.'

Blair pulled open the living-room curtain to the bright shiny day, which bore no resemblance to the frightening night. 'The main thing is that you don't have any guilt or bad feelings. If you want to see a counsellor, we can arrange it through the staff medical fund.'

'Thanks, Blair.' She took the cup of coffee. 'You've both been so kind. I feel awful about spoiling your first day here, Jennifer.'

'What did Blair say? No guilt. Just get on with your life. Consider yourself lucky. It could have been worse. Look forward to going home. And, please, let us know how you are.'

It felt a trite comment but Jennifer didn't know what to say. The episode had unnerved her, but more, she was shocked at Blair's reaction. How would he have felt if it had been her instead of Rhonda? Would he still put the reputation of the resort first?

There were few guests around as Jennifer watched the pretty redhead pick up her small sports bag. A hat and dark glasses shaded Rhonda's face. A box and a suitcase would be sent on the catamaran. Rhonda shook hands with Blair who took Bob, the pilot, aside.

'No need to mention to anyone this was a special trip. I want this kept as quiet as possible. It was just a bad fall, you understand?' said Blair in a low voice.

The pilot looked unconvinced but shrugged. 'Sure, whatever. These things happen.'

Jennifer took Rhonda's hand as she said goodbye.

Rhonda looked miserable. 'I don't know that Sheree bought my story. Can you say something to everyone, explain things, sort of . . .'

'Of course we will,' said Jennifer. 'You're not leaving under a cloud, we'll tell them we just want to make sure you get checked out at the hospital. After your fall.'

Rhonda hugged Jennifer. 'I hope I see you again. And please, don't let this put you off. This island, the reef, it's really, really special. I've loved being here,' she said earnestly.

How can you say that after what's happened?

143

'I'm sure I'll settle in. Look after yourself, Rhonda.'

With Rosie away, and Blair acting manager, Jennifer was left to her own devices. She moved the table and chairs from the small front balcony of the cabin next door to the rear courtyard, setting them up under a tree, and here she had her breakfast of fruit, cereal and pot of tea. Blair had promised to send over a toaster as their kitchenette was sparsely supplied with utensils. She hadn't bothered to pack such items, thinking more about personal things and her work needs.

Guiltily she thought about the computer and box of papers she'd pushed into the back of the closet the morning she'd arrived. Her enthusiasm for Professor Dawn's book and her need to know she had work and an objective to achieve during the next few months here had utterly vanished. She still felt tired, mentally, physically, emotionally. She put it down to the humidity and heat, the languid lifestyle and lack of focus. She hadn't seen a newspaper or watched TV and had to force herself to listen to the morning news on Don's little radio. Events on the other side of the world, even in Sydney, held little interest for her. She was in a cocoon here and she wondered when and what she'd become when she finally emerged. She felt a pang of remorse at not having contacted her mother or Vi and Don other than a fax telling them she'd arrived.

Their cabin was serviced so after breakfast she left the unmade bed, the dirty dishes, her wet towel flung over the bath. It was unlike her, she hated to leave a mess each morning but here she had no routine, nothing familiar around her. She wandered over to the reception area and looked in the recreation room library for a book from the help-yourself shelf.

She watched guests setting off on their morning activities – diving, fishing, a reef walk, kayaking around the island, sailing in small boats, carrying a hamper and beach towels to a secluded picnic, an underwater trip on the sight-seeing submarine.

Others claimed their favourite reclining chair by the pool, setting out towels, sunlotion, books, magazines, sunglasses, a small table ready for snacks and drinks. Some would spend the day there playing cards, chatting, reading, drinking exotic drinks or chilled wine and icy beers in tall glasses, sleeping off their drinks till it was time to change for sunset cocktails.

There were no squealing children in the pool or running around the grounds. Under fourteens were not permitted at the resort, and there were few special events for teenagers. Most were there to share the experience of the island and reef with their parents.

She'd seen on the weekly calendar of events a lecture and video presentation by a marine biologist to acquaint, she presumed, overseas visitors with the 'History, Science, Heritage and Mystery

145

of the Great Barrier Reef'. Through the year visitors could go with a naturalist from National Parks on a bird-watching tour, turtle observation tour during egg-laying season and, later, a chance to observe the hatching of the eggs.

As she walked past the pool she stopped and caught her breath, her chest tightening. Standing with several young men in boardshorts and brief swimsuits, she saw Willsy the TV host. They were laughing and kidding around wearing dark glasses and holding breakfast beers.

He saw Jennifer across the pool and lowered his sunnies to give her the once-over with an appreciative flirty smile. Furious, she turned and walked quickly away as Willsy's mates pushed him into the pool.

She nodded at the young woman on reception and walked to Blair's office, hovering in the doorway. 'Can I come in?'

'What's up?' He was glued to the computer screen on his desk.

'That awful man, Willsy, he's goofing around at the pool. They're all drinking, for God's sake. He even looks pleased with himself.'

Blair jumped up and pulled her into his office, closing the door. 'Listen, Jennifer, hush up. There's nothing we can or should say. What's got into you?' He kept his voice low.

'I think it's despicable. Can't we let him know that we know what went on last night?'

'That won't achieve a thing. You can't accuse someone and, besides, we promised Rhonda we'd

146

say nothing. Anyway, they're leaving on the cat tomorrow. Just keep out of their way. What are you doing today?'

'I was going to sit by the pool. I won't now.'

'Get a picnic hamper, go and explore, find a bit of beach. The tide will be full by lunchtime. Have a swim, it's magic, you don't have to go out far. It's perfect at high tide, just wade in to your waist, it'll be like crystal. At low tide you have to watch for rocks in the shallows.'

'I don't know about that.'

'I know you're not a beach person but, for crying out loud, we're surrounded by a lagoon. At least go and lie under a palm tree. Work on your tan.'

'What about your lunch?'

'I'm eating here at my desk. Trying to get through a bunch of stuff.'

'I'll see you then.' She left his office feeling like a chastised child.

The mid-morning sun was hot. She ordered her lunch hamper and went into the boutique to buy thirty-plus sunblock, and passed Doyley on the way out.

'Hey Jennifer, settling in okay? Bloody dreadful about Rhonda taking a spill. Not like her to get so pissed.'

'It was dark, I guess. She's sorry she didn't have a proper goodbye party.'

'Ah, we'll try to catch her up on the mainland if she hasn't left. So what do you think of our little paradise?'

'It's a great place for a holiday, that's for sure. I'm taking a picnic and a book off to find a shady tree. I'm not into growing melanomas if I can help it.'

'I'm with you. Stick to a whiter shade of pale. There's a terrific little cove around from Coral Point. You can't get there from the beach at high tide but you can if you take the track over the headland. Bit of a hike, not many people bother. But it's worth it.'

'Thanks, Doyley. See you.'

Jennifer put on her swimsuit and a large floppy hat, pushed a towel in her cotton shoulder bag with the sunblock, her book, radio, room key and a bottle of water. When the picnic hamper arrived she found it to be a huge basket with napkins, glasses, plates, cutlery, chilled fruit juice and food in little containers. She took out some fruit, the juice, a bread roll, and corned beef and salad, tied it in a plastic bag and added it to her carry-all. She slipped on canvas shoes in case she had to climb over rocks or a rough track, and set off.

At the point, she turned in from the beach and spotted the narrow track leading over the headland away from the main path that headed back towards the resort. This was new territory and she hesitated, then continued. At the top of the headland there was a clearing, an informal lookout. Someone had strung a hammock between two trees. While it wasn't a great height the slight rise and cleared top of the point gave a vista straight out to sea. Sooty Isle sat at the edge of the horizon, a tiny blip in the flat blues of ocean and sky. The reef was covered by the tide, which sloshed around the base of the point. Apart from a fishing boat churning through the movie-set backdrop, it looked like a painting. Sooty Isle intrigued her, maybe she would go over and see it. Even stay overnight. It looked a calm enough trip, even for her. Jennifer turned away and as she moved down the scrubby slope of the small hill she saw on the path ahead the figure of a tall man. He was standing with his hands clasped behind his back, an old leather peaked hat squashed on greying hair. He wore patched cotton pants pulled in with a wide leather belt and a faded blue shirt. He was watching something in a tree.

She stopped, worried this might be the perving Patch. She waited. Then saw what he was studying. In the tree a massive twiggy nest was heaped into the topmost fork. Perched to one side was a large bird. Its underbelly was white and its head, back and wings were a mottled brown, though its wings had creamy tips. It seemed to have a ruff around its neck. The bird leaned forward into the nest, feeding its young. Jennifer took several slow steps forward.

Without looking at her the man said softly, 'It's a sea eagle. She's got two young 'uns in the nest.'

'What's she feeding them?'

'Fish. She's a great diver. Grabs fish in her talons just below the surface. Marvellous to watch. They've been here for years.'

'Oh. You've been coming here for a long time . . . ?' *Damn, it must be the dirty old repair man.*

They said he was harmless. Looks to be. 'Are you the Mr Fix-it?'

He gave a brief chuckle, still not taking his eyes off the bird.

'Lordy, don't mix me up with that old reprobate Patch.'

The osprey spread its magnificent wings – the long feathers at the wingtips like elegant fingers, its tail a delicate fan – swooped from the tree and then soared over the sea.

'How beautiful,' said Jennifer.

The man turned to look at her for the first time. 'Yes. While you're here you should spend time observing our birds. It's a good opportunity.'

'Oh, I'll have plenty of time to do that.'

'Ah, you're working at the resort then?'

'No. My husband is. I've just arrived.'

'Well, you'll be able to explore at leisure. There's much to see on the island. And in the sea.'

'I'm not much of a seafarer. Apart from the birds and when the turtles come in, what else is there?' Jennifer glanced around as if expecting suddenly to see obvious and entertaining things to do. The scrubby headland and empty sandy tracks leading nowhere in particular didn't look very interesting.

He pushed his hat back, thrust his hands in his pockets and began walking at a leisurely pace along the path. 'Well, now, it depends on what you're interested in. Do you work, have any special passions?'

She glanced at him and, seeing a slight smile on

his face, Jennifer decided he was a nice old fellow. There was a calmness to him. A man who no longer hurried and had time to watch birds and, probably, chat at length. She was rather glad of the diversion. 'I'm working as a research assistant to Professor Matt Dawn, organising his data and writing it up for his book.'

'Why don't you write your own book? What's it about?'

Jennifer paused before answering, sensing this was not a general or polite enquiry she could dismiss with a bland remark. This man's question required a thoughtful response. 'Well . . . my interest is in biology and ecology. As a naturalist I'm interested in a general science degree. I grew up on a farm with few playmates,' she felt yet again the stab of loss over her brother, 'an only child, so the world around me, all the living things in the bush and how they related to each other, became important.'

'It seems to me you're in the right spot if you're a naturalist. In between writing why not just wander about the island? See what question comes to you.'

'That's an interesting way of putting it,' said Jennifer. She was warming to this old gentleman by the minute.

He tugged at his hat. 'The way I see it research is about answering questions, but first you have to know which ones to ask. Often you can look for things and never see them. Other times, when you least expect it, there they are, fish, turtles, birds, insects . . . going about their business. Rather like life, when you stop seeking, stop charging after something, it drops in your lap.'

'You're a bit of a philosopher. Do you live on the island?' asked Jennifer. He'd obviously thought a lot about research. His perspective seemed so fresh compared to her university teachers.

'I'm just an old fisherman, a boatie. A beach-comber you might say. I washed up here over thirty years ago.' He stopped and held out his hand. 'My name is Gideon.'

'I'm Jennifer.' She paused, wondering why she didn't want to use her married name. Or her unmarried name. This connection with the old beachcomber had nothing to do with Blair. Or her mother.

'So, Miss Jennifer, where are you off to this morning? You look like you're set with provisions – and a good book I hope.'

'I was going down to the little beach around from Coral Point.'

'Boomerang Cove. Yes, that is nice. Secluded. A favourite spot for the honeymooners. Now that we have made our acquaintance and we are both local residents, may I invite you to my side of the island? It's something of a private club.' He grinned.

'Do you go to the resort at all? What was here when you . . . washed up?' The path narrowed as it turned in from the cove through massive piso-nias, some almost twenty metres tall with thick chunky branches blotting the sun, so they walked in single file, Jennifer following Gideon's old canvas tennis shoes that had peepholes for his big toes and no laces.

'I knew the old boy who first settled here. His yacht gave up the ghost so he camped here and then started bringing stuff over from the mainland, he liked it so much. Originally he was fishing but with no refrigeration that was too hard so when he discovered that thousands of turtles came here to lay their eggs he latched on to the idea of a turtle soup factory.'

'No! That's awful. They're protected,' exclaimed Jennifer in horror.

'Not back then. He prospered for a while, then went bust so he set up a few cabins and a lot of sailors stopped in here, and spread the word. Then he started bringing a few visitors over for holidays. That was back in the sixties.'

'It must have been very unspoiled then.' Jennifer ducked under branches in the thicket of trees. She sensed they were in the centre of the island. It was still and hot, no smell of the ocean and no seabirds.

'There were no amenities, if that's what you mean. But we didn't know much about conservation and protection of the reef and sea species then. People sailed off with as many fish as they could, pretty shells, lumps of coral, turtle shells, starfish. Can't do that any more. Nor should we,' he added as they threaded their way through she-oaks.

Jennifer could feel a sea breeze. 'That's cooler,

are we nearly there?' They'd been walking for about half an hour.

'Ten more minutes. You can see why the tourists don't bother me.'

'Aren't you lonely?'

'Aw, I get regular visitors. Lloyd and Doyley bring the boat around to have a fish on their days off. A bit of a gang drop around some Friday nights. Come along, too, if you like. Any time. There are several different groups, communities, here on Branch. And they tend to keep to themselves mostly.'

'Odd, when it's such a small place,' Jennifer was about to ask who they were when the she-oaks gave way to stately spiky pandanus trees balanced on their legs of strong upright roots. They fringed the sand and beyond them was the ruffled blue ocean. 'How pretty.'

They walked out onto the sweep of deserted beach. It was windier, more exposed, than the resort side.

'Does it get wild in storms here?' asked Jennifer, remembering what Rosie had said about cyclones being few and far between.

'You bet. That's why the Shark Bar and my joint are nestled back in the she-oaks.' He pointed along the beach to where a dinghy was pulled up on the sand and tied to a tree.

'Shark Bar? Real bar? Real sharks?' Jennifer was intrigued.

'Of course. That's the private club I mentioned. Very exclusive.'

'Are ladies allowed?'

'I might be old school but I'm very liberated about letting ladies in to share an ale. By invitation of course. Come and see.'

'I'm honoured, Gideon.' She followed him along the shore. 'Is that dinghy what you go fishing in?' It looked very small.

'That's the taxi that meets the yachts and cruisers to bring people ashore and back again. I have a half-cabin putt-putt moored up the inlet. There's an inner lagoon with a channel out to the sea. Very convenient. That's where my little house is.'

Jennifer couldn't see anything resembling a house but in behind the pandanus, backed by a line of she-oaks, she could see a shack made of corrugated iron and timber with a lean-to out the front draped with fishing net to make a roof. The shack itself had a thatched roof. There were no floorboards, windows or doors. Merely three sides with the lean-to facing the ocean. Two tables and chairs were under the fishnet roof, which had mooring buoys, fishing rods and a couple of old circular life preservers on top to anchor it. A length of wood that looked like it had come off a boat had 'Shark Bay' painted on it.

Jennifer clapped her hands. 'How gorgeous! Robinson Crusoe eat your heart out. Or is it Fantasy Island?' She laughed.

'More Gilligan's Island. Come in, have a cold drink. No hard stuff till after three.'

There was an old refrigerator powered by a generator along with several hanging light globes.

A cupboard, makeshift bar and chairs stood on a sandy floor. 'Easy housekeeping, sweep everything out the door. But look at the view,' said Gideon as he put two clean glasses on the bar and pulled a bottle of lemonade from the fridge.

Jennifer was looking at the inside of the unlined walls, which were covered with the names of boats and their skippers. 'You have had a lot of visitors over the years.' She wondered about his family but didn't want to pry. There'd be time to discover more about the fascinating old beachcomber. Already she knew she'd visit again. She surprised herself. What would Blair think if she told him she'd trekked across the island to the remote and lonely side to spend time with some old recluse? Especially after last night. But she knew she wasn't going to tell Blair. Just yet.

They finished the lemonade and Gideon led her through the trees to his cabin. It was a simple wooden building but around it he'd cleared a path edged in whitewashed stones, and to one side there was a table, chairs, a barbecue made from a gasoline drum, a clothes line and a faded beach umbrella. A hammock was strung between trees with a mosquito net looped over it, and a goat was tethered nearby.

'This was one of the original holiday huts from where the resort is now. I lived in a tent for the first few years, but my old bones appreciate a bed these days. That's the siesta hammock,' he said, following her gaze. 'Now I'll take you along the private track to the inlet. The best swimming, and right now the tide is perfect.'

The channel widened into a small lagoon before narrowing as it passed through the sand dune to the sea. It was almost like a swimming pool.

She spotted a shady tree at the edge of the sand. 'I think I'll set up under that tree. How far inland does the channel go?'

'Ah, that's quite interesting. It dribbles away to a bit of a marshy area and goes underground. It's fresh until it meets the seawater. Drinkable in a pinch if you treat it. No sharks or nasties up there, don't worry. I'll leave you to it, Jennifer. You want anything, just holler.'

Jennifer stripped down to her swimsuit, applied sunblock, laid out her towel, made a pillow from her clothes and stretched out in the shade to read. But soon she dozed, the book falling from her hands. When she woke up she was hot. The sun had moved and she realised she must have slept for an hour or more. She walked to the edge of the small lagoon to splash cool water on herself. She waded in and her feet felt the smooth hard white sand. Then she squatted down, splashing herself. And before she knew it, she pushed off and dog paddled into the still water. She didn't count this as the ocean. This was a very big spa tub. Not like the water she'd finally learned to swim in at school. This felt like her body was wrapped in silk that slithered around her and she rolled on her side and then onto her back. She felt wonderful. She hadn't swum anywhere but in a private home or hotel pool when Blair had insisted. To reassure herself she stood up and found her feet touched the bottom and the water in the centre of the lagoon came up to her chin. She did a slow breast-stroke circuit of the main lagoon but decided against going along the channel in any direction.

She lay in the sun to dry, then ate her lunch and returned to her book. She napped again, finished her juice, dressed and thought she'd explore a little further. She walked around the bend in the channel as there seemed to be a well-worn narrow path. There she saw Gideon's little boat moored beside a wooden landing. But beside it on the grass was a strange contraption. A kind of sophisticated large toy, big enough for two people, with a window in front like an eye, and rudder-like fins on either side. Was it some sort of strange fish trap? It wasn't a boat. It looked more like a plane.

There was a small portable tin shed set back from the shore that had a padlock on its door. Now what was Gideon keeping under lock and key? She decided she'd better return to the resort. She went past Gideon's house and saw that he was stretched out in his hammock, sound asleep. Quietly she walked back along the beach, hoping she'd be able to retrace her steps.

Jennifer felt relaxed and rested. And calmer and happier in spirit. She was, however, somewhat bemused, unsettled, distracted at the events of the day. How had an unshaven, older man, a rough diamond, with no visible means of support, but warmth and intellect, made her feel so comfortable in a few hours?

Her faith in the goodness of people had been somewhat restored. She was still shocked and repelled by the fact that a man with public acclaim, some notoriety, considered successful and popular, had exhibited such a vicious streak. And lurking out there somewhere was an apparent pervert who did odd jobs but spent more time ogling young women.

What made Gideon different? She had nothing to judge him by except her own instinct and intuition. Gideon had given her a sense of security, of independence and, in her heart, he reignited her longing for the father she'd lost, the grandfathers she'd never known. Jennifer decided she would visit the Shark Bar on Friday afternoon. She wanted to spend time with Gideon and she was curious about the other community he referred to. Here she was on a tropical island hundreds of kilometres from what she considered civilisation, so who else was sheltering here?

Jennifer reached the peak of Coral Point and followed the track to where it forked and the sign pointed to the resort. She paused, wondering where the other path led. She decided to take a look. Within a few metres she heard voices and girls' laughter. The path was only wide enough for two people, but through the trees she glimpsed several girls and a couple of men in casual clothes.

To her shock as they came in sight she saw Willsy, two of his friends and four young women. She didn't recognise any of the girls, but then she hadn't met all the staff yet. Jennifer was frozen to the spot as the TV host sauntered in front with what looked to be a cluster of acolytes around him. He stopped.

'Ah, halt, who goes here? A lost maiden, a damsel in distress? Want to join our party?' His face looked red and blotchy and he wore dark glasses.

'We're going to the cove, come along,' called one of the girls. They seemed merry and Jennifer wondered if they'd been drinking. Did these girls know anything about this man and his mates? He looked so affable and attractive. For a moment a doubt flashed into her mind, then the memory of Rhonda's smashed face returned.

'No thanks. I'm just going back to the resort. I've been to the beach.' She knew she sounded prissy. What could she say to these girls?

'Resort is the other way, love. Wrong track,' said Willsy, giving her a second look. 'Haven't I seen you there?'

'Yes. I saw you at the resort the other night. I'm a friend of Rhonda's,' said Jennifer evenly, her eyes not leaving his face.

If there was a flicker in his expression it was veiled behind his sunglasses. He looked away, stepping to the side and ushering the girls past him. 'Don't think I know her. See ya.'

They moved past and the last girl gave Jennifer

a concerned glance. 'Do you work at the resort?' She had a foreign accent.

'No. Be careful of those guys,' said Jennifer in a low voice.

The dark-haired girl gave her a smile and a quick thumbs up. 'Don't get lost.'

Jennifer turned around and took the track to the resort as the group headed off, her happy mood deflated.

That evening, sitting on their little patio before dinner, she told Blair she'd seen Willsy and his mates with a group of girls.

'Listen, the guy is on holidays on a tropical island, he's going to look for a good time. So long as it doesn't get out of control, there's nothing we can do. So, what did you do all day?'

Jennifer looked at her husband then said shortly, 'Sat under a tree, read a book and dozed off.'

'Great. Sounds great. Listen, there's an interesting couple from Switzerland here. I've invited them to join us for dinner.'

'Why? Must we? Can't you entertain them?' sighed Jennifer.

'While Rosie is away, you and I are the host and hostess, babe. Don't be such a stick in the mud. And get a bit dressed up, they're money people.'

Jennifer longed for Rosie to get back. She did feel frumpish. Willsy's arrogance had unnerved her and now Blair irritated her. She didn't feel herself at all. Her body felt very wobbly, not sick, but not well. Maybe later in the week she'd go back to the mainland for the day, see a doctor, have a day trawling round the shops and cafes. The idea made her feel better. She went inside to change for dinner.

7

Moonrise

THE STRETCH OF SAND in front of the resort was becoming very familiar. Jennifer could picture every tree and cluster of rocks she passed each morning on her pre-breakfast walk. She always ended up at the jetty and walked its length.

Peering into the clear green shallows she was occasionally rewarded with a glimpse of the lazy bulk of Methuselah, the grouper who had claimed the expanse between the jetty and the old wreck as his territory. There were always schools of slim silver fish that swam between the boats in a perfectly choreographed formation, changing direction as one. Inevitably other early-morning visitors lamented the fact no fishing was allowed inside the reef. Sometimes graceful eagle rays danced in the deep green water around the pylons or close to shore with balletic ripplings of wings, their long tails trailing.

Jennifer had lost track of the days, each was the same as the one before. Perhaps one sunset was marginally more or less spectacular than another, or the breeze whipped up more strongly today than yesterday, or clouds scudded in at mid-day – threatening a shower that never came – and were gone by late afternoon. She drifted through the first week, sinking into a sun-induced torpor where the day was divided into meals, reading, a dip in the resort pool, cocktails, conversing with strangers.

She couldn't bring herself to set up her computer and start work. She made the excuse to herself that there was no space. But she had no interest either. Her university days seemed a world away. She decided to shake her lethargy by going across to Headland Bay on the mainland for the day.

Rosie was back and Blair was preoccupied and irritable. Probably because he was no longer in charge, Jennifer surmised. Rosie had made a special point of calling on Jennifer and asking how she was settling in.

Jennifer was honest. 'I'm not sure, to tell you the truth. I'm just drifting along like I'm on holiday, but I'm not having a brilliant time. I feel I'm the single person on a Valentine's Day couples' outing or something. Blair takes his job seriously and he might as well be working on the mainland as I never see him until dinnertime and then he's out socialising with guests. I'm afraid I haven't been able to keep up with him.'

Rosie chuckled. 'And I bet all your friends think you're just so lucky to be living on a magic island on the Great Barrier Reef. I know the feeling. You need to have a focus of your own. By the way, any time you want to do any resort activities you get a staff rate. Scuba, the submarine . . .'

'Thanks, but no. I have a . . . thing about the water. It's a miracle I went swimming in the lagoon the other day.' Jennifer wondered if Rosie knew Gideon. She supposed she must, but she didn't mention their meeting to Rosie.

'Oh dear.' Jennifer heard the sympathy in Rosie's voice, the unspoken, *What the hell are you doing here?* 'That's difficult. I thought Blair said you had a project to work on for the uni or something?'

'I do, but I haven't had the energy. In fact I'm going over to Headland today on the morning catamaran. It will be smooth, won't it?'

'Of course it will be. It might get a bit bumpy on the way back if the wind gets up. But that catamaran skims along. I've some pills or a seasick patch if you want. Have you got plans over there?'

'I got the name of a doctor, from Doyley actually. He's a fount of information. I thought I'd have a check-up and, well, a little retail therapy might do the trick.'

'Sounds good,' laughed Rosie. 'Call me when you get back and show me the spoils. We can have a catch-up drink.'

'Great.' Jennifer was looking forward to the day ahead.

Headland Bay was a small Queensland town with big ideas. At the wharf where the catamaran docked there were pleasure boats, a take-away food and general store, a fish and chip shop, a small newsagent and a coffee bar. A large, colourful display poster pictured how the area would look when the proposed Headland Marina Complex was built – berths for luxury yachts, restaurants, shops.

Inside the Branch Island reception area, where several couples were checking in their luggage for the trip back over to the island, Jennifer was greeted by Vera.

'Morning, Mrs Towse. How are you liking the island? This is your first time off it, eh?'

'Please, call me Jennifer. The island is beautiful.' She glanced at the guests listening to the conversation. 'Why do you call it the rock? That makes it sound so barren.'

'Rock fever, luv. It's what you get living on a small island surrounded by a big ocean. If you don't get off every couple of weeks or months, you go a bit crazy. You've only been there ten days or so, right?' She gave a smile and raised an eyebrow and Jennifer felt she was being chided for escaping so soon.

'I have a few errands to do. Some shopping. Where's a good area?' asked Jennifer.

'Oh, we have a big shopping centre, look for signs to Tropicana World. Soon we'll have a fabulous mall, this place is going ahead since the new council got in.'

What a shame. Developers will make this like everywhere else when it could be kept low-key and tasteful. 'Fine. Book me on the late afternoon trip back, will you? See you later.'

Jennifer took the car from the storage depot and as the engine ticked over it occurred to her she could drive away, anywhere. Further north, down south, inland or to the outback. She longed for open spaces, a distant horizon that was not the sea. She longed for anonymity and knowing she had choices. A movie, shopping, cafes, restaurants, pubs. She wanted rain and cold weather. She wanted change. The parade of blue sunny days bored her.

The shopping centre was sterile, the same stores and layout found in any town or city suburb in Australia. But it provided a welcome distraction. She didn't need or want anything in particular but she browsed with the thoroughness of a dedicated shopper and bought a few items.

She drove around the boldly signed 'CBD', which seemed to consist of appliance stores, video and mobile-phone outlets, boat repairers and offices housing small businesses. Further out of town she found the residential streets, a large garden nursery, a few restaurants, a corner store and a newsagent. She wound up the hill to the public gardens, which had a view across the harbour to the sea where the reef with its skirt of small islands drew visitors to its postcard beauty. Blair constantly repeated how lucky they were on Branch, named because it was an island sprouting right from a limb of the Great Barrier Reef.

The fence surrounding the gardens was covered in massed purple, pink and white bougainvilleas and Jennifer realised how Branch was lacking in colourful flowers. She was tempted to go back and buy some bright silk ones, but felt that taking artificial flowers to Branch Island would contravene its ethos of 'nature rules, okay'. Tucked into a green oasis at the side of the public gardens was a restaurant appropriately named The View. She parked and asked for a table on the verandah.

She hadn't been eating well though the food at the resort was regarded as a big drawcard. Blair and the chef were concocting fabulous dishes but to Jennifer these were too elaborate, too much like the glitzy meals in foodie magazines. The guests either went for the dressed show dishes or what Jennifer had named the whole-hog buffet, in her mind more variety and quantity of food than any human needed.

The uncomplicated dishes at The View appealed to her and she ate heartily. She felt so much better she wondered if she should cancel her doctor's appointment. What she needed, she decided, was a regular hit of the outside world.

While she was waiting for her coffee, she turned on her mobile phone, which had been useless on the island.

'Hello, Vi, it's me. I'm on the mainland for a day so we can have a chat.'

'Oh Jen, it's so good to hear your voice. My goodness, we miss hearing from you. Your mum is going to be so cross she missed you. She's down at the club.'

'I miss you too. Is Don okay? And how's Mum?'

'They're good as gold. Now tell me, what's it like? You haven't sent us any emails yet.'

'I'm sorry, Vi. I feel bad about that. But it's like I've been in some cocoon. The days just pass and I haven't been able to get myself organised. Just been playing at being a resort guest. Blair has settled right in and loves it.'

Vi heard the disquiet in Jennifer's voice. 'But you haven't settled in? You needed a rest, sweetie. Recharge your batteries, that's all. Are you doing any work? I mean, how do you pass the time?' Vi couldn't imagine Jennifer just lazing by a pool or doing whatever people did at those flash resorts.

'I've been doing a bit of retail therapy over here in Headland Bay. I'll be fine, Vi.'

'Is that a nice little town?'

'It is at the moment. A holiday place that's the jumping-off point for this part of the reef. Developers are moving in to jazz it up, you know what that means.'

'Oh dear. So tell me more about the island,

your mother is going to want to know every detail. She's playing a comp and they hang about with tea and sandwiches after so she won't be back for hours. Can you ring again before you go back?'

'I'll try. The island and the resort are lovely. Just like the postcards. I'm afraid we have a rather small unit. But it's secluded. There's an empty one next door that they use for visitors doing office work and so on. Blair said we might be able to use it for friends. So we could put you up.'

'All in good time, Jen. You settle in properly. I wouldn't tell your mother that just yet. She's itching to get up there of course. And are the people nice? Have you made any friends?'

Jennifer was tempted to share her upset over Rhonda's beating but didn't want to worry Vi. They chatted and Jennifer tried to make island life sound upbeat, mentioning Gideon as one of the interesting people she'd met.

'What about your old friends, have you heard from anyone?'

'Not really. Communication is difficult. Once I get my computer going . . . I'm about to call Trisha,' said Jennifer, feeling guilty that she hadn't called anyone from what she thought of as her 'old' life. The waitress brought her coffee as she said goodbye to Vi, then Jennifer dialled Trisha, her closest friend from uni.

'What's happened to you? We've been dying to hear. Is it fabulous?'

Jennifer sketched a picture of tropical nights

under the moon, fantastic activities, the glamorous resort, the intriguing island.

'Sounds like paradise. Any famous people there too?'

The question caught Jennifer off-guard. 'There was a TV guy . . . actually, oh God, Trish, he beat up a girl . . .' The words tumbled out in a low whisper and she felt close to tears.

'What! What the hell happened? Who'd he beat up? Who is he?'

'He was drunk. That guy from *Life Starts Here*, the reality show, the host . . .'

'Dougie Wilson? Willsy? Doesn't surprise me, he's an egotistical moron if you ask me. Wasn't he a boxer? God, how bad is the girl?'

'She was bruised and bleeding, he grabbed her on the beach late at night not far from our place and she got away and came to our door.'

'She was lucky by the sound of it. Did he rape her?'

'No. But Trisha, it's all been kept quiet. Please, you mustn't mention this to anyone . . .' The relief she felt at sharing the painful secret was overtaken by worry that the news might get out.

''Course not. But then, who's going to believe her story unless there was a witness? Though you and Blair could testify to what happened. I tell you, guys like that think they can do what they want with women,' said Trisha angrily.

'Rhonda doesn't want anyone to know. Blair was acting manager and it would be bad PR for the resort, he thought.'

'That's for sure, but, shit, what about the poor girl?' said Trisha bluntly and when Jennifer didn't answer, knowing it made Blair look bad, Trisha added, 'Well, at least if anything happens on an island the culprit can't get away easily. It must have been awful for you.'

'Yes. Anyway, she's gone home to Ireland and he's left too.' Jennifer paused. 'It's good to talk about it. I think it rattled me more than I realised. I'm feeling very isolated. I'm not the island type. I know what my mother would say – you made your bed, girl, now sleep in it.'

'What about the book? How's that coming?'

'Haven't done a thing. But I'm starting tomorrow. I feel so much better, Trisha. I thought I was going mad. I came over to see a doctor, but I feel so much better after talking to you.'

'Any time. And any time you want some company let me know. I could take a bit of sun, scuba and snorkelling on the reef. It sounds gorgeous.'

Trisha filled Jennifer in on their mutual friends and her own life before Jennifer glanced at her watch and said she'd be late for her appointment.

She found the doctor's surgery and waited her turn. She flipped through an old gossip magazine until the doctor called her into his surgery. He was an old-fashioned fellow, comfortable in tweed jacket and woollen tie, and she didn't mind him calling her Dear.

He did seem to be thorough and finally he peered at her over the top of his glasses. 'Just as I expected. No surprises here, nothing wrong with you, dear. No wonder you've been feeling "off colour", as you describe it.' He paused and smiled. 'You're just pregnant, that's all.'

'Pregnant?' Jennifer's hand flew to her mouth in shock.

'You hadn't considered the possibility?'

'No. I hadn't. I mean . . . my life, my routine, has been a bit upset, with the move and all . . .' *Oh God, what is Blair going to say? How am I going to tell him?*

'You're fit and young, you'll have to come over from the island for regular check-ups and, closer to the due date, make other arrangements. I assume you'll have the baby here? It's rather a good little hospital. Can't imagine there will be complications. Even though you have little information about your family history.' There was a faint hint of disapproval in his tone.

Jennifer knew nothing of her father's or her grandparents' medical background, nor anything about her mother's except for a few minor problems in the last few years. It had never occurred to her to ask about her or her brother's birth. That was taboo territory.

'So. Congratulations, my dear.' The doctor's attention was shifting to the waiting patients. 'See the receptionist on the way out, she'll give you all the basic information. Diet, vitamins and so forth.' But Jennifer didn't seem to be reacting as he expected. He studied her for a moment, then said, 'You're not pleased about this news?'

'We hadn't planned this. I mean, I went off the

pill after I read how bad it could be. But I thought
. . . we were being careful.'

The doctor airily waved a hand. 'Babies are
heaven sent. You can't always control these
things.'

Jennifer's mind was racing. That's why she'd
felt so odd. Now what? She tried to think laterally.
How would they deal with this? She had nine
months. Less. Blair had a twelve- to eighteen-
month contract and part of their deal had been no
children. Maybe she'd go back to Sydney and have
the baby there, but where would she live? At Vi
and Don's with her mother? She felt her heart sink
at the idea.

The doctor was looking at her.

'I'm just concerned for my husband's job. I
don't think children were part of the package
when he was hired.'

'What about you two . . . had you planned on
a family at all?'

'Well, yes, eventually. We agreed we'd wait, and
be careful . . .'

'Sometimes you only get one chance. How
would you feel if you didn't go through with this
only to find you couldn't conceive when you do
decide you're ready?'

Jennifer bit her lip and he continued in a more
kindly tone.

'I'm not being judgmental. An infant who's
happy, healthy and comfortable shouldn't be too
much trouble. My concern is you and your baby.
But that's why we schedule regular check-ups.' He

turned back to his notes and scratched something on her file. Any further decisions were up to her.

Jennifer sat in the car outside the doctor's rooms in a daze. Eventually she drove to the harbour and parked close to the car storage. The reef cat was coming into the wharf and would be making the trip back to Branch in forty-five minutes.

She watched the holidaymakers disembark looking tanned, relaxed and happy, and wished she felt so carefree. She couldn't adjust to the idea that she and Blair really could create a child. That she would be a mother. This would change their lives. But Blair would not be happy at this slip-up. She felt sure he would love the baby, but she was scared to tell him just yet. She just knew he'd be upset at the upheaval in their lives. His career might suffer and they'd already had a discussion about putting off a family. Would he want her to have an abortion? How did she feel about that?

Jennifer sat with her hands pressed to her belly. She wanted to cry. She felt very young, not ready for this. Could she go through with terminating the baby and never tell Blair? No! She was suddenly flushed with a strong emotion that surged in her like someone had thrown hot water on her. Why was her first concern for Blair and his damned career? She was carrying this child. They would discuss the future together, how best to rejig their lives. But Jennifer resolved with unflinching certainty that the decision about this baby was hers and hers alone.

She returned the car, ordered a cold drink, and waited for the call to board.

Vera spotted her and called out, 'Where's all the shopping? Couldn't find anything?'

Jennifer held up one small bag. 'Just a few gifts. I'll have to come back over, didn't hit all the shops.'

'You look more relaxed. Glad you had a nice day. Got a couple of honeymooners going over this trip. Weather isn't looking crash hot. Still, don't suppose they'll care if they have to stay indoors for a few days.'

Jennifer glanced at the sky, seeing the low edge of dark clouds. 'How bad will the trip back over be?'

'No probs. But stay inside, wind will bring the spray on deck. Do you get seasick?'

'Ah, I'm not sure. Frankly, I'm scared rather than sick. It is safe, isn't it?'

'Safe as houses. I'll get them to put a good video on, and the bar is open. Get a glass or two of champers, you won't notice a bit of see-sawing.'

Want to bet? 'Oh. Maybe I'd better take a seasick pill.' Then she remembered. She was pregnant. She'd better not take anything that could affect the baby. God, how her thinking was changing already. 'Ah, don't worry, Vera. I'll roll with the punches.' Everything in moderation would be her credo now.

She hated the trip back to the island. The water looked bruised. Wind whipped the tops off the greyish-blue waves and Jennifer had the feeling that the light frame of the big catamaran was slithering to stay on top of some irritable creature as if it were an irksome tick on a beast's back. She sat near the air-conditioning vent and glanced at the video showing the wonders of the reef and its islands. While the tourists exclaimed in anticipation Jennifer sipped her glass of champagne and kept thinking about the tiny speck of life within her, trying to get used to the staggering idea that she would be a mother. She hadn't rung Christina back as she'd promised Vi. She had a good excuse with no mobile reception and only a payphone in the resort main area. Phones in the rooms were only connected to the resort reception. Jennifer knew her mother would sense something and drag out her news. She wasn't yet ready to announce to the world she was pregnant.

For two days Jennifer tried to plan how she would break the news to Blair. Over a romantic dinner? Or a sunset drink? Only trouble was they were rarely alone. And it was raining. Warm grey showers swirled around the island, keeping the dive boats at anchor though the fishing boats still went out. It didn't stop visitors from swimming or trudging along the beach. People socialised more indoors, the bar and terrace were crowded with happy drinkers and the table tennis and billiard tables were always in use in the recreation room. Blair decided a big clean-up was in order around the staff quarters and working bees were under way.

Jennifer felt energised too. She was feeling

better, her lethargy replaced by a surge of activity. She set up her laptop on the deck using an extension cord and began to answer the dozens of emails she'd accessed from Blair's office connection. She was working out there with piles of papers around her when Rosie came by.

'Ah, Blair said you were back in busy mode. Though it isn't a very satisfactory office.'

'It'll have to do. I can't believe the backlog of emails,' she said with a laugh.

'Maybe we could find you a corner in an office somewhere.'

'Would you like a coffee?' asked Jennifer.

'That'd be lovely.'

They sat in the back courtyard under the tree. 'Now the rain has stopped, I like sitting out here and watching the birds.'

'The turtles will start coming in to lay their eggs any day. It's an amazing experience. I was never much of a nature lover till I came here. The biggest attraction for me is scuba diving. What about you?'

'Rosie, like I said, I don't like the ocean. I had a bad experience when I was a kid. My brother drowned and, well, there's a whole bunch of issues.'

'Oh, that's right.' She recalled Jennifer's reluctance about swimming. 'No wonder you don't seem happy, well, comfortable here. I wondered why. Blair's appointment must have been difficult. You had to give up your own pursuits.'

Rosie's sincerity and empathy brought Jennifer

to the edge of tears. 'I never thought I'd have to make hard choices and compromise my life for a husband. My mother has always knocked men. She thinks they either mess up your life or leave. She had to struggle to bring me up and she wanted the very best for me. Or what she saw as best.' Jennifer choked up, thinking of the secret she now held within her. She was tempted to blurt her news to the warm and friendly Rosie. She had to keep reminding herself that Rosie was Blair's superior, as she felt her to be more her own friend. Rosie was around forty and her strong, good-natured personality came through in her direct gaze and her straight-talking honesty, which was very appealing.

Rosie leaned forward, recognising the vulnerable streak showing in Jennifer. 'Jennifer, I like you. Blair is very fortunate to have you as a partner. While we work together, I would like you to consider me a friend outside the professional relationship with your husband.'

How diplomatic. Reversing roles. Blair would have put it that one worked for the other, not as a team. 'That's nice of you, Rosie. I felt I knew you from the minute we met. I'm sure Blair will understand and be glad we have a friendship. I suppose it's difficult for you to have women friends here on staff when you're the boss.'

'Ah, that's part of it. It's safer to keep some distance. And frankly, Jennifer, I'll level with you – I'm gay. I doubt anyone here knows, or cares, and that's my business. But I keep my private life private and off the island. I have a girlfriend in Headland and it's a great relationship.' She gave a small laugh. 'To tell you the truth, seeing your lover every two weeks rather than living together every day keeps the romance alive.'

Jennifer's momentary shock dissolved in laughter. 'You know, that sounds like a great arrangement. I hope I'm not being unkind to Blair, but it's true, isn't it, about absence making the heart fonder? Thank you for telling me. Of course this conversation is just between you and me.'

'I knew you'd treat it as such. Which is why I felt okay about telling you.' She put her cup down. 'I'd better get going.' She stood up, giving Jennifer a smile, her voice gentle and concerned. 'I'm not sure how, but maybe there's a reason you've ended up here, and perhaps this is your opportunity to come to terms with your childhood trauma.'

Jennifer was tempted to respond to Rosie's honesty by telling her about her pregnancy, but she felt that would be disloyal to Blair. Nevertheless, she felt better about their situation. While she'd never disclose any of this conversation to Blair, she felt more secure that Rosie would be understanding and supportive about the pregnancy issue. Impulsively Jennifer gave Rosie a hug. 'Thanks, Rosie, I'm glad we had this chat.'

'Hang in there, Jenny. I'll look into finding a better working space for you. In fact, I might talk to some people. See you.' She waved and headed off down the track.

Jennifer watched Rosie's tall shape dressed in

her white shorts and loose flowered staff shirt disappear in the trees.

Blair was on duty the following weekend and he promised they'd do something special on his two days off, Monday and Tuesday. 'How about we go over to Sooty Isle? Have a picnic. Stay the night. And when I have a week's break we'll plan something.' He was feeling a bit guilty at leaving Jennifer on her own, though she seemed to have settled in at last, working on her laptop, and was more cheerful than she'd been.

Jennifer was relieved and decided their picnic off the island, away from his work, would be the right time to tell him about the baby. So late on Friday afternoon she packed up her paperwork and the laptop, pleased with what she'd done, and decided to take up Gideon's offer of calling by the Shark Bar.

The track over to the other side of the island seemed shorter as it was more familiar this time. As Jennifer came through the pandanus to the beach she could hear voices and laughter. She was glad she came. She grinned to herself, remembering the Thank God It's Friday get-togethers she and Trisha had occasionally shared after a week of hard work at the university. The Shark Bar, with its bare floor, thatched roof and rustic amenities, was a far cry from some of the trendy bars and cafes in Sydney where they had their TGIF gatherings.

Gideon, sitting in an old deck chair under the lean-to shelter, spotted her and lifted his hat in greeting. Shyly Jennifer waved to him, rather surprised at the large group of people. They seemed to be all ages. She recognised Professor Macdonald Masters whom she'd first flown over with. There were two other men in their forties, and a group of young men and women she'd never seen before. She caught a foreign phrase or two. It was hard to slot people into categories when they were all very casually dressed, barefoot or in thongs and sandals. Perhaps they were a group off a boat. Though there was no boat anchored and the dinghy was tied securely to its tree.

'Excellent, welcome back, my dear Jennifer. I was hoping you'd come. This is Mac . . . Professor Macdonald Masters . . .'

'Yes, we met when you first arrived.' He shook her hand and smiled. He was holding a beer can. 'What would you like to drink?'

'I didn't come empty-handed.' Jennifer pulled a bottle of white wine from her small backpack. 'And a jar of olives and a chunk of cheese courtesy of the resort kitchen.'

'You'll always be welcome,' grinned Mac.

'You do the honours, Mac, they're your mob,' said Gideon sitting back down.

Mac glanced around at people inside the bar, seated in chairs, several sitting on the ground. 'We'll do it bit by bit. That way you'll be able to remember names more easily.'

Am I going to ever clap eyes on any of these people again? Where have they come from?

A pretty olive-skinned girl joined them and Jennifer recognised her as the girl in the bikini she'd seen several times with Mac heading for the beach. If she was Mac's girlfriend they seemed somewhat mismatched. Mac was in his late forties, lean and wiry with crinkly tracks on his face that showed he'd spent a lot of time in the sun. Behind his glasses his eyes were a keen blue that seemed very bright, or was it the intensity of his gaze? His greying hair, pulled back in a short pony tail, showed a high brow and an intelligent face. His voice was soft but mellifluous. Jennifer's first impression in the helicopter had been of a quiet, almost withdrawn, man. But then he'd courteously sat behind her and allowed the stunning scenery to be the focus of her attention. The olive-skinned girl was very beautiful and when she spoke she had an exotic, South American accent. Mac introduced them.

'Jennifer, this is Carmelita, also called Carmel, Carmen or Caramel. She's from Venezuela.'

'Oh, which name applies when?' asked Jennifer, smiling at the dark-eyed beauty.

'Carmel is easy for Australians. The rest call me Carmen if I get excited and Caramel when I get too brown.'

'I see,' laughed Jennifer, noticing Carmel seemed to have an all-over suntan. 'You're a long way from home.'

'I've been working in the Caribbean, I'm not

183

sure where I'll end up. Depends on my professor here.'

If it was a proprietary remark Mac looked unfazed. 'No, Carmel, it's up to you. You must choose. It's your future.'

Gideon appeared beside them. ''Scuse me, Jennifer, come and meet Rudi, Mac's associate professor. And you must know Lloyd?'

'I don't believe so,' though she recognised Lloyd as one of the resort staff. He was twentyish, and good looking in a sun-bleached hair, over-tanned way. She hadn't seen any of the others before.

'Lloyd is our sailing skipper, and dive captain for the Shark Bar and Mac's crews,' said Gideon, which meant nothing to Jennifer.

'Hi. The rest of the time I'm a boatie on the fishing charters at the resort. I've seen you round,' said Lloyd, shaking her hand with a disarming smile. 'When are you and your hubby coming out with us?'

'She says she's not the seafaring type,' explained Gideon. 'We'll have to get her out for an underwater excursion.'

'No chance of that!' Jennifer was wondering what on earth, if anything, she might have in common with these people. It was like being at a cocktail party where you came into conversations halfway through, where Jennifer was asked her impressions by everyone she met, and it seemed everyone knew everyone else really well. But they were friendly, funny and affable.

It didn't occur to her that she was also attractive, charming and warm.

Gideon replenished his glass of rum and took Jennifer by the arm. 'Come and talk to Mac and me.'

They settled themselves in three chairs facing the sea. The moon was rising and it was a magnificent sight.

'Never get tired of the view. A good way to end the day, no matter what the day has brought,' said Gideon. 'So when is the queen of the deep returning?' he asked Mac.

'Isobel? Soon enough. She's been at a conference in Portugal.' He turned to Jennifer. 'Isobel is a fascinating woman. Very impressive. You must meet her.'

'Really. Will she be staying at the resort?'

'No, with us,' said Mac.

Jennifer looked from Mac to Gideon. 'I'm confused. All these people, are they off a boat? I didn't think there was anywhere else but the resort to stay on Branch.'

Mac glanced at Gideon, then to Jennifer, and chuckled. 'Ah, and never the twain shall meet. You have stumbled into the secret world of Branch Island.'

'The Shark Club?' asked Jennifer in amusement.

'That's by invitation only. Mac is the director of the Reef Science and Research Station here on Branch.' Gideon indicated the group behind them. 'They're all his students and associates. Doing whatever it is they do for months at a stretch.'

'It mightn't look like work, Gideon, but there're five PhDs happening amongst that lot, not to mention the other postgrads – masters and honours students.' Mac turned to Jennifer. 'We're mainly scientists and marine biologists, attached to Southern Star University in Queensland. But we have students from all over the world. Like Carmel. The opportunity to study the reef, its ecosystems, marine life and other environmental issues is highly sought after. I bring a team here twice a year.'

Jennifer felt goosebumps rise along her arms. 'I had no idea this was happening here. Where are you based? Do you come over from the mainland and camp?'

Mac laughed. 'Some might call it roughing it, we have a fairly basic set-up but we have a functioning lab, tanks, work areas and reasonable accommodation. Depends whose turn it is to cook. Of course, the turtle researchers are up all night and they keep waking up the coral researchers who are awake all day and they keep waking the turtle researchers . . . You get the drift – sleep is at a premium.'

'That's where the rest of the original resort went,' explained Gideon. 'The research station is tucked away in the middle of the island.'

'No ocean view, I'm afraid. But we've set up a beach base camp as we got sick of dragging gear back and forth. You must come and have the A-class tour.' Mac grinned.

'I'm staggered.' Jennifer was almost speechless. 'I'd love to see it. Can I come tomorrow?'

They all laughed. And then Jennifer had so much to talk about and so much to ask Mac and Gideon she didn't notice the light had slipped away. Candles and lanterns were lit, a dim light hung above the bar and the mutton birds began returning for the night, shrieking and calling as they flew to their nests.

'Are we barbecuing, Gideon?' called Rudi, who, as Mac's associate professor, oversaw the hands-on day-to-day running of the students' schedules.

Jennifer jumped up in alarm. 'Gosh, I didn't realise it was so late. I'd better head back. Oh, do you have a torch, Gideon?' The track would be in pitch darkness.

'Lloyd is heading back to the resort, go with him,' said Rudi.

'Great,' said Jennifer with relief. She hoped Blair was busy and hadn't noticed she wasn't there. He'd be worried. 'Where is Lloyd?'

'On his boat. In the channel. You can wade out and hop on.'

Jennifer stared at them in shock. 'Oh no, I couldn't.'

Gideon took her arm. 'Lloyd will look after you. Sometimes you have to step outside the circle you've drawn round your feet, young lady.'

Mac stood on the other side of her. 'It's a calm night, after that rain you might see some phosphorescence. Just around the point,' he said gently. 'If you want to join the club, you have to do something you've never done before. Step up now, Jennifer.'

187

For anyone else a boat ride in the calm and starry dusk was not a frightening event. But as Jennifer sat in the small fishing boat clutching the handrail and watching the silhouette of Lloyd at the wheel, she experienced a mixture of emotions. The surface of the water was silvered, still. Like a lid on some nether-world below the sea. It had been many years since she'd had the dream. As a child she'd always felt there was a safe world down there. But as a rational adult she realised she had come close to drowning like her brother and also her father.

For Jennifer her fear of the sea was linked to abandonment and temptation. How easy it would be to slip over the side right now. Lloyd wouldn't hear the splash above the engine noise. Jennifer didn't trust herself. She didn't trust the almighty pull she felt from the ocean that repelled, scared and yet seduced her.

She closed her eyes but Gideon's words came back to her, about stepping outside the circle. She did feel she had drawn a net of safety and security tight around her. Afraid to let emotional challenges creep through. She thought of what Mac had said, of doing something she'd never done before. When she opened her eyes she saw Lloyd sitting comfortably on his swivel chair at the wheel, paying her little attention.

Cautiously Jennifer angled her body towards the gunwale and looped her hand through the metal railing. Holding on tightly, she raised herself to her knees and looked over the side.

Water gurgled past the hull. She took a few short, sharp breaths. Nothing changed. The silvery water rushing past sparkled in the night light. She lifted her gaze, looking past the wake to the flat dark water beyond. It didn't appear sinister or threatening. She continued to stare down into the water.

Then, from those dark unknown depths, a white blob shivered towards the surface. It looked spongy, soft. Childlike. To her horror, Jennifer saw the face of her brother. Ashen-faced, glassy-eyed. A washed-out shape of a once-vibrant boy. Jennifer gasped, felt her stomach heave and put her hand to her mouth to stop the retching.

Lloyd was beside her, a hand on her shoulder. 'If you're feeling sick, hang right over and let it rip. Don't try to swallow it.'

She shook her head, swallowing hard, and looked at him. 'Sorry, I just thought . . . I saw . . .' She looked back at the water where the mucusy blob floated. 'That . . .'

'It's a man-o'-war. Big jellyfish. Harmless. Some varieties have long stingers that can give a nasty rash. The box jellyfish is quite deadly and has tentacles up to three metres.'

She couldn't answer. She saw the pulsing flaps around the circular body. 'Sorry, Lloyd. I'm fine now. Really I am.'

'Good-oh. Shall we go full steam ahead?'

'Let's go.'

'Hang on then.'

Lloyd opened the throttle and the boat surged

forward, the bow lifting slightly. He glanced back at his passenger. Jennifer was grasping the seat and gunwale rail, her face lifted to the night air. Whatever had momentarily ailed her had passed. Instead she looked exhilarated.

There were bright lights, activity on several boats and a few curious people watching from the wharf. As they chugged in to the steps Lloyd cut the engine and called out, 'What's going on, Doyley? Someone get something big?'

'No. Blair's wife's missing. We're going out, they might have to call the chopper in,' shouted Doyley.

'No, man. She's with me. It's all right.'

A siren rang out and a signal flare whooshed in an orange glow off one of the boats. There was shouting and figures ran down the wharf. Jennifer hated the attention and just wanted to be alone back in their cabin. Blair walked back with her.

'You had us worried sick. That was so stupid of you. Not to mention creating bloody havoc.'

'I'm sorry, Blair, I met some really interesting people and I didn't notice it was getting late. And, frankly, I didn't fancy walking across the island on my own in the dark,' she added with some heat.

'You're right,' he conceded. 'I was just so worried. It's so unlike you.'

'Is it?' Jennifer stopped. 'You mean I've been acting like some nervous nelly when I used to be my own person, do my own thing?'

'Yeah. I guess so. I have enough to do with

keeping tabs on all the staff without worrying whether you've fallen in the sea, down a mutton-bird hole, whatever.' They were both thinking of Rhonda.

Jennifer resumed walking. 'You know what, Blair? You can stop worrying about me from now on. Believe me.'

There was something in her voice that caused Blair to bite back any more criticisms. 'Great. I'm glad. So you won't mind if I go back to work? What about dinner?'

'I'll fix myself something. You eat at the resort. I don't need babysitting, Blair. I plan to do some work.'

'Good girl. Have a restful evening. Sounds like you've had enough excitement for one day. By the way, who were these interesting people?'

'No one you'd enjoy. Some university people. A scientist and a beachcomber.'

'You're right. Not my types.' Blair didn't see the tight and furious expression on Jennifer's face.

Later, alone, after having eaten a scrambled egg and a cup of soup, Jennifer sat with her feet on the coffee table listening to the radio and thought about the afternoon. And the trip back. Suddenly she laughed out loud, went and pulled the wine from the fridge and poured herself a glass, lifting it up to toast herself. 'Welcome to the Shark Club, old girl.'

There was a tap at the door.

'Who is it?'

'Rosie. Are you okay?'

Jennifer opened the sliding door. 'Never better. Sorry about the panic earlier this evening.'

'No problem. Good to know the team swung into action so quickly. Gave everyone a bit of excitement for a minute or two.' She held up a bottle of wine. 'Thought you might like some company.'

'Lovely. In fact, I have one open. Come on in.' Jennifer's eyes were bright, her mood merry, which Rosie put down to the wine and excitement.

They finished the bottle of wine and found they had plenty to talk and laugh about.

'I'm glad you've met Gideon, he's a grand old character. A tinker and boffin. An inventor. I've never got time to get over and see him. He cruises over for dinner once a month or so. I suppose I should go,' said Rosie eventually, not making a move.

'We haven't opened your wine,' protested Jennifer.

'Is there something we can celebrate then?'

Jennifer stood up and reached for the corkscrew. 'Yeah. I shouldn't open more wine, but what the hell. Today I did something I've never done before, something that scared me – and I survived. And . . . I'm pregnant! Blair doesn't know and probably won't be thrilled. But, you know what? I don't care.'

Rosie took the corkscrew from Jennifer and reached for the bottle of wine. 'I'm going to have another glass. You stick to soda. Here's looking at you, kid!'

The first mutton bird of the night shrieked outside, but it was drowned out by the peals of laughter from inside the little cabin nestled amongst the sand and trees.

8

Strangers on the Shore

LLOYD STEERED THE LAUNCH into the deep channel of
the outer reef where the turquoise water changed to
indigo above the continental shelf. Jennifer sat in the
half cockpit beside him, sheltering from sun and spray
as Blair held the fishing rod Lloyd had set to trawl
behind, hoping for a strike.

'Are there big fish down there?' she asked
above the engine.

'Used to be . . . fishing has gone off in the last
few years. That's why they're banning commercial
fishing inside the reef, to give stocks a chance to
replenish. Those bloody nets take everything.'

She looked back at Blair holding the long

flexible rod in one hand and a beer can in the other. 'I didn't know Blair liked fishing.' Though he didn't look particularly comfortable.

Lloyd had a similar thought. 'He'll get a shock if he gets a marlin, Spanish mackerel or tuna strike. Living on the island you take up interests you mightn't have had before, I guess. No laid-on city entertainment around here,' he grinned. Lloyd was in his late twenties and had always lived near the ocean. Boats, especially sailing, were his passion.

'So what do you do when you go back to the mainland?' asked Jennifer, imagining that like most of the other young staffers he'd head for a pub, bar or club. 'Go to a footy match?'

'Nope. My breaks are busman's holidays . . . I work in my dad's boatshed out of Headland. He builds and repairs marine craft. Has a big slipway. A lot of boats put in there when sailing up the coast.'

'Hey, Jenny, come and hang on to this. I'm going to the head.'

Gingerly Jennifer edged into the swivel chair bolted to the deck at the open stern. There were padded benches along either side with rod holders so six people could fish at a time. She took hold of the rod Blair handed her with both hands and felt the drag of the lure through the water.

'If your arms get tired, just lock the end of the rod into that slot there.'

'What do I do if I get a bite?'

'Yell for Lloyd, I guess. Want me to take your picture? Show them back home how you've gone native?'

'I think they'd get more of a kick out of seeing you with a fishing rod,' she retorted. Blair was known for having even less sporting prowess than handyman talents.

As Blair disappeared into the small enclosed area in front of the cockpit, which held a tiny galley, toilet and one bunk, Lloyd glanced back at Jennifer. He was glad to see she seemed more comfortable on the boat than she had on the smaller craft on Friday night returning from Gideon's. What a stink that had caused. He hoped it hadn't put Jennifer off hanging out at the Shark Bar. He wished she wasn't the assistant manager's wife, then he'd feel easier about encouraging her to spend time with Mac and the gang at the research station. Jennifer was a university person and he assumed she'd have more in common with them than the resort people.

His musing was broken by a loud squeal from the stern. The rod's tip was now bent low to the water, the line screaming through the reel. Lloyd knocked the engine back to idle and leapt towards Jennifer. 'Flip the reel, stop the line running out. Okay, now start winding in.'

She tried to hand him the rod that now felt so heavy. 'Here, you do it.'

'No, rule is whoever is holding the rod when there's a strike has to play it.'

'I can't! It's too hard,' wailed Jennifer, not liking the situation at all.

He explained to her how to lower and lift the rod, gaining some line in the slack. Jennifer bit her lip as she strained against the powerful fish. Blair began taking pictures and Lloyd stepped back to the wheel, easing the boat around.

'What is it?' asked Blair, amazed Jennifer hadn't just dropped the rod or pushed it at Lloyd. He was relieved the fish hadn't taken the lure while he was holding the rod. 'She's never going to bring it in.'

'Patience, perseverance, pain. It's a private battle between them.'

Jennifer was sweating, her arms ached, but she felt a small thrill each time she gained a few more centimetres of line.

'Take the wheel, Blair.' Lloyd stood next to Jennifer and used an old towel to wipe her forehead and her straining arms. 'Don't let your hands get slippery. Lift as it runs. It's trying to dive, when it gets close it'll try to get under the boat.'

'Why don't we just let it go?' panted Jennifer.

'We will once you've hauled it aboard. It's a battle so there has to be a winner and a loser.'

He stood beside her as she leaned with the straining rod, her back, arms and legs burning as she lifted and lowered the rod to wind in more line.

Lloyd brought the long gaffer pole with the metal hook to the edge of the boat. 'It's getting close.'

Then with a sharp ping the rod snapped free, flinging Jennifer backwards.

Lloyd grabbed the rod. 'Gone. Damn. Bad luck.'

'What did you do?' called Blair.

'Nothing. It just happened,' said Jennifer. 'It was like someone got scissors and cut it. Bang.' She stared into the water, wondering what her adversary looked like.

'Let's have a cold drink.' Blair went below as Lloyd took the wheel and revved up the engine.

'I'm sorry, Lloyd. I hope you haven't lost too much line.'

'Are you disappointed?' he asked.

'Kind of . . . it is a challenge. And I wanted to win it. But I'm glad it escaped. I hope it's not hurt.'

'Probably got a sore lip. Fishing tackle in the sea can be a nuisance. Not as much as plastic bait bags though.'

'I thought they'd be making biodegradable ones by now.'

'They're around but they're expensive. Plastic bags are killers to turtles. They think they're edible jellyfish and then they choke on them.' He paused as Jennifer gazed into the water. 'Any time we don't have a full charter you can come out fishing as a staffie,' he added.

'I'll think about it. Thanks, Lloyd.'

They were outside the shadowy outline of reef surrounding Sooty Isle. A tiny crescent of white sand fringed by low green vegetation several metres above sea level with no visible buildings made Sooty look a very tiny and isolated place to Jennifer.

'How do these coral cays form?' she wondered aloud.

'Basically, billions of coral polyps accumulating

from the supporting reef build up a foundation,' said Lloyd. 'Cyclones and storms break down the coral to make the sand that starts to build up around the reef. I get asked this all the time. Take a breath, what do you smell?'

'Ammonia? I noticed it when we first arrived.'

'Yep. The birds leave their calling cards, which adds fertiliser to the landscape, seeds are blown, carried by birds, or float ashore and germinate, soil develops and, eventually, vegetation.'

'So there's no fresh water, just rainfall?' asked Jennifer.

'In the beginning rainwater soaks down and, being lighter than seawater, sits on top in what we call a freshwater lens. It's salty at first as the island grows, then it becomes less brackish and can eventually feed plants, trees and so forth. But now there're underground tanks and water is carried over in a bad season. We're lucky on Branch, there's some fresh water. Years of rain got trapped and so there's a bit of a stream for much of the year.'

'Umm, interesting. You know quite a lot.'

'Ah, I've been hanging round Mac and his mates,' smiled Lloyd. 'And Carmel is my girlfriend.'

They could see the white silhouettes of several large boats moored in the lagoon. 'Whose boats are those?' asked Jennifer.

'A couple of yachties gone ashore for the day, sheltering for the night. The floating gin palace could be the big bosses'. I heard they might be coming to the island,' said Lloyd shading his eyes as he looked at the distant boats.

'That's who it is,' said Blair. 'The corporate heavies who get to go on junkets around all Reef Resorts.'

'Yeah, the senior staff are always looking to transfer to one of them,' said Lloyd. 'They have some seriously upmarket places in Asia. They just opened a new one in Koh Samui. Rumour has it they want to develop Branch to the same degree.'

'What's wrong with it as it is?' asked Jennifer.

'It's ten years out of date. It could be far more exclusive. Needs new management strategies and ideas,' said Blair. 'We got time for one more beer before we get there?' he asked, diving into the galley.

'Sure,' said Lloyd, but his expression was tense.

'You don't agree with upgrading Branch Resort?' said Jennifer.

'Nothing to do with me. It's between the resort owners, National Parks and the research station.'

'Doesn't Rosie, as manager, have some say?' asked Jennifer.

Lloyd looked uncomfortable. 'I'm just a hired gun. The resort pays me and I help the research station guys and Gideon voluntarily. Rosie has definite views about which way they should go but as manager she has to do what the corporation wants.' He glanced across the water then picked up the binoculars beside the wheel and changed the direction of the boat, gradually slowing. 'Look over there, see, in the water. She's heading for Branch.'

On the starboard side Jennifer could see a dark round shape. As they drew close she saw it was a large greenback turtle, head and shell breaking the surface, her gaze set resolutely on the distant shadow of Branch Island.

'Oh, wow! Blair, look!'

'She's early in the season. Going back to where she was born to lay her eggs,' said Lloyd.

'They travel long distances, don't they?' said Blair. 'Amazing navigation to find their way back halfway round the world to some dot in the Coral Sea.'

They were alongside the female turtle, a few metres away, when her steadily swimming flippers suddenly jerked and she plunged in a desperate dive.

Before Jennifer could ask what had startled the turtle, it seemed a torpedo hit in an explosion of surging foam. A great dark shadow only a metre or two shorter than their boat broke the surface, shaking in a frenzy of white water.

'Shark!' screamed Blair. 'Christ, check it out! Must be seven metres! Move it, Lloyd!' It struck Blair that if the enormous shark took it into its tiny brain to ram them, the boat would capsize for sure.

'Oh no,' screamed Jennifer. 'Look, it's got the poor turtle!'

The shark rolled and flung its head, revealing the curved slash of teeth gripping the struggling turtle. With a sickening crunch the shark gripped the shell between powerful jaws before flicking its tail and shooting from sight in a second, leaving a slick on the still-bubbling surface and a bleeding severed flipper from the turtle. After the thrashing and shouts the silence was frightening.

'Jesus, how big was that! Haven't you got a gun on board to shoot the bastards?' asked Blair.

Lloyd spun the wheel, gunning the motor. 'Tiger sharks get pretty big out here. We're in their territory. That's probably what took Jennifer's fish,' he said shortly.

Jennifer was shaking. The huge killing machine that had sprung from nowhere to strike and disappear in seconds had frightened and unnerved her. It was as she feared – the sea harboured killers. Awful slashing beasts like the tiger shark or silent unseen forces that swept away and swallowed a father and a brother.

Once they were through the channel and inside the reef they cruised across the placid lagoon where the luxury yachts and motor cruiser loomed, almost dwarfing the islet.

'I hope we don't have to swim ashore,' joked Blair.

'Nothing too big can get inside the reef, this is pretty safe in here. We can load up the dinghy. I'll take you guys ashore first and bring your gear to the tent. You know your way around, eh Blair?'

Blair nodded, rolling up his camera in a towel and picking up a small backpack. 'Jenny, grab the small stuff you need and we can go and explore and come back to get our lunch. There's a great spot to swim around the end of the beach there.'

'Exploring sounds better than swimming,' said Jennifer. 'I'm looking forward to the Robinson Crusoe experience.' She figured once they were settled under a tree on a deserted section of beach with their picnic, she'd tell Blair about the baby.

When she stepped from the dinghy and looked around, Jennifer could see a structure with a thatched roof and open sides, supported by thick wooden poles. As they walked through the trees she saw this was a communal dining area with long wooden tables, polished wooden floor, a serving area and a kitchen at the rear. As well as the tables, chairs and benches there were long seats, stylish cane chairs and wicker lounges all covered in colourful tropical-print silk cushions. It was airy though she saw there were light mesh and split bamboo blinds that could be lowered around the sides as well as tall candle holders and flame torches placed outside.

A pretty girl came to greet them wearing the same turquoise and white print cotton of the Branch Resort staff shirts except hers was a simple sarong with a white cotton singlet on top. She was braless, slim and tanned.

'Hey, Blair, great to see you. The big boys are here with a party. They're hoping to see you for lunch on board.'

'Ah, Susie, this is Jennifer, my wife. Susie is the hostess here. Though she does practically every-thing,' said Blair to Jennifer.

'Not really. I just direct the troops. But I did have to cook breakfast this morning. Carol and Geoff were snared by the *Kicking Back*. That's the name of the bosses' cruiser,' Susie said with sparkling eyes and a big smile to Jennifer.

'That gin palace out there?' Jennifer asked. 'Their resorts must be doing well. Don't you feel a bit, well, cut off, being over here all the time?' she asked as they followed Susie along a shady track scattered with frangipani flowers. She hoped Blair wasn't planning to go to lunch with the group on the ostentatious boat.

'We have accommodation for up to ten people but yachts can book to moor and come ashore for meals and entertainment. There's a charge and we try to keep to a certain type of clientele of course,' said Susie.

'Of course,' said Jennifer and neither of them noticed her sardonic tone.

They reached the first of several tent-style accommodation.

'Wow, this is certainly upscale camping,' said Jennifer. 'Reminds me of some very grand permanent tent sites I saw in an ad for exclusive safaris in Africa.'

'We don't run to chandeliers or leopardskin rugs or black staff in tuxedos, but it's very comfortable, very gracious and very romantic, wouldn't you say, Blair?' said Susie.

'It's popular with newlyweds and for private liaisons as well as people just wanting totally secluded relaxation. There are a lot of thoughtful touches Susie came up with. Sooty is in the running for a major tourism award this year,' Blair added proudly.

Jennifer stared at him in some amusement. 'You don't have to impress me or sell it to me. I'm impressed already. All very nice.'

She did like the high tent with polished wooden floors, mosquito net looped over the carved wooden bed and the small wooden deck with comfortable lounges facing the sea. The cleverly screened bathroom had thatched walls and roof, a bush rock floor and a porcelain basin shaped like a giant clamshell. The lights shone from replica triton shells and moisture-loving tropical plants in beautiful stone pots created lush screens.

'This is tent three, the Japanese-style one,' said Blair.

'Each tent has a subtle decor theme – Balinese, Thai, North Queensland. The Japanese one is my favourite, very clean lines, all black and white with splashes of red,' said Susie in a professional voice. 'Each tent is placed for maximum privacy from the other tents, but with a view of the sea. And yet it's no more than a few minutes' walk skirting around the rear of each tent to the communal area. If a guest doesn't want to eat with everyone else in the main area we'll set up a tete-a-tete table and bring the food here,' added Susie.

'For those private liaisons, eh?' said Jennifer. 'So who's here at the moment?'

'We tend to operate on a first-name basis and

of course I can't divulge guests' names,' said Susie smoothly. 'It's up to individuals to share their personal information. I *can* say we have two couples, a woman off one of the yachts who wanted to sleep ashore a few nights. Plus a gentleman on his own. And yourselves of course.'

'And where do you and the staff here stay?' asked Jennifer.

'We have a sort of eco lodge we all share,' she answered. 'Mine is separate as I'm here most of the time, the others rotate from Branch. I either go back there for a break or over to the mainland every three weeks. Well, hopefully I'll see you on board for lunch. They have a great chef with them this trip.'

'We'll probably only hang out for one night,' said Blair. 'Now, what about this lunch, who's going to be there?'

'On that boat? Oh Blair, you're not going to do that are you?' asked Jennifer, distressed.

'Jennifer, of course you're invited,' said Susie. 'It's quite a fun group on board. While Blair is busy with the guys, you'll enjoy the female company.'

'Of course,' snapped Jennifer, more unkindly than she meant. She wished the 'hostess with the mostess' would leave her and Blair alone. 'Blair, can we at least go for a bit of a walk, that swim you suggested and then decide about this lunch? Please?'

'Sure. Catch you later, Susie. Come on, Jennifer, let's change. Our stuff is probably here by now.'

They came to a compromise. They'd spend a few hours together, share a picnic and then Blair would join the owners on the cruiser for drinks.

'It's business, a bit of shmoozing. These guys like me, it's important to keep in with them. They're having a big rethink about the resort and the whole corporation so I want to be in on that.'

'What about Rosie? Shouldn't she be in on it too?'

'C'mon, Jennifer. She's yesterday's news. I'm tomorrow's edition. Just leave it to me. I know what I'm doing.'

For you maybe. What about me? What about our family? 'I hope you do, Blair. I worry you're trying to get ahead too quickly.' Jennifer knew it would be pointless defending Rosie. She was standing in the way of Blair's promotion.

They settled in the shade of a large pandanus leaning over the sand and ready to drop its red seeds to be taken by the tide to grow on some far shore. This end of the beach curved around a coral ledge to a miniature cove.

'Cute place but too hard to get to. You have to pick your way over the coral,' said Blair.

'But you have been there, seen it?'

'Yeah. I checked out the whole place first time here. You can walk around the whole island in fifteen minutes, except for that little corner. Unless you want to cut through all the undergrowth from the centre. Let's not bother. I'm going in for a dip. Coming?'

'I'll set out our lunch.' The spectre of the shark was too fresh in her mind.

Jennifer set out food from a hamper on the cloth and plates provided. In the chiller bag there was a cold bottle of champagne, some wine and fruit juice. She pulled out the champagne and glasses and stretched out in the sun. She closed her eyes.

Had it only been a few minutes when she opened them again? She'd lost track of time and felt as though she was in a different time zone. Through her dark glasses the sun blinded her, flaring into her eyes directly above her as she lay there. Jennifer rolled over and looked towards the sea. In the bright light of sea, sky and sand, her polaroid sunglasses gave everything a strange pink glow. A dark figure loomed over her, blocking her vision.

She rolled sideways with a scream, with thoughts of the perv, of Willsy, of Rhonda's bashed face.

'What the hell?'

She ripped off her glasses to see Blair bending down to pick up his towel.

'What's up with you?'

'I guess I fell asleep. You startled me.'

'What's got into you, Jennifer? You're very nervy these days.' He sat down beside her and pulled on his sunglasses and favourite baseball cap.

Jennifer handed him the champagne. 'Here, pour us a drink to celebrate.'

'What are we celebrating?'

Jennifer laughed. 'What's got into me! I'm pregnant.'

Blair's hand jerked and the glass overflowed as he stared at her in shock. 'You're not?'

'I am. Oh Blair, I know we didn't plan it this way, but I feel wonderful. Aren't you happy for us?'

'Are you sure?'

She couldn't see his eyes behind his dark glasses.

'Very. I saw a doctor in Headland Bay when I went over.' She took the glass from his hand and took a sip.

Blair looked out to sea. 'I don't know what to think,' he said quietly.

'You'll get used to the idea. I've been trying to find the right moment to tell you, so I've had time to think things through. It will be just fine. I can have the baby in Headland Bay, see the doctor regularly.'

'And then what? Have you told anyone?'

Jennifer hesitated. 'No.'

He turned back to her. 'Are you sure about this? I mean, Jennifer, we discussed this. I thought I was being so careful. We can't drag a kid along to some of the places I was hoping to be appointed to.'

'Then we'll go where we *can* take a baby. I mean, how do other couples who work in hospitality manage a family?' She was feeling hurt and annoyed; she knew he'd baulk initially but this wasn't how she'd played the scene through in her mind.

'They wait, the wife goes home, or they end up in a third-rate job,' he said. 'Oh Christ, what a mess.'

Jennifer slowly turned the stem of her glass. 'And these are not options for us. So are you suggesting I . . . have an abortion?' She struggled to keep her voice neutral.

He went to speak, changed his mind, and took a swig of champagne. 'That's your decision,' he said finally.

'Yes, Blair. It is. And if I decide I want this baby – our baby – what then?'

'That's the bloody trouble, what then? Sure, you can waddle round the island for nine months and stay on with the kid for six months, I suppose. But then . . . it's going to hamper my career prospects no end.' His voice was bitter.

'Blair, can't you think about us for once? I didn't plan this, it was an accident. Why can't we just wait and see?' Suddenly Blair's unspoken message seemed very clear to Jennifer. 'You're asking me to choose between you and this baby.'

'That's stupid.'

'You know what, Blair? I'm choosing the baby. And if we can tag along on your rocket ride to wherever, then fine. If not, I promise not to stand in your way.' Tears burned in her eyes and she shoved her glass down, the bubbles soaking into the sand as she jumped up.

'Jennifer, sit down, don't be so melodramatic.

Let me think this through, get used to the god-damned idea for a minute!'

'That's a fantastic reaction, isn't it?' she shouted. 'Why can't you at least be pleased? Anyway, you're going to have the next twenty-one years plus to get used to the idea!' She stormed down the beach.

Blair drained his champagne, reached for the bottle and topped up his glass. He knew he should go after her but they'd only argue more. 'Oh fuck it,' he cursed aloud. He tipped the champagne on the sand, threw down the glass and went back to the tent to change. There'd be drinks on the boat.

Jennifer walked along the beach and stopped at the coral ledge, then decided to go around to get away from Blair, that awful Susie and whoever else was in tent paradise. She was furious, hurt and sad. She had thought Blair was going to be shocked and annoyed, but he could have at least touched her, shown some sliver of pleasure, pride, something. Jennifer was still awed at the immensity of knowing a small being was being created within her. It must be hard for Blair who hadn't had a chance to absorb the concept. All he thought about was his job. Maybe that made him a good provider. No, she answered herself. He was looking after himself first. Well, he'd come round to the idea. It wasn't as if they were living together with no formal commitment between them. And surely once he *saw* his child he couldn't help but love it. Him? Her?

Comforted with this thought, Jennifer tried to

shake off her disquiet. Give him time, give him time. She began to clamber across the exposed white rubble of dead coral. Halfway around, where water dribbled through tiny channels and pools, she hit living coral. And, while it was beautiful, it was also sharp. Carefully she judged each step, looking for a smooth surface, stepping into the sandy bottom of the shallow rock pools. Thoughts of deadly stone fish came to her. Did they live on islands? What did the spiny creature that resembled a crusty stone covered in weed really look like? All she'd heard was they were hard to spot and their poisonous spines killed you in seconds. She decided to clamber up to the scrubby tangle of bushes, vines and clumps of pandanus that ran all the way to the sea ledge.

It took some time and she was scratched and hot but finally she found a cleared track between small she-oaks. It must be the path that came through from the centre of the cay. The tiny cay was certainly unspoiled. She glimpsed the slash of blue water and as she was so hot and sore she decided to splash in the shallows, just knee deep, and cool off before taking the track back to their tent.

She came out of the bush onto a minuscule strip of sand with large rocks at one end. It was pretty. And private. All she was wearing was her swimsuit and a hat. Still, she wanted to strip naked and float in that clear water, but she was too afraid. The sand was scalding hot on her bare feet, so she did a little jig and raced to the water's edge.

A man's cheerful laugh rang out. Shocked,

Jennifer spun around. A man was sitting near one of the rocks, his feet in the water. He gave a wave.

Jennifer ducked down, squatting in the shallows. Who was he? What was he doing here? Wildly she started to plan her escape if he turned out to be dangerous. Run? Swim around the point? He'd outrun, outswim her. Shout for help? Who'd hear?

She watched him for a moment, but he paid her no attention. Then she saw he was reading a book. He was probably one of the other guests Susie had mentioned. God, I'm becoming paranoid about men, she told herself. Thanks to Willsy and the lurking Patch. Or maybe it was the sense of being trapped, of having no escape because she was living on an island. The reef around Sooty and Branch was worse than a jail fence. Impenetrable, lethal, guarded by monsters.

Jennifer closed her eyes, feeling relief from the cool water on her sunburnt back and shoulders, the salt stinging her grazes and cuts. She edged back and sat in the shallows, the water covering her hips and legs, and closed her eyes again. Slowly the tension, anger and physical pain leached out of her and floated away on the rippling wavelets. She lay back, putting her head on the wet sand, and mentally drifted.

'Are you okay? Tide is starting to come in.' His voice was gentle, not wishing to intrude.

Jennifer sat up with a jolt. Surely she hadn't

been asleep. 'Oh, I'm fine. Thanks. Just cooling off.' She scrambled to her feet.

'You didn't come prepared for exploring.' He grinned, looking at her reddened skin and fresh scratches, bare feet. He held out a bottle of water. 'A spare one. Please have it.'

'Are you sure?' Jennifer realised she was parched.

'The cook overloaded my picnic hamper. I have more than enough. Are you staying here or on a boat?'

'Just here for a day and a night, I think. We live on Branch Island.' Gratefully she drank the slightly warm but refreshing water.

'You live there? That must be, well, different.' He caught her expression and they both laughed.

Jennifer tightened the top on the bottle, she'd need the rest for her trek back. Her apprehension had gone. He seemed a nice guy. She studied him properly. Tall, kind of rangy, a bit thin, but very tanned. His eyes were green, he had a warm smile and his tan made his teeth look white. From what she could see under his frayed straw hat his hair was light brown. He looked to be in his mid to late thirties. She then noticed the scar down one arm, a pink slash along the length of his biceps. 'And you? On holiday here?'

'Sort of . . . R and R. It's certainly relaxing. Are you heading back?' He indicated the coral ledge. 'Risky with the tide, it comes in fast. Besides, you can't hurry without shoes. Seems your visit was impromptu.'

'It was,' admitted Jennifer. 'Did you walk here?'

'I have done it a few times. But with the picnic hamper Susie threw in a free ride. She's sending one of the guys in the dinghy to pick me up shortly. Want a lift?'

'Yes please, thanks a lot.' *Here I go again, riding home in a boat with a stranger.* 'I'm Jennifer.'

'Tony Adams. I'll just pack up my gear.' They strolled to where he had been picnicking in the partial shadow of the rocks.

Jennifer sat down, put her sore feet in a rock pool and watched him repack the picnic basket. 'How long are you staying here, Tony? Are you travelling around this area?'

'I'm trying not to travel, done my share of that. This seemed a nice out-of-the-way place to . . . just hang. Places like Branch and the other island resorts don't appeal to me.'

'Too yuppie?'

He grinned. 'That's part of it. I just don't want to have to make the effort to be sociable. Here you can choose to be by yourself and no one cares. They advertise privacy.' He paused. 'Sorry if I sound a bit reclusive or stuffy. I just wanted, needed, some downtime.' He closed the basket and folded his towel and jammed it on top.

Jennifer was curious but didn't want to pry. As they both sat there staring at the ocean she said, 'I'm sorry if I intruded on your peace.'

'Not at all. I was engrossed in my book and thought I was hallucinating when I saw this, well,

215

fairy lady in red bathers dancing across the beach.'

They both laughed. 'I think I've burnt as well as cut my feet,' said Jennifer ruefully.

'Get the first-aid kit from Susie and treat those. Coral cuts can get infected easily. And what brought you to live on an island in the beautiful Barrier Reef? Do you work on Branch?'

'No. My husband does. I'm still adjusting, haven't been here too long. He's assistant manager.'

'And you? How do you fill in your days? I imagine you can only swim, snorkel, scuba for so long. Do you get bored, or not?'

Jennifer had an urge to pour out her feelings to this softly spoken, calm man. There was a stillness to him that she couldn't quite figure out. Like he was waiting for something. Perhaps it was more an alertness that was below the seemingly casual and relaxed surface. 'I don't think it's boredom. Despite the fact I don't enjoy any water things. I'm not fond of the sea. It's more a sense of feeling trapped. Of being uprooted. I was thinking of continuing my studies when Blair got this job.'

'Whose career comes first, eh? What were you studying?'

'I switched to environmental science. Not for any specific reason, it just interests me. I was working at the university. Now I feel a bit adrift. What about you? Are you working?' He had an air about him that was not of a man taking time off work or someone with a set routine taking an interlude. Restlessness, was that what it was about him?

He didn't answer for a moment. A flock of sooty terns swept past, landing in the tussocks of grey-green grass behind them. 'No. I'm between jobs, as actors say. Resting.' Then, as if he didn't want to appear rude by being vague, he added in a rush, 'My last assignment was pretty stressful. Lasted longer than I expected and I got to a point where I couldn't cop it any more.'

Stress leave. He doesn't seem the type. He looks . . . capable. Strong somehow. 'That's getting pretty common these days. Well, more recognised, I guess. My Uncle Don told me war vets came home a psychological and emotional mess and were expected to get on with things as if nothing had happened. I guess people at home couldn't imagine what they'd been through. Now stress seems to be pressure to achieve, keep up with society, get ahead . . .' She sighed, thinking of Blair. 'For what, I sometimes think. Other things in life are more important.' She thought of her mother and she thought of her baby and was suddenly fearful. Would she be a good mother? Would Blair be a good father?

Tony nodded. 'Family. A future. Security. The things my grandparents talked about. Do you have kids?'

'Blair wouldn't have taken the job here if we had. He's aiming for a big hotel in Europe.'

'So life goes on hold for a bit.' He gave her a sympathetic look. 'There's always a trade-off in relationships. Or a compromise. Or one person walks away.' He looked back to sea again. 'And are you enjoying island life?' he asked. It was a polite enquiry but Jennifer sensed something in his voice. Had she given away her feelings about being here? Impulsively she shook her head.

'Not really. I hate the ocean. I have a recurring nightmare about being in the sea.'

To Jennifer it was as if they were alone on a desert island. As if they were seated side by side on a long flight sharing secrets and life stories in the anonymous dark.

Suddenly he blurted, 'Funny you saying that, about the war. Nothing's changed much. I've been in war zones for the last few years. Places like Afghanistan did me in.'

'You were in the military?'

'Correspondent. Newspapers mainly.'

'Oh. That must have been tough.' She thought of the tired faces she'd seen on TV, the deaths of news men and women. It had all seemed so far away and unnecessary. 'This must seem a world away. Well, it is, isn't it?' she finished lamely. There was a set to Tony's mouth and a pain in his eyes. She wished they hadn't ventured into such personal territory. It was too painful.

Quietly, conversationally, looking at the horizon and seeing something else, he said, 'Even here. I hear bombs, sniper fire, screams. On this pristine beach I see bodies, children . . .' He rubbed his eyes. 'Sorry . . . you see why I avoid people. I'm not very good company.'

'How long has it been? Since you got out?' asked Jennifer, not daring to ask about his own family. Did he leave a wife, avoid having children because of what he did for a living? Or had he returned to them a damaged man?

'Eighteen months.' He gave a bit of a smile and stood up as a dinghy appeared around the rocky point. 'They say it gets better with time. Once I start work again I'll have something else to think about, I guess.' He picked up his hamper, towel and book and moved along the beach to where the dinghy was coming in.

'You're going back overseas?' Jennifer walked beside him.

'No. I quit. Might freelance. Maybe do a photographic book. Landscape images, not war.' It was the first trace of bitterness she'd heard.

'There's an old beachcomber, kind of an inventor, on Branch. He encouraged me to take the plunge and do something I'd never done. And was scared to do,' said Jennifer.

'And how did you feel?'

She grinned at him. 'Pretty good. And it gave me entry into his very exclusive Shark Club.'

Tony helped her into the little row boat, settling her in the stern seat. 'I'm not a club man myself. But what's the Shark Club?'

'A shack the tourists don't know about. Dirt floor, cold beer, lanterns, and a lot of interesting locals. Scientists and sailors.'

Tony put the hamper between Jennifer's feet as the boy who doubled as bartender pushed off. 'I reckon there's a story or two there.'

'Remember, to be a member you have to do

something you've never done before. But in your case that might be a bit tricky,' she said lightly.

He smiled, looking calm and relaxed once more. 'Ah, you might be surprised. There are quite a few things I've never been brave enough to do. I'll keep the Shark Club in mind.'

They didn't speak again until they reached the lagoon. Loud laughter ricocheted from *Kicking Back* to shore.

Blair, after returning ashore with Susie and several others, had a nap and joined Jennifer and the other guests for pre-dinner drinks. Dinner in the dining hut was convivial. Jennifer was reserved, letting Blair be the one to joke and chat, matching Susie in entertaining the resident guests and several people from the boats. She could see what Blair had meant about the importance of the social bonding at resorts. People became best friends for a short time and parted with promises to return or keep in touch that they inevitably failed to fulfil.

The corporate heavies stayed on board *Kicking Back* though there was mention they might come ashore later. Jennifer noticed Tony was not present. As soon as she could she made excuses and returned to their tent. She lay between the black silk sheets, watching the water darken, and finally the terns and small creatures fell silent. She thanked her stars no mutton birds nested here. Their mating fights and wails still haunted and awakened her on Branch. By the time Blair staggered into bed she was asleep and so discussion of their situation was once again put on hold.

In the early morning Jennifer eased from bed and walked down to the beach. It was a still and perfect sunrise. There was something so hopeful about a new day when it seemed everything would be all right, problems would be overcome. Would it be a new beginning for her and Blair? She'd wait till later to talk to him. Blair was not an early riser and would be suffering the effects of yesterday for several more hours.

Glancing further down the beach she saw Tony standing at the water's edge, a solitary, stationary figure. Jennifer wondered what he was seeing. This peaceful dawn or haunted memories? Soon he dived into the glowing rosy sea and swam in easy steady strokes towards the horizon.

Jennifer turned and retraced her steps.

At breakfast Blair was sweetly attentive, and Jennifer detected a hint of remorse. Whether for his excesses of the night before, or their tense discussion about the baby, she wasn't sure. However, he did declare that yesterday had been very useful. He didn't elaborate. Nor did he make any mention of their child, their future or indeed tomorrow.

Who was it, Jennifer wondered, who'd said 'Tomorrow is another day'? Well, she had come to her decision and from now on her priority would be her child, it was a pact between herself and her developing infant. Just the two of them. Adjusting to each other. And, after she'd seen the doctor once more, she would break the news to Christina that she was going to be a grandmother. Walking along the beach after breakfast while Blair talked to Susie and her staff, Jennifer held her hands across her belly. 'It's you and me, kid!'

The promise of the dawn held firm. It was a good day.

9

Treading Water

THE TIDE WAS OUT, the exposed reef with its pools
and channels glistened under a sheen of water. The
sea was two hundred metres away, a turquoise
ring stretching to the white crest marking the
outer reef. There were a few people making a
pre-breakfast pilgrimage across the reef, stepping
between the coral outcrops in rubber-soled shoes
or aged laceless sneakers that hung on the side of
the dive shop for guests. Leaning on their long
wooden walking poles they bent and peered
through plastic viewing cones balanced on the surface of the water. Like seafaring shepherds they
followed the sea paths mapped by tide and wind,

observing, rarely disturbing. Occasionally someone could not resist straightening briefly to hold
aloft a bright blue starfish to admire or to photograph. Later in the morning groups would cluster
around a reef guide to learn the intricacies of a
miniature world and its inhabitants, the history of
the formation of the reef on which they stood.

Jennifer continued on her early-morning
walk, a ritual she loved while the day was new.
Blair was not a morning person and Jennifer
rarely lasted the distance in the evenings after
dinner when Blair came to life. He was a charming host with guests, conferred with the chef,
checked staff rosters, and met with Doyley about
any personnel problems. One morning a week
Blair sat down with Rosie to go over what he
called 'the big picture'.

While Blair slept Jennifer walked along the
pristine beach. It was time alone with her
thoughts, which she let drift in and out of her
mind rather than focusing on anything specific. If
it was an uncomfortable or painful thought she let
it go, choosing not to dwell on it. She felt in a suspended state as the days slid by, unsure what she
was waiting for. She put it down to being pregnant, concentrating her energies on this gestation
time. And if the thought came to her – *you can't
spend nine months like this* – she let that go too.

The resort was behind her, out of sight. The
softness of the early light hardened as the sun
became full strength. Her footprints were the
first to mark the sand. But ahead in the dazzling

bright light of sun and sea she saw figures at the edge of the reef. One of the group was pulling a small rubber duckie and, shading her eyes, it looked to be full of plastic buckets. The group were in knee-deep water, some in pairs, some bent over a net. One of the figures began splashing in to shore.

Jennifer sat on the sand to watch this activity. And then she recognised Professor Masters.

She waved. 'Hi, Mac!'

He gave a salute and sauntered over and sat beside her. He was wearing his battered leather hat, shorts and a Greenpeace T-shirt, and carried a small underwater camera and a pair of swimming goggles. 'Isn't this the best part of the day?'

'It is. Though I'm a bit partial to the sunsets too. What are you doing out there?'

'Collecting specimens. Taking pictures of them in situ before putting them in the sample buckets. They'll go into our tanks for observation and monitoring. Eventually they're returned to where they came from.'

'They're students out there?'

'Yes, most are looking at reef ecology. Kirsty is doing a study on coral reproduction, Gary is looking at the impact of pollution on the reef system and Rudi is looking at symbiosis or how certain fish and other organisms live together for mutual benefit out there.'

'Like the little clown fish that lives in an anemone?'

'That anemone has stinging cells that are

225

deadly to other fish and predators, yet the fish is immune. A perfect relationship.'

'You wonder how they found each other.'

'You mean, is it a partnership designed by nature, perfected over aeons of evolution? Or have countless fish died until they developed a strategy and system to protect themselves? It's a fish-eat-fish world down there.'

'Are these the sorts of questions that occupy your days?' asked Jennifer.

'Amongst others,' he answered easily. 'Like, what is it that protects corals and other sea creatures from getting sunburnt at very low tides. The tidal range is nearly two metres here and this sunburn protection could be useful in preventing and curing skin cancers in humans. The natural world is like a great textbook, we just have to crack the code to find answers to help us in the human world.'

'So what is the future for the reef?'

'Essentially our work is to find answers and raise awareness of what's happening to the reef. In 1998, thirty per cent of the world's reefs were wiped out due to a rise in sea temperature. And we're going to see more severe and more frequent events like this. Which will be catastrophic. At this rate it'll be gone in thirty to fifty years.'

'God, it's fascinating work,' said Jennifer sincerely, then added, 'But I can hear my mother commenting that paddling around on a tropical resort island is pretty nice kind of work. She never understood me wanting to be at university. She's got no time for academics or research. Work is not pleasure in her book,' sighed Jennifer.

'She's been reading the wrong books. So, how are you doing? You haven't come to see us again. In fact, why not come now? We're all heading back for breakfast,' he said, jumping up and pulling Jennifer to her feet.

She was touched at their interest in her. 'I'm starving.' She was about to comment she was only wearing a sarong around her swimsuit but knew no one would think that unusual. The rest of the group were wading in and all were in shorts or swimwear.

'I'll go help with the boat. Perhaps you could carry one of the buckets,' said Mac.

As they trailed inland after tying the little rubber boat to a tree at what Mac called the beach camp, Jennifer asked, 'So what am I carrying in here?' As far as she could tell all that was in her green bucket was a bunch of seaweed.

'Small creatures with big appetites, and that common-looking weed has strange properties. It's only found in coral outcrops and Rudi is doing experiments with it.'

It was the first time Jennifer had gone into the confines of the research station and she was surprised to find a completely different setting and community from the resort. It was sheltered at the centre of the island and initially it reminded her of university. The communal dwellings were different from the resort's staff quarters, which were built by cookie-cutter design, an inexpensive version of the more lavish resort suites. Here, buildings seemed to have grown as needs dictated. Awnings, partitions and impromptu work areas were tacked on to and between huts and simple houses. There were a couple of double-storey dwellings, all strewn with scuba gear, wetsuits, flippers, goggles, towels and clothes.

Past the accommodation were two long buildings separated by a series of large cement tanks, plus a series of stands with Perspex aquaria set up. Hoses, motors, pumps and a clutter of implements and tools were scattered around. Further on, a wooden shack with flyscreen doors and windows had a sheltered outdoor eating area with long benches at two big tables. Unlike the staff quarters at the resort, this had an air of also being a workplace. Jennifer longed to see the set-up in the two buildings that were the labs.

'Do you have an office somewhere?' she asked Mac.

'A corner in one of the labs and the dining table in my house. And I share that with Rudi.'

'The table or the house?'

He laughed. 'Both. But we have a system. It gets a bit chaotic if we have visitors as there's a spare room with four bunks. So it's a bit cosy in our small kitchen with one fridge. The students eat in the rec room. There are only three cottages with a kitchen.'

'Who comes to visit? Family? Friends? Work people?' asked Jennifer, suddenly curious about Mac's personal life.

'We try to keep the island a work-only centre. We have an email set-up so we can stay in regular contact. Visitors tend to be other professors, international researchers, and postgraduate candidates. Come on in and see for yourself.'

So I'm none the wiser about your family. 'Can I help with breakfast?'

'Absolutely. I'm a basic cook at best. Though this mob will be hungry enough to eat whatever's going.'

The wooden and prefab structure was screened by frayed lattice and shade cloth making a semi-private courtyard in front. A clothes line strung along one side under the roof overhang looked to be a sort of wardrobe with wetsuits and shirts on hangers. Dive boots, thongs and gym shoes were scattered beneath.

'I've never seen so many wetsuits,' commented Jennifer. 'In all colours too. Do you wear certain colours on a different day of the week?'

'Our American friends bequeathed the fancy jobs to us. I try to avoid black, I feel too much like an edible seal. Though Carmel is doing some interesting research on that.'

Jennifer followed him inside to a sitting room with several sofas, lots of cushions, a stereo in one corner and a large table covered with a laptop, piles of papers and books.

The house was suddenly filled with laughing energy as several of the group arrived and everyone seemed to be talking at once. Jennifer noticed how each one wanted to share news or take Mac aside to talk with him one-on-one. He pulled off his hat, sat on a sofa patiently listening to details of this morning's finds, and made suggestions about specimens, writing up material and next steps.

'Hi, Jennifer, have you been delegated chief cook?' said Carmel. 'Can I help?'

'Yes. I haven't a clue where anything is, what's here?' said Jennifer.

Carmel gave a Latin shrug. 'What is in the refrigerator, or this cupboard? Hah, eggs, chilli sauce, bread, baked beans, last night's chicken. Some fruit. Honey. Is plenty, yes?'

'If you're hungry,' laughed Jennifer. 'And I am.'

'Go for it, then,' said Rudi, coming in with a pile of papers. 'I have to check my tanks. I'll wash up,' he offered.

Suddenly an efficient chaos took over as plates appeared, and helpers made toast, tea and coffee, and sliced papaya into bowls and squeezed lime juice on top. Everyone was talking about their projects, plans and workload. Jennifer felt totally comfortable and at home. Rudi found some frangipani flowers and scattered them along the table set up in the outer courtyard area.

'Very nice touch, Rudi,' said Mac as he sat down. He'd showered and changed clothes, and his wet hair was slicked back, his pony tail in a neat ball at the base of his neck. He sat at the top of the table and the others ranged themselves around him. As the plates of food were put on the table, he gestured for Jennifer to sit next to him. Despite his friendly and casual manner he had a quiet air of authority.

Jennifer kept quiet listening to the exchanges about individual projects and interests. She could see that Mac deftly kept the discussion informal and yet each person was aware of the nuances of each other's work status from difficulties or small failures to a lucky moment or a pleasing result. She wished Blair could be so subtle and sensitive in keeping a team blended and supportive of each other. But then Mac had been doing this for a long time. Carmel had told her that he played the guitar and sang, drank and partied with them, was laid back and pulled no rank. But there was huge respect for him and Jennifer sensed anyone could go to him with a personal as well as professional problem.

She kept her head down, finishing off the spicy eggs and beans, and when she looked for more toast she found Mac looking at her with a slight smile.

He passed the toast and pushed the Vegemite in front of her. 'Try something a bit more traditional. Carmel's meals are known as luscious Latin lovelies. Last year we had a Swede and he pickled everything.'

'Thanks. I'm enjoying this.'

'The food or the company?' he asked gently.

Jennifer put down her knife. 'The company, I have to say. Thanks for inviting me. And if I can see around a bit more, the labs, see what people are doing, it will be the best time I've had since arriving here.'

'Mmm. You'd better become a regular visitor then. Are you settled over there?' He inclined his head in the direction of the resort.

'I haven't felt settled in years,' said Jennifer suddenly. 'I mean in the sense of my own space.'

Although no one else at the table was following their conversation, Jennifer stopped, embarrassed. It hit her that the last time she felt comfortable and in her space, which meant an area that was hers and hers alone, was in her old room back at the farm. How different things were then. Her brother in his little room next door, her parents down the hall. The dogs, the farm noises, the bush sounds. It was a place she knew intimately and where she felt secure.

Out beyond the farm gates was the world, but she was protected by a father tinkering and fixing things and leaning on a fence having a smoke and watching . . . what? And a mother who was different then too. She fussed, she bossed, she muttered, and everyone did her bidding because it was easier that way. And what did it matter because they all had their own secret worlds and fantasies. Then Christina laughed, really laughed, with pleasure and enjoyment. And if she was cross, it was tempered with, 'Well now, this is for your own good, you'll thank me one day.' So you didn't feel you'd been so terribly bad or were hopelessly incompetent. Which was how Christina made her feel now.

'And what would you like as your own space now?' probed Mac. His eyes didn't flicker as he studied her.

'Oh, my needs are simple,' she answered lightly. 'A desk, a quiet corner to set up my laptop and stuff and leave it there. Rosie thought she might find a corner in an office for me. I really do have to start working again. I've dropped out, it's terrible. I've never missed a deadline before. Professor Dawn must be mad as hell.'

'You'd be better working around here. I'll see if we can find you a quiet corner.'

'I don't want to put anyone out. I mean, space seems at a premium. You're working on the dining-room table, for goodness' sake!' Jennifer wished she hadn't said anything.

'Ah, I like the company,' grinned Mac. 'Actually, I like to be accessible. And a lot of useful stuff comes out of what we call the kitchen conferences. The rest of the year I'm in my study, my office at the university, lecturing. Removed from the nitty-gritty hands-on and . . . intimacy, if I may use the word without being misinterpreted.' He got up. 'Bring your toast, I'll give you a tour.' To the others at the table he waved a hand. 'Giving Jennifer a bit of background. Rudi, I'll see you in the lab later and we'll transfer those coral colonies.'

While the two labs were rudimentary, they had all that was needed for the work being done here. The long Besser block rooms were air conditioned, had good lighting, and tables and benches. The floor was filled with temporary large tanks while along one wall was a glass aquarium reproducing a section of the reef. It was temperature controlled and well lit. Jennifer could have spent an hour watching the activity of the little fish, seagrasses and strange squashy sponges that looked like brilliantly coloured slugs. Small jellyfish, iridescent and transparent, moved with pulsating movements like a heartbeat.

Mac showed her how new data were added to the comprehensive monitoring information that would be analysed, with comparative studies and tests done later.

'Jennifer, I know there are people out there like your mother who think all this is a bit of a wank and why aren't we trying to feed the poor, cure cancer or stop wars.' Mac perched on a stool at a work bench. 'We are created in water. A lot of scientists believe the sea is the birthplace of life, that answers to questions about the creation of the planet lie at the bottom of the ocean. And, say, four billion years ago energy from the centre of the earth began to create life.'

'How? In what form?' asked Jennifer.

'Water is an extraordinary substance. Molecules of water helped to link more and more complex proteins together to form DNA, the complex chemical and cellular formation that is the basis for life. So when life forms emerged from water to land they carried water in their cells, as we do.'

'But how does investigating a theory of evolution and creation apply to what you're doing today?' Jennifer was intrigued.

'Sorry to bore you with a lecture . . .'

'Oh, it's not boring at all,' exclaimed Jennifer.

'To get the word out about the state of the reef we need the media, and there's a wall of silence. It was a hot topic in the eighties and a bit in the nineties with the crown of thorns seastars, but now they don't want to know what's really going on. Been there, done that,' sighed Mac. 'The other thing is, we don't know what's down there, on the floor of the ocean. We have more idea what's on the moon than what's on the floor of the oceans of the world. And frankly, we can't keep treating it as a dump and pouring crap into the ocean. There are things down there that are not only worth knowing about and protecting, but that might hold answers to our own future.' He stood up. 'End of lecture . . . for the moment.'

'Mac, I'm really interested. I can't explain but I feel like the world just turned upside down. Like the sea is on top and we are down in some abyss . . .' An image from the dream flashed into her head and she closed her eyes.

'What is it? You okay, Jennifer?' he asked softly.

She opened her eyes that were filled with tears. 'I nearly drowned once, and I remember being underwater, like I *belonged* there. I could *live* there . . . That's why I'm so frightened of being in water, in the sea. I have this uncontrollable desire to stay down there. It's some kind of death wish I suppose, as my brother drowned. And my father, well, took his own life in the sea. Just disappeared. They never found his body. Maybe I'm drawn into the sea looking for him.'

Impulsively Mac wrapped his arms around Jennifer. 'I understand now. But I think your interpretation of your dream isn't right. It isn't a death wish, or that you feel guilty you survived and they didn't.' He was quiet for a moment as Jennifer caught her breath, and he loosened his arms to allow her to wipe her eyes on the edge of her sarong.

'So what do you think is wrong with me?'

'Jennifer, I'm no psychologist but you're a lonely girl who has always tried to please everyone and taken on the burden of being the one left with your mother. I bet every time she looks at you she's reminded of what she's lost. That's a heavy trip to lay on you.'

'I've never thought of it like that,' said Jennifer quietly.

Mac smiled and touched her cheek, 'Sweetie, you're a girl who misses her dad. Her brother. And everything that was safe and secure. We all have holes and pain in our lives – to a lesser or greater degree. My wife and I lost our little girl when she was three. I miss her too.'

'Oh, I'm sorry.' She looked at Mac's kind face and saw the pain in his eyes.

'We have two great boys and we're happy. But there's always that shadow of the one who isn't there. Wondering what she'd look like now, what she'd be doing. She'd be eighteen next month . . .' he caught himself. 'Jennifer, there's someone arriving next week I insist you meet.

And also, go and spend some time with Gideon. Now he's the one who can tell you about the unseen sea.'

They left the lab and closed the door. 'What's the unseen sea?'

'The deep seas, way down in the darkness where no light has ever been. So far down you could put Mount Everest down there and sail right over it miles beneath you.'

In the bright sunlight of the sandy square Jennifer saw her new friends hanging over a large tank housing sea snakes. 'Mac, thank you.'

'Any time. Listen, I'll find you a spot to call your own. Check in tomorrow.'

'I will. Say goodbye to everyone.'

'No probs.' He headed back to his shack and Jennifer wound her way back to the resort through the dappled pisonia forest of fluttering, ever-busy, noddy terns.

Blair was dressed and walking out the door as she came along the sandy path. 'You're late, you coming to breakfast?'

'No thanks, I've had it. I'm going to shower and get my laptop out.' She was about to ask what he was doing today but knew he'd give the response he always gave: 'More of the same.' Which depressed her. But this morning she felt as if she'd awakened from a long snooze and now she was refreshed and energised.

'Okay then. See you at lunch maybe, eh?'

'Maybe.' Jennifer headed for the bathroom.

Blair stuck his head in the door. 'You all right?'

'Yes. Why do you ask?'

'Oh, nothing. You've been funny since we came back from Sooty...' His voice trailed off. He didn't know how to, or he didn't want to raise the subject of her pregnancy.

Jennifer whipped off her sarong with a flourish and spun around. 'I'm fine, Blair. In fact, never felt better.'

Blair closed the door, thinking so far, at least, the terrible things he'd heard about mood swings and morning sickness hadn't arrived.

Jennifer slipped out of her swimsuit and looked at her body in the mirror. Turning sideways only showed her lean flat belly. She rubbed her breasts. Now they definitely felt bigger and slightly painful. She arched her back, sticking out her stomach, and pretended to waddle. Giggling, she stepped into the shower.

After working for a while on her laptop in the rear courtyard she felt too hot and decided she'd print out the notes and draft chapter and work on it inside. She shut the doors, turned on the air conditioner and headed for reception with her disk to ask Rosie if she'd print it out for her as she had no printer with her. Rosie was outside wearing a hat and sunglasses. After Jennifer explained what she wanted, Rosie handed the disk over to Heather at the desk.

'Could you please print this out for Jennifer when you have a minute?' She turned to Jennifer. 'Do you mind waiting a little while? We're just checking out the last lot and getting ready to welcome the next group. In fact, I'm walking down to the wharf to do the meet, greet and goodbyes. Come along.'

They walked to the waiting area at the end of the wharf. Departing guests, surrounded by their hand luggage and souvenirs, waited and exchanged addresses, looked at photos and swapped stories. Rosie chatted, shook hands, hoped they'd return. Jennifer strolled along the wharf behind the laden carts carrying all the luggage to be loaded on the big cat when it arrived.

There were several boats getting ready to head out with guests going diving, snorkelling and fishing. Three or four were always berthed on one side of the wharf out of the way of the cat, which docked on the other side where a gangplank made it easy for people to embark and disembark. The boats continued the colour theme of the resort, clean white hulls and decks, turquoise upholstery. The crews were always neatly attired, as spick and span as their boats. Jennifer admired how competent some of the young women were. One day they'd be driving the submarine giving a commentary, that night they'd be behind the bar on the terrace, and the next day she'd see them behind the wheel of a boat. Blair told her three of them had their captain's ticket.

'Hello again!'

Jennifer looked at the boat tied at the steps and saw Tony Adams with Lloyd. They'd been fishing and Lloyd was putting several fish in a plastic crate with ice while Tony hosed the deck. 'Looks like you've done well. So you decided to come and play and socialise after all,' she said. She went down the steps for a closer look.

'Come on board,' called Lloyd. 'We were about to have a cold drink.'

Tony held out his hand and helped her onto the transom and into the boat. 'I'd be happy to share my fish with you. I'll be leaving this afternoon.'

'I talked him into an outing,' said Lloyd, handing round cold soft drinks.

'It's been very interesting too,' added Tony.

'Great,' said Jennifer, pleased to see that the withdrawn man she'd met on Sooty seemed a lot more relaxed and outgoing.

'There's Methuselah,' said Lloyd, pointing to the great dark shape with the massive head and mouth that could swallow a child in one gulp.

'That's a hell of a big grouper,' said Tony.

'Yeah, we have a couple of them around,' said Jennifer, looking at Lloyd, who explained to Tony.

'There's this big grouper here at the wharf, and there's an old codger who's a part-time handyman who's a bit of a lech. Pervs on the girls. But he's harmless.'

'Some people look harmless but aren't,' said Jennifer tartly, thinking of Willsy.

Tony raised an eyebrow. 'You sound, shall I say, a bit touchy?'

Lloyd chuckled but Jennifer was not amused. Both men looked at her. Jennifer gave a dismissive wave. 'Oh, forget it.' She took a gulp of her lemon drink. 'So, Tony, do you do much fishing? Where are you based now?'

'I've had a flat in Sydney for years, but I'm moving north. Bought a beach house to contemplate the great novel. Might do a spot of beach fishing,' said Tony casually.

'I've been telling him about Gideon, the research centre and what they're doing,' said Lloyd.

'I went and had my first look around this morning. I think Mac is brilliant. I wish I'd had him as a professor,' Jennifer said.

'Why don't you do a course with them while you're here?' said Tony. 'Whether it's official or not, I mean, some of the stuff they're looking into is pretty amazing.'

'That's a great idea. Why don't you, Jennifer?' Lloyd said enthusiastically.

'Oh, I hadn't considered anything like that. I don't know if it's possible. But I'd like to spend more time with them all.'

'Ah, just talk to Mac. He'll fix it,' said Lloyd.

'Well, he did say he might be able to find me a corner to work in. That would give me an excuse to hang around at least.'

'You'll find it a lot more interesting than the resort, I imagine,' Tony said.

'I'm trying to persuade Tony to come back and write about it all,' said Lloyd. 'Wouldn't Blair think that good PR?'

'I wouldn't mention that to Blair, Lloyd. He'll be putting the pressure on Tony to write up the resort. I don't think that's your sort of story, is it?'

'Not really. Though the future of Branch Island, well, the whole reef, from what I'm hearing, could be a big story. We'll see.' He put his empty can in the garbage bin and shook Lloyd's hand. 'Been a great morning. Thanks.' Turning to Jennifer, he smiled and held out his hand. 'If I do come back I hope you'll be doing your research forty fathoms deep, or snorkelling anyway.'

Jennifer laughed. 'I doubt it. Good luck with whatever you decide to do.'

'That's the hard part. Deciding. Please, take some of the fish we caught. See you, Lloyd.' He stepped off the boat.

As the reef cat approached, Jennifer took the two coral trout Lloyd handed her and made her way back along the jetty. Tony was talking to Rosie but she headed for reception to see if she could collect her printed pages and get back to work.

Jennifer ploughed through the notes, drafting Professor Dawn's research on the East Australian Current into coherent prose, but her mind kept returning to the research station. How she'd love to work there. Would it be possible to do some sort of course? She must be able to get credits for it. And how much she wanted to be in Mac's orbit. The camaraderie of the research station group made Jennifer realise how lonely she'd been. Except for Rosie.

She stretched, put the papers to one side and decided to find Blair so they could have lunch together. She was starting to notice how her appetite had picked up. The reception staff told her Blair was down with the maintenance guys so Jennifer asked them to let him know she was in the dining room. On the way to the restaurant she saw Rosie so she went to thank her for getting her file printed.

For the first time Rosie looked slightly harassed. 'No sweat, Jenny. Any time. You getting through some work?'

'Sort of. I spent some time with Mac over at the research station. It's pretty interesting. He thought he might let me do some work there.'

Rosie's face lit up. 'Wow, that'd be perfect for you. I was going to clear out a storage room, well, no bigger than a cupboard for you.'

'Please don't go to any trouble.'

'You'll be better off with Mac's mob. Could lead to anything, you never know.' They fell into step. 'You going to lunch? I was about to grab a bite. Bad morning.'

'I was looking for Blair. Let's get a table. What's up?'

'Ah, I wish I knew. Something's going on with management. Maybe we shouldn't discuss this, but Tony Adams inadvertently dropped a small bomb on me. He's a correspondent turned bigtime journo . . .'

'I met him on Sooty. Is he writing something about this place?'

'God, I hope not.' Rosie sat down and immediately ripped a bread roll apart as it was put on the table.

'Wouldn't that be good?' Jennifer was thinking

how Blair was so publicity conscious.

'Nothing against Tony Adams. We like the glossy upmarket travel leisure stuff that we can control. Tony told me the corporate heads of Reef Resorts were jaunting around on the company boat at Sooty. I had no idea they were in the area. The head office is in Sydney. Why wouldn't they contact me or even stop in here, see how Branch is looking? I don't like secrecy. Especially as they're not my favourite kind of people. Money men who only look at the bottom line. So long as it's in profit they don't care what it costs in human, environmental or PR terms.'

Jennifer decided to keep quiet about Blair hanging out with these men. 'How do you see the business side of this company?' she asked.

'Reef Resorts are an arm of a big international chain of boutique and upmarket eco resorts. The reef group, obviously, specialise in locations near reefs and islands. Fanzio and Holding are the two head honchos in Australia. My, and Blair's, direct superiors.'

'Have you ever met the international heads?' asked Jennifer, wondering why Rosie hadn't been included in the gathering on board *Kicking Back*.

'Yes, I was based in London before Prague and then I wanted to come back to the southern hemisphere. The London office was understanding and switched me to Reef Resorts. Unfortunately I never warmed to Mr Fanzio or Mr Holding.'

'Maybe they're cruising around and will check in later. Maybe they want to surprise you,' said

Jennifer. 'A sort of spot check.'

Rosie didn't look convinced. 'Anyway, how are you doing? Feeling okay? You look great.'

'Eating like a horse. Blair still doesn't talk about the baby idea.'

'It's a reality not an idea. He'll get used to it. You don't look pregnant so it's probably hard for him to take it in.'

'He's normally such a planner. It's unusual for him to just bury his head in the sand and not start thinking ahead,' said Jennifer.

'And you?'

'I haven't been thinking clearly for a long time. But I am now. And, as long as you're willing to let me stay here after the baby is born, that's about as far ahead as I want to think.'

'When are you going to start telling people?'

'After the next doctor's appointment.' She smiled at Blair threading his way through the room.

Blair sat down. 'Am I interrupting a ladies' lunch?'

'Not at all. I'd better get back to the office. Everything hunky dory with the grease monkeys?' asked Rosie.

'Would be if they had all the spares they need. Couple of the washing machines are stuffed. Nothing too major.' Blair headed to the buffet as Rosie left.

'My God, Blair, that's a huge plate of food,' said Jennifer as he returned with a heaped plate.

'You're not being too shy in the food department lately.'

'I am eating for two, remember.'

He ate a few mouthfuls before saying, 'When are you going to tell people?'

She knew he meant the baby but wanted to hear him say it. 'About what?'

'You know. Being pregnant. I think you should tell your mother and Vi and Don. You probably should have it down there. I don't think the hospital over in Headland will be much chop. What if something goes wrong?' He kept eating as he spoke, not looking at Jennifer.

Jennifer didn't know whether to get upset or just laugh at him. She kept her voice reasonable. 'Nothing will go wrong, I'm as healthy as a horse. I don't want to go to Sydney, the hospital in Headland is big enough, it caters for a huge section of the coast and people from regional Queensland. I was planning to get back here a day or so after giving birth. We don't need much gear for the first few months, we're far enough away from guests and staff if it cries . . .'

'Oh God. Sleepless nights . . . What about the baby depression thing. What if you get that?'

'I'm not working, I can devote myself to the baby as a full-time mother. If there are problems, we'll deal with them.' *I'll deal with them.*

'That's good. Because you know what my workload is like. I might have to go to London in a couple of months. A quick trip for a meeting or two.'

'What is going on, Blair?' asked Jennifer in a

low, concerned voice. 'Why are those corporate guys snooping around and not even contacting their manager here or checking out their business operation here? How come you're so cosy with them and your boss doesn't know?'

He looked at her with some surprise and said firmly, 'Jennifer, it's none of your business. And don't say anything to Rosie. She'll be in the loop soon enough. Leave things to me.'

'What do you mean? Your job, your future, concerns me too. And our child. Stop treating me like some dumb juvenile wife,' she snapped.

'Listen, when we got married we agreed I was the breadwinner, I had the assets. So my career came first. We couldn't live on what you were earning. I'm looking to the future where we can have a very, very comfortable life way beyond what I had in Sydney.'

Jennifer sat very still. His words, 'what I had', hit her. 'So I haven't contributed to this marriage?'

'Come on, don't be silly. You did your bit, we were lucky I had a place to start off with. You bought your own car. Good on you.'

'Blair, we could have bought a place together. Started out as equals. You make me feel so . . . dependent.' Jennifer got up.

'Jennifer, I'm just looking after you, like I promised your mother.'

'Thanks very much, but I think I can look after myself.'

Blair caught her hand. 'Don't throw a wobbly in here. You have a kid coming and a mother who's a pain in the neck who's going to get old one day. Hopefully my family can look after themselves. I have to think about these things.'

'All right, Blair, that's very fine of you. You fight your way to the top, go for the big money if that's what you want. I don't think that's what we need.' She was close to tears. 'All I want is for us to be a proper family.' She put on her sunglasses and walked out of the dining room from the side door near the kitchen. As soon as she was out of sight she ran along the sandy path, turning by the dive centre, and flung herself onto the sand.

She sat there thinking about their conversation. Blair thought he was doing what was right and responsible. What upset her more was the knowledge that she had never really supported herself other than as a poor university student for a brief time. And how supportive Vi and Don had been to her and her mother. She'd met Blair and moved in with him. They'd married and now she was following him, barefoot and pregnant. How would she manage if she was on her own with a child? She had qualifications that were of no practical use. She could throw words around on paper that related to subjects she knew about. How useful was that?

She got up and headed back to their cabin feeling depressed and demoralised. She wanted to talk to Mac, hopefully he could give her some advice. And she thought of Gideon. The old beachcomber might have some life experience to share with her. What she wanted was a father figure to tell her it was going to be all right. She wondered what advice her own father would give her if he was around now. Sadly, the memories of a man beaten by circumstances and a domineering wife, preferring to bury his head in the sand and escape on his own, did not bring a lot of comfort.

She felt hot and bothered by the time she reached their cabin. She pulled off her clothes, wrapped her sarong around her naked body and on impulse went and stood under the outdoor shower. It ran hot from the sun before cooling. She refilled the clamshell where the birds had put sand and leaves in it.

She was about to pull off her wet sarong in the privacy of their courtyard but, as she turned to face the bush, she saw a flash of yellow and a man standing watching her. It was the elderly one-eyed handyman, a stupid smile on his face. She froze, the image of Rhonda returning to her, then the smirking face of Willsy – and it rendered the old man harmless in comparison. Seconds before, she was ready to scream, rush inside, feel sullied, her privacy violated. Instead she lifted her arm.

'Piss off, you old bugger!' she shouted.

Deflated, shoulders hunched, he turned and shuffled away.

Later in the afternoon Jennifer walked up to the reception desk and waited for the two guests to complete their check-out before taking the chopper back to the mainland. The last was Tony Adams. He picked up his leather shoulder bag, saw her and smiled.

'Good luck, Jennifer.' He paused. 'Do you need luck? Don't know why I said that. Make the most of your time here, might see you at the Shark Bar sometime.'

'A bit of luck never goes astray. Don't forget the rule to join the Shark Club.'

'I'm taking a small step. I'm taking the chopper back. My last trip in one was rather hairy.' He gave a rueful grin.

'It's stunning. The reef is amazing, you'll enjoy it,' said Jennifer.

Bob, the pilot, appeared in the doorway. 'All set? Camera ready?'

Tony nodded, gave Jennifer a short wave and walked outside.

'Okay now, Jennifer, what can I do for you?' asked Heather from behind the desk.

'I wanted to use Blair's office and phone my family. We have to let them know some news.'

'Sure, he's out for a bit. Help yourself.'

Jennifer walked into Blair's neat office, trying to frame the words to tell her mother she was going to be a grandmother. It was not an announcement that came easily to her, she was unsure how Christina would take it. You never knew with her mother. Vi and Don would, of course, be thrilled, as was Blair's family.

She thoughtfully hit the numbers that would connect this island to the suburban house in Sydney.

10

Serpent of the Sea

THE OFFICE WAS AIR conditioned, Blair had his desk facing a wall, the window behind him. On one wall was a large map of the Great Barrier Reef. Next to it Blair had hung his favourite picture of a castle in Liechtenstein that was now a five-star hotel. Jennifer rested her head on her hand, holding the phone to her ear, glad the door was closed as her mother droned on and on, detailing weeks of minutiae, every trivial event in her life since Jennifer had driven away. Vi and Don were scarcely mentioned.

'Mum . . . Mum, 'scuse me, but can I jump in? The calls from here are really expensive.'

'Oh. I see. Well, if you don't want to talk to me, I'll get off now then.'

'It's just that I haven't had a chance to *do* any talking,' Jennifer said lightly. 'Why don't you ask Vi to get on the extension so I don't have to repeat everything?'

'Oh, I thought you'd called *me*. Very well, I'll get her, though I could tell them what you say later.'

'Whatever. It's –'

There was a click as Vi, who'd been hovering, picked up the phone, anxious to hear the news, knowing that Christina wouldn't share everything at all. She'd drop little snippets over the next few days in front of other people. Jennifer is doing this, told me that. Oh, didn't you know that, Vi? Goodness, must have slipped my mind.

'Hi, sweetheart, how's everything?' came Vi's cheerful voice.

'I was just about to tell Mum my news, so I want you to know too.'

'We can't chat, Vi, this is expensive for her.'

'Mum, just let me get it out, will you! . . . I'm pregnant.'

There was an excited squeal from Vi, silence from Christina.

Then, 'Are you sure? Could be a false alarm, you know. Don't get so hysterical, Vi.'

'Of course she's sure, or she wouldn't be ringing us up. Ooh, this is wonderful. When, when?' gushed Vi.

'Have you seen a doctor? Obviously you can't

252

stay on that island in the middle of nowhere. You need a good doctor. I'll make arrangements down here with Dr Martin. Now, when are you coming back home?' Christina was businesslike and efficient.

'Why's she have to go to a doctor down here, Tina? Aren't there good doctors up there, Jenny? That place where you go shopping?'

'Yes, Vi. Headland Bay. I've seen the doctor and there's an excellent hospital here. All very handy.'

'You can't be serious. You can't stay in the middle of the ocean and have a baby,' snapped Christina.

'Is Blair thrilled?' asked Vi, trying to get Christina off this track.

'Er, I think so. I mean, we're both still getting used to the idea. It was a bit of a surprise.'

'I hope he's making arrangements to move back here as soon as possible. You need your family now,' said Christina.

'Let's not rush things, Tina. So what are your plans, sweetie? Do you feel okay? Don will be thrilled . . .'

'I'm fine, Vi. No morning sickness. Just eating a lot.'

'Don't you get fat, Jennifer. That flab is hard to lose after a baby.' Christina's authoritative tone cut across Vi's weepy happiness.

'Did you get the email pictures?' asked Jennifer, now desperate to change the subject.

'Ooh, yes, we looked at them on the computer

screen. It's a real tropical island, all right. Must be hot,' said Vi.

'Everything is fine. I'm back into work mode and in fact there's a very interesting bunch of scientists and researchers here from a Queensland university.'

'Fancy that. That'll be interesting for you, luv.'

'Typical. Those uni types playing around on some vague sort of research. For what? Sounds like a good excuse for a holiday to me.'

'I knew you'd say that, Mum.' Jennifer laughed. 'I'd better go, I'm in Blair's office. We send our love, give Don a hug and I'll keep you posted after my next appointment with the doctor.'

'You look after yourself, Jenny.' Vi then added, 'By the way, what do you want? Boy or girl?'

'Vi, so long as the child is healthy, that's all that matters. Next you'll be asking her for names. And you haven't even started to think about that yet, have you, Jennifer?'

'Not really. Well, I hope you're pleased for us.'

'I'm just very worried about it all.' Christina tut-tutted.

'You said your living quarters were small, how on earth are you going to manage a baby in there?' asked Vi suddenly.

'Vi, she's not going to stay in that place!' Christina's voice had that tinkling glass-breaking sound Jennifer recognised. 'You leave everything to me, Jennifer. I'll send you a letter soon.'

'I'm fine, everything's under control, Mum.

Bye, Vi. Bye, Mum.' She quickly hung up. The conversation had gone as she thought. She hoped Vi could keep a lid on Christina's ideas of 'helping'.

Jennifer passed Lloyd outside the boutique.

'Your fish are in the staffie freezer. Tell the chef when you want one cooked for you and Blair. Or else ask Doyley to whack it on our hotplate.'

'Great, thanks heaps.' Maybe she and Blair could have dinner alone at their place, talk quietly, share a bottle of wine. Make love. It had been ages.

'Thank Tony. Oh, and Mac said to call over tomorrow. Bring your stuff and move in!'

She went back to work with renewed enthusiasm knowing this was the last time she'd have to set up her laptop and work on a temporary table. Good on you, Mac.

It was even better than she hoped. Mac showed her to a small room that was air conditioned with empty floor-to-ceiling shelves and a long desk under the window.

'It's our storage lockup when we're not here. Computers, diving equipment, all that kind of stuff gets put in here. So the following season it's waiting for us. Saves carrying gear back and forth. Should suit you all right.'

'Absolutely. This is fantastic. You're sure I'm not throwing anyone out?'

'No way. And if you need company, Rudi's lab is next door, the canteen rec room is across the sandy square. My place is always open so use the kitchen, help yourself to tea, coffee, food, whatever.'

'Mac, you're so kind.'

'No slacking off is all I ask. Get that book done. I'd be interested to talk to you later about maybe writing something for us. But finish what you're doing first.'

'You've never read anything I've written. Is it academic, esoteric, historical, scientific?'

'Don't worry about that for now. But do put some time aside for when Isobel is here. I think you'll enjoy her. She's an amazing woman. You might want to write about her. Though I think Lloyd got that journo Tony a bit interested.'

Jennifer spread her things around her, settled down to work and hardly noticed the time passing.

'Want a coffee break?' Rudi was smiling in the doorway. 'I'm going to make a brew.'

'I'd love one.' Jennifer stretched.

'Come next door. I have the makings in my lab.'

She followed him into the cluttered laboratory. 'Where are you from originally, Rudi? Your name and your faint accent. I can't place them.'

'My family were from St Petersburg. I came here when I was ten. Went to the University of New South Wales. And don't tell anyone, but my name is Rudolf. Now, how do you like your coffee?'

Jennifer walked around looking into the various glass tanks as he poured the coffee. 'Milky, please. Why did you choose to study sea plants?'

'I know they don't look that important individually, but they're a foundation of a food chain and have been part of the marine ecosystem for over two billion years. And gorgeous to see. Swimming through kelp forests off Tasmania or over the seagrass meadows near the reef is unreal.'

'You make it sound like a day in the country,' she said, laughing. 'And are the forests filled with beasties?'

'There is some weird and wonderful marine life down there, for sure. I'm interested in the chemical side of what's in their tissues and fibres that protects them, stops fish eating them.' Rudi drained his cup. 'It could have applications in medicine, pharmaceuticals, genetics, or even chemical warfare . . . who knows?'

Jennifer was thoughtful. 'The work, research, that's being done here maybe isn't so esoteric after all. So all you guys paddling around on the reef under the sea . . . what you find out could benefit humanity or mean big bucks?'

'Possibly. We don't often look at the whole picture. Scientifically it's a step-by-step process on a small scale until there's a breakthrough and you can move forward, if not in leaps then at least in the right direction. It's just satisfying to get confirmation of a hunch or theory.' He refilled their coffee cups. 'Though I have to say, there has been interest in what I'm doing from some strange quarters. I leave all that stuff to Mac as he's head of the program. Though I'm hoping Isobel might turn up some new specimens.'

'So who is Isobel and how does she fit into the picture?' asked Jennifer, intrigued.

'Ah. Here, I'll get on the net and you can read for yourself. She's very famous in our world, but not so well known by anyone on the street I guess.'

Jennifer settled herself on a stool in front of Rudi's computer as it downloaded a photograph of an attractive, cheerful-looking dark-haired woman in her fifties. She was wearing a colourful wetsuit and sitting at the edge of a reef in the Caribbean. 'Queen of the Dark and Deep' scrolled across the screen beneath her photo, followed by a string of links and websites. Jennifer chose one and clicked.

For the next hour she jumped from story to story, from photos to interviews with the astonishing Dr Isobel Belitas. Inspired by the legendary Sylvia Earle, the world's leading aquanaut, Isobel had become fascinated with the world beneath the sea – 'where our future lies'.

Jennifer read how the Brazilian-born, American-educated Isobel had made dives deep into the Mariana Trench – a slash in the ocean floor one thousand eight hundred metres deeper than Mount Everest is tall. Here Jacques Cousteau had taken down his bathyscaphe in 1960 whereas Isobel, in a special diving suit, was strapped to a small submersible that took her more than three hundred and eighty metres below the surface where she released herself and walked on another part of the ocean floor for nearly three hours.

Looking at the pictures of the strange underwater

vehicles developed over the past decades in which adventurers and scientists had tried to find what was in the darkest reaches of the sea, Jennifer was struck by their similarity to the odd winged machine she'd seen next to Gideon's shack.

'You coming up for air?' asked Rudi, entering the lab. Jennifer hadn't heard him leave and, glancing at her watch, hadn't realised how absorbed she'd been.

'It is fascinating. I can sort of understand why you get so . . . immersed in all this. She's a brave and fearless person, or just crazy.'

'You can decide for yourself on Friday night,' said Mac, coming in the door. 'She'll be at Gideon's. We're having a welcome-back party for her.'

Jennifer returned to Professor Dawn's notes on the history of the East Australian Current with an early observation of it from explorer Lieutenant James Cook in May 1770 as he charted the coast of Australia. It was off Cape Byron, the most eastern extremity, that he became aware of the surge of the surface stream, tens of metres deep, that travels down Australia along the Coral and Tasman seas.

Professor Dawn was only one of the many scientists who have studied the EAC for more than two centuries. But as he showed with modern technology, this travelling body of water can be mapped and observed from earth observation satellites, with ocean monitoring and measuring equipment and also from research vessels.

Professor Dawn's dry descriptions took on new meaning for Jennifer as she imagined Dr Isobel Belitas inside, or strapped to, a small underwater machine chugging along beneath the sea, observing and sending back information from the sophisticated miniature equipment attached to the submersible. It was science fantasy, the wild tales of Jules Verne, space exploration upside down! Jennifer turned off her computer, overcome with feelings she couldn't describe.

She waved to Mac. 'Going home for lunch. See you later. And thanks again.'

Mac, sitting at a table in the shade with a graduate student, going through her papers, gave Jennifer a brief wave in return.

In the middle of the day the pisonia forest was still and hot. No breeze stirred the strange sticky fruit and leaves. Even the noddy terns were silent and less active. Instead of returning to the resort she turned down the track leading to Coral Point and when she came to the small headland she was surprised to see Blair in the distance, standing with two men, gesturing around and out to sea, admiring the view.

She called out, waved, and could tell by Blair's body language he was uncomfortable.

'I thought you were busy working,' he greeted her.

'I'm on a lunch break. Have you had lunch yet?' She looked at the two men, recognising them from head office, and smiled. 'Nice to see you again, Mr Fanzio, Mr Holding.' She put out her hand, annoyed Blair hadn't bothered to include her.

'Hello. We were just talking about lunch too. Please call me Joe and this is Reg,' said Fanzio.

Jennifer glanced at Blair, 'Ah, you were on *Kicking Back* when we were at Sooty. Beautiful boat.'

Blair's eyes had narrowed and he was sending her some signal but she had no idea what. 'It's the company boat. Reg and Joe are just here briefly to see how things are running,' said Blair. 'A flying visit.'

'Oh, is Rosie hosting drinks or anything?' asked Jennifer innocently.

'No time, unfortunately, just a stopover visit to our outposts,' said Holding, separating his lips and showing teeth, his eyes cold.

Joe, the fatter, redder and balder of the two, made a bit more of an effort. 'So how are you enjoying being out here? Blair says you're doing some writing. Very good to have a portable occupation when your husband is so . . . involved.'

Jennifer gave Blair a bright smile. 'Oh, he's definitely very involved with it all. The staff and guests love him.'

Signals were still flashing from Blair, who turned away from the view. 'Well, shall we? Have that lunch?'

The men glanced around as they walked away from the headland. 'Fabulous location. Spot on.'

'Just got to make it work. Counting on you, Blair.' Holding jabbed Blair in the arm.

Jennifer was walking slightly ahead as Blair came alongside. 'We're having lunch on the boat, it's at the wharf. Sorry I can't ask you, business. Rosie has a meeting with them too,' he added for her benefit. Then as the men, talking in low voices, dropped further behind them, he said, 'Don't mention being pregnant. Might hurt my promotion.'

'Already?'

'Just talking future plans, you never know.'

'So where do you plan to park me and the baby if we're not included in your future plans?'

'Don't be silly, just play along,' he hissed. As they reached the divide in the track he kissed her quickly on the cheek. 'See you later on. I'm just taking them down to Boomerang Cove for a bit of a looksee.'

'Nice to see you,' called Jennifer and turned onto the resort path. The men gave a desultory acknowledgment. Jennifer had the distinct impression they couldn't care less if they never saw her again or would they even recognise her if they did. 'Jerks,' she thought. 'How did they get to be senior executives?'

She didn't see Rosie for the next two days and Blair was vague about the meeting, but seemed cheerful and more loving than he'd been in a month. They started making love again, but he avoided what she thought of as real intimacy. No cuddling, talking or lazing in bed together in the afterglow of sex. He either fell asleep or leapt from bed, rushing to get ready for work, leaving Jennifer to her solitary morning walk.

On Friday morning Jennifer asked Blair to come with her that evening to Gideon's Shark Bar.

'That weird old guy that Lloyd and the uni people hang out with? I don't think so.'

'Have you ever met Gideon?'

'Would I want to? You go if you want. I'm off to Sooty, we're looking at some refurbishments. Maybe another tent. So I'll stay over there. Will you be okay? How will you get back? No more dramas, please.'

'I'm not sure. If you're on Sooty is Rosie on duty here then?' It struck her as odd that Blair would be looking after upgrades and refurbishments rather than the manager.

'Yeah. But I don't want you walking across the island at night after a few drinks. Take Rosie with you, someone can cover for her.'

'I might come back by boat,' said Jennifer with a cheeky air.

Blair gave her a look. 'Don't put Lloyd through that trip. You're just not meant to go on boats.'

'Speaking of boats, *Kicking Back* didn't stay long. What's going on with those two company boys? They're not exactly impressive, are they?'

'Just because they were dressed casually . . . those guys are worth heaps. And they run a squillion-dollar business. They have other connections as well as the resorts.'

'Really? Like what?'

'Nothing to do with hospitality. I'm not sure.' Blair sounded evasive.

'Blair, I don't think you should suck up to those guys. If they're only part of the board, corporation, whatever, who is the really big boss?' she asked.

'The chairman is Sir Giles Blake. A Brit. No one ever sees him. His family owned Reef Resorts before it went public. He's probably some old geezer who goes to the board meetings and has no other involvement. Sends his rellies off on fancy holidays to the resorts they own. Who knows? It's middle and senior management, guys like Fanzio and Holding, who are hands-on, running things.'

He went into the bathroom. Jennifer dropped the subject, deciding to quiz Rosie. She hoped she'd come along tonight.

'You bet I'm going over there, I've already made arrangements,' said Rosie when Jennifer stuck her head around her office door. 'Isobel is a truly fabulous gal. You up to coming with Lloyd and me in his boat? He's off duty too.'

'I guess so. Sure, why not? Nothing could be worse than the first time. And I'm a member of the Shark Club now.' Jennifer felt happy, liberated.

'Good for you. See you down at the wharf at six.'

Lloyd and Carmel were on board waiting for them. Lloyd helped Jennifer into the boat and gave her hand a slight squeeze. Rosie sat beside Jennifer as they sped away from the wharf.

Rosie shaded her eyes. 'I love looking back at the resort from the water. It's tucked in there so discreetly, really blends in. What a relief it's not a high-rise monstrosity.'

'Where's Blair?' asked Carmel. 'Is he holding the fort?'

'He's on Sooty Isle. Working over there. Just for today and tomorrow,' said Jennifer. She caught Rosie's eye and saw her discomfort. Was Blair upstaging his boss? She'd have to speak to him. Rosie was an understanding woman but if he was jeopardising her career everything could backfire on him. When the time was appropriate she'd talk to Rosie. And Blair.

But it was Lloyd who asked one of the questions Jennifer had been thinking about. 'I saw *Kicking Back* was here for a bit, Rosie. Pretty quick inspection, wasn't it?'

'Only an informal visit. Not exactly social, though I had a quick drink with the slick boys – as I call them. They're cruising around. Got some women on board and no wives. Not really serious business. Hardly came ashore.'

'Oh, I saw them up at Coral Point. And Blair took them down to Boomerang Cove,' blurted Jennifer without thinking.

Rosie looked stunned then shrugged. 'I'm not going to worry about it. They had no complaints as far as I could tell, that's the main thing. The board and chairman are in London, the slick boys are the Australian arm. Unfortunately I answer to them.'

'Are you going to London for the next meeting?' asked Jennifer cautiously.

'No, that's not my call.'

Carmel sensed Rosie's tension and diverted the conversation. 'I am so excited to meet Dr Belitas. How often is she here?'

'She was here about eighteen months ago. She hadn't been to Branch for a couple of years before that. It depends on her schedule, I s'pose. Mac will know more. If she has a project here she'll spend weeks, maybe months. She sometimes stays at the resort for a break but mostly she's at the research station. She's a ball of energy, that's for sure.'

'She's very down to earth for someone so famous,' said Lloyd.

'Yes, I looked her up on the net. Odd that some people can be so respected and known in their field and yet unknown to the general public,' said Jennifer.

'Depends what general public you refer to – the followers of the tabloid press and TV soaps, or people who take their news and reading a bit more seriously,' said Rosie. 'If you talk about the queen of the deep and extreme feats, some people will know of her.'

Jennifer kept quiet. *I'm a country girl. Ask me about droughts, bushfires, flooded creeks, plagues of locusts. I haven't had any interest in marine science.*

Lloyd cut the engine as the day drifted into lilac twilight and the small boat slowed, heading for the shore of the little lagoon near Gideon's shack. Carmel jumped out into the knee-deep water and pulled the boat until it stopped on the sand.

Rosie, holding her sandals, her long peasant skirt bunched up in the other hand, swung her legs over and dropped into the water. 'It's only ankle-deep, Jenny.'

Lloyd threw the rope to Carmel, who trudged up the beach to secure the boat. 'I'll hop off and help you down, Jen.'

'I'm fine.' She swung her legs over and jumped almost straight onto the shore. She rolled down the legs of her cotton pants to cover as much skin as possible. Early evening was the midges' favourite feasting time. Rosie handed her some repellent.

'I hear revelry,' said Lloyd, heading towards a glow through the trees.

Single file they approached the Shark Bar. The burst of music from an old ghettoblaster on the bar was heart starting. Rosie swung her hips. 'Dig that beat.'

Jennifer laughed. 'Salsa!'

Carmel danced past them. 'No, calypso!'

Gideon had turned on the coloured party lights along the sagging thatch of the roof; outside, the flame torches burned with the tangy odour of citronella. Lanterns, candles and the electric light over the bar flickered with the shadows of moving figures. At first Jennifer thought everyone was dancing. But, like moths around the flame, the crowd hovered, swelling and receding around an unseen magnet in the centre.

Gideon, looking even more genial than usual, rose from his favourite chair to welcome them.

The others were quickly swallowed in the throng except Rosie who headed for the bar and poured glasses of wine.

'So, Jennifer, what's your latest news?' Gideon dropped his arm around her shoulder.

'From Headland Bay? Nothing too exciting I'm afraid.' She held back from sharing her news for some superstitious reason, or shyness, she wasn't sure.

'And have you been working on that book of the absent professor?'

'I have, very much. Thanks to Mac. He gave me a cubby hole to work in at the research station.'

'Do I hear my name? Glad you came.' Mac had extricated himself from the group. 'Everyone is talking at once and the music . . . let the excitement dissipate. Grab a seat outside.'

Jennifer glanced inside, disappointed she hadn't yet met, or seen, the famous Isobel Belitas.

'Don't worry, I'll introduce you to her shortly,' said Mac.

Rosie handed Jennifer a glass. 'Have a red wine. Medicinal purposes,' she winked.

'Do you come over here much? How well do you all know each other?' Jennifer asked Rosie. Mac, Rosie, Gideon. Each came from a different world on the island, yet they seemed so comfortable, so compatible.

Jennifer watched the streaks of light change colour in the evening sky. She wondered for a moment what Blair was doing. But then there was a shuffling of seats. Mac stood up. And there was

268

Isobel, being shown to the empty canvas chair next to Jennifer.

She was tiny! Jennifer was struck silent as Isobel Belitas held out both her hands. Wide, dark-brown eyes, short wavy dark hair. And a smile, a huge smile, that dominated her face. A diamond earring caught the light and twinkled. Her hands were small, soft but strong. She wore a rich musky perfume redolent of night flowers. She was in red. Was she fifteen or fifty? There seemed no difference. She radiated energy, warmth, delight.

'A new recruit. How good to meet you. We have a lot to talk about, yes?' Her voice was throaty, slightly accented though more musical than Carmel's. Still holding one of Jennifer's hands she sat beside her. Jennifer felt she was under some incredible spotlight as Isobel turned her gaze on her.

'We do, I mean, I hope so. I've been reading about you on the net,' said Jennifer shyly.

'Hah. Don't always believe everything that's out there. But I hope you found some of it . . . interesting?'

'Oh, yes. Very much so.'

Mac and Rosie moved to replenish drinks, pass food. Gideon leaned back, his arms behind his head, paying little attention it seemed.

'And you are here because of your husband. Have you been here long enough to decide how important this place is?' asked Isobel.

'I'm not sure what you mean. You mean the

work being done at the research station?'

'What I am saying is . . . Are you happy he brought you here? Do you hate being away from this island, these waters, when you go?' She cocked her head, the brilliant smile now faintly quizzical.

Jennifer sensed there was more to her question. She thought a moment before answering. 'At first I hated it. I'm acclimatising. If it wasn't for Mac, Gideon, everyone else, no, I wouldn't like it here. Except . . .' She turned away, looking at the tranquil sea in the distance.

'You have, as they say, unfinished business,' said Isobel gently. 'I understand that.' She patted Jennifer's hand. 'Even if you don't.'

Gideon sat forward. 'I've told Isobel what little I know about you, Jennifer. And what I feel. And about the book you're doing for that professor.'

'And what do you want to do? For you?' asked Isobel, her eyes sparkling.

'I wish I knew. I feel quite envious of you all . . . having such interesting projects and plans,' began Jennifer.

'What's the book about?'

'Oh, it's a work by one of the professors from Sydney Uni, where I studied. He's been looking at the East Australian Current . . .'

'Oh, I know it! I have been in it. I call it the serpent,' said Isobel. 'It starts here in the Coral Sea, travels often around four knots and makes enormous eddies and flows,' she waved her arm in a snaking motion, 'like a serpent. It brings up nutrient-rich waters from deep below. And that makes fish happy.'

'Talking of sea creatures, are there lots of whales?' asked Jennifer.

'More and more. When I first came here we hardly saw them, and the waters of the reef are their nursery, where they have their babies,' Gideon explained. 'Their numbers are way up now since we started watching them instead of killing them.'

'Have you heard the whales sing?' Isobel asked Jennifer.

She shook her head. 'Maybe on a CD. Can you hear them under water?'

'Oh yes. You can come and listen if you like.'

'Under water? Near a whale? Not me!' laughed Jennifer.

Isobel studied her for a moment. 'One of Mac's postgrad students is running a research project on DNA monitoring of the whales. A genetic study to find if they are family groups and how they relate to one another. The DNA samples will show that. We'll take you out when we collect skin samples. They leave small pieces of skin on the surface each time they breach. We call it sloughed skin.'

'Jennifer is not at home on or in the sea,' commented Gideon.

'Maybe that will change,' said Isobel. 'You strike me as a young woman about to make some big change in her life.'

'Ah, Isobel, the clairvoyant. She is very perceptive,' said Gideon.

'She is indeed,' said Jennifer. 'I am definitely going to change. I'm having a baby.'

'Wow, what news! Wonderful, wonderful!' Isobel clapped her hands.

Gideon reached over and clasped Jennifer's hands and called for Mac and Rosie. 'Gather round, gather round. A toast.'

'Please, please, Gideon, don't make a fuss,' said Jennifer, rather embarrassed.

'This news deserves a big fuss.'

As attention turned to Gideon, Jennifer and Isobel, Rosie stepped forward and held her glass aloft. 'Here's to Jennifer's baby . . . now known as baby Branch until he, or she, arrives.'

'And may she make her first swim right here,' declared Isobel, raising her glass towards the shimmering moonlit lagoon. There were more congratulations, the music was turned up, glasses were refilled and Jennifer was the centre of attention as Isobel sat beside her, watching and smiling.

Later, travelling back in the boat with Rosie, Lloyd and Carmel, Jennifer reflected on the happy evening. She was glad they'd made a fuss. The news was out and she'd enjoyed everyone celebrating. Blair probably wouldn't be pleased now the whole island knew. But it wasn't something that could be hidden forever. Jennifer patted her tummy and thought of Isobel. What a powerful personality, she certainly lived up to her reputation. She had promised that she would go and spend time with the diver and scientist the following afternoon. And Jennifer had an odd feeling that, as Isobel had predicted, her life really was about to change.

11

Submerged

ROSIE SAT AT HER desk, doodling on a sheet of
paper. She was frowning, the cup of coffee beside
her was cold. Despite the soft hum of the air conditioner, she could hear laughter and voices of
guests at the reception desk.

She rubbed her hand across her eyes. She had
a headache. Patch had just told her that the maintenance team was having problems repairing the
desalination plant, which was on the blink. Thank
goodness they had storage tanks to last for a week
or more. The rainwater tanks were low. Workmen,
waste and water: the three major problems in running a resort on an island.

Blair appeared in the doorway wearing white shorts and a plain turquoise shirt with a white turtle embroidered above his name tag. He was tanned with an air of charm and confidence that added to his attractiveness. The thought crossed her mind that with Blair's appeal and Jennifer's golden good looks, they would produce a beautiful child.

'Come in, Blair. Few things I'd like to talk over. Close the door if you wouldn't mind.' This was unusual. Rosie ran an open-door policy of accessibility at all times.

'Sure. What's up?' Blair pulled the chair to one side of the desk and crossed his legs in a nonchalant pose so it didn't appear that Rosie was in a superior position on the other side of the desk.

'The barge has just delivered the weekly supplies. Seems the part for the pump has arrived,' he said conversationally.

'Do you know what Fanzio and Holding are up to?' she asked bluntly.

'Up to? You make it sound like they're doing something . . . illegal.'

'I'm just wondering. You've had more to do with them than I have,' she said pointedly. 'Showing them around, socialising on Sooty and on the boat. Now this.' She slid a letter across the desk with the logo of Reef Resorts International on it.

'What is it?' Blair didn't seem particularly curious.

'First off, it is a request from head office in

London for a young man to come and work here, preferably on the dive boat.'

'Whose kid is he? Son of one of the heavies being sent out to the colony before going to Eton?' said Blair.

'Quite possibly. I don't recognise the name. Odd that it's head office making the request and not a minion further down the line. The other more concerning thing is they are informing me that a team from HQ will be doing an inspection of Branch Island Resort with a view to – quote – upgrading facilities – unquote. What do you make of that?'

'Sounds reasonable. This is a pleasant eco resort – classy, quiet, back to nature, that sort of thing. Maybe they're thinking we should be more . . . ultra, *über*, chic. International style. That sort of thing,' said Blair.

Rosie thought the words rolled out a little too glibly. 'And you think that would be a good thing?' Her face gave nothing away though her eyes narrowed slightly.

Blair chose his words with care. 'I know you don't think so, but look what's happening in other places round the world. There's a demand by rich people for eco tourism in style and comfort. They'll pay thousands of dollars a day for the right place in the right setting.'

'Spending a lot of money doesn't guarantee a developer will manage a world heritage site better than just leaving it be,' argued Rosie. 'Anything that's pristine, places that time forgot – and there are a few – are going to be damaged simply by people going there whether it be in a tent or a ten-star resort.'

'Some might disagree. There are examples of scientists treating protected areas as their own private playgrounds and not looking after them environmentally because there's no outside monitoring. Whereas a tourism concern would have to comply with extensive restrictions and requirements.'

'You've obviously given this a lot of thought,' said Rosie somewhat sarcastically. 'If our company is planning to upgrade this place, they'll have a hard time convincing me, the university that runs the research station, and the media. Let's wait and see what this visiting team has to say.'

'The media can work for both arguments. It depends who the journo is or what publication, doesn't it?' said Blair. 'And I don't think there's a serious team coming out here. I figure Fanzio and Holding have pretty much got the picture after what they saw.'

'You can't be serious. How much did they see? They have no idea of the importance of this island, the reef, the work being done,' said Rosie, think-ing Blair had no real idea either. 'What did you show them? Did they visit the research station?'

'Not that I'm aware. Anyway, what's the prob-lem, Rosie? The more upmarket the company goes, the better the job opportunities, I say.'

'That's one way of looking at things. For me, being manager here isn't just a job. Sure, it's important for guests to have a good time, but the real privilege for me is to help them become aware of the beauty of nature and how special and sensitive the reef is. You dived on it yet, Blair? Snorkelled?'

'Been too busy. I get a good feel for nature on Sooty. I reckon this resort can have it both ways, a far plusher, chic resort here on Branch with a day trip or a couple of days going rustic on Sooty. Low key, laid back. I like it over there.'

'So I gather,' said Rosie tartly. 'Okay, Blair, I just wanted you to be aware of what was going on and keep an eye out for the English kid – Gordon Blake. And there's no need to let the rest of the staff be any the wiser. He's just another backpacker with a bit of hotel experience working here for a month or two.'

Blair strolled from the office, leaving Rosie feeling she'd come off second best. She had no doubt Blair was scheming behind her back by getting cosy with the slick boys. Blair was ambitious, nothing wrong with that, but Fanzio and Holding were middle management with a small say when it came to the international board that made the big decisions. Still, Rosie felt concerned enough to alert Mac to what was in the wind.

Jennifer was working in what she now considered 'her office' next to Rudi's lab. She could, at last, see the end of Professor Dawn's book, which she'd now subtitled in her mind 'The Serpent of the

Eastern Seas' after Isobel's descriptive analogy. Though, as she thought to herself, dry old Dawn wouldn't agree to such a poetic title on his work.

'You look pleased with yourself.' Isobel's smiling face peeped around the door.

'I am, I am!' agreed Jennifer enthusiastically. 'I'm almost there. My boss, Professor Dawn, has emailed me to say he's "delightfully surprised at the quality of the interpretation of his research material". Must have given him heartburn to say that.' She pushed back her chair. 'Come in. What have you been doing?'

'Talking to Rudi, listening to his theories. He's trying to prove that what people think are the insignificant plants in our seas hold cellular secrets to cures for ills and diseases on land. Like rainforests, but underwater.' She perched on the other chair Jennifer had borrowed from the rec room. 'Ah, Jenny . . .' She pronounced it *Jeneee*, which made Jennifer smile to herself. It was a pleasing, intimate way of saying her name that, up till then, she'd always thought a bit boring. 'How little we know of these things and then they have disappeared before we can fully explore their potential.'

Jennifer gazed at Isobel. She was casually dressed in navy bermuda shorts, a red T-shirt, white canvas plimsolls and a floppy cotton hat with a wide brim. Her skin was smooth and olive, she wore little make-up except bright red lipstick. 'Your work sounds so important and intriguing. So Isobel, why do you do what you do? I mean, how does it fit in with your life? Do you have a family?'

'It is my passion. I could not do otherwise ever since I discovered the world beneath the sea. I lost my husband to the sea . . .' She stopped, seeing the swift change of expression on Jennifer's face. 'No, not like your father and brother. I mean diving became my lover, my life. My husband left me and I do not blame him at all. He is a banker.' She gave a shrug. 'We have two nice boys. They are married. So . . . I am free. I hope that doesn't sound selfish. Perhaps it is. Which is why I give my time and my work to serve the cause of the oceans.'

Jennifer didn't answer immediately. In a few sentences Isobel had summed up her choices. She had changed her life and she was fulfilled. And famous for her dedication and her inspiring work. 'You make it sound simple. I hear stories of how women turn their lives around . . . I wish my mother had been more like that. She's quite dependent. On me, her brother and his wife. Not that she would agree.'

'And what about you, Jennifer? What are your future plans, dreams, ambitions?'

'I'm having a baby. That seems to take care of the immediate future, I guess. It depends on Blair.'

'Why?' asked Isobel gently. When Jennifer didn't answer for a moment she added, 'Having a baby doesn't mean your life goes on hold. I found it a very energising and enriching time. I tackled some of my more challenging tasks in the early months. Why don't you?'

Jennifer looked at her computer, knowing she was on the last chapter of the rewrite of Professor

Dawn's book. What would she do with herself for the next twelve months? 'Once I have the baby I'm sure that will keep me busy. But until then – I don't know. My options are a bit limited.'

'Nonsense. There's a whole incredible world out there. You can help secure its future. You have an environmental degree, you can help us.' Isobel jumped off her chair and grabbed Jennifer's hand.

'No, no. You're talking about marine biology . . . I couldn't. The ocean freaks me out. I worked with National Parks in bushland, nothing to do with islands, reefs, the ocean . . .' Jennifer shook her head, starting to feel panicky. Isobel was so sweet and smiling but the force of her personality was over-whelming. The expression 'velvet steamroller' came to mind.

'Jennifer, you have choices in life. Take them or lose them. I'm showing you a path. It's not diving over the continental shelf or anything.' She drew Jennifer to her feet and linked her arm through hers, propelling her outside. 'Don't you believe people meet, cross paths, for a reason? A season perhaps?'

'Possibly,' said Jennifer reluctantly. But inside her head there was an insistent voice, *Listen to her, listen.*

They started to walk in the sunshine. 'There's meeting someone new and then there's *connecting* with someone. You understand the difference?'

'Yes.' *Mac. Gideon. Tony. You. A connection, an indefinable something.*

'Are you happy, Jennifer? Do you wake up each

morning and can't wait to rush out of bed, seize the day . . .'

'Not really.' Jennifer gave a short laugh. 'I can't ever remember feeling like that. Well, maybe when I was a little girl. Before I lost my father and brother.'

'And what about your husband?'

'He is very ambitious. Has his career all mapped out. Loves his job.'

'And you? He loves you?'

They were walking past Mac's house, follow-ing the path back towards the resort. Isobel still had her arm through Jennifer's.

'Yes.' She felt uncomfortable. 'It'd be pretty awful if he didn't, with the baby coming and all.'

'He's happy, excited about your baby?' Isobel felt Jennifer stiffen slightly and she loosened her arm, adjusting her hat and sunglasses. 'I am asking too many questions. That is my way. We're nosy people.' But she looked at Jennifer, still waiting for an answer.

'He wasn't at first, we'd decided to wait for a few years. But . . . he's getting used to the idea.'

'Hmmm.'

They walked in silence into the pisonia forest where the air was thick and wet. Isobel wiped beads of perspiration from her lip, taking off her hat to fan herself. Jennifer felt a trickle of moisture between her breasts. They both stopped to watch two noddy terns arguing over where to attach a leaf to a half-built nest.

'Every couple has their domestic disagreements,'

commented Jennifer. She was thinking about their lack of nesting. 'Our baby is probably going to sleep in a box on the floor,' she tried to joke. 'Rosie is being very accommodating about letting us stay here with the baby till Blair's contract is up. Then, hopefully, we'll settle somewhere a bit more permanent.'

Isobel was dismissive. 'Babies don't need expensive equipment. So long as she is close to you, that's all she needs. Milk, cuddles, crooning, hearing the sea and the birds. Perfect.'

'Oh Isobel, I don't know if you are being a Pollyanna or just trying to make me feel good,' sighed Jennifer. 'I wish everything was as easy as you make it sound.'

They continued walking and came to the junction of the path.

'I am going to see Gideon,' said Isobel.

'I'll go back to the resort.' Jennifer felt she should thank Isobel but wasn't sure what for. If anything, she'd made her feel restless and resentful. That she could be doing other things, leading a different life.

Isobel touched Jennifer's cheek. 'My dear girl, let me help you. You know what is wrong with you?'

Jennifer was about to retort there wasn't anything wrong with her, but reflected on how she'd been feeling a moment before. She looked down at her sandy feet in her casual sandals and simply shook her head.

Isobel rested her finger under Jennifer's chin,

lifting her head so they looked into each other's eyes. 'You've lost the magic of childhood, of wonder. Of truly seeing. You can't be a good mother to your own child until you share that again.'

Inexplicably Jennifer's eyes filled with tears.

Isobel smiled. 'We shall find it. Together. That's what friends are for, yes?' She squeezed Jennifer's hand and turned down the track. Isobel glanced back at Jennifer standing at the intersection of the sandy paths and wondered if the girl realised she was at a crossroads in her life. She hoped Jennifer had the courage to take the path of self discovery.

Jennifer couldn't find Blair so after eating and cleaning up their kitchenette she walked down to the resort wharf. It was mid afternoon and as always it amazed her that, despite there being over a hundred guests at the resort, it always looked empty. Where did they go during the day? She saw Lloyd hosing down the deck of his boat. She wandered down and gave him a hoy.

'Hey there, Jennifer, how's it going? Hear you've hunkered down at the research station.'

'My home away from home. How's it with you?'

'Come aboard. Just back from a trip. Want a cup of tea?'

'Why not!' She went down the solid ironbark steps and, steadying herself on a pylon that had once been a forest giant, took Lloyd's hand and stepped into the boat.

'You're getting to be a regular now. Why not come out for a fish with us next trip?'

'I couldn't stand to watch them die. Plus, I'd probably be seasick. My condition, you know,' she laughed.

'No such luck. About the fishing.' He turned the gas on under the tea kettle. 'It's a worry . . . hardly any bloody fish out there any more.' He pointed to two black marks on the edge of the gunwale.

'See that – forty-five centimetres. Anything under that size has to go back. Which means most of the fish the tourists catch. They whinge, of course, a fish that size'd feed one or two people.'

'I don't imagine they pay money to come and catch something that'd fit in a small frying pan,' said Jennifer.

'Branch isn't known as a major game fishing place. But there's always been good sport fishing out there. Tag and release, get your photo taken, that sort of thing.' Lloyd gazed thoughtfully out to sea.

'You're worried about the effect on tourism?' asked Jennifer.

He turned to Jennifer. 'Nah, not really. I mean, I'm twenty-nine, I can turn my hand to a lot of other things. No, I'm worried about the future. Of the reef. For most of the gang here it's just a job.'

'You've spent too much time with Mac and Gideon,' said Jennifer with a small smile.

'Yeah.' He got out the mugs. 'Do you know much about Gideon? What his interest, his passion in life is?'

'This island, as far as I could make out. I feel badly I haven't shown more interest in him. He's been so attentive and helpful to me,' said Jennifer.

'That's his way. Actually, Gideon is quite an inventor. He has some sort of engineering degree. He was a pilot in the war. Now he's building submersibles. Don't know why he didn't join the navy,' mused Lloyd. 'He says gliding about underwater is more like flying. Anyway, that's where the connection with Isobel comes in.'

'That funny machine I saw!' exclaimed Jennifer. 'Is that what it is?'

'The sharkmobile we call it. Operates on aerodynamic pressure and principles like a space craft. I don't understand it. I just drive the boat and help them launch it.'

'They've tested it? Does it work?' she asked incredulously.

'My oath. Old Gideon has been down quite deep, he's taken pictures and videos. They're a bit dark and blurry but he reckons he's seen some amazing things.'

'Is that why Isobel is here?' Jennifer felt her skin tingle at the idea of going down into the ocean depths in a plastic machine with windows and small fins like a fragile but sleek fish.

'Partly. They keep it a bit quiet, don't want tourists gawking, media people hyping it up. And you know it's dangerous. The university doesn't want a failed experiment on its hands. Take sugar?'

'No thanks, Lloyd. Isobel, is she attached to the university too?'

'No, she has her own research organisation that has American funding. Ask Carmel about it. Or better, talk to Isobel.'

'I will.' She watched Lloyd stow the fishing gear. 'You know, in a way it might be more interesting for tourists to know what the research station and the scientists and students are doing than sitting in a boat hanging a line over the side with no idea what's down there.'

Lloyd pointed to his depth sounder. 'Yeah, seeing a school of fish as a yellow blob on the radar screen isn't as exciting as being in the resort submarine and going eyeball to eyeball. You should try that. It trundles along with the passengers below the surface and the top half out of the water.'

Jennifer shook her head. 'Why is everyone trying to get me under water?'

'That's why people come here. All the other stuff, the fab resort, tropical island, idyllic lifestyle, turtles, fish, birds – they're all trimmings. It's the reef. The reef is the drawcard. They don't call it one of the wonders of the world for nothing. You gotta see it, Jennifer.'

She held out her hand to be helped back onto the steps. 'Thanks for the tea. Say hi to Carmel. See you, Lloyd.'

Jennifer walked through the resort thinking she'd have a nap in the new acquisition Doyley had found for them – a hammock – which they'd strung between trees in the courtyard of their unit. But to her surprise she saw Mac and Gideon coming towards her. Gideon wore long cotton pants, a colourful shirt, sandals and his leather hat. Mac, while in shorts, looked spruced up in an ironed shirt.

'Howdy, Miss Jennifer,' said Gideon, lifting his hat.

'This is a nice surprise. What brings you into the resort? Having dinner here tonight?'

'I believe we will,' said Gideon. 'Will you join us? We're Rosie's guests.'

'We're having a bit of a meeting at Rosie's place,' added Mac. 'Keep it under your hat.'

Jennifer wondered if that meant not to mention it to Blair. 'I'll see you later then.'

Lying in the hammock, listening to the distant, constant rumble of the waves breaking over the outside reef, birds rustling and murmuring in the trees, a heron squabbling with a seagull over possession of the clamshell under the shower, Jennifer felt like she was curled in a canvas womb as the world around her went on with business as usual. She felt in limbo, waiting. For the birth of her baby? A new direction in her life? Some sign from Blair that they would be together in the rocking chairs surrounded by grandkids one day?

Later that afternoon Blair changed clothes and glanced at Jennifer lying on the sofa reading. 'I'm going for a sunset cocktail with some Yank visitors. Want to join us? I've no idea where Rosie has been all afternoon.'

'I'll be up for dinner. What's been happening? How are things going?'

He gave her a quizzical look. 'As ever. Why? Should anything be happening? Maybe I should ask you the same.'

Jennifer dropped her book. 'I've nearly finished Dawn's book. I'm wondering what I can do to occupy myself.'

'Relax and do the things they say – eat right, exercise. Think how lucky you are to be here and not working right up to the baby's arrival. Maybe if you're bored you should consider going back to stay with Vi, Don, your mother.'

'Are you mad? There's nowhere to stay. Unless we throw the tenants out of our place. I'm not bored, I'm considering my options. I could do a further degree or at least do a course through the research station and uni. Or Mac suggested I might write something for them.'

'Now who's mad? Why get into something you can't finish? I'll speak to Rosie, maybe you could work in the office, even reception, guest activities, something like that.'

'I didn't think spouses were allowed to work. And I'd hate that.'

'I can pull some strings.'

Jennifer sat up. 'What do you mean, I couldn't finish, anyway?'

Blair turned away, smoothing his hair, adjusting his belt. 'Maybe we could cut this contract short. If I get a good job with Reef Resorts International. There are big plans for this company in the works.'

'And you're part of them? I wouldn't believe

everything that Mr Fanzio and Mr Holding have to say.'

'Listen, Jennifer, I'm doing you a favour. Don't get involved with that uni mob. It's quite likely the research station could be closed. Now don't say anything, you just never know, that's all.'

It occurred to Jennifer that Blair regretted saying what he did. She got up and went into the kitchenette. 'Want a cup of tea?' Then casually, 'So why would the research station close? I thought they were doing useful work. And it's been there long before the resort was here.'

'It's sitting on land adjoining Coral Point headland . . . Land is valuable. Who knows what a developer could do with it.'

'It's too far away for the resort to extend on it. And you couldn't have two resorts. What mad idea are those guys hatching?'

'Don't jump to any conclusions,' said Blair irritably. 'And don't repeat this. It's speculation. There could be a journalist coming in to write up the resort – don't give her any wild ideas.'

'What sort of journalist?'

'A glossy travel mag. I'll probably take her and the photographer over to Sooty as well.'

'When are they coming? I'd like to go to Sooty again.'

'Don't know any details. When are you going back to Headland Bay?'

'I have a doctor's appointment next Friday. Maybe I'll do some baby shopping. A few basics.'

'See who's off duty and take one of the girls

with you. Doyley says a couple of the new girls are hanging out to hit the shops and stuff.'

'So I'll see you at dinner? I was hoping to join Rosie.'

'I'll be with the Yanks and Susie, she's over from Sooty. We're trying to persuade these Americans to go over to the isle and do some deep-sea fishing. They have plenty of dough and a lot of rich friends. They're crazy about the scuba diving they've done here.'

'Everyone says we have to see the reef. Maybe on your day off on Sunday we could do something? I mean, not scuba. But go sailing, just spend the day at the beach, what do you say?'

'We'll see. I don't want to arrange something and then have you freaking out.'

'I'll try not to do that, Blair. I'm working on being a kid again. Fearless, adventuresome, excited to seize the day.' She smiled.

Blair didn't seem to be listening. 'Whatever. See you for dinner.'

Jennifer got dressed slowly, deciding to wear a long wrap skirt and camisole top. The skirt was softly draped and she wound it around her larger waist and swelling stomach. She rather liked her fuller breasts and she took trouble with her make-up. As she walked along the path she plucked a frangipani blossom and stuck it in her upswept hair.

Doyley grinned at her as she entered the terrace bar. 'You look, what's the word they use for brides and mothers to be? And not necessarily in that order . . . radiant. Yes. Glowing.'

'I've had a relaxing afternoon.' She glanced around. 'Is Blair about? Or Rosie?'

'Blair is out on the lawn with the zillionaires. Rosie sent a message to ask you to her suite for a drink before dinner with some pals.' Doyley raised an eyebrow. 'Everyone wants your company.'

'I'll just say hello to Blair and arrange to meet him later.' Jennifer heard laughter and saw the group, two couples, obviously the Americans, and Susie and Scott from Sooty. Susie was sitting in a deep cane chair, Blair perched on its arm. She saw Jennifer and nudged Blair. He stood up as Scott began to drag over another chair.

Jennifer shook her head. 'Don't bother, please, I'm not staying. Hello.' She nodded at Susie.

The two American men rose and beamed at her as Blair introduced her. Jennifer saw the approval in their eyes and warm smiles from their wives.

'How darling you look. Blair, she's lovely. And congratulations too, my dear.'

Susie stood up. 'Nice to see you again, Jennifer. Hope we see you over on Sooty Isle. You must be busy.'

'I am actually. I'll be sure to come over with Blair next time and stay for a couple of days. Lovely to meet you all, I'm just meeting some friends. See you at dinner.' Jennifer gave a wave and sailed outside feeling pleased with herself despite the unease she felt about 'sexy Susie'.

Rosie opened the door of her suite. Mac and Gideon were sitting on the sofa. 'Hi, good,

Doyley gave you the message. Come and have an aperitif.'

'How beautiful you look, Miss Jennifer,' smiled Gideon.

'You both look pretty spiffy too.' She sat down.

'We try to make an effort when we come to this bit of the island,' Mac said. 'Can't let Rosie down, have her entertaining a bunch of scruffy boffins.'

'Blair is entertaining some bejewelled American matrons, hubbies in golf shirts and plaid bermuda shorts. And the Sooty siren, Susie,' said Jennifer, raising her glass and taking a sip.

'Cheers.' Mac and Rosie exchanged a look. 'Jenny, we've been having a bit of a pow-wow and we don't want to put you in an awkward situation,' began Mac, 'but Rosie is concerned and so we thought we'd be up-front with you.'

'It's about Blair and those two slick boys, isn't it?' said Jennifer. 'What are they up to?'

'We're not sure. Except they don't wield much power internationally so they can't do too much harm. Big dreamers, opportunists. There's always someone with an eye on the main chance,' said Rosie. 'I've come across them a lot. It's just that here, on Branch Island, I'd hate to see them try and turn this into a mega resort.'

'We're a bit worried there is a campaign afoot to discredit the research station or make the resort look bad, something to give them some leverage,' said Mac.

'If they do their homework they might change their mind,' said Gideon. 'I wouldn't worry too much.'

'Blair said that Fanzio and Holding wanted to do a report on the possibility of upgrading the resort, whatever that means,' said Jennifer. 'There's a journo coming in to write a glitzy story. For some travel magazine.'

'I don't like the sound of that. It hasn't been run past me,' said Rosie.

'If they want to change the resort they're hardly going to have it written up in glowing terms as it is,' mused Gideon.

'I don't trust journos coming in on freebies,' said Rosie. 'Maybe they're paying their way, as they're supposed to, and we won't know who they are.'

'Nothing wrong with that,' said Mac. 'I'm more concerned about the research station. The university board gets toey about bad publicity.'

'Why don't you get your own PR man in, write up all the interesting work being done,' said Jennifer. 'Carmel's whale genetics study, Kirsty's coral reproduction, Rudi's plants. And what about Isobel? And you, Gideon? Lloyd was telling me about your hubble-bubble, diving-bell thingy.'

They all burst out laughing.

'I've never heard it described like that,' chuckled Gideon. 'I keep a low profile, thanks. No one knows me and I prefer to keep it that way.'

Rosie was looking thoughtful. 'It's not a bad idea to get some other publicity, stuff that promotes the island as a conservation centre. Not the sort of place you'd expect to find spas, flunkies and a casino.'

'What about Tony Adams? I thought Lloyd had talked to him about a story on the research station,' said Jennifer.

They all looked at each other, remembering the serious, reclusive war correspondent.

'Do you think he'd be interested?' asked Rosie. 'He's exactly the type of journalist we need. Someone prepared to do a story, not an investigative piece exactly but an in-depth article. Or series of articles. Plus he's a very good photographer.'

'Ask him,' said Gideon. 'And we say nothing.'

Jennifer sat through dinner, smiling, nodding, listening, asking an occasional question about life in Minnesota, bored rigid as the woman talked about her kids. Susie, on the other hand, was bubbly, effusively promoting the resort and Sooty Isle. Jennifer wondered if she received a commission for every guest who went there. When they all left the dining room, heading for the bar and a nightcap, Jennifer excused herself, pleading tiredness. Blair took her to one side.

'I might be late, these guys like to party on. I forgot to tell you, Aunty Vi rang. Nothing dramatic apparently. Maybe you'd better call them. Use the phone in my office. I told Heather on the desk.'

'You could have told me before dinner,' said Jennifer. 'Vi wouldn't ring here unless it was important.'

'I didn't speak to her. But the message said it wasn't urgent.'

'It's something to do with my mother. For sure,' sighed Jennifer. 'Don't be too late, Blair.'

He lifted his shoulders. 'Why not? I can walk home, it's business.'

'Fine. Please yourself.' Jennifer was tired. She went in to reception and asked Heather if she could use the phone in Blair's office.

'Vi, it's me. Is anything up? Sorry to call so late. Blair just told me you rang.'

'How are you, sweetheart, feeling all right?'

'I'm fine. Never looked better, I'm told. What's the problem?'

'It's your mum. She has a bee in her bonnet.'

'Why am I not surprised? What is it?'

'Ah darling, maybe you should come and visit. Talk her out of this hair-brained scheme. She misses you such a lot. We all do. You seem so far away . . .'

'What hair-brained scheme, Vi?'

'She wants to be near you. Help with the baby.'

'Well, I understand that, but look where I am. She can't come here.' *Thank God.*

'She's moving to Headland Bay. She's found a unit. Overlooking the water, no less. With two bedrooms.'

'Oh, no. Holy shit, I don't believe it. Sorry, Vi. I mean she hasn't moved, rented it, signed anything yet? Has she?'

'She's being vague. You know how she just changes the subject when she doesn't want to tell you anything.'

It's called evasive and devious. 'Yeah, I know. Well, what do I do? I don't want to get you in the poo so she knows you rang.'

'Call her for a chat in the morning. I won't say anything. I just thought you'd better know, luv.'

'You bet. Thanks so much, Vi. Is Uncle Don okay?'

'We're all fine. Wish we could see you.'

'Maybe I'd better come for a flying visit. Baby shopping, seeing a doctor, something like that. Settle her down.'

'Oh, I'm so relieved, Jenny. We've been that worried. She gets an idea and no one can talk her out of it, or say anything.'

'Don't worry. It's a silly idea. We could be gone from here in six months. Be in Europe or something. You never know with Blair.'

'Oh dear. I don't like the sound of that. That's even further away. We'll never get to see that baby.' She sounded teary.

'Vi, I doubt it will happen. But we have to make Mum understand that Blair's career will have us moving around. While he's heading up the ranks we could be sent anywhere for any length of time. That's what we tell her, okay?'

'I get you, luv. I'll leave it to you. Sorry if I bothered you.'

'Vi, thank God you did. We'd better nip this in the bud. Don't worry. I love you lots.'

'Same here, darling. Look after yourselves. You and that wee one.'

A trip back to Sydney. Jennifer liked the idea,

even if it meant dealing with her mother. She could deliver the work to Professor Dawn, talk about further study. Isobel's voice echoed in her mind as she washed her face and got ready for bed. *We all have choices. Some we make and some we stumble over. It is up to you to change the direction of your destiny.*

Jennifer looked at her shiny face smeared in cleanser in the mirror. Blue eyes looked back, steady, unflinching. 'Looks like I have some decisions to make,' she said aloud. And, for once, she didn't feel insecure or the need to ask for someone else's opinion, whether it was Blair's, Vi's, a professor's or a girlfriend's.

C'est la vie. She reached for the box of tissues. 'Christina, you're a worry,' she said aloud. 'But you're not winning this one.'

12

Reef Walking

JENNIFER SLID OUT OF bed as the tiny alarm clock tingled. Blair stirred but didn't wake. It was dark. Three a.m. This is crazy, she thought. But she was alert and up for whatever Isobel had planned. They'd agreed to meet on the beach outside the terrace bar. It was cool, so Jennifer wore a tank top under her T-shirt, put on her canvas reef shoes, grabbed the torch and tiptoed outside.

There was a shriek followed by moans and soft feathery scufflings as she stepped into the hunched shapes of mutton birds along the path. Neither she nor Blair heard their nightly courting and squabbles any longer, even though they sounded like babies being murdered. She still wondered why the birds chose to make holes in the middle of pathways. The resort placed boards over these with 'Caution. Mutton Bird Nest' stencilled on top.

Jennifer turned off the torch as she came into the resort grounds. She could see well enough by the dim illumination from lights at the base of trees and along the pathway. There was also enough light from the moon, which was high and cast a glow in the sky and on the surface of the quiet ocean. She walked past the swimming pool where the trapped water shone in the pearly light. The tide was out, leaving a creamy stretch of sand between the coral ledge and the heavy rocks at the base of the resort seawall.

A firefly light flickered and she judged it to be Isobel walking, stopping, waving the beam of her torch. Jennifer went along the wooden walkway and found the steps leading to the sand. She was halfway along the beach heading for the water's edge when it occurred to her, what if it wasn't Isobel? Glancing behind her, Jennifer saw the low buildings of the resort apartments, doors and windows open to the sea breeze. One shout or scream and people would raise the alarm. She wasn't afraid, but the memory of Willsy's attack on Rhonda still troubled her.

The torch light beckoned her and she could make out the small neat figure of Isobel against the silvery backdrop of the water.

'We have a perfect night,' said Isobel softly.

'I've been here for an hour and there's a lot to see.'

'Really? It's dark. Empty looking,' said Jennifer, falling into step as they walked away from the resort.

In response Isobel stopped, touched Jennifer's arm and pointed her narrow beam of light at the shining liquid-like sand. 'Look, see the bubbles and bumps? This is feeding time, all manner of animals are sifting through the wash, filtering nutrients. See?' She had a stick in her other hand and she scraped away the sand to expose a busy mollusc and sea worm, burrowing in their sifting search for food. 'And look here . . . no disguising itself.' The outline of a perfect star lay just below the surface. 'It's taking in water and pushing it out through its porous upper side.'

Jennifer bent down and smoothed the sand from the starfish, marvelling at its beautiful pattern. They swung their torches further up the beach, catching scuttling, prancing crabs emerging from holes to race after minuscule prey or furiously burrowing from sight, leaving a tiny bunch of sand grapes as a locked door behind them.

They shone their wavering torchbeams into the shallows where flashes of small glinting fish were being steathily followed by an ominous dark shadow that suddenly flicked its tail and rocketed into the middle of the fish, shattering the school into seeming shards of glass.

'Reef shark. Small and harmless,' said Isobel.

They continued walking, alert to small sounds,

swinging their torches in unison when they heard a scratch or a plop or a rustle from the fringe of undergrowth at the top of the beach. There were no large dunes, the sand petered out into waxy grasses and vines that thickened around the roots of the pandanus and what Isobel called the sea trees. But the soil was sandy until further inland where it was enriched by the layers of bird droppings, leaves and seeds built up as the vegetation, fed by rainwater, flourished.

A slight breeze stirred the pearly water and Isobel sniffed the air. 'Dawn is coming. I always feel its presence. The temperature changes, the air and water stir, birds waken, these night creatures creep away. It is the best time of the day.'

'I remember waking up early and lying in my bed back at our farm,' reminisced Jennifer. 'I was little and I'd listen to the cattle, the birds' dawn chorus, hear my dad put his boots on and clump down the hall, the sounds of him making that first pot of tea. My brother and my mother always slept in, waiting for Dad to bring them tea and toast. But we always had the first pot, him and me, quietly in the kitchen. He'd go and do chores and I'd sit outside in my dressing gown, the dew melting or the frost crunchy on the grass – we had an outside dunny. Then I'd sit on the back step and watch the world come to life. Then Dad'd come back and make more tea and toast and wake the house. I don't think my mother even knew my dad and I had that quiet time together. We hardly ever spoke, but he might point out something, or come back and say, "Molly had her calf." Something like that.'

'Lovely,' murmured Isobel.

'And what I remember most, apart from the sense of a special time with my father – even though he might be across the paddock – was noticing little things. Dad said I was a great observer of nature. And I realise I've lost that. Well, till now. You're opening my eyes again.' Jennifer paused. 'You and my dad would've liked each other.' *Despite my dad being reticent, scared of my mother, insecure. Strong and vibrant and clever as you are, Isobel, I still think you two would have had a rapport.*

'Anyone who opens a child's eyes to the world is a special person. So you miss him?'

'My father? I hardly knew him, so I don't miss him as a person. I only remember him as a cipher, bossed by my mother. I miss the *idea* of him, of having a father figure. He might not have been the sort of father I wanted, but at least being there – even in the shadows – is better than the dependent, obsessive relationship I'm left with – just Mum and me.'

'Do you ever think that not having a male role model has affected your relationships with men?'

'Relationships?' Jennifer gave a hollow laugh. 'Can't say I was lucky enough to have had a series of inappropriate relationships. Blair has been it.'

'Your mother likes him? She's probably happy you didn't have unhappy dalliances, yes?'

'Isobel, my mother wouldn't approve if I'd

married a charming handsome crown prince of never-never land. No one was ever going to be good enough in her book.'

'Oh dear. And is she happy about the baby?'

'You never know. She can't come out and say, "Wonderful, terrific, I'm thrilled." Straight off, she goes into negative or organising mode. I have no idea what I'm doing. I should do this or that. I suppose it's to make her feel wanted.'

'Yes. And you've spent your life trying to adjust to and address her needs. What about yours?' asked Isobel. 'You can't please everyone else all the time. What about looking after you?'

Please don't ask if Blair nurtures me. 'I'm doing that now. Health and stuff.'

Isobel touched Jennifer's arm. 'Because you're pregnant. I mean in general, looking out for your needs, mental, emotional and intellectual. Not just physical.'

Jennifer couldn't answer. There wasn't anyone that fulfilled those needs. Carefully she said, 'I suppose I get a little bit of all those things from different people.'

Isobel nodded to herself and they walked a little further in silence. The intimacy of the night was fading. They could now see well enough and they turned off their torches.

'There, up ahead, that's what I want to show you.' Isobel quickened her step but Jennifer couldn't see anything.

'There are her tracks. She hasn't come back down yet.' She pointed to a single set of distinctive tracks leading from the water to the top of the sand.

To Jennifer it looked like the imprint of a set of tyres with a strange tread. A single straight line ran up the centre between them. 'Is it a turtle? What's that line between the tracks?'

'The base of the female's shell as it drags through the sand. She'll still be laying. Don't stand in front of her.'

Isobel followed the tracks to the edge of the sand and vines where a huge hollow had been dug. There, in the centre, the enormous green turtle was laying her hundred or more eggs, one by one. Quietly they sat behind her to one side, awed by the concentration and effort of the old turtle.

Jennifer was moved, empathising as a mother-to-be. 'She's crying! Look at the tears rolling down her leathery old face,' she whispered.

'No, it's a secretion to stop her eyes drying out. But I always think it must be stressful for them. These turtles were born here, and they swim vast distances back to this same spot to leave their eggs, and then they never see their babies hatch to live or die. Only about two per cent ever survive,' said Isobel.

'So many predators,' sighed Jennifer. 'I feel like such a voyeur, do you mind if we go now?'

'I know how you feel. It always disturbs me when groups of tourists watch, chattering, taking photographs.' Isobel got to her feet. 'Let's cross down the beach to Coral Point and go to Gideon's for breakfast.'

'Will he be up?'

'If not, we'll wake him,' said Isobel cheerfully. *Blair would have a fit if I woke him up and brought someone home for breakfast.* 'I'm ravenous. Sounds good.'

Just before they reached the end of the beach they saw the flash from a camera.

'Early-morning tourists,' said Isobel.

Three or four people were standing in a group and in the lavender light Jennifer could make out the gouge marks in the sand. One turned as they approached.

'The poor thing, what an effort. We watched her bury this huge heap of eggs,' he pointed to an obvious mound in the sand, well above the high-water mark. 'And it's taken her ages to get this far.'

'A long night's work,' agreed Isobel.

Jennifer watched the exhausted turtle dig in her flippers and drag herself a few centimetres forward. She waited, gathered her strength and heaved her enormous shell dome once more.

'They're so graceful and move so easily in the water,' one of the tourists said.

They continued to watch as the growing dawn cast a pink wash over the wet sand, the surface of the sea and the turtle's barnacled shell. There was a mutual sigh as the turtle reached the edge of the sea and, rapidly now, pushed herself into the water. Soon all that could be seen was the top of her shell and her head, beady old eyes focused on some distant place.

'See you next year,' someone called.

'Come on, there's another turtle back that way.'

The group headed towards the resort and Jennifer and Isobel started on the path over the small headland. They stopped in the pisonia forest to watch the morning mayhem of noddy terns beginning their day, laughing at the hundreds of pairs squabbling, kissing, preening, nest building.

Isobel nudged Jennifer as they walked towards Gideon's shack. 'I smell bacon and coffee.'

A short while later the three of them were relaxing in old canvas deck chairs in front of the barbecue hotplate where Gideon had put two thick pieces of bread to toast and soak up the remains of the egg, sausages and bacon drippings. The morning sun shone on the sea.

'So you were turtle-spotting this morning, Miss Jennifer? You'll have to be there, when they hatch. What else have you planned for our keen student, Isobel?'

'Just awakening the senses. She has been modest about her accomplishments. Mac suggested she enroll with him to do honours,' said Isobel. 'And having a baby is no reason not to,' she added. 'Mac will supervise her research. If she gets first-class honours she can go on to a doctorate.'

'I am tempted, I have to admit. It's just completing it if we move overseas as Blair is threatening. He's so mesmerised by the slick boys, as Rosie calls them.'

Isobel shrugged and waved a hand. 'Pshaw, I

wouldn't pay any attention to such plans. Rosie says they're opportunists with no clout. Corporate politics, corruption, wheeling-dealing. They just want to make swift dollars for themselves. They won't help your husband's career, they'll use him. Believe me, I have seen masters at work in such matters.'

'We're interested in you, Jennifer lass,' Gideon said. 'There's a lot of exciting work happening here. It might all appear to be a university summer camp, but there's government interest in what Rudi is turning up, for example.'

'What government department might that be?' asked Isobel. 'Fisheries?'

'They're a bit vague, which flags secretive to me,' said Gideon. 'Mac will find out more, I guess. It's to do with plant toxins.'

'Chemicals, biological warfare?' laughed Jennifer.

'Do not jest, young lady. The secrets under the sea are just being sniffed at. Though,' he gave a small bow in Isobel's direction, 'our esteemed friend here has garnered much kudos and many accolades for her research, her achievements as an oceanographer and her daring exploits.'

Jennifer nodded. 'I know you say the information on the internet isn't always accurate, but I've done a bit more homework on you, Isobel. How you dived in one of the first submersibles with a lock-out chamber so you could leave the vehicle under water, go and explore, and come back with samples.'

'Like the moon astronauts,' agreed Gideon. 'Plus living under water in a special laboratory for several weeks for a secret government experiment.'

'And I was four months' pregnant when I did it.' She grinned.

'I thought you were most famous for doing the world's deepest dives,' said Jennifer.

Isobel gave a casual shrug. 'Whatever it takes to achieve the end. Yes, we want to know more about what is in the deepest, unknown part of the ocean. But if my exploits draw the attention of world decisionmakers and thinkers and make them understand the need to protect oceans, that is more important.'

'Hence we have a mutual effort here.' Gideon gestured with his thumb behind him. 'We mightn't have all the money that outfits like NASA have, but we're brave – some might say foolhardy – warriors and explorers.'

'He means we're either the Wright brothers or Einstein – so far no one has bettered our efforts,' said Isobel.

'That's not hard. No one knows about us,' laughed Gideon.

Jennifer realised their light banter had a serious edge. 'You're not seriously going down again in the ocean in that machine of yours, Gideon?'

'Please, I take offence. The sharkmobile may be experimental but it's created from solid principles that we know work,' said Gideon.

'Gideon has engineering and aeronautical degrees as well as marine experience,' said Isobel.

'We're not out to break world records, we consider ourselves scientific detectives.'

'Spying in the deep. Who's for more tea?'

'Is this research being recorded in some way?' asked Jennifer.

'Mac has that under control. Plus it seems we will have an outside observer from the media,' said Gideon.

'The media? Is that wise?'

'Only if something goes wrong,' laughed Isobel. 'We are being guided by Mac. He's been talking to the journo and he seems sympathetic and supportive.'

'He was here before. You met him, Jennifer – Tony Adams. He's going to write us up for some serious, quality magazine,' said Gideon.

'The war correspondent? He was nice. Seemed genuine,' said Jennifer, wondering why Tony had agreed. He'd seemed so lost and unsure of his career plans.

'But no one is to know. It's not a tourist story,' said Isobel. 'Maybe best you don't mention it to your husband. And when will I meet him?'

'Come over to the resort and have dinner with us. And Rosie. I'll invite Mac and Gideon too. It will be nice to entertain some of my friends instead of being with Blair's buddies.'

'Lovely. Now I must get back. Gideon, I'll see you with Rudi and Mac later this morning. And thank you for breakfast.' Isobel got to her feet.

'I'll help you clean up, Gideon,' said Jennifer. 'And Isobel, thank you.' She hugged Isobel in a rush of affection and a feeling she couldn't describe.

As Jennifer carried their dishes inside she saw on the long rough wooden table large sheets of paper with designs and specifications. Photocopies of photographs and graphs were piled beside them.

'Would you like me to explain in more detail about how the submersible works? I had my first dive in Cousteau's bathyscaphe in the 1960s and I was hooked. Gave up flying for diving.'

Two hours flew by. Jennifer was entranced at Gideon's stories and plans and dreams. He told her of his brilliant academic life, how he upset his parents by joining the airforce, marrying a girl from the Cook Islands, and embarking on a life that took him from being a seafarer, a teacher, an amateur scientist and a shipwright to being a coconut plantation owner.

'And now beachcomber. My wife died two years ago. I have a son who runs a business in Rarotonga in the Cook Islands and looks after his mother's family. My daughter lives in England. Very proper. I visit them. Maybe the grandchildren will come and stay here with me sometime.'

'I think grandkids would think you and this place utter heaven,' said Jennifer. 'I wish I had a dad, a grandad like you.'

'You can borrow me any time. In fact, what say I be a stand in grandpop for that little mite when she comes along?' He pointed at Jennifer's neat bulge.

'Wonderful! Thanks, Gideon. I don't know

why you and Isobel say she though. It might be a he.'

'I never argue with Isobel,' he grinned. 'If she says it's a girl it will be.'

Dinner the following night at the resort was Jennifer's evening. She sat between Mac and Gideon, Rosie and Isobel sat on either side of Blair. Blair was uncomfortable. Jennifer noticed Isobel seemed to be plying him with questions and she knew he'd hate that.

Doyley had gone to some trouble to set their table in a far corner of the verandah and moved in several large potted palms to give them extra privacy. Rosie had ordered some good wine and the staff on duty were attentive and cheerful, not just because their two bosses were at the table. Everyone liked Jennifer even though they didn't see as much of her as they saw of Blair. In the kitchen the staff gossiped, pleased to see Jennifer was in control of the evening. Blair was patently bored and as dessert was served he excused himself to see to the other guests.

'You stay and enjoy yourself, Rosie. I'll do the rounds.' He left the table, nodding to Isobel. 'It's been interesting to meet you.'

'And for me also.' She smiled but her eyes were coolly appraising.

Later Gideon and Isobel left, and Rosie, Mac and Jennifer returned to the terrace bar. Rosie excused herself after one drink.

'I might sneak away, seeing as Blair is holding the fort. It's been a fun evening, thanks for organising it, Jenny.' She stopped at the bar and spoke to Blair who was chatting with some new arrivals.

'So you like Isobel, eh? I knew you two would get on,' said Mac.

'Oh Mac, I can't thank you enough for introducing me to everyone. It's saved my life here. I'd be crazy without you all to talk to, and what's going on at the research station. Thank you, thank you.' She squeezed his hand.

Mac looked pleased. 'You're one of the gang now. I gather you spent time with Gideon and seem *au fait* with what he and Isobel are doing. Why not get more involved?'

'In what way? I mean, could I really switch to marine biology honours?'

'We can arrange it. If you go for first-class honours it would be an intensive year and if you get it you can apply for a PhD scholarship. My other thought, after speaking with Isobel, is the writing. I read what you gave me of Dawn's book. You have a lovely sensitive style. You make him look far better than he is. A bit unprofessional to say that, but I read his notes and your rewrite. I hope he paid you well.'

'Slow down, Mac. If I can work on my honours degree in a practical way while I'm here and then, wherever Blair and I end up, hopefully I can consider the PhD, though how I'd manage the practical side if we end up in the mountains in Europe or something . . .'

Mac held up his hand. 'One thing at a time. Get your honours first. I'll assign you to one of the teams. Does Rudi's work interest you? Or Carmel's?'

'Yes, Rudi's interests me. But then so does everyone's. I'll have to find my way a bit. Having stayed away from the sea as far as possible.'

'Be guided by Isobel. Our other thought is we'd like you to document and write up some parts of Isobel and Gideon's experiments.'

'I thought Tony Adams was coming to do that.'

'On a different level, for a different audience. You could collaborate, share information. Yours would be more academic with the aim, because of your writing style, of reaching a mainstream audience as well.'

'Mac, I have to go to Sydney next week, let me think about it while I'm gone.'

'No medical problems?' he asked, looking concerned.

'No, I'm seeing the doc in Headland on the way. I feel great. Have to settle my mother down. She's fussing, wants to move closer.' Jennifer rolled her eyes.

'Understandable.'

'Mac, believe me, you wouldn't want my mother in close proximity.'

He leaned towards her. 'Jenny, I know family can be a pain, and I know your history, but when you don't have them around, you can have regrets.'

Jennifer looked into his kind blue eyes and knew he was thinking of his lost daughter. 'Dear Mac, thanks for that. I've had years of regrets. Much as I miss having a father, I can't help feeling angry at him for pissing off and taking the easy way out. Even *he* couldn't cope with my mother. So I'm saddled with a hurt, bitter, lonely, dependent woman.'

'You have to think about your life, your future, your child now.'

'I know. Isobel has made me see that.' She straightened up. 'So I'm off to Sydney to do battle with mother's quips and forked tongue,' she laughed.

'Drive carefully. When you come back I'll have all the paperwork for you to start work. You'd better tell Blair.'

'No point really. Why give him something to gripe about? So long as I'm occupied and happy, that's all he wants.'

'You two don't share much,' said Mac, draining his glass and standing up.

'Ah, I don't know about that.' Jennifer patted her tummy. 'We share this.'

Mac kissed her cheek as he wished her goodnight, but his eyes were sad. 'Like I said, be guided by Isobel. Thank you for dinner.'

The drive to Sydney was uneventful until she approached Hornsby and hit the early evening traffic. Jennifer drove past Blair's house in Glebe.

He'd asked her to make sure the renters hadn't damaged the property, and they hadn't as far as she could see from the outside. As she slowed the car she thought of the time she'd lived in this terrace with Blair and it seemed a lifetime ago. She'd never felt attached to the place because Blair had bought it and decorated it.

She now felt more at home in the tiny cabin on Branch Island. The anonymity had given them equal opportunity to make it their own space. Blair took little interest, setting up his favourite personal items in his office. Jennifer had her bits – driftwood, an abandoned bird's nest dropped from a tree, pictures, posters, books and CDs – around her. Having a work space at the research station had made a difference. As she drove to Vi and Don's she thought she might drag out some favourite cushions, photographs and her framed degree, stored in Don's shed, to take back.

Jennifer had given Christina ten days' notice of her visit so she could rearrange her social life and they could go shopping, do some things together. She was trying to work out how and when to tell Christina, in a firm but loving way, that moving to Headland Bay was a crazy idea.

It was dusk as she drove into Vi and Don's. Jennifer pushed open the front door, calling, 'Yoo hoo, anyone here? Mmm, what smells so good?'

Vi came bustling to the door, wiping her hands on her apron. 'Oh darling, it's so good to see you.' She stepped back and patted Jennifer's belly.

'You're starting to show! Jenny, this is so lovely. Don, Don . . .'

'I'm here, luv.' He was beaming, and hugged Jennifer. 'You look terrific. Lookit that suntan. Come on, come and sit down, you must be tired. I couldn't do a drive like that any more.'

'I am weary.' She looked around, 'Don't tell me Mum is out somewhere?'

Vi and Don exchanged a quick look. 'Kind of, come on, luv, sit down first. How about a nice cuppa, or do you want a sherry? Maybe you shouldn't, eh?' Vi bustled into the kitchen.

Jennifer sat at the breakfast table. 'A cold beer wouldn't go astray, if you've got one, Don.'

'Oh, he's got a little fridge out there with his birds, haven't you, luv,' said Vi as Don headed out the back door. 'He loves to sit there with a tinnie and watch those birds of his when he comes home from work. If it relaxes him, why not?'

'You bet. So, where's Mum? How is she? I thought I told her I'd be here today.'

'Oh you did, luv. She had it circled in red on the calendar. Oh Jen-Jen, I don't know how to tell you,' Vi sat across from her, twisting her apron.

'What? Has she had an accident? Is she sick? What is it?'

'No, no, nothing like that, luv. She's gone. Up and went. We tried and tried to talk her out of it.'

Jennifer went cold and closed her eyes for an instant. 'God, what now. Gone where?'

'Headland Bay. Packed and flew up yesterday. We didn't know whether to ring your mobile to try and stop you coming. Don thought it'd be too late. We didn't think she'd really go. But she did.'

'You might need something stronger than this.' Don put the cold beer in front of her as Vi leapt to get a glass for Jennifer.

'You mean she's gone to visit me when she knew I was coming down here? I suppose she knew I'd give her an earful.' Jennifer poured the beer into a glass and gulped the frothing brew.

'It's not a visit, Jen,' said Don quietly. 'She's gone, bag and baggage.'

'Told everyone her daughter needs her and with the baby on the way you wouldn't be able to live on that island.'

'Damn her!' Jennifer thumped the table, tiredness and frustration hitting her. 'Well, she'll just have to move back. Sorry Vi, Uncle Don.'

'She said she'd paid a year's lease on that place,' said Don. 'Hasn't even been there.'

'It could be horrible,' Jennifer said.

'Don't say that, she thinks you're going to stay there too,' said Vi. 'We saw the brochure from the real estate people, it looks very nice.'

'Well, she can't stay with us on the island. You didn't mention about the empty unit next to ours?'

Vi shook her head. 'I wouldn't worry about that. She doesn't like the idea of going over there at all. What are you going to do? She might be able to get a refund on the apartment if someone else takes the place over.'

'Who's going to make her move?' asked Don. 'We talked till we were blue in the face.'

'I wish I'd known she was really going to do this. You know how she talks and never follows through. Anyway, you'll have your home back, just the two of you, after all these years.' Jennifer choked up, thinking how good they were. How they'd opened their home and their hearts to her and her mother and never complained.

'Family, luv. What can you do? We always said you have a home here. You will bring the little one to visit?' asked Vi, looking teary.

'You bet, you can have her all to yourself too. But we'll bring you up to stay. You'll love the island.'

'And what does Blair think . . . about your mum moving there?'

He sees it as my problem. 'He doesn't know too much. He has enough on his plate, I didn't want to worry him,' said Jennifer.

'Well, maybe it won't be so bad. You can go over and see your mum, have lunch and things when you see the doctor,' said Don, reaching for another beer.

'While I'm here let's do just that. Found any-where new to eat, Vi?'

'She's planning on doing a lot more fancy cooking,' said Don. 'You know your mum didn't like anything a bit, you know, foreign.'

'Then we'll lash out, try a few places, and I'll go back earlier than planned. She is naughty, though, running off without waiting to discuss it with me,' said Jennifer.

'You know your mum, luv.'

'I do indeed, Vi. That's the trouble.' *Being away from Christina makes me realise how much easier and happier life can be*. 'Anyway, my other big news is I'm doing a uni course. Maybe some writing for them, and planning to study. Over dinner I'll tell you all about these great people and what they're doing. I'll go and freshen up first.'

'You do that, luv.' Vi and Don looked at each other as Jennifer left the room. 'Poor darling. Tina's not going to give her or that baby a minute's peace.'

The drive back to Headland Bay passed in a blur. Jennifer ran through a dozen scenarios in her mind, till she was just too exhausted to think further. She played a John Butler CD and pulled into a motel for the night. She drove away early the next morning and by lunchtime was in Headland Bay. She unloaded a couple of boxes and bags at the wharf, asking Vera to get her on the cat.

Vera gave her a surprised look. 'You're back early, aren't you?'

'Yep.' Jennifer smiled. 'Can't wait to get back.'

'Do they know?' Vera busied herself with the reservation list.

'I'm my own boss, Vera. I'll just return the car to storage.'

While waiting to board the cat, Jennifer ordered a coffee and looked at the happy faces of visitors waiting to go to the island. She kept wondering if she'd spot her mother. Somewhere in the sprawl of units and holiday rentals along the seafront Christina was settling in to her new home.

You didn't call me. I'm not calling you, thought Jennifer and joined the passengers getting on the catamaran.

Once the safety spiel had finished and the video of the reef was playing, Vera came over to Jennifer. 'Congratulations, by the way. How are you feeling?'

'I never thought I'd say this, but I'm looking forward to getting back to Branch.' She patted her tummy. 'And now I've a lot more to keep me occupied.'

Doyley was on the wharf with Rosie, greeting and directing the new arrivals.

'Hey, there's Jennifer! You're back early.' Doyley leaned over to speak to Rosie.

'Should've let us know you were coming back early.' Rosie took Jennifer's bag from her. 'Come and have a coffee and tell me how it went.'

'I'll go back to the unit first . . .'

'Nah, come on. I'm anxious to hear. Doyley, can you take Jennifer's stuff over to her place?' Rosie looked at Doyley, who took the bag. Both looked a bit grim.

'Any other stuff?'

'Heaps. Went baby shopping. You know what I mean, got a few essentials and non-essentials too.' Jennifer laughed.

Rosie took her arm and steered her past the tourists.

'What's up? You look tense,' said Jennifer.

'Few problems. Anyway, I'll fill you in on our news. Let's see, that journo Tony is back. Plus, I've got a new staff kid who's arrived from England. No one is supposed to know but he's someone's son. I feel like I'm being spied on.'

'You do seem frazzled, Rosie.'

'Never mind me. What's your news?'

Jennifer blurted out her news about her mother moving to Headland.

'So you haven't confronted her? When are you doing that?'

'When I feel strong enough. I just couldn't wait to get back here. There's something to be said for getting away from it all on a small island.'

Rosie turned away. 'Look, I have to deal with something a bit urgent. Meet me over at reception. There's, er, some mail and stuff for you. I'll be there in a minute.'

Jennifer shrugged as Rosie hurried off and caught Doyley's arm and spoke to him. Passing two of the housekeeping staff, who cleaned Jennifer and Blair's cabin, she smiled and nodded to them.

The girls stopped, mumbled a greeting, looked at each other, then said a hurried goodbye and raced away.

Jennifer passed the boutique and remembered she wanted toothpaste.

'Hi, Lesley –' Before she could say anything, the girl behind the counter gave her a strange look.

'I thought you were away!'

'I decided to come back early. Why? What's going on around here?'

'Oh, nothing. Just the usual.' Lesley put the toothpaste on the counter with what Jennifer thought was a forced smile. 'Anything else?'

Jennifer walked from the shop and found Rosie waiting for her.

'Um, your mail has been sent over. Not to worry.'

'Rosie, what the hell is going on? Everyone is being really odd, cagey kind of. Is Blair all right? Where is he?'

'Working. He's around. He wasn't expecting you back today. Come over to my place and have a coffee.' Rosie asked Jennifer about Sydney, shopping, trivial stuff, as she made the coffee.

Jennifer could tell she wasn't interested in what she was saying. 'Rosie, tell me what's going on? What's happened?'

'We're friends, right? And I'm Blair's boss. There's something you should know and I think it's best I tell you. It's hard to keep secrets in a small community.' She placed their coffee mugs on the small table and sat down. Jennifer just looked at her, faint puzzlement in her clear blue eyes.

'Damn Blair, this is hard.' Rosie took a breath. 'Blair has been having a bit of a fling. I'm sure it's nothing serious, but he was stupid and he's been caught out. Probably normal for a man with a pregnant wife, feeling trapped a bit . . . Oh shit.'

'What!' Rosie's words didn't make sense.

Rosie winced. 'Jenny, I know this is hard . . .'

'What do you mean – a fling?' Jennifer's voice was a whisper. 'Do you mean seeing someone, or . . . sleeping with someone? Who? Oh God, don't tell me. That Susie. Right? Right?' Her voice rose.

Rosie nodded miserably. 'Yes. He was over on Sooty and they came back together, nothing wrong with that. We had a meeting. But two mornings later one of the housekeeping staff came and told me.'

'He had her in our place? In our *bed*?' Jennifer thought she was going to throw up. Tears sprang from her eyes. 'The bitch. I'm having his *baby*!'

Rosie touched Jennifer's hand. 'Blair is just as much to blame in my book. I'm sorry, Jenny. I spoke to him and she's gone back to Sooty. I hate to tell you this, but everyone knows. It's between the two of you now.'

'Oh God, how could he?' She dropped her face in her hands. 'Why? Why Rosie? What've I done? I've never been mean or horrible to him. We didn't fight before I went away . . . Is it because I'm pregnant? How could he?'

'Jenny, stop blaming yourself.' Rosie would have hit Blair if he'd appeared at that instant. 'That Susie is a devil, she eats blokes, I reckon. Blair was stupid.'

'I can't go back and sleep there. Not now.'

'You can stay here, there are a couple of empty suites.'

Jennifer couldn't stop the tears. She jumped to her feet, pacing around the room. 'It's so cruel.

How could he hurt me like this? Upset me? What about the baby?' she almost shouted at Rosie. 'And everybody knows! I feel awful. What am I going to do?'

'Jenny, don't get hysterical. Calm down. Listen to what he has to say.'

'Yeah, what *can* he say? Sorry? That's not enough, Rosie.'

Rosie was inclined to agree. 'Much as I'd like to, I can't get rid of Susie easily, she's on a contract . . .'

'I hope I never set eyes on her. How could she? She knows I'm pregnant, she knows everyone would find out. It's like she, they, did it deliberately to hurt me. Why?'

'I don't think they planned this, Jenny. It just . . . happened. Thrown together in a romantic place too much . . .'

'Well, I can't stay here, that's for sure. I feel such a fool. Everyone must be laughing at me.'

'No, they're not at all. Blair is very silly. This is going to undermine his authority with the staff. He's made things very difficult for himself.'

Jennifer turned her tear-stained face to Rosie. 'No, the staffies won't give a shit really. They all sleep around, have their fights and *flings* . . . If only my blasted mother wasn't over there I could move to Headland and commute here.'

'Give him a chance, Jenny, what with the baby coming. Don't let him be the one to push you out of your home. He can stay in one of the staff quarters.'

'I'm starting my marine biology course. See, every time I go to do something, get a life, Blair gets in the way.'

Rosie had been trying to be placatory and comforting. Personally she had little time for Blair other than as an employee. 'Leave him then.'

Jennifer didn't answer and looked away.

'Sorry. I shouldn't have said that. Listen, ride it out for a bit, keep your distance, don't do anything rash. You have to decide if, and how much, you love this guy. And don't let the baby influence that decision,' Rosie said firmly.

'That's easy to say.' Jennifer was in tears. She picked up her coffee and sipped but had trouble swallowing and put it down.

Rosie leaned over and wiped the milk from Jennifer's top lip with a napkin. 'You do what you feel is best for you. Not Blair, not the baby. We're all here for you. Isobel too. Now are you ready to see Blair now or later? He doesn't know you're back.'

'I'll go for a walk. Think about things for a bit. Does Isobel, Mac, Gideon know? Of course they must.' Jennifer stood up, her knees wobbly. 'I feel like I've walked into a brick wall. You know what's the most terrible thing at the moment? My mother. She's going to say, "I told you so." And she's going to say, "Men, you can't trust them." And she'll want me to move in with her. And she'll be so goddamned smug!'

Rosie tried not to smile. 'Leave your mother to Isobel and me. Just take it day by day. Go and see

Mac and Gideon and everyone at the research station. I'll have your things sent to suite twenty-five. What will I tell Blair?'

'I suppose he's hiding out with that Susie somewhere, doesn't want to see me,' said Jennifer. *How could he do this to me? And . . . why am I not really so surprised?*

'And dinner? Want to eat in here with me? I'll have something sent in.'

'Rosie, as the whole thing is public knowledge, I'm not going to run away and hide, like I've done something wrong. Could you ask Doyley to reserve a table in the middle of the dining room for Blair and me, please? And tell Blair I'll meet him there at eight p.m.'

Rosie blinked. 'You sure?'

'Don't worry, Rosie, there won't be any ugly scenes.' Jennifer opened the door.

'Pity, could've provided a bit of dinner entertainment for the guests,' joked Rosie. Her eyes were soft and sympathetic. 'Good for you, Jenny.'

'Thanks, Rosie. You're a pal.'

'You betcha. See you.'

The afternoon sun was losing its heat. People were straggling back to their rooms before the ritual of sunset drinks. Jennifer walked and walked, her mind whirling. She stopped, wondering where she was, and had no memory of how she got there. *This is ridiculous. I'm walking in my sleep. Isobel told me to walk with my eyes open.* She was on top of Coral Point, at the very edge of the small windswept peak with the great view across the ocean. The sweep of little Boomerang Cove was to one side, the beach leading back to the resort behind. One path led into the trees and across the island to Gideon's side, another branched off to the research station. The beach track went back to the resort. Somewhere there was a small track down to Boomerang Cove.

'You all right, mm . . . miss?'

She spun around to see old Patch standing behind her, hands in his pockets, one eye covered by his trademark black patch, the other eye popped out like an old poached egg. 'What do you want?'

'You're nnnnot going to jump, are you?' He stuttered, and took a step forward.

'Why would I do that?' she demanded. 'You stay back there. In fact, just go away. Leave me alone. Follow someone else,' Jennifer shouted.

'I jest want ttto help them. Young girls, they get inta trouble.' He had a whiney voice compounded with his stutter.

'Hello there!' Another man sauntered up the track from the trees.

'My God. Tony, it's great to see you!' Jennifer rushed past Patch, and grabbed Tony's arm, clinging to it tightly. 'I was just heading to the research station. Walk with me.' She half dragged him back the way he'd come.

'So long,' Tony nodded at Patch, who watched them for a few moments then shuffled away.

'Thanks for turning up.'

'Er, nice to see you. This is quite a welcome.

However, I was going the other way, to the resort.'

'No. Walk with me to Mac's. It seems I can't be trusted on my own at the moment.'

'Fine. You seemed to handle the old fellow quite well. What's his story?'

'God knows. Who cares. He's just the resident watchdog.'

'Oh, I see.' He looked bemused. 'So how are things with you?'

Jennifer glanced at his tanned face and smiling green eyes. His open expression indicated that he hadn't heard about Blair's affair.

'Tony, don't ask. Just let's walk and look at nature.' Jennifer took definite striding steps, staring ahead, trying to make her mind a blank.

'Fine,' said Tony easily. 'When we meet nature will you introduce me?'

Jennifer slowed her big angry steps, let go of his arm where her nails had dug in, ran her hands through her hair and almost smiled. 'Sorry. I am a bit overwrought.'

Tony didn't chat and Jennifer sensed he was unaware of what had happened, not that it would interest him. It was an easy silence, neither feeling the necessity to make idle talk. As they strolled, Jennifer's heart gradually stopped thudding, her breath slowed and, while there was a dull painful ache in her head, she felt slightly better. Almost a normal person. She could breathe without her breath catching or tears filling her eyes. As they walked through the thicket of trees and birds, something relatively large crashed across the track and stood in the dappled light.

'What was that?' Tony stepped cautiously off the path. 'Good grief, it's a little goat.'

Jennifer recognised Gideon's milking goat. 'Naughty girl, she's escaped.' She picked up the end of the chewed rope and drew the white doe to her. 'Tony, meet Nature.'

He smiled and patted the goat, who promptly butted him.

'Sometimes Nature can be cruel.' Jennifer laughed as if it was the funniest thing she'd ever thought or said. Then she stopped as she saw Tony giving her a quizzical look. 'Take no notice of me. It's been a difficult day.' *And it's going to be an even more difficult evening.*

Leading the goat, they walked into the research station to find Mac. And return Gideon's newly named goat.

Jennifer got ready in suite twenty-five, wishing she'd taken something more dressy to Sydney. She was not going to go back to the cabin and run into Blair. There was a tap at the door.

Rosie stood there clutching a bottle of champagne. 'Some Dutch courage. Want a drink before dinner?'

'I don't think I should. We'll probably have some wine with the meal.'

'Good thinking. I'll stow it to wet the baby's head. Or any other occasion you can think of. You look gorgeous.' She walked in and circled Jennifer, whose skin had a soft, luminous quality. Her eyes were bright and her shining hair fell in smooth waves to her shoulders, reminding Rosie of a 1930s movie star.

Jennifer looked down at her loose black velvet pants, held up with an elastic waistband, and her tailored man's-style white linen shirt. She had simple black sandals on her feet. 'I feel a bit underdressed. I wanted to make some statement, look smart and not like a schooner under full sail.' She smoothed the shirt over her protruding tummy.

She's thinking of Susie and not feeling good about herself, thought Rosie. 'Listen, no one can compete with a blooming, beautiful mum to be. But I know what you need . . . I'll be right back.'

Jennifer put on her perfume, one Blair had given her, and tried to think what to say, but her mind was a blank. Maybe he'd do all the talking and she could take the high moral ground.

Rosie came back into the room with a black box. 'Here, the finishing touch. Wear these.' She opened the box to reveal a rolled black leather band with a gold clip. Suspended from the necklace was a perfect Broome pearl hanging from a diamond clip. Two matching pearl and diamond earrings were beside it.

'God Rosie, they're stunning!'

'Aren't they just. Bev and I took an anniversary trip to Broome and lashed out. It's great with that outfit.'

Jennifer's eyes sparkled. 'Can I really borrow them? Just for tonight?'

Rosie took out the necklace and Jennifer turned around, lifting her hair as Rosie clipped it on. 'You feel a million bucks when you wear a great pearl. And the earrings.'

Jennifer stepped back and looked in the mirror. 'Wow. I love them.'

'Classy, elegant, glowing. The only words for it. You go in to dinner and stand your ground. Let him see you're the very best thing in his life.'

Jennifer walked into the dining room through the main doors. Often she and Blair nicked in through the side verandah door by the kitchen. Tonight, she walked slowly and deliberately across the length of the room, held her head high, aware of sidelong glances from the staff but also conscious of some admiring looks from guests. Blair was at the table. Doyley had a candle and a silk flower on their table that was central but discreetly screened by a few pot plants. Nevertheless, traffic to the buffet passed close by.

Blair half rose from his seat as the waiter pulled out Jennifer's chair. She gave the young waiter a dazzling smile, settled into her chair, smoothed the napkin the waiter flicked into her lap and finally looked at Blair across the table. His face, lit from below by the candle, had a somewhat spooky expression.

As the waiter hovered, Blair leaned across the table. 'Champagne, wine? Or lemon lime bitters?'

'A white wine, thanks. I'm being judicious. I'll switch to mineral water later.'

'Do you mind – I've ordered a bottle of red.'

Why should I? You've never asked before. 'Please yourself. What are you going to eat?'

They dithered over the choice of food as a means to delay any in-depth conversation and Blair's bottle of wine arrived. He lifted his glass. 'You look terrific. How was your trip, your mother? You came back early, didn't you?'

'I had a nice visit with Vi and Don. My mother has moved to Headland Bay, in anticipation of the big event. Figures I need her.'

'My God, she's there already? Where's she staying, what're her plans? She's not thinking of coming over here?'

'No, she hates the idea of being on an island.' *I know that feeling.* 'Actually, I didn't see her. Typically, she didn't tell me she was moving.'

'So you drove all the way to Sydney to find she'd gone? That'd be right.'

Although she agreed with him she bristled. 'I guess she was over anxious, I didn't give her much notice.'

'What are you going to do?'

He meant about Christina but it gave Jennifer the opening she'd been looking for. She folded her hands on the table.

'Do you mean about my mother or about us?' Seeing a quick guilty flicker in his eyes, she pressed on. 'Specifically about you and that girl. Susie.'

'Jesus, Jennifer, what are you talking about?'

'You know very well.'

'I've told you not to listen to gossip.' He took a large gulp of wine.

'Blair, don't try to deny it, at least give me that.'

Blair topped up his wine. Jennifer's glass of white had yet to arrive. 'It wasn't anything.'

'You slept with her,' she hissed.

'What do you want me to say then?'

'Sorry would be a good start.'

Blair didn't answer and Jennifer felt vulnerable despite her anger, but wasn't going to show it. 'Was it me? Why did you go off with . . . her?'

He twirled his glass, avoiding her eyes, and didn't answer.

'Just tell me what I did wrong, Blair. So it won't happen again.'

'Keep your voice down. It won't happen again.'

'How do I know that? Is it because I'm pregnant? I'm ugly? You don't want this baby?'

'Jesus, Jennifer, get yourself together. No. I don't know why it happened, for God's sake. Maybe I was lonely.'

'Lonely! You're always surrounded by people. I'm the one who's lonely.'

'How can you say that when you spend all your time with those other people? Talking academic stuff. You treat me like I'm some dummy because I didn't go to uni.'

Jennifer was stunned into silence as the waiter, who'd been waiting for an appropriate pause, placed her wine in front of her and quickly moved away.

'You've never told me that before. Blair, I don't think that at all. You're the one who's clever, entrepreneurial, who makes the money.'

'Don't tell me you don't have ambitions. I always feel you're just going along with my career plans until something better comes along for you.' He looked so crestfallen, so hurt, Jennifer was bewildered.

'I guess I had dreams, I wasn't sure how to achieve them. I felt trapped by what my mother expected me to do, become . . .'

'Your mother has a lot to answer for.'

'We can't blame her for this! I suppose I wanted it all, as they say. It didn't seem such a big ask. A husband, both of us with careers, a family one day. Why is that impossible?'

'I thought we had that. I wanted a wife who supported me, who had her own interests as well, and, when kids came along, we'd deal with it. What's so hard about that?'

They stared at each other with the uncomfortable realisation of the other's position and feelings, and the knowledge they might have wanted the same thing but were coming from different directions. That they'd never talked about each other's goals and dreams.

'So where do we go from here?' asked Jennifer.

'I have a job to do, a contract that keeps me here. You're my wife. I thought you'd agreed to support me in my job.'

'You sound as if I haven't done that,' she snapped, hurt by the unfairness of the insinuation.

'Come on, Jennifer. You did nothing but complain about being here. You hardly ever came and socialised with guests, got to know the staff, did things that help me. Instead you're off with those university people who have nothing to do with this resort.'

'That's so unfair of you. I've done everything you wanted,' she hissed, trying not to raise her voice. 'I'm the one who gave up my career, you recall.'

'You were happy enough at the time. What about all the bullshit about writing some book for that professor? What've you done? Got pregnant, that's been it, and that's not helpful in my situation.'

'Well, excuse me. You had nothing to do with that? It wasn't planned, we slipped up, but you can't blame me. And what's the problem? Rosie is quite happy for us to stay on after the baby is born until your contract is up.'

'Yeah and then what?'

Jennifer's anger was ignited by the bitterness, the accusing tone, in his voice. 'Blair, you went off and had an affair.'

'So we put this behind us. Learn from it.' Blair was sounding brisk.

'That's easy for you to say.'

'Jennifer, don't start –'

'Blair, I cannot go back into that unit, our bed, as if nothing has happened.' She tried to sound calm but she felt her fury rising at Blair's total lack of acceptance that he had betrayed her.

'Come on, don't be ridiculous. Grow up. What do you want to do, go and live with your mother?'

'You'd like that, wouldn't you? Well, I'm not leaving you alone over here.'

'Jennifer, that's unfair. C'mon, I said nothing is going to happen. It was just . . . Oh, never mind, do what you want.'

'Time, a little time, that's all I want, Blair.'

'Fine. Talk to Rosie, see if you can stay in that suite for a bit. Of course, the staff will love to gossip about this. You're not making it easy for me.'

Why should I? 'Let's just leave things for the time being, please, Blair. Time out.'

13

Beyond the Reef

THROUGH THE MISTS OF sleep Jennifer heard
early-morning calls of seabirds, lapping water
and surf breaking on the reef. A soft, salty
breeze curled over the second-floor balcony, lifting a curtain. She opened her eyes in a strange
room and, as the previous day and evening came
back to her, she started to cry. It was like a bad
dream. If only. Dinner with Blair had been difficult. She just wanted to get away from the
resort. Pulling on shorts and a T-shirt from her
bag, which she hadn't unpacked, she dressed,
slipped on sandals, a hat and dark glasses, and
left the room.

The staff were setting up for breakfast, the clatter of plates, cutlery and chatter drifting across the grounds where one or two early risers were walking or waiting to go into the dining room. Jennifer had arranged to meet Isobel at the research station as soon as she woke up.

'Come at dawn, any time. Wake me. It doesn't matter. Tell me how things went with Blair and how you feel,' Isobel had urged.

The door to Mac's cottage was open, a dripping swimsuit hung on the clothes line at the entrance, and Isobel, a towel around her dark curls, was wrapped in a cotton kimono, her feet up on a chair as she sipped a mug of coffee.

'Good timing, the pot is still hot. Or do you prefer Australian tea to Brazilian coffee?'

'Maybe strong coffee is a good idea. I'll get it. Anyone up?'

'Just me, I've been for a swim. And Rudi is kayaking around to Boomerang Cove for exercise.'

The kitchen was cluttered: dishes, remains of a meal, empty beer cans, wine bottles and papers were spread over the table. Mac's guitar lay on the sofa. It reminded Jennifer of her uni days. She sat on a director's chair next to Isobel. The sun was lifting above the screen of trees. 'I feel disoriented. Out of my routine. I'm sad, hurt, but also mad.'

'Mad is good. How was dinner?'

'Awful. I thought it would be better to be in the public gaze rather than shout at each other on our own. We ended up shouting in whispers or hissing across the table.'

'Did you achieve anything, come to any conclusion?'

'Not really.' Jennifer was reflective. 'We just went round in circles.'

'He can't deny he is in the wrong.'

'He doesn't, but he's trying to pass it off like it was my fault! Being pregnant when we didn't plan it, not supporting him in his career, blah blah blah. Shit, why does he think I'm here? Thinks I've been hormonal, moody and distant. Being pregnant is no excuse. That kind of stuff.'

Isobel chuckled. 'Outrageous. When in the wrong, shove the blame. Never apologise, never admit you were wrong. Say women are hormonal. I know that type. How did you leave matters?'

'Up in the air. I think he feels it was a brief fling, I should be understanding and we'll go on as before. I wonder if he'd feel like that if it had been me!'

'And what do you want to do?'

Jennifer rubbed her eyes. 'I don't know, Isobel. I just said I need a bit of time to . . . adjust. The awful, sad thing is we both seem to want the same thing and the other doesn't see it that way.'

Isobel was quiet for a moment. She could see very clearly they were going in opposite directions. Finally, she said gently, 'Sometimes one partner hasn't grown up properly, or begins to grow and goes in a different direction. It happened to me.'

'How long have you been divorced?'

'Years. I had two little boys, but I managed. I

had supportive parents even though they believed marriages endured, no matter what.'

'What went wrong?'

'In the beginning, nothing. I tried to have it all. My problem is that my passion is difficult to share – unless you dive with me! I have always been incredibly motivated, I go at something to the exclusion of all else. So juggling a home life was hard. It was not a traditional relationship. Scientists are obsessives, like some poets, musicians, painters. I can't turn off my curiosity and that strained the marriage ties until they broke.'

'You're a big success and famous and contributing to science. Has it been worth it?' Jennifer hoped she wasn't trespassing into personal territory too much, but she needed to ask these questions.

Isobel sighed. 'Jenny, that was my choice in life. Yours might be different. I would have preferred to stay married but the urge to explore and seek answers to help save oceans is, for me, an irresistible force. I also know I could not have fought it.'

Jennifer mulled these comments over, thinking again what an indomitable woman Isobel appeared to be. Then she too sighed. 'If only I wasn't pregnant. It adds an unfair dimension, puts pressure on me to make things work out. Plus, there is my mother champing at the bit over the ocean waves.'

'Ah. Maybe you could go and spend some time with her?'

'No way. She'd sniff something was amiss and pounce on me. I'm not getting out of the way and making it convenient for Blair and that bitch Susie. And, I don't want to go. I like it here.' She gestured around her. She was about to say she wanted to get on with her work with Mac and the others. To be with Isobel and Gideon.

Isobel tilted her head, looking at Jennifer who had stopped mid sentence.

'My God, I don't believe I said that!'

'Go on.'

'That I like it here. I do! I really do. I *never* thought I'd say that.'

'Why? What do you like?' asked Isobel.

'The island. Being surrounded by water. It brought back nightmares. Now . . . knowing what the others are investigating, it's so important.'

'And what else?'

Jennifer spoke slowly, trying to analyse and articulate these new feelings. 'The beauty, the lifestyle, that we are coexisting with nature, the animals. We have to adjust to them rather than the other way around. But mostly it's the people. You, Mac, Gideon, everyone here at the station.'

'Perhaps we have interests in common – that's very powerful glue,' said Isobel.

'Friendship glue. Is that what it is? Still, I can't help thinking you are very special people. It's more than a friendship . . . I can't quite explain.'

Isobel touched her hand and smiled. 'You don't have to. Now, what were you saying?'

Jennifer took a breath. 'I like the idea of a book, and if Mac thinks I can do it – I will.'

'Brava! The best thing you could do.' Isobel was pragmatic. 'However, you have to consider your domestic arrangements. Are you prepared to go back to the marital home and bed?'

Jennifer was silent. She tried to imagine things as they'd been with Blair. And would they still be the same?

'It's a hard one, yes?' prompted Isobel.

'Yes. I suppose I should try, to be fair to us both. We do have a child on the way. But you know what? In thinking about our life together these past years, and especially since being here on Branch, we've hardly shared anything. Maybe that's not unusual in young couples with busy careers. I'm gone when he gets up, in bed when he comes home. Our interests rarely overlap.' She drew a tight breath. 'I'll try to do what he wants, socialise and play the hostess and so forth. I'll have to make more of an effort.'

'So will he,' said Isobel.

Later Jennifer went into her little workspace next to Rudi's lab. She spread out the papers from Mac and studied them. Yes, she decided. She could do this. She wanted to do this.

'Hi. Am I interrupting?' Tony Adams poked his head around the door. 'You're at it early.'

'Come in. I'm starting a new project – doing more studies.'

'You finished the book for the deadly dull professor?' He sat and stretched his long legs. He was wearing khaki shorts, a blue shirt with the sleeves rolled up and a cotton vest with a lot of pockets. She thought he looked exactly as a foreign correspondent should look.

'I have. He's pleased. Did Mac talk to you about my doing a book on the exploits of Gideon, the sharkmobile thingy, and Isobel? I don't want to cover the same territory, tread on your toes though.'

'Different readership. We're coming from separate perspectives. But it would be helpful to collaborate. There's a lot of ground to cover.' He patted one of his pockets, took out a packet of Lifesavers, popped one in his mouth and passed her the packet, looking thoughtful. 'I sense there's quite a story lurking here. Or several stories. Can't put my finger on it.'

She tossed him the peppermints, which he stowed in his pocket, smoothing the flap. She grinned. 'What do you keep in all those pockets?'

'Old habits. From the war, being on the run. Everything from chocolate, glasses, pen, paper, cassette tape, digital camera, American dollars, cigarettes.'

'You smoke?'

'No. Did for a while but gave it away. Offering American cigarettes is a good way to get people to talk to you. Well, used to be. So what's your take on this place?'

'On the island as a whole? You know, even though it's a small place it's like three separate states or three separate tribes. There's the resort with the staff and the tourists, there's the research

344

station and the scientists, and then there's Gideon and the wildlife.'

They both laughed.

'And the reef out there as a living border keeping invaders at bay,' added Tony.

'So where are you starting?' asked Jennifer.

'Supposedly Captain Cook discovered the reef. But there's evidence that probably Portuguese and Spanish explorers were here centuries before 1770. And I've been skimming scientific stuff, how reefs are formed and some fascinating early references to coral.' He pulled a small notepad from another pocket and read out. 'The poet Ovid and the Roman author Pliny describe coral as a soft plant underwater that hardens in air. And two millennia later a French scientist finally identifies coral as being formed by minute animals. What had previously been considered flowers were truly more like upside-down jellyfish – cnidarians.'

'So the reef is a living formation, each generation growing on the skeleton of its parents until the colonies become hundreds of years old and the reefs develop over thousands of kilometres,' said Jennifer. 'And incredibly beautiful.'

'Especially when seen from underwater, undisturbed. But what intrigues me is what Gideon and Isobel are after – what's way, way below the reef? Do you believe in monsters of the deep?'

Jennifer shuddered. 'I don't even want to think about it. You do the underwater research, thanks.'

Isobel appeared in the doorway. 'Ah ha. The collaboration begins, eh?'

'How can Jennifer write about the mysterious wondrous reef without seeing it?' Tony said. 'What did Gideon say about doing things you've never done before?'

'A journey begins with a single step, Tony. It is a process. Like having a baby,' smiled Isobel.

He looked at Jennifer. 'Oh yes, I heard. Congratulations. That's why you are looking so . . . healthy,' he finished, looking slightly embarrassed.

'Tony, the tide is out. Remember what we did yesterday? Why not take Jennifer and show her what is the tip of the iceberg, shall we say?' Isobel smiled at Jennifer. 'A simple reef walk. Go, get some fresh air. Off you go.' She waved at them and headed for Mac's.

'You'll need rubber shoes. Let's go to the resort and get a walking stick and viewing cone. Sunblock, hats, the lot. Disguise ourselves as tourists,' said Tony.

'Sorry, you don't have to do this. Isobel is a very definite sort of person,' said Jennifer.

'But I want to. She opened my eyes to so many things!'

'She's good at that. Well, I suppose . . .'

He touched her lightly on the shoulder, remembering what she'd told him about her childhood trauma. 'We won't go near the edge of the sea. Just the inshore bits. Okay?'

They walked through the pisonia forest and took the track to the resort, chatting animatedly about the various research projects Mac's students were undertaking. Suddenly Jennifer stopped, realising she'd got to her and Blair's cabin.

'Is something wrong? Have you forgotten something?' asked Tony.

'Ah, no. It's all right. I'll just run in for the sunblock.'

'I'll wait here.' He sensed her discomfort.

Jennifer went to the rear courtyard, slid the glass door open and pulled the drawn curtains. She always left them open. The place smelled different. Was it another woman's perfume, or her imagination? The girls had been in to clean, but instantly she saw things were out of place, not as she left them. Different CDs were lying around. A couple of magazines she never read were on the coffee table. Despite the folded clean towels and Blair's tidy array of shaving and hair products, something looked out of place. The bottle of nail polish. Not hers. She grabbed the tube of sunblock and hurried outside, avoiding looking at the bed. No. She could not come back and live here with Blair. Not yet.

Rosie was on what the staff called her walkabout – a casual wander through the grounds, staff area, recreation rooms and entertainment areas. But her eagle eyes were taking in sloppy or unattended tasks, staff not properly dressed, any untidiness or uncleanliness. She saw Blair talking to a pale young man in the staff uniform and walked up to them with a smile.

'Morning, Blair. Welcome, you must be Gordon.' She extended her hand.

'This is Rosie Jordan, the general manager. This is Gordon Blake, from the UK. I'm just giving him the rundown and orientation tour.'

The boy's handshake was limp. 'How do you do. Pleasure to be here, at last.' His voice was plummy, his smile thin, as if he could just about muster the energy for conversation. The casual, colourful staff uniform looked incongruous on him.

'Have you come direct from the UK? No other travel in Australia?'

'Not yet. I hope to see more.'

Rosie thought this odd. 'Branch is a small island. Australia is a very big island – well, continent,' said Rosie brightly. 'I hope you do see a lot more. Working here you'll be able to save money to tour.'

'Quite.' He looked to Blair. 'Where do we go next? Is it possible to see outside the resort area? I'd rather like to see the science research facilities on the island.'

Rosie tried not to feel like he was dismissing her. She continued to smile. 'Oh, you're interested in marine research? We do overlap from time to time. I'm afraid the research staff are only permitted to the resort on an invitation basis. It's reciprocal, as we all have our jobs to do and social interaction is kept to a minimum. Sometimes some of the scientists give a lecture to the guests.'

Blair heard the needles in her voice and

decided to move the new staffie on. 'We'd better get along, quite a bit to cover yet.'

'I hope you enjoy your time here,' said Rosie.

Gordon Blake gave her a polite smile and turned away with Blair. 'Well, he didn't seem even faintly intimidated by me,' thought Rosie. Arrogance of a wealthy upbringing, for sure. Why has he been sent here? Is this the new trend, to send sons to the tropics rather than to a cattle station in the outback? She'd ask Doyley to keep an eye on young Mr Blake, see how he settled in.

Jennifer hadn't noticed the time pass. She'd been hesitant at first as they picked their way across the edge of the exposed coral. She was glad she had her 'shepherd's stick' to help her balance as she waded through the water in sandy patches to step up onto the dead coral. Pools, and tiny channels, ran between the limestone rock formed by millions and millions of coral deposits and bodies of molluscs, worms, algae, sea urchins, starfish and sponges that had over time become rock-hard reef.

Tony bent down and lifted a clump of brain coral.

'Isobel talked of the power of the individual, it takes just one coral polyp to secrete lime and make a hard cup around itself, then multiply each growing polyp into colonies that become cities, then countries, then whole nations of coral! By dying, living things build and create beautiful forms.'

'And within their borders all manner of inhabitants, the good, the bad and the ugly. Very fanciful,' added Jennifer.

'It's the symbiotic relationship between everything that's intriguing. The tiny algae, plants that live in coral tissue, use sunlight to give the coral oxygen and carbohydrates, while the coral gives the plants a home, carbon dioxide and waste products as fertiliser. The food chain ranges from minuscule planktonic animals to great whales. Right along the line they all depend on each other. That our world was so constructed,' he sighed.

'But isn't the most important thing for the reef clean water at the right temperature?' said Jennifer.

'Therein lies the rub – global warming is apparently killing off great chunks of the reef. Mac's mob are doing serious research into the effects. Not to mention the water pollution.'

'Even out here . . . hard to believe, isn't it?' said Jennifer.

Tony pointed at a brilliant orange fan of soft coral that was lazily swaying in a rock pool. 'It's the colours that amaze me. Why are some fish and coral such vivid colours? And others totally camouflaged? Do you think the colours obvious to us are seen the same way by other animals?'

'One of the grads is studying colour vision and how sea creatures perceive their environment. Apparently reef fish and little creatures like shrimp have retinas far more complex than ours,' said Jennifer.

'I think I'll come back in my next life as a marine biologist. There's so much to investigate, and it's a pretty good lifestyle,' laughed Tony. 'What interests you most in what the gang at the research station are doing?'

'There's so much! Andy's acoustic study is fascinating. We know about whale songs and dolphin-speak, that clack and click language. But the idea that fish can communicate is pretty amazing.'

'He's deciphering vibrations, underwater sound waves?'

'Yeah, I liken it to high-pitched whistles dogs can hear and we can't. But whether it's movement of their fins, swim bladders, gills banging, who knows? And how sophisticated are their messages?'

Tony shook his head. 'As technology improves with sonar equipment, hydrophones, whatever, I guess they'll learn more and more. But, talking with Mac, the overall sense I get is a kind of quiet urgency to protect and save the reef – mainly from humans.'

'Yes, I think Rudi's work is interesting, too,' said Jennifer. 'Perhaps because I can see a practical reason for it. Chemicals derived from marine organisms that can cure cancer maybe, add UV compounds to paint to make it last years longer in the sun, that kind of thing. He talks about coexistence too, the reef fish that live in anemones, a marriage of poisons that is quite common, one protecting the other.' Jennifer stopped. Was that

351

the relationship between her and Blair? Her and her mother? At times poisonous but each needing the other?

Tony didn't seem to notice her pausing. Peering through his viewing cone held on the surface of the water, his American baseball cap pulled low, he said, almost to himself, 'It's better than television. It's like being God, sitting in the sky peering down at all the doings of this little universe.' Without looking up he added, 'Makes all our day-to-day dramas, joys, tragedies, seem a little insignificant in the big scheme of things.'

For Jennifer, the casual comment hit home. Tony had no interest in her personal life, no knowledge of what had transpired between her and Blair. Well, she assumed that was the case, while everyone else on the damned island seemed to know the details. He was still a reclusive, introverted person, he wouldn't have been interested anyway. In the big picture maybe the rift between her and Blair wasn't such a massive event, but to her the hurt and unfairness burnt with a constant pain. She straightened up, wondering why her back was aching. 'Oh, we've been here two hours!'

Tony was also surprised and glanced at his watch. 'The tide is turning, we'd better head back. Follow me.'

He placed his feet carefully, the water was rushing in to the channels and once again Jennifer was glad of her walking stick. She hadn't realised they'd moved across the exposed reef so far that they were only a few metres from the drop-off point into the deeper water. It was behind her now and she concentrated on following Tony's feet in the old reef shoes. Occasionally she lifted her head, looking towards the postcard picture of the strip of sand, the line of palms half hiding the resort, coloured dots of people on the beach and along the reef.

As they pulled off their shoes to hang them on the side of the dive shack with the other array of shoes, cones and walking sticks, Jennifer felt more relaxed than she had for ages. 'That was fascinating. Thanks for the tour.'

'I don't know as much as Isobel, or have her flair for presentation, but I'm glad you're venturing forth.' He gave a warm smile.

'She's very enthusiastic, isn't she?' agreed Jennifer. 'Do you want a coffee?'

'I'll pass, thanks. I'm going to talk to Rudi. Apparently there's some agency interested in his work. I'd like to find out more. What are your plans?'

Without thinking about it she found herself saying, 'I have to go to the mainland this afternoon. My mother has moved over there. Grandmotherly anxiety or something. Maybe we could talk with Mac, about the book, when I get back?'

'Sounds good. The team are starting to get the submersible ready for a test dive. Enjoy your visit with your mother.'

She stood up. 'I'll try. I hate being fussed over.'

He laughed. 'Enjoy it while you can.' He walked down to the beach, heading for the track to the research station. Jennifer hoped Blair was busy and she could slip into their cabin and pack her things for the mainland. She couldn't put off her mother any longer. Just as well. There was a note from Blair on the coffee table, delivered, it seemed, by one of the housekeeping girls. 'Your mother keeps ringing. For God's sake call her and go over.'

As she gazed around, again Jennifer was overwhelmed by a sense of being trespassed on, that this was no longer her, their, private space. Trying to remember what she'd left in her bag in the resort suite she hurriedly grabbed clothes, personal items, her laptop, file of papers, several books, Vi and Don's radio, bundled them into Blair's sports bag and dragged it into the courtyard. She gulped the humid air and sat down, unsure what to do next. The heron was back at the clamshell under the shower. It was a graceful creature, but as a seagull warily approached, it sprang forward and the seagull swerved away with a sharp screech. The heron ran its sharp beak through its feathers, pleased with itself. The seagull simply waited for another opportunity. Jennifer looked at the arrogant grey bird. 'You're beautiful, but you have mean, yellow eyes.'

Leaving her bag, Jennifer took a roundabout route to reception to book herself on the cat and see Rosie. She felt utterly depressed, heavy hearted, faintly nauseated and too sad to cry.

What had happened to her life? She was having a baby, she had little money of her own, a disastrous split in the relationship with her husband, and had no idea what was going to happen to them, to her.

Behind the staff quarters, she passed the big shed where the resort vehicles and machinery were stored. There were workshops and the maintenance and utilities offices. A man was working on repairs to a boat that was on a trailer behind a small four-wheel drive. She saw Patch talking to a young staff member she didn't recognise. They were deep in conversation and neither man noticed her walk quietly past.

Rosie was standing outside reception talking to some guests. Jennifer hung back until Rosie had given the couple directions. Then Rosie, looking concerned, came over to her.

'You look so down, sweetie. How are things with Blair? How did the dinner go? What's the plan?'

'No plan,' said Jennifer miserably. 'I felt like I was getting my life together. I'd start the course with Mac, do the book with Tony, Isobel and Gideon. Now,' she shrugged, 'I'm going over to see my mother and I don't know if I should come back.'

'Take a couple of days' break, see how you feel.'

'This is not a good time to be visiting my mother.'

Rosie spoke firmly, wishing she could shake

Jennifer. 'Listen, you can't let this get on top of you. I know you're hurt and upset, and she'll spot that right off. Why don't you change tack – instead of expecting the worst, assume this is a new start. Share the baby with her.' Rosie stopped talking as Jennifer didn't look convinced.

'And then what? Where do I go, what do I do, Rosie?' She was on the verge of tears again.

'Do you want to stay in the suite?'

'Not really, thanks. I hate being in our apartment. I can just . . . sense them there together.'

Rosie took her arm. 'Talk to Mac. I'll talk to him. And listen, I'm due for two days off. I'll take them tomorrow and meet you over in Headland. Come and have lunch. Meet Beverly, my partner.'

'Rosie, that would be great. You can meet my mother.' She managed a smile.

'Done. Give me your mobile number. I'll ring you tomorrow sometime. Don't worry. You mustn't stress the baby. Will you tell Blair, or do you want me to pass the message on?'

'He sent a note. He expects me to go to Headland. There's not much else to say. Besides, I don't want him to . . . make any plans while I'm away.'

'He wouldn't dare. Don't worry, I'll talk to Mac, see if he can set you up in accommodation at the station. They have plenty of student share places, but they keep a couple of spots for their visiting VIPs. Like Tony. I'd put you in the empty cabin next to Blair's and your place, but that seems a bit pointless. Don't worry, it'll be sorted out by the time you get back.'

'Thanks so much, Rosie.' Her practical help and friendship meant a lot to Jennifer. 'Would you mind asking Mac to let Isobel know?'

'Sure thing. How about we go and have a slap-up lunch, then you can catch the cat.'

'I didn't have any breakfast. Sounds great.' Jennifer felt better.

Rudi was peering down a microscope, watching the cells on the slide meld and change colour. He made a note of the activity and gave a start as there was a voice at the door of his little lab.

'May I come in?'

'Er, yes. Sure. How can I help you?' Rudi looked at the young man, trying to place him.

'We haven't met, Dr Orlov. I'm a new arrival, Gordon Blake.'

For a young man he was very self-assured, thought Rudi. Very upper-class British accent. 'Are you a student?'

'Actually, I'm working at the resort for a while. On a bit of a sabbatical. I understand there's not a lot of fraternisation' – he gave a disarming smile – 'but I'm frightfully interested in the research you're doing. If I'm not intruding, could we chat a few minutes? I've read about your investigation on the net.'

'Ah, you are a student then. A graduate of . . . ?'

'I'm attending London University . . . I'm travelling before settling into my business degree. My father wants me to follow in his field, but I must say I'd like to know a bit more about your research. I'm more interested in medicine.'

Rudi thought his approach a bit unorthodox. 'Very enterprising of you. Can't help you other than explain what I'm doing. Be quite some time before I have anything conclusive to report. But the initial results and leads are quite promising.' Rudi switched effortlessly into lecture mode. The young man was polite, attentive and had a ready supply of surprisingly in-depth questions.

After forty-five minutes of talking, showing samples and discussing the plants in his tanks, Rudi glanced at his watch. 'I have a meeting in fifteen minutes. I can run you round the station in ten, give you a bit of a feel for what we're doing, but after that you'll have to come back another day – if you're interested.'

'Absolutely. I'm most grateful to you.'

'Give me a bit of time and I could point you in the direction of further work in the field. Some names and places where you might apply.'

'Excellent, I'd appreciate that.'

The meeting was being held in the living area of Mac's little house, but the group gathered around the dining table, papers and notebooks in front of them, had the air of a board meeting or formal conference. Mac gave a brief rundown of the status of each of the graduates' work, the projections and assignments for everyone in the next three weeks. Tony sat quietly on the sofa in the background, taking notes. They went round the table, with each person present, students and scientists, raising problems, making requests, recounting small successes or failures.

Mac turned to his associate professor. 'Rudi, do you have anything to add?'

'When the coral spawns I'd like to see it documented on video as well as stills. We can do that more easily with the control tanks outside. But I think there should also be observations recorded in the sea, if we can.'

'Could we use Gideon's submersible?' asked Carmel. 'I don't like the idea of swimming in coral sperm.'

'Possibly. It has strong lights, it'd be fantastic to be right down in it when all the coral spawn,' said Kirsty. 'Like driving through a pink underwater snowstorm.'

'How are your results going, Rudi?' asked Carmel.

Mac raised his hand. 'If I can jump in here. As you know, Rudi's toxicity investigations are proving to be quite intriguing. And there's been a great deal of interest from outside the university.'

'How's that?' asked Andy, whose audio-sensory study of whale and dolphin songs and language had attracted a lot of public interest, while his studies on fish communication were little known.

'Andy, what you're doing with the whale songs is touchy-feely stuff. The general public love it. Rudi's work, as it's developing, is showing potential for bio-technical, chemical, industrial applications. And that means, potentially, big investment. So I'm asking you all to keep what we're doing here to ourselves.' He swung around and indicated Tony. 'While Tony is an independent writer, he has agreed not to publish any material without the consent of Rudi, myself or the chancellor.'

'So who's interested? We normally have trouble getting any kind of publicity for our work,' said Kirsty.

Mac fiddled with his pen. 'Unfortunately, some of Rudi's results were posted on the website and there was interest from a couple of companies. I don't have to tell you guys how competitive it is to attract funding for research programs. We compete with other unis for students, money, resources, acclaim, you name it. As you know, our funding also depends on the quality of our research. There are other people working in the same fields and so we don't want anyone to pinch, copy or discredit what we're doing. While I know you all want to get your qualifications, make a name and get work, we mustn't forget one of the prime reasons we've chosen to work in the field of marine research.' He looked around and Carmel raised her coffee mug.

'Here's to the seas of the world!'

'To the reef,' said Rudi. 'May it survive.'

'It's got about thirty years at the rate it's going,' said Mac. 'Now, let's talk about Isobel Belitas and her work. She's asked for volunteers to assist, hopefully for some accreditation or acknowledgment, in her beyond-the-reef survey.' All hands around the table shot up.

'She's not seriously considering really deep dives in Gideon's sharkmobile, is she?' asked Tony.

'Up to two hundred metres, yes, for beyond the reef to a thousand metres, plus she's bringing the Sea-Life over from the US. It's pretty revolutionary, up there with what Hawkes and Co are designing.

'God, that's one of the world's most advanced marine machines. It'll cost zillions,' exclaimed Andy.

'She's got massive support from institutions and private foundations,' said Rudi.

Mac spoke quietly. 'As you know, the Pacific Ocean has an average depth of four thousand two hundred metres, the bulk of it unexplored. For a start, commercial concerns – fishing, energy, oil and gas, biochemical industries – are interested. But research has to be done sensitively and co-operatively. The days of drilling the Great Barrier Reef for oil, minerals and lime for sugar cane fields are over.'

There was silence at the table for a moment. Rudi spoke first. 'It's a huge field with many opportunities. A bit like conquering space. A universe filled with alien creatures, unknown geological features, ancient shipwrecks, even clues to the origin of life.'

'That was the study which found multibillion-year-old Archean microscopic life forms in ancient lava, wasn't it?' remarked Kirsty.

'Yes. So what Isobel and others are concerned about is that industry doesn't overtake science.

Hence the need to have human involvement in deep ocean discovery.'

Tony sat with his pen poised, too fascinated to make notes. 'It's a big story all right. But you know what interests me the most? Not the commercial or scientific applications, but the marine life. What creatures, life forms, are way down there.'

'We can only guess. We know some – giant squids and jellyfish, huge eels, bizarre fish and, of course, the sharks,' said Rudi.

'Sharks way down in the deepest part?' asked Tony.

'Having no swim bladder helps them to manoeuvre more easily in the deep. Quite incredible creatures. It's a strange world down there. We could find the equivalent of the Loch Ness monster or keys to our own future,' said Mac.

'It's a lot to think about,' said Tony.

'Any questions, Tony, get back to me. I'll do my best, but there's no one who's an expert in this area!'

'The first explorers down there will be the experts,' said Tony.

Jennifer walked two blocks from the waterfront up a hill and, glancing at the address on the piece of paper in her hand, realised the cream-brick block of units called 'Ocean Tide' was where Christina was living. She went into the lobby past the wall of letterboxes and found the buzzer beside number eight. The metallic buzz was cut off by Christina's voice.

'Yes? Who is it?'

'Me. Put the kettle on.'

'Well, you might have rung! I look a mess. Come up, come up. Turn left out of the lift.' Her voice was laughing. Pleased.

Christina stood in the doorway, watching Jennifer come down the hall. Each swiftly appraised the other. Jennifer was surprised to see her mother wearing bright orange shorts and an orange and white flowered T-shirt.

'Turn sideways, let me see how much you're showing. Why're you wearing a man's shirt, haven't you got any nice maternity outfits? We'll have to go shopping.'

They embraced awkwardly in the narrow doorway, and Christina turned into the apartment.

'Mum, people don't wear those ghastly things they wore in your day.'

'No, they let it all hang out. I've seen them. Young girls walking around with their bellies hanging over their jeans. Disgusting. I hope you don't expose yourself over on that island.'

'How about tea? I'm dying for a cuppa. This is nice . . .' Jennifer walked through the small sitting room to the tiny balcony. 'You can see the ocean. Branch Island is way over there.'

'Come and see your room. I'm not very organised yet, haven't found where the decent shops are. Mavis downstairs says there's a great warehouse thing where you can get stuff so cheap . . .'

'What kind of stuff? This is okay, isn't it?' She ignored the reference to 'her' room.

'Well, baby stuff, of course. Where's the poor thing going to sleep?'

'Mum, let's get this straight. I'm not moving in, we can use those porta-crib things. We don't need any *permanent* arrangement.'

Christina froze with the kettle aloft. 'You can't possibly stay on that island before, during or right after the baby comes. I have moved from Sydney – lock, stock and barrel – to help you!'

I didn't bloody ask you to! And you didn't ask me! 'That's terrific of you, Mum. Really appreciate your help. But Blair and I can manage pretty well.'

Christina plugged the kettle in and flicked the red On button. 'I don't think Blair is the type to actually help. Like doing things, feeding, bathing. Pacing around when it bawls with the colic.'

You're probably dead right there. 'Mum, I'm not going to have a colicky, crying baby.' *Think positively, Rosie said.* 'Anyway, that's a long way off. Let's talk about you. I didn't expect you to uproot yourself. I thought you were happy at Vi and Don's. The club, your friends . . .'

'Family comes first, Jennifer.'

Haven't you heard of letting go, cutting the apron strings? 'But, Mum, what are you going to do here? I can't be here all the time, every week. I can't move from the island. Blair now has an eighteen-month contract – though he could be posted to Europe at the drop of a hat too. I'm starting a uni course over there, and there's no problem keeping the baby with us after it's born. As a matter of fact,' Jennifer seized at a straw, 'Blair's boss, Rosie, the general manager, is here for her break. You could meet her, we could have lunch tomorrow.'

'I doubt such a person would be interested in meeting the likes of me.' Christina took down mugs from the cupboard. Solid, cheap, rental stuff, Jennifer noted. Then she added, 'And, Jennifer, you don't have to worry about what I'll *do*. I have a lot to do, and I already know people. People who enjoy my company. You act like I need a nursemaid.'

'Good for you, Mum. You've just arrived in a new place, a new state, after years being with a family in one place. It must be a bit strange. What about a job? You can't afford to do this.'

'You'd be surprised.' Milk and a plate of Jennifer's favourite biscuits were put on the tray. 'I've tucked something away for just such a rainy day.'

'Mum, this isn't a rainy day. That money is for you. Blair and I are doing fine. Having a family is part of being married.' She saw the pursed lips. 'It's lovely of you to be here, but once the baby is settled into a routine –'

'Then you won't need me any more and I can be dismissed, sent away like some hired help.' She poured boiling water into the teapot.

'Mum, let's take it day by day. You just can't plan things . . .' *And don't we both know that.*

'How long are you renting this place for?' Jennifer looked around. There didn't seem to be very much in the way of personal decor. Christina certainly hadn't nested. The pot plants, pictures, cushions, all looked to be rental furnishings.

'For as long as you need me.'

You mean you need me. 'Thanks, Mum. Well, let's have that tea. So, what have you been doing? Checked out the town? Trust you to know people after a few days.'

'Jennifer, how long are you here for? You are staying with me, I hope?' There was a lost, pleading look in her eyes.

''Course I am. Having lunch with Rosie tomorrow, have to see the doctor, but maybe you and I could look around for baby gear. Some sort of a pram that you can convert to a carry bed.'

'I know exactly what you need . . .' Christina was away.

Jennifer sipped her tea, her mother's familiar voice droning on and on with all her ideas for baby trappings. The sun began to sink and Jennifer thought of the tourists preparing to watch the sunset from one of the most romantic spots in the world. The happy honeymooners believing this was the start of a blissful life . . . Had she and Blair felt like that? She couldn't remember.

When finally she did take her bag into the second bedroom, she found her mother had decorated this one room. Jennifer was touched. Her long-forgotten doll, Molly, was propped up on the bed. Her old dressing gown, which she'd left years before at Vi and Don's, was laid at the foot of the bed.

Christina hovered. 'Just thought it might make things a bit homey . . .' There was a rare catch in her voice. 'We haven't had our own place, just the two of us, for such a long time.'

'I know, Mum.' Jennifer didn't want the dam inside her to burst. 'Things change. Be two-and-a-half of us in here soon enough.' She tried to smile.

'Are you all right, Jen-Jen? Really all right?'

Please don't let me say anything about Blair. 'Yep, just great, Mum. Bit tired, that's all.'

'How about I make a nice dinner? One of your favourites.' She bustled away, happy.

Jennifer lay on the bed and pushed her knuckles into her eye sockets.

14

Ebb and Flows

THE THREE WOMEN SAT at an outdoor table on the terrace of The View restaurant, overlooking Headland Harbour. Rosie put on her glasses and studied the menu. Beverly poured sparkling mineral water and smiled at Jennifer.

'She reads a menu like it's homework. What do you feel like?'

'Whatever Rosie wants to try. I'm used to this, Blair is the same.'

Jennifer liked Rosie's partner Beverly, who was in her mid thirties, tall, striking and thin with short dark hair. A contrast to the big-boned, rounded Rosie who'd visited the hairdresser that morning and had a vivid scarlet rinse through her red curls. Beverly was a nurse at Headland Hospital and had filled Jennifer in on the staff, routine, scandals and systems of the regional hospital.

'Sounds like the incestuous life of an island community,' said Jennifer.

'I suppose it's inevitable that people working closely together in a confined space can get over-involved,' said Beverly, and Rosie threw her a glance at her inadvertent remark. 'So how has your mother settled in?' asked Beverly, changing the subject. 'Does she know anyone here?'

'The lady downstairs. Mum is pretty good at chatting people up – superficially, you know, socially. She never lets anyone get too close. I'm hoping she'll join the tennis club again.'

'Ooh, I play. Would she like me to take her along?'

'That'd be great. Do you play, Rosie?' asked Jennifer. She'd never seen Rosie indulge in any recreational activity at the resort. Sitting around at Gideon's had been the most relaxed she'd seen the general manager.

'I'm not about to blow my credibility with the staff by being seen in a tennis outfit, or a swimsuit lazing by the pool. I do snorkel but I go out with Lloyd and Gideon and Mac's mob.'

'She's a strong swimmer. We have a pool at our apartment,' said Beverly. 'I'm the poolside with a book and a pina colada type.'

Jennifer thought they were a well-matched couple, comfortable with each other, both with careers and a shared life as it suited them. She enjoyed the older women's intelligent and amusing company. If it hadn't been for Rosie and Isobel, close female friendships on Branch were hard to find. She enjoyed Carmel, Kirsty, and the other grad students, but they were wrapped up in their work and relationships. Although they were only two or three years younger than Jennifer, she was married, unemployed and pregnant. Rosie was a great support on the island, understanding Jennifer's personal issues without being disloyal to Blair. She and Rosie knew each other well enough not to compromise their friendship.

Isobel, now she was someone very special. While Jennifer knew that Dr Isobel Belitas was hugely respected around the world, she felt such empathy, such a link to this woman, which she simply couldn't explain to herself.

Rosie caught her thoughtful mood. 'What are your plans? Want to go for a stroll along the harbour foreshore this evening? Have a drink? There's a cute little bistro and bar down where the proposed marina will be. Bring your mother.'

'Actually, I might do that. Just a quick drink, we might go for a walk and I'll take Mum to dinner.'

'Join us, we'll eat at the bistro probably,' said Beverly.

'I don't want you to be overrun with Mum. But to meet and suggest the tennis would be great. Thanks so much.' Jennifer smiled, then, remembering the reason she was there, 'Mum knows nothing about any problems with Blair.'

'And nor should she. Everything will sort itself out, Jenny, don't worry,' said Rosie comfortingly.

Jennifer wondered whether she should tell her mother that Beverly and Rosie were a couple, but decided not to. Her mother would enjoy them and find Beverly a friendly, helpful woman.

'You didn't give me any notice, but I've stocked up the fridge anyway. Mavis downstairs wants to meet you. I thought afternoon or morning tea tomorrow? When are you seeing the doctor? Has he done one of those sound machine things?'

'Ultrasound. Not yet, Mum. I just want to chill out a bit. What've you been doing?'

Jennifer let her mother ramble on. The talk was all about the town, what Christina had been doing, who she'd met and what she'd seen in baby stores. She didn't ask about the island, Jennifer's university work, or Blair. She eagerly agreed to meet Beverly and Rosie for a sundowner.

Headland Bay waterfront and harbour was not Monte Carlo, but in the setting sun, the rigging tinkling on moored yachts, people walking along the seafront, sitting in the small park, fishing from the wharf where the Reef Cat was locked down for the night, kids on bikes outside the fish and chip shop, the coffee shop and bistro doing a steady trade, it was a cheerful and pretty rest stop between the sunny day and the oncoming cooler night.

Christina was entranced. 'Well, this is a find. I'll have to come down here more often.'

Jennifer introduced Rosie and Beverly, who handed Christina a glass of champagne.

'How extravagant! I suppose one glass won't hurt me. Of course, Jennifer can't have any, being in the family way.'

Christina sparkled, told vivacious, outrageous – untrue – stories that kept Rosie and Beverly laughing. She was immediately enthusiastic about joining the tennis club.

'And are you retired, Christina? Not looking for work?' asked Beverly, thinking the energetic sixty-something woman would be an asset in a town full of retirees and casual workers.

'Oh, I don't have any skills to speak of . . . not like my talented daughter here.'

'Mum, that's not so –'

Rosie cut Jennifer off at the pass. 'There're a lot of opportunities up here. Talk to Beverly, she says the hospital is always looking for people. Workers and volunteers.'

'It'd be good to fill in the time and meet people,' added Jennifer, hoping that if her mother got a job it would dilute her desperate interest in her life.

'And make a bit of money. I'm happy to introduce you to the right people in the health system,' said Beverly.

'Why don't you give Christina your phone number?' suggested Rosie, 'And you two can work things out . . . tennis and so on.'

As they were exchanging numbers, Rosie suddenly said, 'Blow me, the slick boys have become a trio. What do you suppose they're doing?'

Jennifer quickly looked behind her to see Fanzio and Holding with a young man who looked familiar. 'Who is he?'

'That's the young pommy bloke who's arrived to work on staff. Referred by head office, obviously some bigwig's son,' said Rosie. 'Arrogant young jerk. I think he's more interested in the research station. He was at uni but is taking time out to travel. Sounds suss to me.'

'You mean he didn't pass his year so Daddy has sent him abroad,' said Beverly. 'Surely he's not working in the kitchen, or cleaning?'

'That's Blair's area. He's the one who's been dealing with them all. The kid must be well connected if he's strolling around with the slick boys.'

'Why aren't they wearing ties and sitting behind a desk in Sydney?' asked Jennifer.

'Perks, I'd say. Didn't you say they had girlfriends on the gin palace boat?' Beverly asked Rosie.

'Yeah. I hope they don't see us.'

'Well, that all sounds intriguing,' said Christina. 'So, Jennifer, are we going to dinner? Or shall I make something?'

'There's a great take-away gourmet joint down the road,' said Beverly.

'Oh, we don't eat that sort of thing. Waste of money, and you never know how clean those places are,' said Christina.

Jennifer grinned at the girls as she stood up, 'No, Mum, I promised you dinner at a nice restaurant. See you both later.'

As Christina got up, Jennifer glanced at the three men getting onto a small tender to go out to the luxury cruiser *Kicking Back*, which she had spotted at anchor. 'I know where I saw him before. He was at the maintenance shed. Talking to Patch.'

'God, whatever for?' wondered Rosie. 'I think I might be keeping closer tabs on this Gordon Blake.'

Two days passed quickly. Christina was a whirlwind of activity and Jennifer was longing for a rest, not so much the put-your-feet-up rest that her mother kept suggesting, but a mental break from the constant chatter and talk of Christina being there to help with the baby. If Jennifer mentioned the island, Blair or Rosie's being supportive about their staying on, Christina's conversation swerved in a different direction. In the evening they watched TV as they'd always done, Christina controlling the remote and browsing through a name the baby book.

'Luke. No, I don't think so, too religious. Hollister . . . too American. Hector, no . . .'

'Apparently it's going to be a girl, Mum.'

Christina looked up sharply. 'Oh, who says so?'

'Isobel. The famous oceanographer I told you about.'

'What would she know? It's too early anyway,' sniffed Christina.

'She's such an interesting woman. Amazing what she's done and plans to do. I really like her. She's very warm, very special . . .' Jennifer clammed up, halting the compliments.

'I thought these scientist women would be very mannish. It is a man's world. How old is she? Does she have a family?' Christina's eyes hadn't left the quiz show but there was a critical tone to her questions.

'Mum, science isn't a man's world any more. In fact, women have always been in the forefront, they just never got the credit. I have a Bachelor of Environmental Science degree! And Isobel is in her fifties, I guess, with two grown sons, and divorced.'

'I bet she was more interested in her work than her family. See where it's got her. I hope you realise what your priorities are.'

'According to Isobel, being happy and fulfilled should be my priority.' *I'm on thin ice here, but what the hell.*

'Family should be your priority. But I don't suppose you're going to listen to me when you have some world-famous clever lady scientist to advise you.'

And by family you mean you, not my husband. 'Family will always be important in my life, Mum. Such as we have. Why haven't we kept in touch with Dad's side of the family? My baby must have second cousins out there somewhere.'

Christina swung her feet to the floor from the fake leather ottoman. 'There's cake left out there, want another cup of tea?'

'Why won't you talk about Dad?' persisted Jennifer.

But Christina was in the kitchen and would not be drawn and Jennifer was too emotionally weary to fight her.

In her little bedroom with her mother sleeping noisily in the next room, Jennifer wondered about her father. How would he have felt about being a grandfather? With the baby growing inside her she was thinking more and more about family. What kind of family would she and Blair create? What baggage would they pass on to this child and any future children? Now all the vague stuff she'd read and heard about blaming your parents for trauma in childhood, and later life, took on new meaning. She hadn't resolved her own parental issues, what on earth was she going to dump on her child?

The doctor's appointment went smoothly. Jennifer introduced her mother to the doctor in the waiting room, and as she went to follow them into his room, he politely asked Christina to wait outside.

Jennifer thanked him. 'My mother is well-meaning but over anxious.'

'Very normal. What about your husband? Does he plan to be present at the birth?'

'Oh. I hadn't thought that far ahead.' Jennifer tried to imagine Blair in a mask and hospital gown, holding her hand or whatever fathers did at that time. Was he the squeamish type? She didn't know.

'Most couples do childbirth classes. It's up to you. There is a new birthing centre at the hospital. I don't go in for the waterbirth business. We'll have to book you in soon. You're both coming along just fine.'

Christina grilled Jennifer on her weight, blood pressure, diet, extra vitamins and what the doctor had said. 'He looked a bit of an old codger. Does he know what he's doing? Is he up with the latest things?'

'Of course. He did tell me my calculations were out, so I'm at least four months' pregnant. He also asked if Blair was going to be at the birth,' said Jennifer.

'Good grief, you don't want that. Take my word for it, men can't cope with that sort of thing. Of course, if you did want someone there, you know I'm here.'

'Thanks, Mum. I'm sure Dr Thomas has a good team on hand. Now, how about a coffee?'

Jennifer was thoughtful. The idea of Blair and her mother being involved with the birth unsettled her. She kept feeling she and the baby were a unit, an extension of each other, and no one else was involved. She felt protective and selfish. She didn't want her mother or Blair to be part of the process. As her mother ordered the coffee, chatting to the woman behind the cappuccino machine, Jennifer tried to rationalise why she felt like a single mother. She and Blair had created this child from an act of love. Or was it love? Sex had become routine and unadventurous. The passion had dissipated after the first two years of their being together. If she was brutally honest with herself, she knew she agreed to lovemaking as a means of keeping Blair happy and easy to get along with. Times she'd refused him, or pretended to be asleep, had meant a sullen and moody Blair the following day. Which annoyed her. It was her body and he had no right to make her feel she had done something wrong in not wanting to have sex. Had that been the reason he'd slept with Susie? It wasn't fair to blame her pregnancy. She had to face it, she simply didn't want to make love to Blair. She never instigated lovemaking, she acquiesced. It was pleasant enough but there was no emotion, no mental connection to him.

Jennifer rubbed her brow as she felt beads of sweat break out.

'Jennifer, what's up? You look terrible.' Christina put the cups on the table.

'Ah, just a hot flush thing. I'm fine.' She reached for her glass of water. 'Anyway, I'm due to go back to the island.' She'd made up her mind. She was going back, but not to Blair. Not yet.

Her mother came down to the harbour to see her off. 'I'm worried about you, you're so quiet. I wish you wouldn't go all that way out there. What if you get sick?'

'I'm not going to, Mum. I'm as healthy as a horse. The chopper can fly me straight to hospital if necessary. Now, you be sure and call Beverly and get into that tennis club.'

'I certainly will. Oh my goodness, look who's over there!'

Jennifer spun around to see who her mother was ogling. In the middle of a group was a man, hair spiked with gel, dark glasses, a bold Mambo shirt open over his bare chest, and white shorts. Three young women who looked like caricatures of sexpot starlets seemed to be attached to him. A video cameraman walked backwards in front of them, a sound recordist attached by his sound umbilical cable held a fluffy boom microphone aloft.

'That's Dougie Wilson, the TV star,' whispered Christina, in awe.

'Bloody Willsy,' muttered Jennifer. 'What's he doing up here?'

In the resort check-in area she found Vera. 'What's going on with the media circus on the wharf?'

'They're doing a segment for Willsy's TV show. What a pain in the bum he is,' she said shortly.

'Vera, this is my mother, Christina Campbell, she's seeing me off. Willsy isn't going to the island, I hope?'

'Not to Branch. He's on that monster cruiser. Doing a fishing charter. They might go to Sooty.'

Jennifer shuddered. 'I hope I don't have to see him.'

'I rather like him on TV,' said Christina. 'Cheeky, bit of a larrikin, but you know how they are these days.'

'I heard there was some heavy partying when he was at Branch last time,' said Vera. 'Frankly, I don't think they'll be doing much fishing. That boat is meant to stay in port and party, or rip over to Hawaii or New Zealand.'

Jennifer didn't answer. How could he dare to come back up here? She'd seen the photos of Rhonda as a bridesmaid back in Dublin and the last she and Blair had heard she was working in her father's office and hating it. She'd knocked back a job in a pub that would have paid well. She confessed she was nervous around drinkers and wouldn't work in hospitality again.

From inside the glassed-in waiting area they watched the group being filmed and finally Willsy and the girls boarded a sleek speedboat that zipped from the wharf through the moored boats to the luxury cruiser, *Kicking Back*. Jennifer wondered if the slick boys and the young English staffie were on board. She didn't care especially. She just hoped the cruiser didn't come to Branch.

Rosie wasn't getting back to Branch until the next morning, so Jennifer made a quiet return to the island. She'd rung Mac and he'd confirmed that she could stay at the research station. They'd agreed that the best way to explain this was to say she'd been hired to write about the station's current activities for an academic journal and had formally begun an intensive study course under

Professor Macdonald Masters and Dr Isobel Belitas. This news item was written up in the resort's daily newsletter.

As the big white catamaran nosed out of the harbour a feeling of anticipation and relaxation struck Jennifer. There was a visible letting-down of hair, a more relaxed attitude amongst the passengers as they kicked off their shoes, had a glass of champagne, began to get into holiday mode. She felt it too, as people around her set out to have a good time. This was an interlude of blue space between the familiar mainland and the speck of green on coral that was now her island home.

Doyley saw her and gave her a big smile. 'How're things in the big smoke? I'm off tomorrow for a whole week.' It seemed the news item in the Branch newsletter hadn't made much of a ripple around the resort.

'Don't rage too hard. What's news here?' asked Jennifer as brightly as she could. While she was glad to be on the island she felt uncomfortable about the new arrangement.

If Doyley saw anything odd in the assistant manager's wife moving out he didn't show it. 'All quiet on the western front. Good luck with your studies, by the way. When do you want your gear moved over to the station?'

'Oh, I haven't decided what to take yet. Where's Blair?'

'He's in his office.'

'Ah, have you heard anything about a TV crew coming here?' She hoped Blair hadn't arranged for Willsy to film the resort.

'Nope. Whenever they do it's a nightmare for the guests.'

'Thanks, Doyley, see you later.' Jennifer headed to reception.

Blair was coming out as she approached. He gave her a warm smile. 'Hey, is everything all right? How's Christina?'

'Settling in. She'll be okay. So long as she stays there . . . though she doesn't seem to want to cross the water, thank heavens. And the doctor is pleased with my progress,' she added pointedly.

'Oh, good.' There was a slight pause. 'Do you want to have lunch with me?'

'Thanks, but I think I'd better check in at the station. I'm going to stay over there for a bit, Blair, just for a break. And I'll be busy with all the projects happening.'

'So I read in the newsletter,' he said dryly.

'Blair, do you know anything about Willsy and a film crew coming here?'

'Shit no.' He looked shocked. 'Why?'

'I saw him at Headland. I also saw Fanzio and Holding and that young staffie from England. Rosie pointed him out. It looks like they're all on *Kicking Back*.'

Blair looked stunned. 'No idea.' He didn't look pleased at being left out of the loop. 'They could be cruising further north.'

'Don't those two executives do any work? Vera thought they were going fishing.'

'Yeah? For what?' Blair gave a short laugh. 'Did Rosie talk to them?'

'No. Anyway, so long as that Willsy doesn't have the gall to come here.'

'No one knows anything. We can't stop him, especially if he's with corporate people. So don't say anything to anyone. And if they're filming, well, it could be good for us.'

Jennifer turned away. 'I don't agree. But that's your area, Blair.'

'So when will I see you?'

'I'm packing some clothes. I'll go backwards and forwards, if that's all right. Keep up appearances,' she said, trying to smile.

'Well, how about dinner sometime soon? Rosie will be back, I'll be off duty.' There was a hint of gallantry in his manner.

'That'd be nice. I'll give you a call from Mac's.' It occurred to her he could walk over and have a look around, find out what she was doing. But she wasn't inclined to suggest it, and he hadn't asked. She decided she preferred keeping her two worlds separate.

Jennifer went to the cabin and added clothes, toiletries and towels to the bag she'd taken to Headland and left it in the courtyard. Doyley had promised that someone going to the station would drop it off for her. She changed into shorts and hurried to her new accommodation.

She waved to several of the researchers as she

went into her work area and found a note from Tony stuck to her laptop. 'If you're back by two p.m. come to Gideon's. Bring notepad! Going for a dive!' The station was quiet, and she wondered what was going on.

There was a buzz of activity at Gideon's. Through the trees she could see a group at the edge of the lagoon where Lloyd was at the helm of the cabin cruiser and Rudi and Carmel were in a tinnie. Between the little aluminium outboard and the fishing boat floated Gideon's submersible. It looked more like a super sea beast gleaming silver and white, the clear nose cone and bubble windows looking like a transparent snout and eyes. The hatch on top was open, with Gideon, in a black wetsuit, perched on top and Isobel, in a purple wetsuit, in the water beside it. The great fishlike seaplane was tethered by ropes held by Lloyd in the fishing boat and Carmel in the tinnie.

Tony waded from the water and came towards her. 'Good timing. This is quite an effort.'

'I had no idea this was happening. Are they really going to dive?'

'A serious test run. Tide and conditions are perfect. Gideon will pilot, Isobel will observe, plus one other. You or I have first option.'

'Not me. No way.'

'I suspected as much. There's a video camera on board, but they say it's not the same as being there, so to speak. But you should go with Lloyd.'

She hesitated. 'All right. What's the plan?'

'Apparently they're checking the state of the reef around here in the marine park, then they'll go outside the reef for a test dive to one hundred metres. Later they'll do the bigger depths off the continental shelf.'

'I can't believe Gideon built that thing.'

'Its specifications and design are similar to a lot of the submersible manufacturers'. It's a huge business going in all directions. Gideon has added a few clever design features.'

'Using his aeronautical engineering, I suppose. It really does look like an underwater plane. Or a shark! Are you nervous getting in it?'

He looked at the craft and grinned. 'Sort of. But Isobel is so experienced I feel safe with her. And Gideon, I have to say, does seem to know what he's doing.'

'He should,' said Rudi, joining them. 'Don't worry, you'll be so gobsmacked by what you can see you won't think about anything else.'

They headed slowly out of the lagoon into the deeper water, the fishing cruiser towing the craft with the three adults strapped inside in harnesses. They had audio contact with Lloyd's boat.

They ran through a checklist and then Gideon's voice announced they would begin descending and fly under their own power. The line was dropped, Gideon pushed the control stick that was electronically linked to the thrusters in the rear, and the sharkmobile shot below the surface in a roar of bubbles, its passengers seated in the pressurised cabin. Like a plane it banked to starboard and slid swiftly down and away from the cruiser.

Jennifer's heart lurched. She glanced at Lloyd who was looking at his sonar screen. 'Is it safe?'

'They can move quickly, it's very manoeuvrable. Unlike the old subs, which were like hot air balloons with ballast tanks,' said Lloyd. 'It's my dream to build one. I wish I'd gone to uni but I just wanted to get on the water and help my dad. I did my apprenticeship with him as a shipwright, but he prefers boats that stay *above* the water. Gideon is my teacher now.'

'About submersibles? How can he afford to do all this? Or has Isobel subsidised him?' asked Jennifer. Now that she'd seen the sharkmobile in action she was stunned at its sophistication. This was no tin, plastic and string job, but high-tech alloys with specially treated viewing windows and electronics. Folded underneath the short wings or fins were manipulators – mechanical arms that could be controlled to pick up objects. The array of geophysical instruments in the cockpit was way beyond her understanding.

Lloyd cut the motor, dropped the anchor and sat back in the swivel chair at the wheel. 'Gideon doesn't say a lot, but he must have access to money somewhere. Isobel helped for sure, she has the backing of all kinds of people interested in her work. She's very open in what she's doing because she wants the world to know about protecting the oceans. But with others . . . there's a lot of secrecy.'

'Big money at stake, I suppose.'

'Yeah, when it comes to industry uses. But there was a team of oceanographers from Scripps Institute out here a year ago. Man, what I'd give to go to San Diego and study there. Even just to work on one of their research ships. They told me some of the stuff being investigated on a global scale. If they're investing around two hundred million bucks, there must be some pay-off.'

They sat in silence for a while, then a seagull with one leg flew down and squatted on the top of the cabin. Lloyd went to the locker, pulled out his bait bucket and handed the seagull a fish. 'That's Hoppy. Lost his foot when he got caught in fishing tackle floating in the water. Some fisherman had a tangle, cut it off, and threw it overboard. We found Hoppy with his foot almost severed by the nylon and his wing tangled up as well. Nursed him back to health and he's learned to manage with just one foot. He follows us when we come out fishing for a free feed.'

'Talking of fishing, I saw those guys, Fanzio and Holding, over on the mainland. They had that Willsy and a bunch of groupies with them. Said they were going out fishing.'

Lloyd looked surprised. 'Yeah? Wonder who they've got as crew? That's not a boat for fishing unless they take a small craft along with them. They didn't seem the fishing type anyway.'

'It's just an excuse to get away with a bunch of girls, guys and booze,' said Jennifer.

'And the rest,' said Lloyd.

'Drugs?'

'When Willsy was staying here he was offering hard stuff around. I don't think Rosie knew. Doyley tried to keep a cap on it.'

'Did Blair know?'

Lloyd looked uncomfortable. 'I doubt it. Frankly, I think he's been more impressed with the resort execs. Don't want to be rude about him, but he's working on a promotion, I'd say.'

'Blair is ambitious,' said Jennifer noncommittally, wondering how much Lloyd knew about her and Blair's problems.

'I don't think those two blokes carry a lot of weight in Reef Resorts. Well, not according to Gideon. Speak of the devil.'

At that moment Gideon's voice crackled over the radio. 'We're traversing the southwest end of Scarf's Reef, doing one more run, and will head back inside. Over.'

'Roger, Gideon. We're anchored as instructed. Over.'

'We'll surface within fifty metres. Visibility is good. Over, out.'

'I wonder how deep they've gone,' said Jennifer.

'Isobel is looking at the condition of the reef to see if the bleaching is happening there as well as in the inner reef. Or any other problems like another crown of thorns infestation.'

'Maybe they can spot where the big fish hang out,' said Jennifer.

'That's for sure. Trouble is, they move,' said Lloyd, laughing. 'I've had people out fishing and I can see a school of fish on the depth sounder right under us and they won't touch a damned line.'

'I feel bad catching those big fish,' said Jennifer.

'Well, maybe Carmel and I can persuade you to come sailing one day.'

Jennifer liked Lloyd and had confidence in him. 'I respect your seamanship, Lloyd, but I'll have to work up to that. Does Carmel sail?'

'I've taught her. In fact, we've been planning a day out with Isobel, Gideon and a few others. Some friend of Isobel's is coming in with a decent-sized schooner. Very solid, stable boat. It'll be a fun day.'

'I'll think about it,' said Jennifer, and meant it. 'How serious are you and Carmel?' she asked, thinking how well suited they were despite their very different backgrounds.

Echoing her thought, Lloyd said, 'We're very close. I think I love her. I mean,' he grinned, 'how do you really know?' And went on, 'We come from very different families. Hers is quite rich, I think. But she and my dad get along famously. What's really important is we like the same things, we're both really interested in what we're doing here. Like, my resort job is a way to earn money. Learning from Gideon and following what everyone is doing at the research station, that's our passion.'

Jennifer looked out to sea and didn't speak for a minute. His answer made her feel hollow and brought home yet again the chasm between her and Blair. Suddenly there was the welcome distraction of the sharkmobile breaking the surface of the water and slowly gliding to a halt. It gently pitched and rolled as Lloyd shipped the anchor and sped towards it. Once alongside, the hatch was opened, a line attached, and Isobel slid into the water, nosing the craft to the side where the protector buoys stopped it bumping against the hull. Gideon and Tony were helped aboard, both grinning broadly.

'I guess we don't have to ask how it was,' said Jennifer.

'God, you have to do this! Just have to!' exclaimed Tony, showing the most bubbling enthusiasm she'd ever seen in him. His face was one huge smile, his eyes sparkled and he seemed unable to frame the words to express himself. So he grabbed Jennifer and gently shook her. 'It's bloody fantastic! You must see it!'

Gideon was unzipping the top of his wetsuit and shaking water from his silver hair. 'It was rather good. The craft went well, thought we had a stall at one point when we hovered on the spot, but it performed well on the whole.'

'So what did you see?' asked Lloyd.

'You can see for yourself next trip,' called Isobel as she climbed onto the stern. 'There are still some fish around. And up to twenty metres the bleaching is not so obvious. The deeper you go, of course, there's not enough light for coral. What's alarming though is that the water temperature is slightly up. Not good for coral.' She pulled her goggles off and smiled at Jennifer. 'It's very beautiful and we shall get you into my world one day. Soon.'

Lloyd was handing out cold drinks, Tony was taking photographs, so no one paid much attention to her last remark.

On the way back to the island, slowly towing the sharkmobile, Gideon wrote up his notes, and Isobel, sitting on the bow, spoke into a dictaphone. Lloyd concentrated on manoeuvring the boat and the fishlike plane following in its wake like some strange pet.

'I never thought I'd see you at a loss for words,' laughed Jennifer.

Tony shook his head. 'Me either. At first I felt disoriented. I was worried I'd feel claustrophobic but it was like a surround movie, I was just in it. The oddest thing is losing your sense of what's up and what's down. That machine is amazing.'

'Underwater flying.'

'It's got to be the closest thing to it. Funny seeing how Isobel and Gideon related to each other. Different to how they are just around the place. I felt I was in safe, knowledgeable hands, that's for sure. I'd better write up my impressions too, before they dissipate.'

Jennifer felt left out and wished she didn't have such a phobia, if that's what it was, about the sea, especially under water. 'Then I'll write up my impressions of *you*. Has anything ever made you feel such euphoria before?' she asked.

He lowered his eyes, his smile soft. 'Being in love, I suppose.'

Lloyd handed Tony a can of beer. 'Figured you might be ready for this.'

Tony took the beer and pulled the ring tab and handed it to Lloyd. 'You figured right. Thanks.'

Back at the research station there was a group sitting at tables outside the canteen discussing the dive. Mac took Jennifer aside.

'Your room is cleaned up, there's fresh linen from the resort and your gear's in there. I reckon it'll suit you okay. Keep your work space next to Rudi, your quarters aren't big enough really, and you don't want to be stuck in your room all the time. It's the upper floor so you have a bit of a balcony. They're really jerry-built so if there's a cyclone, get out.'

'You're joking, right?'

'Er . . . no. The main block of the research station meets regulations, but the rest of the buildings have kind of evolved, so they're not exactly legal. Tony is on the lower floor, but he's a quiet fellow. You have to share the shower and loo but it's just the two of you. You don't have to use the shower block the students use. Though that's where the laundry is – but I imagine you can send your stuff over to the resort.'

'Mac, this is great. I must say it's been easier than I thought. Even Blair is being nice.'

'Now this isn't a holiday camp, mate. You have to knuckle down if you're serious about studying.' His eyes were smiling.

Jennifer hugged him. 'Mac, I'll do this. For me, but also for you. Lead on.'

The so-called VIP accommodation was at the end of the sandy 'main street' that ran past the building with the labs, the student accommodation with canteen and amenities block and the section of small shanty-style cottages where Mac and Rudi and the senior PhD candidates were housed. Isobel had the best of the two double-storey units. The structure did look wobbly and, glancing up, Jennifer wondered about the strength of the wooden balcony. A flight of outside steps led to her level. The bathroom was at the rear with a clothes line stretched across a scrubby cleared patch before the pisonias and she-oaks rose in a screen. Being far from the students, it appeared to be a quiet area.

She went up the steps and found an open-plan sitting room and kitchenette with a bedroom and the balcony. It had basic furniture, bare floors with some rush mats, and split-bamboo blinds at the front window that screened the balcony from her bedroom. She lay down and stretched out to test the double bed and found she was looking into trees. Her bag sat in the middle of the floor. It was unadorned student digs, and it suited her just fine. She wasn't here to nest, or holiday. It was a place to lay her head, dress, and think a bit.

Dinner was a shared event in Mac's house with Carmel, Rudi and Lloyd cooking pasta. Isobel, Gideon, Mac and Tony sat with Jennifer in the living room and around the dining table. There was much chatter, banter, discussion and debate.

She drifted to Rudi, who was making salad. 'Can I help?'

'Don't wreck the system. It's a sort of roster or short straws. You'll get to clean up or take your turn in the kitchen next time. So, are you settled in okay?'

'Haven't made the bed or put anything away as yet. And I love it. I guess I'm meant to be a poor student. I feel really comfortable. Happy.'

He smiled at her. 'That's good. You need a clear head to think and write and study. Don't worry about all the personal stuff. These things have a way of working through the system. You have Mac and Gideon and Isobel on your team. You've got it made.'

'And you, Rudi. I like being your neighbour.'

He handed her a slice of avocado. 'That's good. Pop into the lab tomorrow. I'm finding some interesting results.'

She stayed up late and didn't notice Tony leave. She and Isobel walked barefoot back to their units. There were lights on in a couple of the students' rooms, some muted music in another.

At her unit they paused. Isobel's was opposite, Tony's lights were off. Isobel turned off the torch. The moonlight was pale, filtered by cloud. Mutton birds moaned in the distance.

'As soon as you are awake, tap on my door. We'll go for a beach walk, yes?'

'Okay. Great.' Jennifer yawned. 'It's been such a wonderful night. I know we all have to go back to our respective families and lives, but this is so cool. I feel so . . . free.'

Isobel spoke quietly. 'It's mental and emotional freedom. You carry it with you and so you make your life what you want it to be. Sleep well. Tomorrow – work begins.'

Jennifer tried to be as quiet as she could going up the steps so as not to wake Tony, but in the unfamiliar setting she tripped, cursed and stumbled inside. Looking at the unmade bed, she pulled off her clothes, grabbed a sheet and wound it round herself, turned on the overhead fan and fell onto the bed, too tired to bother with anything else. As she drifted almost immediately to sleep, the thought came to her that this was hardly the way to live or example to set for her baby. But Isobel's words about emotional freedom also came back. Jennifer slept soundly and serenely.

15

Below the Surface

THE MORNING LIGHT WAS pushing through the trees as Jennifer rolled on her side in the unfamiliar bed. She loved waking with the light. Blair always insisted on sleeping in a blacked-out room. She stretched, realising she was naked in a hard narrow bed with just a sheet flung on it. Then she remembered her late night. She hoped she hadn't made any noise falling up the stairs in the dark.

Jennifer wound the sheet around her and stepped gingerly onto the little wooden balcony. Isobel said to meet her early, but surely not this early. Jennifer peered at the double unit opposite, trying to see any movement.

'Morning, fair maiden, how did you sleep?' called a soft, amused voice.

Jennifer looked down to see Tony on the track below. 'You're up early. Have you been for a walk already?'

'Yes. I like this time. Making the first footprints on the new day. Are you settled in up there?'

'I hope I didn't wake you last night.' She glanced down at herself wound in the sheet that trailed behind her. 'And no, I'm not organised. Didn't even make the bed or unpack. I didn't see you leave the gathering.'

'I made a quiet exit. I'm making tea – would you like one? Or a coffee?'

'Tea would be great. I'll try the shower and change. Be there in a flash.'

He had squeezed fresh juice, the tea was made and the smell of toast made her hungry.

'Can I scrounge a piece of toast, please? I'm starving, and I have to meet Isobel and I've no idea when we'll be back.'

'I borrowed a toaster, no one is up this early so it's been handy. I even have Vegemite. Or a banana?'

'Can I have both? Not together,' she laughed. 'I have a good excuse to pig out.'

He looked at her slim figure, tanned legs in shorts, the loose T-shirt barely hiding the neat bulge of her belly. 'Are you feeling okay?'

'Doctor says I'm fit as a flea. I have a lot more energy now, thank goodness. Felt very draggy for a while there.' *Or was it depression?* 'Just as well, seeing I'm embarking on a fairly big project. I was thinking maybe I should go through your, Gideon's and Isobel's notes for an overview. I see this effort as being more in the style of a journal. Like the old-time explorers and adventurers wrote of their travails on expeditions and such.' She bit into her toast.

'Sounds good, better discuss it with Mac. And what about your honours project? You're going to have a lot of writing to do.'

'That's why I'll do as much hands-on stuff as I can while everyone is here. Once Mac packs up and heads back to uni for the new term, I'll be on my own. Apart from some of the researchers. And I'll have a lot of long days to fill in.' *And I'll be back in the unit with Blair.* The thought depressed her for a moment. Well, it was still a few weeks away. 'How's your magazine story coming along?'

'The first article is about the endangered reef. It was shocking to see the sad, grey, lifeless banks of coral. I had a long talk to Rudi and to Mac and Isobel. Like you, I'll stay on as long as they're here. When the main group of people leave I'll go to the mainland. Seems a lot of the problem for the reef is pollution from the coast.'

'Farming and developments. It's tragic knowing what's running off into the ocean.'

'Rudi has found traces of industrial toxins in marine plants and animals. Amongst other things. His work is another story.' Tony refilled their mugs with tea. 'There's a lot of confusion and varying theories over the crown of thorns starfish and the future of the reef. Will take a bit of unravelling.'

'So, Tony, what are your commitments?' asked Jennifer. 'You don't seem as . . . sad as last time we talked.'

'It comes and goes. It's easier to forget the wars and tragedy on the other side of the world when you're in a paradise like this. Or anywhere in Australia, for that matter.' He busied himself with milk and adding more hot water to the teapot, then said, 'I'm coming to terms with things. Life doesn't always pan out the way you expect.'

You can say that again. 'I hate people who tell you life is what you make it. You can't change fate and so on.'

'Maybe you can't change destiny, but you can take some control of your circumstances rather than letting events roll over you.' He gave a rueful grin. 'I think I've been a bit of a rudderless ship, adrift on the sea of happenstance.'

'They say optimism and self-confidence breed success.' *Well, Blair says so.* 'I'm more shy, I guess, and I probably miss opportunities. So now you've taken back control of your life?' asked Jennifer, wondering if he was aware that she was just embarking on this process.

'Subconsciously I made choices. I'm here, and not in the Middle East, for starters. And a wound is healing that I didn't think ever would.'

Before Jennifer could probe more into his enigmatic reply, Isobel appeared in the doorway.

'I smell toast. Irresistible.'

'I'll make you coffee. I keep some on-hand just for you.'

'What a neighbour. Fantastic. Are we the only ones up and about?'

'Around here, yes. I went to the beach, there's always an early bird or two about. And I saw that old bloke with the eye patch. He was fiddling with the pool pumps at the resort,' said Tony.

'Patch. He's an oddball. They call him the resident perv, although he's more like the resident spy. He sees everything, I reckon – even with one eye! He always pops up here when you least expect it,' said Jennifer. 'He gave me the creeps in the beginning. I think he's a bit pathetic now.'

'Some of the local colour, eh? So, what are you two up to this morning?' asked Tony.

'A small excursion,' smiled Isobel.

Jennifer and Isobel walked along the beach past the resort.

'How well do you know Tony?' asked Jennifer.

'As well as he wants me to know him. I don't pry. He shares small parts of himself on occasion.'

'He referred to some wound he'd suffered. He meant emotional, not the scar on his arm, I assume.'

'He won't mind me telling you,' said Isobel slowly.

'Oh, don't break any personal confidences,' said Jennifer quickly, thinking of all she'd shared with Isobel.

'No, you should know. He doesn't speak of his love affairs but he did lose his heart in Afghanistan. He'd seen so much death and destruction he thought he was immune. Until in a hospital one day he saw a young girl, about six, who was badly hurt and orphaned. He said she just reached out to him as he went past and that was it. He met the old uncle and decided to help her. I think he had contact with her for nearly a year.'

'What happened?'

'She was killed travelling into Pakistan. He blames himself. And he misses her. I think he felt if he could help just one child, at least, then some small good would come out of the whole horror of that war.' Isobel lifted her shoulders. 'But wars go on. Children die.'

Instinctively Jennifer folded her arms over her belly. 'Poor Tony. He seemed uncomfortable about my pregnancy. Now I understand why. In comparison, no matter what happens, my child will have love and protection.'

Isobel noted, but ignored, the 'no matter what happens'. She touched Jennifer's arm. 'Your baby is a great gift. To all of us.'

Jennifer didn't understand exactly what she meant and they walked in silence, enjoying the early morning. A few people were about but as they neared the resort, Jennifer was shocked to see *Kicking Back* moored in the lagoon. Gordon Blake was disembarking from the little motor launch that belonged to the luxury cruiser. Spotting Doyley unloading departing guests' luggage at the wharf, she went over to him.

'Hi, Jennifer, how's it?'

'Good, good. Listen, Doyley, are Fanzio and Holding back over here? I saw them with that Willsy guy in Headland.'

'Yeah. They're not stopping. On some fishing charter. They just dropped off a new staffie. Don't know how come he's hanging out with them.'

'Who knows? Maybe it's who you know. Just thought I'd ask.'

'See ya, Jennifer.' He nodded at Isobel and started up the electric cart.

'Why are you curious about these people?' asked Isobel as they followed the beach towards Coral Point.

'Maybe I'm being unfair, but I just don't like them. Blair thinks he'll jump the promotion queue by hanging out with the resort executives, and when that TV guy was here there was a bit of a drama. I think it's strange the way they keep coming up here.'

'This is a very beautiful part of Australia. So many people want to come to see the reef. Experience the idyllic island life, eh?'

'So what are we doing at Gideon's?' asked Jennifer, wondering why Isobel had insisted they wear their swimsuits. 'We're not really going sailing, are we?'

'Of course we are, but it's work as well.'

There was no one around. They went past Gideon's house and saw the goat tethered out of reach of the vegetable patch, the Shark Bar, and the sharkmobile pulled above the high-water mark shrouded in netting and tarpaulins. The dinghy was tied to the tree, but standing at the edge of the lagoon was Gideon. A sleek sailboat was anchored next to him.

'Whose boat? We're not going out in that, are we? It looks so . . . frail,' said Jennifer.

'It's a lovely little sloop. Very light, very manoeuvrable. Sailing without an engine is a special experience,' said Isobel. 'It has a shallow draught so we can skim over the reef.'

'Oh no. Is this the surprise, a sailing lesson?'

Gideon turned and, seeing them, gave a salute.

Isobel took Jennifer's hand. 'We've talked about our paths crossing, for whatever reason. I think you feel as I do. There is a bond with us, yes?' Jennifer nodded, her eyes not leaving the white boat that looked as flimsy as a butterfly perched lightly on the calm aqua water. 'So if I ask you to trust me, you will agree? There is a reason I want you to take this step with me.'

Jennifer still didn't speak. What would seem to be a casual event, with some light-hearted teasing, some reluctance on her part to get into the boat, she knew had more significance.

'Will you agree?' continued Isobel. 'To do as I ask, and put your trust in me and let go of any feelings, any doubts, you may have?'

'You make it sound . . . scary.' Jennifer's voice was a whisper.

Gideon came towards them. 'Good morning,

Miss Jennifer. Are you ready?' His smile was gentle, his eyes soft.

'For what?' Jennifer tried to laugh. Isobel had not let go of her hand.

'Let Isobel show you. There are just the three of us and it is a perfect morning.'

They walked to the water's edge and Gideon, wearing old khaki shorts, waded into the water and held the boat as Jennifer and Isobel followed. A life-preserver was hung over the side and Gideon used it to pull himself out of the water. The sand was cold under her feet. The bottom felt like corrugated cardboard, soft, ridged with lines of the movement of the tide and waves. The water came up to Jennifer's waist and Isobel lay forward and stroked sideways to the boat, still holding Jennifer's hand as she waded slowly.

At the boat Gideon leaned over the side. 'Put your foot in the ring, use it as a step.' He took her hand and Isobel put Jennifer's hand up on the hull, helping her to swing herself onto the boat.

Jennifer was shaking. There was little space so she crouched in the shallow cockpit. Gideon and Isobel perched on the hull, their feet on either side of Jennifer, who hugged her knees. Gideon loosened a line and the sail seemed to catch its breath in a gulping intake, then billowed out in a huge puff, making the boat slide swiftly forward. Jennifer squeezed her eyes shut. No one spoke and Jennifer braced herself, feeling the boat heel, terrified they were going to turn over. But the rush forward, the straining sails, the swishing water, the sense of speed, compelled her to open her eyes.

'Where has the wind come from?' she exclaimed. The water looked only slightly ruffled, the craft barely touching the water as they skimmed across the lagoon towards the wider sea.

'You can't see the wind, but it's there. Like many things in life,' grinned Gideon.

'Sit up here beside me,' said Isobel. 'Be ready to duck under the boom when we change tack.'

Gideon changed direction several times as Jennifer began to relax in the narrow boat. Once she glanced up to the top of the mast, but mainly she kept focused on what was close at hand: her feet, Isobel's hand holding a rope, a shiny metal cleat, water splashing along the edge of the hull. She did not look behind, or to the horizon, but tried to be in the present, accepting she was sliding along the surface of the sea, blue water on top and all around, and also endlessly beneath her. Isobel reached over and touched Gideon's arm and he turned the boat so the sail luffed and they slowed as if the wind had been turned off. Swiftly he dropped the sail and swung onto the bow, slipping the reef pick over the side on to a sand patch. Gradually the boat steadied and stayed in place.

The little boat with three aboard was low to the water and Isobel stretched out and peered beneath the surface, then sat up and pulled from a small locker two sets of fins and facemasks with snorkels attached.

Jennifer recoiled. 'Oh no. No way!'

'Couldn't be calmer. It's perfect. No current to speak of either,' said Gideon.

'I'm not a good swimmer. I really didn't swim till I was a teenager and then just in a pool.'

'It's very shallow here, perfectly safe. Jenny, all I am asking you to do . . . is look from here, like this.' Isobel spat in her facemask, swilled around some seawater, shook the mask and held it to the surface of the sea. 'See the clarity, a little magnification but it is a window to a magic world.' She put the mask on her head, pulled on the flippers, swung her legs over the side and slipped into the water.

Holding on to the side of the hull, Isobel smiled up at Jennifer. 'I want you to follow. Gideon will give you a line to hold on to. Just to get the feel of this.'

Jennifer desperately didn't want to disappoint Isobel, who smiled cheerfully as she bobbed beside the boat. But this was asking too much of her.

Gideon showed Jennifer the white nylon rope with a loop on the end. 'You can hang on to this or put your arm through it. You saw how she treated the facemask, but first the feet.'

'Gideon, I can't do this . . .'

'You can. You're ready. Isobel would not bring you out here if she didn't believe you are. Trust her, Jennifer.'

Her hands were shaking as she pulled the plastic flippers onto her feet. 'I can't move in these things. I'll trip, they feel so awkward.'

'Sit on the side of the boat, hang your legs over

the side, let go and slide in. Try to move your legs as if you are walking and the flippers will keep your head above water. It's called treading water. Remember to spit into the facemask to stop it fogging up.'

I'm not going to do this. But she copied what she'd seen Isobel do, pushed the facemask on her head and immediately opened her mouth, gasping for air as her nasal passages were blocked.

'You can try the snorkel later. Just get a sense of this. I can haul you back in a flash.' He held up the rope reassuringly.

'Don't go far, this won't take a minute. I'm in and then I'm out,' said Jennifer.

'Push yourself out from the boat and just let go,' instructed Isobel. 'I'm right here beside you.' She held out a hand.

There was nowhere to go. Jennifer closed her eyes, gulped a mouthful of air, shoved herself away from the boat and fell, clumsily, splashily, into the water. She bobbed below the surface but before she opened her eyes her head was out of the water and Isobel had her arm. The water was refreshing, it felt silky on her skin.

'See how effortless you feel with the fins? Now, put your face to the surface, look through the mask.' Isobel still held her arm, her body close to Jennifer who had the rope from the boat looped around her wrist.

Jennifer stuck her face into the water. It was like opening a dirty window and seeing clearly what was outside. She saw her fins waving as she trod in watery space. She saw the clearness of the water. And then – a ledge of coral, bright yellow-orange and olive green. It looked close enough to stand on. She pointed her toe but the flipper didn't reach. She lifted her head and gulped a mouthful of air.

'It's not as close as it looks. Now come with me, do as I do. Trust me, Jenny.' Isobel took her hand and stretched out horizontally, 'Swim with me, just kick one, two, three, slowlyyy . . .'

Jennifer instinctively kicked and felt her body surge forward with the power from the fins. Isobel kept pace then stopped.

'Watch me, then we'll do it together.'

Before Jennifer could answer, Isobel took a breath, flipped down, her fins flashing out of the water as she did several strokes down towards the coral, then angled her body up, breaking the surface.

'Ready?' She took Jennifer's hand and drew a breath as Jennifer did the same, and then they were both kicking down towards the colourful ledge. Jennifer felt her facemask press against her face but her initial sense of suffocating passed as the clear brilliance of the scene mesmerised her. The coral appeared to glow it was so bright. Small, dazzling-coloured fish darted in cheeky hide and seek. Seagrasses swayed like artful land-scaping. Then she was being pulled up and was treading water again. Isobel grinned at her.

'Ready to go down again?'

'How long was I down there? It seemed ages.'

'Seconds. We'll get the snorkels. If we swim a few metres over there the reef is higher and you can float and breathe and study it more closely.' She put the snorkel in place beneath the strap of Jennifer's facemask and showed her the mouth piece.

'Bite on this, just breathe normally.' She adjusted her snorkel, put her face in the water and Jennifer heard her rasping breathing through the short plastic pipe. Isobel took out the mouthpiece and explained, 'If you take in any water just blow it out – like a whale. Follow me.' She swam off and Jennifer followed, unsure but trusting, the rope held by Gideon floating behind her.

She wasn't sure when it happened, but Jennifer felt like she was lying on top of a waterbed, supported and safe, watching a movie, face-down. Occasionally she glimpsed Isobel's red swimsuit as she dived down below to look at something more closely. Jennifer was content to float on her front, gazing at the oceanic garden beneath.

Maybe it was because she was above and not below the sea, and it was calm and beautiful, that no ghosts or fears came to haunt her. She also felt she was only seeing the superficial picture, that to dive or be in the submersible would give her more of a sense of the excitement Tony had felt. She lifted her head and glanced around. She couldn't see Isobel, or the boat. Instantly she felt her throat constrict. A dozen horrific scenarios flashed into her mind – from the movie *Jaws*, to the report of divers abandoned by a dive boat, to her own childhood nightmares. She pushed the mouth-piece away and started to swim, flailing with no thought to direction, and found she was crying out but her mouth was full of water. She had a sense of waves closing over her, as if night had fallen, that she was being pulled down into a dark and fearful place where bones and bodies lay.

She struggled, then a firm arm came from behind, across her chest and grabbed her under the armpit. 'It's all right. Calm, Jenny . . . you're having a panic attack, take deep breaths . . .' Isobel's voice was strong, insistent. Isobel side-stroked, pulling Jennifer along until she caught her breath and freed herself.

Panting, she trod water and saw the boat behind Isobel. 'God, what happened! I thought I was drowning, going down, something.'

'It's not unusual. Stay still, reorient yourself.'

'I want to get out.'

'No! Stay here. Just a few moments. See, the water is calm, blue. The boat and Gideon are there. And down there . . . you can still see the colours. How lovely they are . . .' Isobel's voice was steady and soothing.

Gradually Jennifer caught her breath, her heart stopped racing and she was able to look down into the water once more.

By the time they swam to the boat and Jennifer handed Gideon her mask, snorkel and flippers while she was still in the water holding on to the life ring, she'd regained her confidence. Isobel pulled herself into the boat, then she and

Gideon reached over and both helped Jennifer on board.

'I feel so clumsy with this bulging tummy,' laughed Jennifer.

'She's laughing, this is good,' grinned Gideon. 'Well done, girl. Well done.'

Isobel pulled up the anchor, Gideon set the sail and they tacked about.

They glided into the lagoon. 'As soon as we're ashore someone put the billy on,' said Gideon.

'I could definitely eat something,' sighed Jennifer.

'Help yourselves. There're eggs, fruit, goats' cheese, good goats' milk too,' said Gideon.

This time Jennifer jumped over the side and waded ashore, carrying the bag that held the snorkelling gear. Isobel followed and they went to Gideon's house. As Jennifer dumped the soggy bag outside, Isobel hugged her.

'I am very proud of you. You know what you did this morning?'

'Something I never thought I would!'

'There is no going back now, Jenny. You've crossed a line.' She tapped her head. 'In here, you've made up your mind. And, if you wish, I can help you really start to uncover and use all that potential I know is inside. Use your brain, your heart, your life, to *do* something. Having a baby is wonderful and it will fulfil you in many ways as nothing else can. But, Jenny, children grow up and they leave. And you have to let them go. And then, then, you must have your life too. So start now.'

411

'I wish my mother knew that.'

'Eventually your mother will be your child, and you will be the mother. Live your life, explore, learn, love.' She smiled. 'Now, let's have a real breakfast!'

Jennifer was concentrating at her computer, notes and tapes scattered around her. At first she didn't hear the tap at the door. Then she looked up, surprised to see Blair standing there.

'So this is where you hang out?'

'Sorry, I didn't hear you, come in. What's up?' Jennifer looked concerned.

'Ah, nothing too important. Thought I'd stroll over and pass on a message from your mother.'

'Oh no, what's up? Do you want a coffee? Come next door to Rudi's.'

He followed her next door to the lab. 'Christina was quite perky. She wanted you to know she has a volunteer job, up at the hospital. Be handy for you, won't it?' He smiled and looked around the lab. 'God, what goes on in here? All the aquarium tanks are empty.'

'Not really. Rudi is studying the plants. Toxins, pollutants, genetics.'

'Fascinating,' said Blair dryly. 'Are you comfortable? Doyley reckons they rough it over here.'

'Nice of you to worry. I'm fine. Tony, Isobel and I have what's called the VIP digs. I'll show you round if you like.' *Thank God I tidied up after my sail.* 'Hey, know what I did this morning? I went

412

for a sail, jumped overboard and snorkelled over the reef.'

'You did! Whose boat? Not on *Kicking Back*?' He looked alarmed and Jennifer had the impression he was mad he might have missed out.

Deflated, she stirred the instant coffee. 'No, Blair. I was out on the reef with scientists, not starlets.'

'I didn't think you were into water sports. Thanks.' He took the mug of coffee from her. 'Can I see around?'

'Sure.' *Just dismiss the fact I jumped into the sea like it was no big deal.* 'I've got my honours research subject defined, which is great. A lot more observation and interviews to do.' She paused and, when he didn't ask, she explained, 'I'm studying the breeding success of the green turtles on Branch Island.'

'Oh, really. Listen, your mother also asked me to tell you that Vi and Don have let the house.'

'Whatever for?'

'Doing the nomad trek. Got a caravan and have hit the road. I think the plan is they get up here in time for the baby's arrival. When is it again?'

'Oh Blair,' she sighed and almost smiled, 'you're so interested, aren't you? The doctor tells me I'm four months gone. Do the sums. But how can Vi and Don just leave? What about his precious birds? Is the tenant looking after them?'

'Ah, no. Seems someone pinched them. Don was a bit upset.'

'Oh God, that's dreadful. He loved those birds. Who'd do that?'

Blair shrugged. 'Dunno. They've let the house to pay for their trip. S'pose Vi thought it'd take his mind off it. So, show me round then.'

Jennifer led him outside. 'That's the main lab, and that's Mac's house over there – he shares it with three of the postgrads.'

They kept walking, but Blair didn't seem interested in his surroundings. 'So you could travel, move, in say seven months?'

'Move? Where? I thought you were on a contract to stay here for a full eighteen months?' said Jennifer, feeling suddenly disturbed.

He shrugged. 'I'm working on a promotion. I thought you'd be pleased. You weren't exactly crazy about this place.'

'Blair, if you think those people – Fanzio and Holding – are going to jump you up the queue, I think you're mistaken. And I think you underestimate Rosie's capabilities.'

'Listen, you be careful what you say to her. She's my boss, remember.'

'She's my friend!'

'So who's more important?' He stopped in the middle of the track and glared at her.

Jennifer bit back her angry retort and drew a long breath. '*We* are supposed to be. You and me. We're going to be parents. We have a commitment together for life – no matter what happens.'

'What's *that* supposed to mean?'

'I don't know. I don't feel very settled, do you?

414

Please, let's not argue in the middle of the path.' She saw Kirsty and Rudi coming towards them and she turned away from the canteen to the end of the sandy road where the two double-storey units faced each other.

'I'm up there. Do you want to see?'

'I guess so. I'm here.' He followed her up the outside stairs. 'So who else is in here?'

'Tony has the place below and Isobel is across the street. At the moment she has both floors. The bottom is her office.'

Blair stuck his head in the door. 'God, you've got less room than at our place.'

'There's enough. I have the work space next to Rudi, we share meals at Mac's or the canteen, or I can eat at the resort. How are you managing?'

'Oh, fine. At least our place gets serviced. This is going backwards, for God's sake. You lived better at uni in Sydney. You can't stay here with a baby.'

'I don't intend to.'

They headed back down the steps. 'What do you intend then?' He glanced in at Tony's open door. 'This is all a bit cosy. What's he staying on the island for?'

'Writing some articles on the future of the reef.'

Blair turned at the foot of the stairs and lowered his voice. 'I hope he's not going to write anything negative. Nothing to put off tourists.'

'Why should you care, Blair? You don't care about the reef, the manta rays, the dolphins, turtles, birds, any of it. All you want is to look good, isn't that right?'

'It's my job! I'm trying to earn a decent living. We're going to need more money. Kids are expensive. The better I do my job – the higher the resort profile – the better I'll look to management. The place has just crept along under Rosie's management. I can do a lot better.'

'Like getting TV people such as Willsy in here?'

'I wish. His show rates. Nah, Joe and Reg say they're working on a few ideas and they'll include me. I guess that's why they're cruising around the area.'

'I thought it was a fishing charter.'

'Maybe they don't want another developer to get wind of their plans.'

'Develop? You're not serious! That's the last thing this area needs. Where?'

'Forget I said anything. It's no big deal. Maybe just an upmarket sports lodge somewhere. Nothing's decided yet.'

You mean no one's told you anything. 'Blair, don't get into anything like that. If what the researchers are finding is proved right, the government might stop any further tourism in this whole area.'

'Bullshit! What do you mean? Like what?'

'So now you're interested. Just more of what we know already. There're too many people using the area for recreation, for commercial uses, and it's suffering from farms and building along the

Queensland coast. One of Rudi's studies proves that.'

'A few sea plants don't prove much. Listen, what else are they finding out?'

'Maybe when I look at the impact of divers, recreational and commercial boating and fishing on the behaviour of turtles and whales and dolphins, then even a study I'm doing could show the negative effects of people on the reef eco system.'

'Oh, Jesus. Now you sound like one of those greenie academics. Seriously, Jennifer, I want you to tell me just what they're trying to prove here. It could be important for me.'

'You mean important for your career, not that it could help save the reef in the long run.' Jennifer was looking at Blair with disdain.

'You know something, Jenny, every time we talk it comes down to my job versus what you're doing – or trying to do. Why do you disagree with me all the time? You act like it's a bloody war. Pretty soon you're going to have to make a decision. Or come to your senses. Once you have the baby, you'll be out of here. You'd better get used to the idea.'

'Why do you disagree with *me* all the time? You don't even try to see my side of things. You totally dismiss me!'

'Calm down, don't make a scene. Whatever happens between us we have to rub along somehow because of the kid. So you'd better look at your priorities and get used to the idea.'

'That your career is more important than mine?'

Blair nearly laughed aloud but seeing Jennifer's set lips and narrowed eyes decided to downplay how juvenile he thought she was being. 'You can dabble with your studies while we're here, but you'll find it all less interesting, and more time consuming, with a baby.'

'Blair, answer me this. If I want to, and I can continue my work here, and I can manage to look after the baby at the same time, would you object?' Jennifer spoke in an even, steady voice to make what she was saying absolutely clear.

'What about me? Or are you saying you'll do your thing and I'll do mine?' His voice was sharp edged.

'Something like that, I guess.'

He dropped his gaze from hers and turned away. 'Then you're being stubborn and silly. This is no place for a baby. Go to Headland, stay with your mother, have the baby and by then I'll know what I'm offered.'

'And I'll know where I stand and what my prospects are too, I hope. Fair enough. But, Blair, don't try and bully me. And don't treat me like a child.'

'You'd better grow up, Jennifer. Fast.'

'I am. I realise I am, Blair.' She turned away and Blair strode back to the resort.

Jennifer walked into Mac's house. He was marking papers, his laptop on the dining table had a picture on the screen of a reef fish similar to one she'd seen on the reef itself. 'Can I have a coffee?'

'Help yourself. How's the morning been?'

'Eventful. A showdown with my husband, and I took the plunge. Literally. I got in and had a look at the reef from under water. You're right. It's unreal!' Suddenly she didn't know whether to laugh or cry.

Mac leapt to his feet, his eyes shining. 'You did it! I'm so proud of you. There'll be no stopping you now.'

'Yeah. I think that's what Blair is afraid of. He thinks I'm regressing, but I think I've just seen a bit of a path through the wilderness.'

Mac grabbed her and they did a jig around the cramped room. 'Isobel was right. You're one of us. And a proper member of the Shark Club now! There's a barbie at Gideon's tonight. We'll celebrate. And Lloyd said he had some news to share.'

Jennifer went back to her computer, trying to settle back to what she'd been writing before Blair's visit.

Later in the afternoon she went home to have a short rest before going over to the sunset barbecue. The door to Rudi's lab was shut, he was either out or working, and Tony didn't seem to be around. Though she could hear a murmur of voices from Isobel's downstairs office.

Jennifer lay on her newly made bed, to rest her mind and her body for a little while. It had been a big day. She was proud of herself for getting in the water out at the reef, and Blair's dismissal of it had hurt her. How little he really knew her. Indeed, how little he realised that she was changing. Isobel was right, she'd taken a step and there was no going back.

The research station was quiet, two of the students were sitting outside the canteen and Kirsty was sitting by one of the outside tanks in the last of the sunlight, reading a book.

As Jennifer came through the trees on Gideon's side of the island, she could smell smoke from the barbecue and hear voices. Gideon and Lloyd were cooking meat and onions; Mac, Tony and Isobel were seated at his outside picnic table. Carmel was setting out plates. 'Here she is!'

Jennifer pulled up a chair. 'That smells so good.'

Tony grinned and got up. 'I'll help you with the table, Carmel.'

Isobel began to slice Gideon's homemade bread and Mac dribbled olive oil over the salad when Tony returned with a bouquet of roses and a large jug.

'Best I could do. Gideon has a singular lack of vases.'

'Good grief,' gasped Jennifer. 'Where on earth did those come from? Whose birthday?'

Tony handed them to Jennifer. 'These are for you. To mark the occasion of your first visit to the reef.'

Jennifer was speechless. Isobel put down the breadknife and lifted her glass as Gideon and Lloyd came to the table.

'To Jenny . . . and our water baby!'

As they raised their glasses, Jennifer buried her

face in the velvet petals and rich, sweet aroma of the roses. 'You guys ... How ... ? I so miss flowers. And things being protected I don't dare pick even a leaf!'

'When we told Tony this morning he raced to the resort and ordered them from Headland and they came on this afternoon's cat,' explained Isobel.

'They're from everyone,' said Tony, looking pleased that Jennifer was so touched.

'This is so thoughtful. Thank you ... all, so much.'

'Don't expect roses every time you dive now,' said Gideon. 'But a toe in the water had to be acknowledged.' He raised his beer.

Jennifer looked from Gideon, to Tony, to Mac and Isobel, their delight and pleasure shining in their eyes. 'So what do you expect next? I'm supposed to go down in that machine of yours, Gideon?'

'At the very least!'

They all laughed as Jennifer shook her head at Isobel, who gave an expressive shrug.

After dinner, she walked back to the research station with Tony. He held the torch and she carried the roses.

'What a lovely evening. I'm going to sleep well.' She touched the roses. 'This was really sweet of you.'

'Oh, Isobel was so proud and pleased. I understand it was not an easy thing for you to do. Confronting old fears.'

Something in his voice gave her the impression he too had faced old fears. But she didn't ask. Tony had a way of quietly sharing bits of himself when it suited him. Jennifer had noticed that he was more comfortable asking the questions than being asked about himself.

'So what did you think of Lloyd's news about getting the loan of a yacht for a month?' asked Jennifer. 'Rosie is being generous, allowing him to start his own private charter trips for guests.'

'He'll do well, eventually. He knows boats, the area. He's young and personable. It's a bonus for the resort.'

'I'm sure he'll go out on his own when he can. He and Carmel seem to have a few dreams,' said Jennifer. *What dreams did Blair and I share? It seems so long ago.* 'Goodnight, Tony.' She went upstairs and placed the roses on her little table, and as she was about to change she remembered that the book she wanted to read was back by her computer. There was so much material to get through. So she headed downstairs, calling out to Tony, 'I'm just going back to my office for a book.'

'See you tomorrow.'

The lights were on outside Mac's house, several people were still awake in the graduates' rooms. The light above the outdoor tanks near the main building shone on the quietly bubbling, breathing water.

Jennifer grabbed her book without putting on the light. Rudi's door was closed and she wondered why he hadn't come to Gideon's barbecue.

422

Maybe he was at the resort, or off the island. She hadn't seen him all day. She was anxious to share her news, so she tapped at the door.

'You in there, Rudi?'

The blinds were drawn so she tried the door in case he was working inside. The room was silent except for the gurgle and hum of the water filters. The light from the fluorescent tubes in the tanks was eerie and blue. But there was a terrible smell, the air was putrid. She knew something wasn't right. She found the main light switch and flipped it on.

Rudi was lying on the floor, his face blue from the reflected light. He was very still. Jennifer ran outside, yelling.

16

Sea and Symbiosis

IN THE DARK NIGHT, the helicopter rose beside the beach, lights flashing, kicking up a flurry of sand.

'Bloody lucky Bob was spending the night here,' said Blair.

Jennifer stood mutely beside him, her arms wrapped around herself, still in shock. Mac had acted swiftly, Carmel had given Rudi CPR, and Rosie had called the chopper pilot out of the restaurant and alerted Headland Hospital. What was puzzling everyone was what had happened to Rudi.

'Do you want a drink? Stay here?' asked Blair. 'I'm on duty. Can I help?' He sounded concerned but a bit helpless.

Jennifer shook her head. 'Thanks. I'd better get back to see Mac and the others. Try to find out what happened.'

'Heart, maybe. You won't know till the hospital sees him.'

'Mac said he was healthy as a horse. He thinks something happened in the lab. The smell was like gas, rotten eggs.'

'You shouldn't expose yourself, then. Be careful. What was he studying again?' asked Blair, suddenly interested.

'Toxins, poisons. Substances in some marine plants are deadly. Like stone fish, blue-ringed octopus and cone shells. Kill humans in a minute.'

'Jesus, Jennifer, that's dangerous stuff. No wonder he looked half dead.'

'I hope he'll be all right. Mac has notified his family.'

Blair was thoughtful. 'I don't think any of this should be made public. Just let people think it was a health thing.'

'Bad for business, eh?' snapped Jennifer. 'There's Tony over there, you tell him that.'

It was a sombre group gathered in Mac's living room when Jennifer and Tony came in.

'The chopper has left and the ambulance will meet them,' said Tony. 'Any theories yet, Mac?'

'It seems Rudi was working in there with the windows and door closed and he'd been boiling down liquid from a specimen. We figure it became so concentrated the fumes got to him. Lucky that Jennifer went in when she did.' He glanced at his watch. 'It's late. Let's get some sleep. Lloyd will take me over to Headland first thing in the morning.'

'You'll let us know the minute you hear anything?' said Carmel.

Tony, Jennifer and Isobel walked slowly back to their units.

'Blair didn't want any publicity about this,' said Jennifer.

'I doubt it would concern guests planning to visit the resort. It's more a problem for the research station. Any accidents reflect on the director of research, so Mac is in the firing line,' said Tony.

'Still, tourists from overseas are not so sanguine at hearing about pretty shells and hidden creatures in rock pools that can kill you,' said Isobel.

'That's tabloid stuff. I try to write more substantive things,' said Tony. Then he grinned. 'Did that sound stuffy?'

'Yes,' said Isobel, with a throaty chuckle.

'I wish I could laugh as easily as you, Isobel,' sighed Jennifer.

'You're upset about Rudi,' said Tony quickly.

'No, I mean, yes, I am,' said Jennifer slowly. 'But I keep hearing Blair tut-tutting, so conscious all the time of his job, what people think of him, being Mr Charm, but you know, we hardly ever laugh together. Before I met everyone around here, with all their teasing and jokes, I think I'd lost my sense of humour somewhere.'

'We'll help you find it,' said Isobel.

'I know how you feel,' said Tony. 'I didn't have a lot to laugh about, places I've been, things I've seen the past few years. But I agree with you, Jen, being here with this group loosens me up. Makes me feel, well, relaxed, not afraid to be myself. I'm coming out of my shell a bit.'

'Like the turtles?' said Jennifer, smiling.

Isobel looked from one to the other. 'Interesting. You both take things too seriously. But look how you've both changed since being here. On an island you can't run away. And it's a private world, so there's few people to see you go a bit crazy.'

'You'll have to join the Shark Club,' said Jennifer.

'Now there's a challenge,' said Isobel. 'Do something you've never done before. Something that you've been too scared, too shy, to do.'

'I'll sleep on it,' said Tony as they reached their units. 'Let's hope it's good news in the morning for Rudi.'

'He'll be in my prayers tonight.' Isobel blew them both a kiss. '*Boa noite*.'

Jennifer tossed and turned uncomfortably in bed. Her belly felt distended and bloated. She got up and went to the small chair on what she thought of as the wonky balcony. She sat in her nightshirt – an antique cotton working-man's shirt she'd picked up in the markets. The bird mutterings were becoming familiar, she felt she knew the family groups and now she understood more of their habits and rituals. The sounds of the mutton birds didn't disturb or distress her as they had in the beginning. She sat there for a while and, still feeling restless, decided to go for a short walk towards Mac's cottage. She thought of the sandy, tree-lined track with the scattered housing, though all was quiet and, for once, everyone seemed to be asleep.

A dim light shone behind Tony's split bamboo blind. He was either sleeping or reading. She tip-toed down the steps in her bare feet and followed the white sandy path past the cottages, canteen, lab block and outside tanks; past the shower and laundry block to where the trees began to meet overhead and the path divided to the resort and towards Coral Point. Here she did a U-turn and began to walk back to the far end where the VIP housing was tucked away.

She heard the birds groan and complain as they leapt and resettled themselves. She knew the sound well, it happened when they were socialising, or when they were disturbed from their night-time nesting positions. Someone or something had jostled them.

She spun around and saw the flash of a small light. It waved up and down, signalling her. Jennifer stood stock still as a figure came into the moonlight from the darker canopy of trees.

'It's only me. I didn't want to scare you.' Tony walked towards her.

'Couldn't you sleep either?' whispered Jennifer.

'Not really. I thought I heard a funny noise. I guess I'm feeling spooked. Did you hear something too?'

Jennifer looked down at her nightshirt. 'No, I was in bed. I felt uncomfortable and I guess I'm upset about Rudi.'

'Want a nightcap, a hot chocolate or bouillon? I can offer all or any.'

'Really? You are organised. Hot milk might help.'

In the moonlight Tony switched off his torch and they turned and walked silently past the cottages. They came to the big outside specimen tanks, the large cement ones and the students' glass aquariums on stands.

Both heard the noise at the same time. Tony grabbed Jennifer's arm and motioned her to stop. Neither spoke. It was a scraping sound, metal on cement, as if something were being dragged. They were out of sight on the other side of the raised deck that held the big tanks. Tony peered around the tank stand, then put his mouth to Jennifer's ear.

'Someone's in Rudi's lab.'

They waited a few moments, hearing movement. Jennifer pulled Tony's face close to hers and whispered. 'What do we do?'

'Nothing. Just watch for a minute.'

There was a clink and movement from a shadowy figure. They could just make out someone moving a container onto some sort of trolley or barrow.

'That's one of Rudi's specimen containers, like an oxygen tank. He was using it to distil liquid gas after boiling the plants,' whispered Jennifer.

'The stuff that knocked Rudi over. Why would someone steal it?'

'Rudi said that treated properly it's a powerful tranquilliser or potent knockout drug that can kill. My God, who'd know about this?' Jennifer was suddenly frightened. She clutched Tony's arm.

'There's only one person. On foot. They won't want to be found out. I'll go round that side and make a lot of noise. Here, take this torch, it's metal. When I shout, start banging on the tank. That'll rouse the neighbourhood.'

'Why don't we just rush up at him, her?'

'If someone wants something that strong that badly they might be armed, or throw it at us. Who knows. Let's not take a chance.' Tony bent low and silently moved away and Jennifer had a flash that he was no stranger to dangerous situations.

Suddenly a door slammed. Tony coughed and called out, 'Is someone there?'

Jennifer started slamming the metal torch into the iron tank stand, shouting, 'What's going on?'

Lights were snapped on, voices calling. The figure dashed from the lab block up the track into the trees. Tony ran after the slim shape but knew he'd never find whoever it was in the maze of dark scrub. There was distant cracking of branches, shrieks from snoozing, irritated birds.

'What the hell . . .' Mac reached the lab as

Tony and Jennifer came from the shadows. Carmel and Lloyd were next to appear.

'Bloody hell, what's going on?' demanded Mac.

'Someone was in Rudi's lab.' Jennifer rushed forward with Tony's torch turned on. 'Look . . .' she shone the light on the metal cylinder and two heavy glass jars, strapped to a luggage hand trolley from the resort.

'Christ. They knew what they wanted,' said Mac.

'Who was it?' asked Carmel.

'Don't know. Who'd want this so badly?' asked Tony.

Mac was silent for a moment as he looked at the abandoned equipment. 'I'm not sure. Hopefully Rudi will be able to throw some light on it. In the meantime, let's lock this up.'

Kirsty appeared, rubbing her eyes. 'Is something wrong?'

'An uninvited guest,' said Lloyd.

'Someone tried to steal stuff from Rudi's lab,' said Carmel. Then, looking around the shocked group, she gave a bit of a smile. 'Maybe we'll know more tomorrow. In the meantime . . . this is an interesting fashion parade.'

Kirsty laughed. 'So now we know everyone's first choice of sleepwear. Very eclectic!' She held up the edge of her short rosebud nightie.

Jennifer looked around and had to laugh. She was in her nightshirt, Mac was wearing a sarong and for once his hair wasn't tied neatly in a pony tail but fell around his face in a silver-streaked bob, Carmel was in a tank top and cotton leggings, Lloyd in boxer shorts with funny-faced whales on them, Tony was wearing white shorts and a University of California T-shirt.

'I got dressed first. I wasn't sure if there was something or someone out here,' said Tony with a grin.

'That's no excuse! You certainly got us all out in short order,' said Lloyd.

'Let's go to bed. Whoever it was won't be back. I want to wait till morning and have a good look around. Don't touch a thing,' said Mac as everyone began to disperse.

'Still want that hot milk?' said Tony as they reached their units.

'Yes, please. Now my mind is whirling,' said Jennifer. She curled her legs under her on Tony's small sofa as he put milk in a mug and put it in the microwave. 'Why would someone want Rudi's samples? Do you think Rudi was deliberately knocked out, that it wasn't an accident?'

'Not a nice thought. He told me he was still in the early stages of separating the toxins and analysing their strength.'

'Did he say what it could be used for?' asked Jennifer. 'I never took comments about biological warfare very seriously. I mean, out here . . .'

'Apparently it affects the nervous system, immobilising it for extended periods. Like a heavy tranquilliser. As Rudi put it, there's a fine line between getting the body to shut down in a state of suspended animation and knocking it out completely. That's where later experiments come into it.' He took the milk out, stirred in some honey and handed the mug to Jennifer. 'I'm having a small straight Scotch.'

'Do you think Rudi was testing it on himself? Or was it an accident? Just breathing the fumes would be enough, surely. It was the smell that bowled me over.'

'Let's hope Rudi can tell us tomorrow. I doubt he would have tried it on himself, it's too early a stage of development.'

'It must be serious warfare down below the ocean with plants and fish releasing this kind of stuff at one another,' said Jennifer, sipping her milk. It was warm and sweet and exactly what she needed.

'Experiments have gone on for years with poisons like this. All that James Bond–type stuff. I seem to remember some spy being killed with a bump from an umbrella. They knew there was a lethal poison in the tip, but couldn't identify it, or it disappeared. This stuff might be the next generation.'

'God, no wonder there's competition for access to scientific research. But people like Rudi don't set out to find killer toxins. He's looking at the symbiosis between fish and their environment.'

Tony threw back his Scotch. 'The world is a toxic place on many levels. We're all battling our environment, taming, conquering, destroying it. Rudi's analogy was that despite the sea creatures and marine plants all having some defensive or aggressive mechanism for survival, they have managed to adjust and survive side by side for millions of years. The whole system started to cave in and get out of balance when humans arrived on the scene.'

'I suppose you thought about that when you were in those war zones,' said Jennifer quietly.

'It does make you start to see how stupid unwinnable wars fought out of ignorance and for the wrong reasons are.' He put his glass down. 'Come on, off to bed. Will you be able to sleep okay? You're not scared or anything?'

Jennifer stood up and handed him her mug. 'That was great, I feel more relaxed. And, no, I'm not too worried. The bogyman will get you before me.'

Tony smiled. 'Think of me as the guard dog on the doorstep.' He opened the door as Jennifer stepped past and turned to him.

'G'night, Tony.' She started to yawn.

He inclined his head and kissed her on the cheek, and then on the lips. Two swift brushes that surprised her with their tenderness.

'What was that for?' she asked with a soft smile.

He grinned. 'Dunno. S'pose I just joined the Shark Club. I've never done that before.'

'Kissed someone?'

'No. Done something I've wanted to do but never felt brave enough to actually do it. You took the plunge today, so, I guess, did I.'

They looked at each other for a moment from either side of the doorway.

'It only means I think you're special, Jennifer. Keep going forward. You're going to be all right, you know that.'

'I think I do. I think you're going to be just fine too.' She turned and started up the steps.

'It's this place,' said Tony.

'And the people. Sleep well.'

She went into her room and inhaled the scent of roses. Curled on her side, cradling her child within, Jennifer slept peacefully.

The next morning Jennifer joined Mac and Lloyd in the resort cruiser to go to Headland to see Rudi. Rosie saw them off.

'I heard there was a break-in at Rudi's lab. Any idea why, or who?'

'Can't say, Rosie. Was amateurish though, didn't look like a well-planned event. Spur-of-the-moment thing.'

'Why do you say that, Mac?'

'Didn't bring any of their own gear to put stuff in or take it away. They were using a trolley from your joint.'

'Do you think it was one of the staff? Who'd be that interested?' said Rosie in surprise. 'How would they have known?'

'All the staff knew when Rudi was flown out,' said Jennifer. 'You know how they gossip. Maybe Blair has some ideas.'

'I'll talk to him when we get back this afternoon,' said Mac.

They piled into Lloyd's old station wagon that Vera allowed him to keep in the parking lot at the wharf, and Jennifer rang her mother from her rarely used mobile.

'No answer. She might be playing tennis. Or even working at the hospital.'

At reception they were directed to the high-dependency floor where Rudi was still under observation. Jennifer asked if they could find out whether her mother was in the hospital.

'I really couldn't tell you who the volunteers are on duty. What's her name?'

'Mrs Christina Campbell.'

'Oh, Tina. She's a card, isn't she? If she comes by is there a message?'

'Mention that her daughter is here. Just visiting,' she quickly added.

Only one of them was allowed into the four-bed ward where patients were being monitored. Mac went in while Lloyd and Jennifer sat outside. He came out fifteen minutes later, Jennifer and Lloyd scanning his face for some indication of Rudi's condition.

'He's going to be okay,' Mac said.

'Phew. What happened?' asked Lloyd.

'Let's get a coffee. I'll tell you what I know. He's being moved into another ward later today. His mother and brother are coming up.'

'He could talk, tell you what happened?' asked Jennifer as they walked down the wide blue hallway. She noticed the tropical flowers on the nurses' desk, the colourful pictures of Queensland flora, fauna and favourite locations. It seemed more like a tourist office than a hospital.

'Yes, not that it helped. Says he has no idea. He must have blacked out.'

'Oh my Lord, Jennifer . . . Are you all right?'

There was a flurry behind them and they turned to see Christina, in a blue-and-white striped uniform, hurrying towards them.

Jennifer held up her hands. 'I'm fine, Mum, don't panic!'

She hugged Jennifer, her eyes flicking down to her belly. 'You might have told me you were coming.'

'We're just visiting a friend who got sick suddenly. I was about to call you, I asked if you were in here on the off-chance.'

Christina turned to Mac, giving him a candid stare. She ignored Lloyd, who was hanging back slightly.

Mac held out his hand with a smile. 'I'm Macdonald Masters. It was rather a sudden dash over from the island. Fortunately our friend is recovering.'

Jennifer could see her mother taking in Mac's pony tail, faded Hawaiian shirt over a university T-shirt, cotton cargo pants and rope sandals. 'Professor Masters is the research director at the station run by the university on Branch Island. And this is Lloyd Dane, who runs the charter boats. He brought us over.'

'Oh, I see. And what happened to your friend? At least it's nice to know you can race across if you need to.'

'The island might seem isolated out there on the reef, Mrs Campbell, but with the helicopter and a fast boat, you can get here quicker than sitting in a city traffic jam,' said Mac.

'I like your uniform, Mum. What do you do?'

'We're the Sunshine Girls. We bring free magazines, books, sweets – if they're allowed – all kinds of little gifts to patients. We visit people who don't have people to come and see them, wheel them outside for a walk, perhaps.'

'Bringing a little sunshine into people's lives, eh? I like it,' Mac said, smiling.

Christina didn't smile back. 'We take our job quite seriously. In fact, I've been asked to help out in the respite unit down the road as well.'

'Good on you, Mum. And how's the tennis?'

'They're quite a nice group. Mind you, I'm so busy I can't spend a lot of time just socialising,' said Christina as they got to the lifts.

'We're going down for a coffee. Can you join us?' said Mac.

'I don't want to take you away from your friends. Can you spare me some time, Jennifer? Or are you rushing back?'

'We did come over in a bit of a rush.' *How come you make me feel guilty so easily?*

'It's okay, Jenny, we needn't go back till late this afternoon. I'm going to see my dad about the yacht we're leasing. Please come along, Mrs Campbell. Have you been north of Headland Bay?' asked Lloyd.

Christina looked at the handsome young man

as if seeing him for the first time. She beamed. 'Why, no. I'm afraid I don't drive. How far away is it?'

The lift doors opened and they walked to the small coffee shop off the lobby. Mac and Jennifer followed Lloyd and Christina. Mac grinned at Jennifer. He knew Christina had dismissed him as a university hippy while she found chatting to fresh-faced, clean-cut Lloyd far more appealing.

They sat at a small table and Mac went to the counter and ordered a pot of tea, coffee and carrot cake.

'And how long have you been over on that island, or do you stay on boats?' Christina asked Lloyd.

'Grown up with boats, my father is a ship-wright. He's restored an old yacht that we're going to charter for guests at the resort.'

'Lloyd knows Blair, of course,' said Jennifer.

'He's my boss, along with Rosie. But, like Jennifer, I spend most of my time at the research station when I'm not on a boat.'

'Is that so? And how does Blair feel about that?' Christina raised her eyebrows towards Jennifer.

'He's very understanding. Mac is supervising the course I'm doing,' Jennifer said.

'I thought you were writing something. Well, once the baby arrives, you'll be too busy for any of that. Now, Lloyd, my brother and his wife are coming up this way. Perhaps they could go for a sail, fishing or something?'

Jennifer was about to leap in and say it was rather expensive but Lloyd nudged her foot under the table. 'I'm sure we can arrange it.'

'That would be wonderful. Poor dears, they've had a terrible time. Did you hear what happened, Jennifer?'

Before Jennifer could speak, Christina, holding centre-stage, plunged on. 'Just terrible. My brother has been breeding birds for years. Now – they're all gone. Like a family, they were. He's devastated.'

'What happened?' asked Lloyd.

'Oh, it was terrible. Don was playing bowls and Vi had gone into town for the day. When he came home he found the wire cages had been cut and all the birds were gone, stolen. My brother had been breeding some unusual-coloured parrots and budgies. The police said it was a professional job,' she added.

'From a suburban backyard? Were they valuable? I know he adored his birds,' said Jennifer.

Mac put the tray on the table and passed around the carrot cake slices. 'It's not uncommon. It's easier to steal birds bred in captivity than to capture them in the wild.'

'They went around the pet shops to see if anyone was trying to sell them. No luck,' said Christina.

'They'd be out of the country by now. They get big bucks for them. A black cockatoo could fetch several thousand dollars in America. They pay hundreds of dollars for sugar gliders or baby wallabies.'

'Good grief. Is it legal?' asked Christina.

'Most of the time, no. By the time they end up with reputable dealers, shops or a licensed seller, it's impossible to trace where they came from.'

'Don't forget the internet. I bet most stuff is sold through sites you can't trace,' said Lloyd.

'Well, fancy that. Who'd have thought anyone would be interested in Don's little hobby?' said Christina.

'He must be so upset, not to say out of pocket,' said Jennifer. She was watching Christina eat her carrot cake. She had her little finger cocked and held her fork as though it were made of fragile crystal, placing tiny mouthfuls through rosebud-pursed lips.

'The nurse said we could pop back and see Rudi late this afternoon,' said Mac, to break the silence that fell over the table.

'And what's wrong with your friend?' asked Christina, fork poised, finger cocked. Like playing ladies' tea parties, thought Jennifer.

'We don't know. Rudi was working on an experiment in his laboratory and keeled over . . .' Mac stopped at a frown from Jennifer. 'Could have been anything.'

'Someone tried to steal his work too. Must have found something interesting,' added Lloyd.

'That all sounds very unsavoury,' sniffed Christina. 'Rudi, is that a Russian name? My goodness, it sounds like a spy novel. I hope you're not around any of these dangerous-sounding experiments, Jennifer.'

Jennifer laughed. 'Now, Mum, don't start on some conspiracy theory. Do you like that cake? You seem to be . . . picking at it.' Jennifer couldn't resist asking and wanted to shift the focus of the conversation. She didn't want Christina to have more ammunition to try to get her off the island.

Christina put her fork down and neatly dabbed at her mouth with the paper napkin. 'Well, as you've drawn attention to me, I'll tell you. Since I've been working around the aged you can't help but notice as people get older their manners go downhill. I want to make sure I don't start losing my social graces.'

They all laughed. 'Mum, you're young! I wouldn't worry. If you start drooling I'll let you know.'

'Goodness, Jennifer, you don't have to say things like that. Even if I am about to become a grandmother,' said Christina stiffly.

Mac downed his coffee. 'Well, if we're going north, we should hit the road fairly soon. Are you joining us, Christina?'

'We can take you home to change,' said Jennifer.

'Very well. A little trip would be nice. I don't get away much, you know,' she sighed.

Lloyd and Mac, catching Jennifer's eye, kept quiet.

In the car Christina was a different person. Mac and Jennifer sat in the back and Lloyd drove with Christina, who was keeping up a bubbling narrative of amusing stories about people at the hospital. Lloyd laughed and Mac made a few dry asides that either went over Christina's head or she chose to ignore.

Lloyd's father, Heath, was under a boat hauled up on a boat cradle in the slipway. An older, weathered version of Lloyd, in his paint-spattered shorts, old shirt, canvas shoes and cotton hat, he nonetheless managed to look at ease, comfortable in his surroundings. Jennifer suspected he was not a man at home in office garb or surroundings. He whipped off his hat, and offered a shy smile and a firm handshake.

'How's that pal of yours?'

'He'll be fine, Dad. We can't stay long. How's our boat?'

'She's in the water. The seams have settled, no more water coming in. Just a bit of the frilly stuff to do. Upholstery, galley gear. She'll be ready next week. I'll bring her over and take that cat back, eh?'

'Great. Tony and I will take her for a test run.'

'Tony sails?' asked Jennifer.

'Didn't you know? He's done a lot of sailing in his time. I reckon that's one of the reasons he's settled on the coast,' said Mac.

'Do you like boats, Mrs Campbell?'

'No, Heath, I don't. I married a farmer and lived in the bush for many years. Though I was originally a city girl. My husband disappeared in a boating accident.'

Jennifer looked at her mother in surprise. It was the first time she'd ever heard her mother refer to her father. The phrase was almost glib the way it tripped off her tongue.

'Sorry to hear that. Well, come and have a look then. For an old girl she's scrubbed up well.'

'You've put in a lot of work, Dad,' said Lloyd as he followed his father through the clutter around the boatshed. Heath Dane held out his hand and escorted Christina over the slips and past several upturned dinghies, empty paint and diesel drums, rusting bits of boat rudders and other boat accoutrements that he was obviously reluctant to throw away in case they came in handy one day. Christina seemed unfazed, almost flirtatious.

'There she is, on that blue buoy next to the cruiser.' They looked at the freshly painted old wooden sloop, the sails furled, the deck polished, the hatch and trim painted a deep blue.

'Wow, she's lovely,' said Mac.

'She's come up real good, Dad. You'd never know she's twenty years old.'

'She's had a bit of a facelift and cosmetic touches, but, like a beautiful woman, age enhances her character.' He nodded at Christina who gave him a big smile.

Mac, Lloyd and his dad rowed out to the yacht for a closer look as Christina and Jennifer sat on the jetty in the sun.

'They seem nice enough people,' said Christina conversationally. 'Not Blair's type though, I would have thought. Seems to me you and Blair have rather different interests over there.'

How can you tell? I'm not saying anything.
'It's a small place, we overlap. He's pleased I have an interest as he's so busy.'

'And the baby?'

'Great. I feel really good.'

'I meant Blair. I hope he's going to be a modern father.'

'Sure he will. We have to share the workload where we can, of course. I mean, his job is more important . . .' Her voice trailed off. Jennifer felt irritated that her mother had brought up the subject.

'Because he's the breadwinner?'

'One of us has to earn an income. I won't be earning much of a salary until I finish my honours.'

'I suppose I'll be doing the babysitting.'

'Thanks, Mum, but let's wait till I have a job, eh?'

'I can't imagine what sort of a job, you just seem to study odd things. But, Jennifer, if you ever need money . . . I have a little tucked away.'

What Jennifer thought of as her mother's disingenuousness disappeared and she sounded genuine and concerned for the first time that day. *How had she picked up on the rift between her and Blair?* 'That's lovely of you to offer, but I can cope, really I can. I've learned a lot over there. About myself and managing my life. I have some very special friends.'

'That's nice for you. Be careful though. People hanging about on an island don't sound very *stable* people. And this friend in the hospital . . . they're not into drugs, are they?'

'Mum! You're reading too many thrillers,' laughed Jennifer.

'Oh, I hear things. You'd be surprised. A man was stabbed on a boat just last week. Headland Bay might look like a casual holiday town, but I've heard about more crime than I ever did in Sydney.'

'You didn't take any notice of such things in Sydney. And you weren't working in a hospital or talking to gossipy small-town people. Now come on, let's have a bit of a look around.'

When the three men returned they walked back to the car.

'You want to have lunch with us, Dad? Just fish and chips at the co-op?'

'Thanks, son, better get this job finished. I'll be in touch before I bring your boat over.'

'We'll bung on a bit of a party. Sort of a chris-tening. What do you say?' said Mac.

'Ah, no fuss. But I wouldn't mind catching up with old Gideon.'

'You're on. We'll have it at the Shark Bar.'

'Sounds good. How's the resort getting along? Making money or are those blokes spending it all?' asked Heath.

'What blokes?' asked Jennifer, suddenly alert. 'Do you mean the slick boys?'

'Those resort bigwigs cruising around in that gin palace. Saw them the other day at the provi-dores taking on supplies for a bit of a trip,' said Heath.

Jennifer rolled her eyes. 'Some job. They never seem to be in an office.'

'They can justify it by saying they're checking out the scenery, I suppose,' said Lloyd.

'They took a lot of stuff on board. Don't know why they don't call in to Sooty or any other place up the coast. They have a funny crew, none of the locals who normally crew charters,' commented Heath.

'Maybe they're talking business and don't want outsiders listening,' Mac joked.

'I heard there's a floating brothel up here,' said Christina.

They turned to Jennifer's mother in surprise as she hadn't seemed to be paying much attention to their conversation.

'What! *Who* have you been talking to, Mum?'

'I don't live in a shell, Jennifer. I do see people from time to time,' she said airily.

Earlier you were saying you never got to socialise. 'Really? What kind of people? Where was this?'

'At the tennis club.' She gave a cheeky grin, pleased with the bombshell she'd dropped. 'There's a retired detective who plays on Thursdays. He has a story or two.'

'Well, I hope Reef Resorts' boat isn't being used for anything untoward,' said Jennifer.

'You should ask Blair about it,' said her mother. 'Thank you so much, Lloyd. It's been a lovely outing.'

In the late afternoon Tony walked along the beach towards the jetty, turning in to the resort. The helicopter was sitting on its pad and when he passed the pool he saw Rosie and Bob the pilot sitting at a terrace table. Rosie waved him over.

'Like a drink, Tony?'

'A light beer wouldn't go astray.' He sat down, putting his camera on the table. 'You had a bit of a late dash last night,' he said to Bob.

'Handy I was here. Hope Rudi's okay.'

'We'll know tonight when Mac gets back,' said Tony.

Rosie had an envelope on the table, which she pushed across to Tony. 'On a flight this morning, Bob spotted *Kicking Back*. Thought we'd be interested. Take a look.'

Tony flipped through the photos. 'Nice work if you can get it.' Stretched out on the deck of *Kicking Back* were three women sunning themselves topless. Fanzio, Holding and two other men were seated on the flying bridge.

'They were heading out to sea. Quite a way out. Maybe they're going to Hawaii,' said Bob. 'Thought I'd take a few shots of the bosses for Rosie.'

'What have you been up to, Tony?' asked Rosie, more out of politeness than interest.

'Wandering around. I ended up having a very interesting conversation with your maintenance fellow.'

'Patch? You talked with him?'

'That's tricky. He's got a terrible stutter,' said

Bob. 'Poor bastard. One eye, a stutter and a reputation as a pervert.'

'Has he ever molested anyone?' asked Tony.

'The staff girls complain he's a bit of a peeping Tom. I don't think he's ever touched anyone. There's gossip but no one has ever complained officially. I think he's harmless. We keep him on as he's been here since the place was built.'

'He does feel some sort of proprietary interest in what goes on,' said Tony. 'He hinted he was keeping an eye on things.'

They all laughed.

'What else do you know about him, Rosie?'

'Patch? Came with the territory. He knows his job. I rarely have direct dealings with him, apart from occasional exchanges when there's a problem. Gideon told me he had some family trauma and he was kind of guaranteed a job here. He is a good mechanic, fix-it man.'

'He's well read too. Have you seen the books in his shed?' said Tony.

'Yeah, I noticed them when I got some oil from him one day,' said Bob. 'If he wasn't so shy and speaking wasn't so difficult for him, I'd try and chat.'

'What were you talking to him for, Tony?' asked Rosie curiously.

'I noticed the luggage trolleys were stored up there. I wondered if he knew one had gone missing last night. He went a bit quiet. I reckon he knows who borrowed it.'

'Someone was trying to carry off Rudi's stuff

when Tony and Jenny interrupted,' Rosie explained to Bob.

'You think it was Patch?'

'Don't think so, Bob. But I reckon with a bit of patience Patch might have some interesting things to say.'

17

Parting of the Waves

A WEEK LATER ON a blustery white-capped, tossed-sea day, Rudi returned to the island, his reappearance kept low-key. Mac knew he was concerned about the break-in, especially as they'd discovered that a small phial that held some of the potent extract was missing.

'It's so new, I can't imagine how anyone knew what I'd stumbled across. Other scientists have made similar discoveries, it's just these particular marine plants hadn't been tested before. And who knows what the effects are? If my reaction to the fumes is any indication, it's powerful stuff.'

'It has to be someone on the island who heard

what you were finding and figured they could use it somehow.'

'You mean one of our researchers? I don't think so,' said Rudi vehemently. 'Besides, until I was bowled over I hardly knew what I had myself.'

Mac was thoughtful. 'It's not a nice thought, but it wouldn't be the first time a researcher or student has sold or passed on information. But I think I know this group pretty well and it's not one of them.'

'One of them could have mentioned it to someone outside our group though,' said Rudi.

'I think a round-table discussion might be helpful,' said Mac.

Tony spread the latest batch of photos on the table in his room. He separated one group out and studied them before putting them to one side. They were a series of informal shots he'd taken of Isobel and Jennifer over the last few weeks. He smiled as he looked at the two women – candid scenes at meals, at Gideon's, walking on the beach, the two of them bent over notes outside Mac's, arms around each other's waists at the lagoon. It was an intimate portrait of a flowering friendship, of two women a generation apart who now had a bond of respect and warmth, one learning from the other who gave knowledge, advice and a sharing of experience. As a male and an outsider, Tony found the relationship touching, intriguing and, if he was honest, one he envied.

The photos for his second feature article on the research station and its work, he put in another pile. Mentally he reviewed his story plans: **The Endangered Reef. Loss of a World Icon.** *A look at the formation, the life it sustains and its imminent destruction by humans.*

Lady of the Deep. *Dr Isobel Belitas, world-renowned oceanographer mapping the last mysteries of the planet – the unexplored world at the bottom of the sea.*

Saviours of the Sea. *The scientists, researchers and students unravelling answers from the ocean that could save humanity.*

Island of Sun and Shadows. *Apparently insignificant, a small island that's part of the Great Barrier Reef, home to protected species, international tourists, scientists, is also where several characters have washed ashore: beachcombers, boaties, business entrepreneurs and budding biologists.*

On paper it sounded bland. But when he thought of his cast of characters . . . Gideon, Rosie, Jennifer, the slick boys, Rudi and Patch, and what he'd observed of the two different communities of resort and research station, he saw a bigger picture. From the scientific work, the nature and wildlife, the tourists wanting sun, sea, sex and sunsets, the young research graduates and the resort staffies, to the mysterious activities of Fanzio and Holding with the speculation of what they might be up to with or without company knowledge, and the break-in at Rudi's lab . . . well, that sounded like an in-depth story.

He put his notes in a pile and decided to go for a wander around the resort. To anyone watching, it appeared to be a casual meander through the bird-filled trees, past the landscaped resort units and further away to where the main laundry, machinery, generator, water tanks, vehicles and equipment were housed. Camouflaged, muffled, as far from guests as possible, this was the engine room that ran the resort.

Outside the machinery shed where repairs and maintenance were done, Tony spotted the shambling figure of Patch carrying a length of metal pipe. He stopped, greeted him, and with his hands clasped behind his back Tony strolled beside Patch as he clamped the pipe into the vice.

As they chatted, the older man straightened, adjusted his eye patch, took off his towelling hat, ran his fingers through his grey hair and then reached for a cigarette from his shirt pocket. Tony listened patiently, nodding occasionally, his arms folded in front of his chest as the man talked slowly through his stutter. Nobody witnessed the conversation, and stubbing out his cigarette the old man returned to the thread-cutting fixture on the vice. Tony watched for a moment or two, spoke again, and walked slowly away with a studied casualness as if the encounter was all part of his morning walk.

Jennifer sat with Mac at the table in his cottage, feeling overwhelmed and frustrated. Piles of folders and papers were beside her and they both were studying the image on his laptop screen of a turtle hatchling.

'So, if I'm looking at the analysis of turtle reproductive success on Branch Island I should be out there taking the temperature of the nests, right?' said Jennifer.

'Yes, the temperature inside the sand mound where the eggs were laid will determine the turtles' gender.'

'Thirty degrees and above, they'll be female; twenty-eight degrees and below, they'll be male,' said Jennifer.

'And in between mixed.'

'So if part of the nest is shaded by a tree, does that mean those eggs will be male?'

'Quite possibly. That can be part of your research. As well as the number of eggs each female lays through the different breeding seasons.'

'And out of those three or four egg-layings, how many hatchlings survive,' added Jennifer. 'And the mother isn't there to see them. Probably just as well. Crocodiles also have their sex determined by the incubation temperature, don't they?'

'Yes. And I have a theory that so were dinosaurs, which explains why they died out. Apart from the meteorite that crashed into the earth, causing a global catastrophe. As the earth cooled during the Cretaceous period sixty-five million years ago, it must have affected the eggs, so eventually only males hatched and with no females they died out.'

'See, you can't do without us,' laughed Jennifer. 'Have you published this theory?'

'I was thinking about it until some guy in America floated it. You've got to publish or perish in academia, Jenny. Luckily, you're a fine writer. It can often make the difference between first-class and second-class honours. And we want you to get first-class, then you can go straight for the big doctoral scholarship.'

'But there's so much to get through!' she wailed. 'Look at all this stuff. I could spend every minute of my time just reading.'

'Train yourself to speed read and pick out what's applicable. Find the right references. You'll most likely have at least a hundred and fifty to two hundred cited references for your thesis. And be prepared for the stress and hassle towards the deadline. It always happens.'

'Can I really do this, Mac? And have a baby at the same time?'

'What's Isobel say?' he asked with a smile.

'Naturally she says I can. I have to find the balance. That I'll be thankful to have something to think about between nappies and feeds. And to turn off from paperwork to cuddles and coos.'

'Sounds like Isobel. Jenny, you've committed yourself and I have a lot of faith in you. While I'm here I can supervise your research in the field and your analysis. And for the couple of months I'm away I can still monitor your work and send you electronic PDF files of photocopied reference material.'

'Rosie says the full satellite network will be up and running in two weeks so we'll have much better internet communication access,' said Jennifer.

'Nonetheless, you still have to attend a couple of weeks at uni, but I'd prefer you to come with a draft of your thesis. But that's still a way off,' he said as she sighed and looked discouraged.

There was a tap at the door and when Jennifer saw the turquoise and white resort shirt she thought for a moment it was Blair. Her immediate reaction had been annoyance at his intrusion and in that second she realised how damaged her feelings for her husband were.

'Yes, mate? Need something?' asked Mac.

Gordon Blake smiled at Jennifer. 'Blair sent me. When you have time, could he see you at the resort. So, how are things going here? Heard you had a bit of a problem.' He took a step inside.

Mac glared at the young man. 'Oh, and what was that?'

'Glad to know Rudi is all right. Seems this research work can be a bit dangerous.'

'Sure can. Sharks, groupers, stone fish, deadly stingers, the bends, you name it,' said Mac in a tight voice. His irritation surprised Jennifer. He was always so mild and patient with the younger students and staff.

Gordon's eyes darted round the room, settling on the laptop. 'Turtles, eh? Is that what you're studying?' he asked Jennifer.

'Their breeding,' she said briefly, picking up on Mac's cue. 'Would you mind telling Blair I'll see him for a drink before dinner on the terrace. Thanks for bringing over the message.'

'No problem. Be seeing you then.' With a nod he sauntered back outside.

They watched him go and didn't speak for a moment. Then Mac said, 'That pommy kid comes from a money family, for sure.'

'How do you know?' asked Jennifer.

'That blasted arrogant air. Like no one can intimidate him. He has a right to go wherever and do whatever he wants.'

'Now, Mac, your humble origins are showing.'

'Bloody oath. Must be my convict ancestors.' He relaxed. 'Curious he was interested in Rudi. I'll put that on the agenda for this afternoon's meeting.'

Jennifer gathered up her papers. 'I'll let you get on with things. Thanks for all your help.'

As Jennifer passed Tony's door he called out. 'Hey, before you go upstairs. Are you going to Mac's round-table this afternoon?'

'I just left him. I have a few things to do, plus I have to meet Blair. Will you fill me in later?'

'Sure will. I've been mooching around. That young English staffie, Gordon, what does Blair know about him?'

'I'm not too sure. I think he's connected to

head office. He's been hanging round with those slick boys. And Willsy. Blair sees them too, I think.'

'Mmm. Patch told me the young English staffie took a trolley from the shed – surreptitiously.'

'Like the one at Rudi's break-in?'

'Seems to be. What do you suppose Gordon would want with some potion Rudi was experimenting with?'

'It'd give a drink a helluva kick.'

'If it didn't kill you, it'd knock you out for a week,' said Tony. 'Rudi told me Gordon had been dropping by to ask what he was doing. Said he was interested in medical research. Rosie doesn't know much about him.'

'I'll see what Blair knows. He's the staff liaison man.'

'Mac is a bit worried as there has been some undermining of his project here. Some poor reports at the university about the quality of work being done.'

'That doesn't count until the students finish their courses and results are in,' exclaimed Jennifer, suddenly alarmed at the idea that marine and environmental studies could be axed.

'Sounds like gossip and innuendo. In the halls of academe they probably imagine there are sex orgies on the beach and nude swimming by moonlight,' said Tony, laughing.

'I'm sure that's gone on amongst the resort staff. The researchers seem focused on other things,' said Jennifer. 'Blair has talked about the bed-hopping and romantic entanglements.' Including my husband, she almost added.

'Mac is affable but he runs a tight ship just the same,' said Tony. 'How are you going with your research? He's thrown you in the deep end, it seems.'

'I'm staying afloat,' she grinned. 'I hope I can keep up with our project. What else did Patch have to say? I'm not sure what to make of him. He gave me the creeps in the beginning.'

'He's a loner, that's for sure. I think he's a non-sexual peeping Tom, if there is such a thing.'

'You mean he just wants to be part of everything, know what's going on, what people are doing, without being involved?' asked Jennifer.

'Something like that. Gideon knows more about him. But then Gideon knows everything about this island. Wait till you read my notes on him. His life alone would be a book.'

Jennifer flung up her arms. 'Please, no more writing assignments, I've got too many now!'

She made an effort to do her hair and make-up and decided to stop by her and Blair's cabin and find a dress to wear to meet him for drinks. I've gone a bit feral, she thought to herself. Wearing baggy shorts, loose shirts, sandals, no make-up and a hat had become a comfortable uniform. She'd bought some loose sundresses in Headland Bay and hoped she'd be able to get away with them until the last few months of her pregnancy.

Despite her clothes being in the closet it didn't feel as though she'd ever lived in this cabin. Being regularly serviced and with Blair away so much, it was very impersonal. She quickly changed and decided to leave her shorts and shirt in the laundry hamper. She was shocked when she lifted the lid to find a flower-printed silk top. With her fingertips she lifted up a sheer nightdress. Beneath it were G-string panties in lime green. Jennifer slammed the lid down on the articles and felt sick. She opened Blair's closet and found women's tops and trousers snuggled up to his clothes. In the bathroom cabinet were cosmetics and a packet of condoms.

Jennifer stood in the middle of the bathroom feeling numb. Susie was becoming a fixture. And she wasn't sure how she felt about it. Resigned. Disappointed that Blair was lying to her. Again.

She sat by the pool terrace, watching the sun begin its shimmering slide below the horizon. Couples surrounded her. They all seemed to be in love, touching each other affectionately, arms around each other in the pool, rubbing their bodies together. An old couple at a table held hands, an anniversary perhaps.

'Hi, Mrs Towse. Can I get you something?'

Jennifer smiled at Bruce, the handsome blond surfie-looking guy she'd seen dancing and flirting at the staff barbecue when she'd arrived. She'd felt he was a peer then; now she felt old beyond her years. 'I'll wait till Blair joins me, thanks.'

'Er, he sent me over. He's tied up on the phone for a few minutes.'

Jennifer stood up. 'I'll go for a bit of a walk then. Thank you.' She was annoyed and knew it showed.

She headed for the walkway along the edge of the resort grounds and saw Isobel coming along the beach. Jennifer walked down the path onto the beach, took off her sandals and went towards her. Isobel was wearing white linen slacks and a brilliant scarlet and gold silk top with a matching sheer scarf. With dramatic gold jewellery and make-up she looked glamorous and exotic. Jennifer had become used to her casual uniform of khaki shorts, shirt over a T-shirt, her dark hair tousled or squashed under a cap and little make-up on her tanned skin. Isobel radiated with the health and energy that drove her to work long, physically taxing hours. She tired people half her age but Jennifer found her company exhilarating. Being with Isobel was like plugging into a power grid.

'Hi there . . . where are you off to?' Isobel called.

'Meeting Blair. What about you?'

'Dinner with Rosie. What's wrong?' She slipped her arm through Jennifer's. 'You look lovely, except for the unhappy face.'

'I pulled this dress out of Blair's unit and found Miss Susie seems to have taken up casual residence. They know I'm going in and out of there. What if I'd walked in on them? He promised me it was over.'

'What are you going to do?'

'It doesn't seem to have registered with him that I'm having his baby. It's like the rules don't apply to him, he can just do what he wants.'

'Do you think he'll change when the baby comes along?' asked Isobel quietly.

They walked along the beach, arms linked, Isobel's top reflecting the colours of the sunset sky.

Jennifer took a long, deep breath. 'I suppose not.'

'And how do you feel about that?'

Jennifer stopped, pinched her arms, and wobbled her head. 'Numb. I must be, I can't seem to feel. What's that mean?' She resumed walking, they were almost back at the pool.

'I'd say you are becoming resigned to the fact your marriage is over. You've known a long time. This other girl, Susie, she's a symptom, not a cause.'

'It's pretty shocking to think I'm walking out of a marriage when I'm pregnant. Why aren't I angry? More upset? More scared?'

'You've gone through that stage. What you have to do now is think about yourself and your baby.'

'Oh, Isobel, it's so sad. I feel like such a dud. I've stuffed up my life. Before the baby is even in the world, its family is screwed up.'

'Not necessarily. Two secure, confident individuals who love their child are better than a miserable couple who surround the baby with bitterness, anger and frustration,' said Isobel calmly.

'I can't help thinking about my mother. What our lives might have been like if my dad and brother were still around. She's so hurt and angry at the world. I often feel she looks at me with some kind of hatred – that I'm here and they're not.'

'Don't beat yourself up and let her make you feel guilty about something over which you had no control,' said Isobel firmly. 'Subconsciously she might feel that way, but it isn't deliberate. She'd be hurt to think you believed her capable of such unkind thoughts.'

'Sometimes she acts that way. She's a magnificent martyr. I became the centre of her universe, I'm all she has, and it's been a hard burden to live with,' blurted Jennifer.

'And now you're afraid she will rule you – and your child. Did Blair ever step forward between you and your mother? Protect you? Stand up for you? Lay down the law to your mother?'

'God, no. He kept his distance. My mother was *my* problem.'

'Then not having him around isn't going to change things very much between you and your mother, is it?' said Isobel reasonably. 'You're growing up at last, standing on your own feet, making your own decisions. You aren't running away, you're embracing big challenges and dealing with them. Be proud of that.'

'You always make me feel good. That I'm stepping up to things I never dared think about.'

'Did you think you'd be a mother, doing a

degree, writing a book, being part of something as important as investigating the future of a world icon like this reef?'

Jennifer had to laugh and she shook her head. 'No way. I don't think Blair or my mother – or me, for that matter – really comprehend what I'm embarking on.'

'One foot after another, dear girl. Now, what were you meeting Blair about?'

'I'm not sure, he asked to see me.'

'Get in first. Tell him there's no point staying together, and start sorting out the nitty-gritty.'

'Are you serious?'

'Are you?'

Jennifer drew a deep breath. 'Yes. I am. If I don't do it now while I have the courage I'll end up like my mother – bitter, miserable, feeling I've missed out.'

'Be decisive. Take control of your life. You have responsibilities to yourself and your child, and a parenting relationship with Blair. Get on with it.'

'God, that will shock him. You make it sound easy.'

'It's easier than you think. Once you've made up your mind you see the road more clearly. And you need a clear head to continue your work. A degree will lead to job opportunities. Everything you do now is with a goal and aim in mind for your future and your child's.'

'How on earth am I going to tell my mother?'

Isobel smiled. 'See, you've already decided.

You know, I think she'll be pleased to have her daughter back. And there will be a few I told you so's.'

'That's for sure. My worry is that she'll want me to move in with her and she'll interfere with raising the baby.'

'Mothers do anyway. Try not to think too far ahead just yet. While you're here some of us will come and go, but you'll always have a network and an extended family.'

'I can't imagine not having you around. I'll miss you so much . . .' Tears sprang to Jennifer's eyes.

'We'll always be in each other's life from now on, don't worry. You will come and stay with me, to visit and perhaps to work together. Maybe you will write my life story one day,' she grinned. Then added more seriously, 'I want people to understand what I'm doing and why. That our oceans can be the saviour of the planet.'

'So after you and Gideon dive in the shark-mobile, you'll be leaving? It scares me to think about it.'

'I have to go to Brazil, to the Caribbean, Hawaii and then return here – before our little baby arrives.'

'I'll be on my own for two months, except for a couple of researchers doing field work – birdos and coral people. Tony will be gone, leaving me with a huge pile of notes and tapes.'

'And you have your own work to do. It will be a good time to be alone. You need to heal, learn to be on your own, learn to know and like yourself. And I am always a phone call or email away. If you need me, I will come.'

'Oh, Isobel, that's so sweet of you . . .' Jennifer stopped, her face registering . . . surprise, a slight apprehension.

'What is wrong?' Isobel turned to Jennifer who had her hands pressed to her belly.

'Flutters, ripples. A spasm. What's happening?' There was a note of worry in her voice.

Isobel rested her hand on Jennifer's belly and smiled as she felt the tremor.

'Your baby. She's going for a walk.'

'Really? It's the first time I've felt it move. Oh my goodness.' Tears sprang to her eyes and she grinned with delight. 'It's really happening.'

'Yes, darling, you really do have a little person in there. What a funny, no, *appropriate* time for her to announce herself. She agrees with you.'

'I don't feel so alone. Oh God, this is scary. But wonderful.' Jennifer felt elated.

'Now, are you ready to make your speech to Blair?' Isobel straightened her shoulders and, despite her petite size, exuded an air of authority.

'I wish I had your poise.' But Jennifer did suddenly feel more confident and knew Blair was not going to intimidate her any more. There was a pang and an ache, her ego and female pride were dented, but she also knew that no matter what happened to her and Blair they were forever inextricably linked through their child. And that gave her some comfort.

She saw Blair sitting at the table waiting for her. Isobel kissed her quickly on the cheek.

'Be strong, be pleasant. Don't make any rash decisions,' she told Jennifer. 'See you tomorrow. Or, if you need me, rap on my door.'

'You're wonderful,' said Jennifer. 'Thank you.'

Blair sat in stunned silence after Jennifer's short, unemotional speech. It was probably the lack of tears and hysteria that rattled him most.

'You don't think you're over-reacting?' he finally asked.

Jennifer merely cocked her head and raised an eyebrow, which seemed to infuriate Blair.

'Don't play games with me, Jennifer. This is ridiculous. You can't announce you're leaving me just like that.'

'It's not exactly out of the blue,' she retorted. 'We've been struggling for months before your, er, indiscretion.'

He ignored the reference to Susie. 'How can you be on your own and manage a baby? Even with your mother's help? And what about finances? You can't support yourself.'

'Not yet. I was counting on your help – financially – until I finish my honours and then we'll reassess our position. I'm sure a family lawyer can sort out something.'

His expression changed, his mouth tightening. 'If you make this public it could be very difficult as far as my job's concerned. We came as a couple. I can't afford to have my career compromised. And I have no intention of selling my house in Sydney to keep you playing with a bunch of long-haired uni people. Get real, Jennifer.'

'That's just what I'm doing. Mac will let me stay at the station and Rosie will help me if I need her to. And most of all there's Isobel.'

'God, you women stick together,' he said in exasperation. 'In fact, all those people are influencing you, I reckon.'

'Yes they are. Thank God. I'm not going to be a doormat any more, Blair. I'm growing up – at last. And as long as I'm here, I'll continue to grow.'

'Well, I wouldn't count on staying at that research station. There's trouble brewing.'

'What do you mean?'

'The company is planning on making changes. Keeping that tacky old university research joint on prime Park land isn't one of them.'

'Who says? If you know something tell me now. Any financial mess I get into won't help you. Isobel is encouraging me to stand on my own feet. You should be pleased.'

'You pay too much attention to that woman. She's got in your ear with some feminist bullshit. What are you going to do when she's not around?'

'I'm asking Isobel to be godmother. She'll always be in my life,' said Jennifer.

'I might have something to say about that. And I doubt your mother would approve.'

'What you and my mother think about it doesn't concern me.'

'It's my child too!'

'You should have thought about that before sneaking around with Miss Susie – or anyone else.'

'There isn't, nor has there ever been, anyone else.'

'Then I hope you'll both be very happy.'

The rapid exchange ceased and they glared at each other.

'Jennifer, this is a mad thing you're doing. I wanted to see you tonight to tell you that I'm going to London. Just briefly, for a job interview. Joe and Reg have set up an appointment for me.'

'The slick boys? And what do you do for them in return?'

'Stop calling them that. They're executives. I thought you'd be pleased about London.' He paused, 'Maybe you should come. Get away from here, see things in a new light.'

'Do you want me to?' *I bet you've already asked Miss Susie of Sooty Isle.* When he didn't answer, Jennifer sighed. 'Blair, we're on different trajectories now. I'd only hold you back. We want different things. Nothing is going to change the situation, unfortunately. Do what you want.' *You always have.*

They were quiet, each thinking of their own future.

'I just hope you will make an effort to do the right thing by your child. And me,' said Jennifer.

'Of course I will.' Under the sincerity there was a touch of relief in Blair's voice.

You think you're being let off lightly. 'Blair, we could fight over money, over custody, over a lot of things. But what's the point? Just a lot of pain and bitterness that I don't need. You mightn't think much of my playing around with a bunch of academics, but be glad I'm making some effort to have a future and a life. And trying to support myself.'

He stared at her with a mixture of surprise and grudging respect. 'You really feel strongly about this stuff? If you think you can do something with it, then good on you. Maybe we're both heading for bigger things, as you say, in different worlds. Funny, we never talked about this early on,' he finished awkwardly.

'Yes. Maybe we were too busy to talk about our dreams and expectations. You assumed I'd do what you wanted, and I didn't know what I really wanted out of life.'

Blair gave a pained smile. 'You married me to get away from your mother.'

At first Jennifer was shocked at the unfairness of his remark, but she soon realised that he was right. 'I hadn't thought of our marriage like that. Mum isn't an ogre, but I did feel a bit claustrophobic, I hadn't lived enough, for sure.' *And now I'm right back where I was in some respects.*

'I always felt I never measured up to your mother's impossible expectations,' said Blair.

'When I'm involved in big plans and projects she might see me in a different light. At least I'll be able to provide well for my kid.'

'No one could measure up to my mother's expectations, Blair,' Jennifer said, but her mind was racing with his last comment. 'What plans do you mean?'

'Jennifer, let me share this but keep it confidential. Fanzio and Holding have big plans. They're getting some Asian investor to put up a whack of money and they're planning to develop sporting lodges – really upmarket private clubs – in a few special spots around the world. South Africa, New Zealand, Aldabra in the Indian Ocean and Branch Island. I can be part of the whole deal, not just an employee.'

Jennifer didn't look as impressed as Blair hoped. 'Be careful, Blair. I'd be doing some background checking if I were you. I suppose Willsy will be involved?'

'Why do you say that?' asked Blair in surprise. Then he added. 'I believe he might be.'

'You only think so? Blair, I'm really not that interested but I wouldn't trust Holding and Fanzio for a minute. I'd just hate to see you taken for a ride, money-wise. For purely personal reasons, of course.' She tried to smile.

'Jennifer, this doesn't sound like you. You've changed.' He didn't sound pleased.

'And so have you. Maybe we both have. And that's why we're not happy together any more,' she said sadly.

They looked helplessly at each other, with honesty, no defences between them.

'What went wrong?' asked Blair.

You were having an affair for a start. 'Please, let's not go there,' said Jennifer. She didn't want to re-examine the question of why Blair felt the need to have that affair. 'What's more important is what we're going to do about it.' Jennifer stood up. 'If you want to keep this private while we're on the island it's going to look odd living separately, or with other people,' she added pointedly. 'In case your big deal doesn't come off with Fanzio and Holding, you might want to ask head office in London if Reef Resorts International can move you to a position without a spouse. Say your wife and baby want to stay at home.' *Though where home is, I have no idea*, thought Jennifer.

'That's a good idea.'

'Let me know what you're doing. I'll be here till the baby is due. Goodnight, Blair.' *This is really goodbye.* She turned away, not wanting him to see the tears in her eyes.

Blair watched his blonde wife walk away from him and felt a sudden rush of panic. Then guilt. Then relief. Then, as his mind switched to the plans outlined by Fanzio and Holding, exhilaration. *Jennifer will be all right. I'll do the right thing by the baby. How expensive could a small kid be? Jennifer will want to send it to uni. By the time I've got to think about school fees, I'll be a rich man. No worries. Susie is ambitious too, we think alike. But I'm not going to get tied up again, no way. I like the idea of freedom.*

Jennifer left the resort and walked slowly back to the research station. She knew every twist of the path through the pisonia forest. The evening shadows shivered in the night breeze. How insecure she'd felt, how fearful at walking here when she'd first arrived. The shock of the attack on Rhonda had lessened, though she still despised Willsy and hoped Blair wouldn't be involved with him and the slick boys in any business venture. Even the strange and disturbing presence of Patch appearing at unexpected moments worried her less. While she'd never really spoken to him, she accepted Mac, Tony and Rosie's assurances that he was harmless. A bit odd, but harmless.

The path divided and one of the girl staffies, late for her shift, hurried past, giving Jennifer a wave.

There were few people about, most were getting ready for dinner, relaxing or working. She walked to the end of the station's main drag to where the VIP cottages were tucked away. As she reached the duplex she shared with Tony, she stopped, catching her breath.

Music swept from inside. Such music. Jennifer stood transfixed, her eyes closed as the orchestral washed over her, lifting her in a great burst of sound so she felt she was zooming and spinning above the trees, above the island. Lost in some enveloping blue world, scenes and moments from films that had moved her flicked on and off. She felt her heart was going to burst. She wanted to cry, to laugh, to be wildly embraced, to feel utterly passionate about a lover. In those seconds she was uplifted and overcome with joy and a sense she could achieve *anything*. She opened her eyes.

Tony was smiling at her from his doorway. 'Wonderful, isn't it? I tend to play music when I have a bit of writer's block.'

'It's brilliant. Makes me feel I could write a masterpiece!'

'Speaking of writing, can we meet soon for a run-through of where we're at? I'll be taking off for a bit and while my editor is happy enough he reckons there're a couple of other features I could be doing.'

'Overseas again?'

Tony's smile faded. 'No. Even though I'm out of the war zones, I'm not ready to stay behind a city desk or write about wankers – pardon my language. I'm trying to persuade him to let me spend time doing my own investigations.'

'Do you want to talk tonight? When are you leaving?' It would seem strange not to have him downstairs. While they lived literally on top of each other, and were collaborating on a book, they spent little time together alone, they were mostly with the group.

'Couple of days. I want to cover Isobel and Gideon's dive. There's a documentary film crew coming as well. And I promised Lloyd we'd go for a sail and a bit of a fish when he gets back from South America.'

'So he's really gone to see Carmel's parents? I

bet they want to check him out,' said Jennifer. 'I'm sure they'll like him.'

'He wants to ask for her hand in the old way,' said Tony. 'Lovely, isn't it? He's nervous because her family is old money.'

'Our Lloyd will do okay. Anyway, if they say he's not suitable, Carmel seems the type to run away with him.'

'Ah, the impetuousness of being young and in love.' Before Jennifer could say anything he turned inside. 'Come down for supper. Give me half an hour or so to whip something up.'

'I'll help open a can or something. That'd be great.' She hurried up the stairs, glad she wasn't going to be alone this evening. She was still coming to terms with the fact she'd told Blair she was leaving him. While ending the foundering marriage seemed the right thing to do while Isobel was there, alone in her bed, feeling her baby move inside her, maybe she'd regret taking a stand, thought Jennifer. She wanted to talk to Rosie but didn't want to jeopardise Blair's position. She knew she'd have to explain things to her at some stage, or Rosie would figure out what had happened.

Tony had rigged up a barbecue at the back of the duplex and was standing over a steaming red emperor, testing it with a satay stick.

'Help yourself to a drink inside. There're some nuts but I wouldn't advise nibbling too much.

Doyley donated the fish, he's been out with guests and is on duty tonight.'

'Smells wonderful. What can I do? I'll pass on a drink. I had one earlier – and, boy, did I need it.'

'You can throw the salad together. It's all on the bench.'

Tony had turned the music down and a different, more mellow David Bridie CD was playing. Jennifer tossed the salad, found some olive oil, made a vinaigrette dressing and looked for some paper napkins. There was a dresser in the tiny sitting/dining area and she went to look there. She didn't find any, but on a shelf Tony had some wine, several books, CDs, notebooks and, to her surprise, propped up were several photographs, including two of herself – one walking along the beach at sunset and another of her sitting by the seawall reading some notes. She studied them curiously and then looked at the other photos. Seeing a pile, she picked them up and looked at them all, stunned at Tony's knack for composition, capturing a moment, someone's personality, in an instant. She wondered why he wrote when he was such a terrific photographer.

She went to ask him and was curious to see Patch standing beside him. They were looking at a sheaf of papers. They looked secretive and it unnerved her. She stepped back inside and neither noticed her.

A few minutes later Tony came inside, put the papers beside his laptop and said cheerfully, 'Fish is done. I'll set up the card table outside, okay?'

He'd gone to a lot of trouble with a candle and a shell borrowed from Rudi's lab as a table decoration.

'It looks lovely. I hope that's not one of Rudi's poisonous cone shells.'

'I checked it out. Display purposes only. And we have to give it back. No shells are to leave the island.'

'Leave only footprints, eh?' She sat as he held the chair for her.

'I'll take away a lot from here,' he said quietly.

They talked about the book, and ran through other highlights of the work being done at the research station.

'Mac wants a positive spin and something splashy,' said Tony. 'He keeps muttering about backstabbing, badmouthing and general undermining back at the uni and elsewhere. Do you know anything about that?' he asked Jennifer carefully.

'Universities can be very gossipy and competitive, but I think it's generally kept in-house.'

'Not when there's funding money at stake. I've been making some enquiries . . .' He paused. 'Ah, this is a bit delicate but I wonder if you know that Blair is part of a group that's hoping to build a string of quasi-elite sports clubs in sensitive, special locations?'

'Blair and I don't share a lot these days.' *Why don't I tell him we're separating?* 'But he did mention it and I advised him against getting into bed with the slick boys and their pals.'

'Wise. They must have done their due diligence, but my suspicious nature wonders why they're persisting, and I suspect it could be a front for something else.'

'Like what?'

'That's the missing part of the puzzle. However, if the research station is discredited and gets closed, Reef Resorts, who lease their part of the island, probably figure that another lease could be taken up by another entity for their private club. The university doesn't own the land or the research station. Only the facilities.'

'But that wouldn't be good for the Branch Resort, would it?' said Jennifer. 'Does Rosie know about this?'

'Fanzio and Holding are executives with Reef Resorts, they're in a prime position to push this exclusive club through, provided they can raise the money. I've talked with Rosie, and she thinks it's pie in the sky. She works for Reef Resorts but she's very supportive of what Mac and his mob are doing.'

'The nature thing, the birds, turtles, the reef, that's what visitors come to Branch Island for. Not some plush private club,' said Jennifer. 'And the marine research being done here is crucial to learning more to preserve the whole system.'

'I agree. But people who want to make big money make their own rules. Private and discreet gambling included. Well, that's in the plans for some of the other clubs, I understand. I could be jumping the gun, so until I find out more I can't say anything.'

'It's just too awful to think about. Corporate greed, machinations and abuse of power. It's all such short-term thinking. No matter how supposedly eco friendly they claim to be, it'll disrupt the nature cycle that's gone on for centuries!'

'I agree, Jen. Just think about those great old turtles you're studying. How do they navigate hundreds, sometimes thousands of kilometres across the oceans to return to the spot where they were born in order to breed?'

'I think about that,' sighed Jennifer. 'It might sound silly, but I've wondered at the effort of those female turtles and then they swim away never knowing if the babies hatch and survive. Do you think they're drawn back here because they too were born here in a place that's safe, beautiful and peaceful?'

'We all carry imprints on our souls of our earliest memories. Maybe even before birth,' said Tony.

Jennifer idly prodded her food with her fork. 'I hope my child has happy memories.' *Poor little thing isn't getting off to a good start with its parents splitting up.*

'Why not? This seems a special place for nurturing, surrounded by beauty, peace, nature, loving friends.' He paused, looking embarrassed.

Jennifer smiled at him. 'What was your childhood like?'

'Uneventful. Nice. Well-to-do suburbia on Sydney's North Shore. A lot of sailing. You'd like my family. You hear a lot about childhood baggage, I brought my dark moments on myself later in life. I'll come good. This break here has been very healing.'

'But now we have work to do.' She didn't want to pry further.

'Yeah. Another reason I'm going back to the mainland – to do a bit more unravelling of the network of companies that is Reef Resorts International. They all operate independently except for two or three executives on the board in London.'

'How do you do that? Do you have someone to help you? I wouldn't know where to start,' said Jennifer.

'I have a very valuable little black book of contacts. Finding the right person in the right place is the key. Often people don't know they have information. An amiable chat can often shed light into a dark corner.'

Over coffee they mapped out the format of the book and left the final section with a big question mark over the heading – *Future Directions*.

'I know you have a lot to read for your own work, but if you can skim through some of this you might find it interesting, useful. Something might strike you that I've missed,' said Tony.

Jennifer curled up in bed and read until she couldn't keep her eyes open. She fell asleep, feeling more peaceful than she had in many weeks, perhaps it was because she had made a painful decision and was feeling in some control of her life at last. Even if she was on her own, she remembered Isobel's advice to use this time to learn about herself. And she wasn't totally on her own. This circle of friends on the island gave her great strength. The evening with Tony had been relaxed, interesting and warm. He mightn't have known it, but he'd helped her cross a bridge in her life.

18

The Sunless Sea

To Jennifer, Branch Island, which she'd once thought of as an insignificant dot, now seemed the centre of the universe. She was awake early, feeling refreshed and energised. She headed for the beach, loving these dawn walks.

She decided to reverse her normal walk, going in front of the resort and past the research station beach base. There were scattered clouds obscuring the sunrise, a possibility of a tropical shower. Nevertheless, the air was warm and the sea calm. Where the resort had constructed the sea wall and boardwalk, the low tide exposed the rocky channel that led to the deeper water. Jennifer glanced up at the far wing of the luxurious suites, shuttered and quiet amongst the trees. She was about to head out onto the deserted stretch of beach swept clean by the night high tide when a movement caught her eye.

Jammed amongst the rocks, low down in the channel barely covered with rivulets of the lost tide, a huge turtle struggled, flippers straining to pull the heavy bulk of ancient shell across the eternity of coral flats on its long march to the sea. She glanced back and saw the old female had come in to shore to lay her eggs in a position where in earlier times no obstruction of cemented rocks had stood between her and her birth place. How far had she come, so late in the season? The clear marks of her ascent to the dune were treadmarked in the virgin sand. Unless she got back into the sea she would die, stranded here to boil in her shell in the sun.

Jennifer didn't pause as she changed direction and stumbled across the sharp, coral-encrusted rocks, glad for her light rubber shoes. The turtle was resting, heaving, teary old eyes sad and glazed. Doggedly she resumed the jerking pull, scrabbling four centimetres up the rocks, only to slip back, pulled by gravity and the weight of the massive barnacled dome on her back.

'You poor old mother.' Touched by the persistence of a mother following a prehistoric instinct, Jennifer crouched, shoving and pushing to help. Panting and straining, she seemed to make little difference. She stood up, looking around. There

484

was no one in sight, no tool that would assist her. Who could she call on to help? The rule of the resort came to her – nature rules. If this was to be this turtle's fate, so be it.

'No, I can't leave you here.' Some mothering, female bond surged in Jennifer. She lay beneath the peak of the turtle's egg tube, shoved her shoulder under the point of the shell and, taking a deep breath, lifted and pushed. There was a crunch and grinding noise, and, with back flippers paddling in the air, the turtle was lifted up over the rocks onto a smoother, flatter surface. Here the rocks were smaller obstacles and leverage was possible. Slipping, sliding, Jennifer pushed and pulled, the turtle levering its weight so together they made gradual, bumpy, grinding progress over the coral flat.

Jennifer stood and gazed at the distant break of water, so far away. But to her left she saw the deep watermark of a channel.

'You stupid female! You're just going in a straight line, the way you've always done. Look over there, go sideways and we can get into the channel and swim.'

Stubbornly, the turtle resisted. Every cell in its body was programmed to the map it had followed for generations. But Jennifer was persistent, the old turtle tired. It slipped and tilted over a rock, facing more to the side than to the sea. They inched along, the turtle distressed. It struggled, but some will, some maternal force in Jennifer, gave her strength and tenacity and she finally tilted the old turtle into the shallow channel. Feeling water under its flippers, the turtle struggled forward with renewed energy. Jennifer was worried it would try to return to its former trajectory, so she hung on, now both of them dragging and scratching through the narrow channel with the water up to Jennifer's knees.

Then there was a gap, and a surge of water, and the channel dropped away to sudden depths. Jennifer held on to the great shell as the turtle started to swim, its head out of the sea, its gaze set on some distant horizon.

It happened so quickly. The turtle was stroking determinedly ahead, carried by the washing current. Jennifer, clinging to its back, was swept into the deep narrow channel, heading to the white surge at the edge of the reef. In seconds they were through the choppy foam and suddenly in clear, gentle water. The turtle dived, swimming strongly, easily, and Jennifer gasped, shut her mouth and loosened her grip as it slid below the surface. The cumbersome beast was now weightless, moving gracefully through the blue water.

The connection between them slipped away. The turtle tilted, swimming deeper, a flash of creamy undershell and a slight turn of the head. Did she see in that glassy, beady eye a look of knowingness, of gratitude? Jennifer was floating, still holding her breath, now aware of the seagrass waving and swaying, the wavelets above washing over the ledge of coral. She kicked, stroking upwards, and gasped for air.

In a minute she had paddled to that ledge,

grasping at the soft coral, and pulled herself back into the channel where against the run of water she hauled herself shorewards with kicking legs and stroking arms until she could stand. Wobbling and tripping, her feet scraped the sand while she waded and then scrambled across the rocky shallows to the beach.

She fell onto the sand, her arms and legs scratched and bleeding, but overwhelmed by a sense of triumph. Something told her this was going to make her a better scientist – she had been there with her subject and had shared an innate if brief connection.

It had been a week of building expectation as Dive Day approached. Isobel had arranged for a documentary film crew to be there and several visiting scientists had arrived at the research station.

'I thought it was just Isobel and Gideon. Why are so many people interested?' Jennifer whispered to Mac at an informal dinner.

'Conditions are extraordinarily good. She said if the dive with Gideon went well they'd maybe be more adventurous and bring over the Sea-Life from Hawaii. We're talking revolutionary winged micro submersibles. Isobel feels time is running out for the reef.'

'Yes, she's driven, all right. Are they trying for some record, or just seeing what they can find?'

'Every deep dive is important. Publicity raises awareness of how precious the reef is. Most deep sea life seems to be in the fourteen to twenty thousand feet band. But of course there're other things to be investigated in the deepest waters of the ocean. After all, the coral species found here are similar to those found right through the Indo Pacific region, but the stuff in the deep water is unique.'

Rudi joined them. 'Like weird creatures and the origins of man?'

'What's your theory on our evolution? Do you think we came from the sea?' Jennifer asked Rudi.

'What do you think, Mac?' Rudi turned to their professor.

'This is a social occasion, I'm not going to theorise. Except to say . . .'

Jennifer and Rudi chuckled. 'Go on, Mac.'

'Well, some say life originated in extreme environments, high heat, for example. And the hydrothermal vents deep in the sea contain organisms existing in conditions similar to the first life forms on the planet. Philosophical debates as to man's origins aside, the fact that our food chain is based on energy from the sun, which doesn't reach the deep sea, means life forms down there rely on a different energy source – that which shoots out of those vents.'

'And not just energy – the biomedical industry is spending a fortune looking for useful enzymes for genetically based medicines and industrial chemicals and processes,' said Rudi.

Mac nodded. 'I know your field is marine medicine research, Rudi, but energy reserves are vital too. How much oil is in the seabed? And what about the deposits of gravel, sand, manganese, tin, gold, diamonds? We want to know what minerals are in deep ocean ridges and deep-sea volcanoes.'

'I'm understanding more and more why Isobel's work is so important,' said Jennifer. 'It's not all airy-fairy save the ocean stuff. There's serious investment and business at stake. But mining the ocean is a risk.'

'I still think marine-based medications are going to help cure human diseases,' said Rudi. 'Coral reefs hold chemicals that will help fight cancer, AIDS, diabetes. We're just starting to find out the molecular potential of the sea.'

'Then do you think we should be mining the seabed?' asked Jennifer.

Rudi shook his head and shrugged, but before he could answer Tony suddenly appeared beside Jennifer.

'Hey, there's dancing in the street. Someone has a speaker outside their room and everyone is dancing. Want to join me?'

'Sure. Though I haven't danced in a while,' said Jennifer, thinking back to her uni days and crowded pubs with unknown bands.

'Me either. I got used to Eastern music, which isn't so danceable.'

They left Mac's crowded house, threading past dancers, just as the music changed to a ballad. Tony shrugged and they drew together at the edge of the sandy path lit by the lights from inside the cottages and several security spotlights on buildings.

Tony turned to her and Jennifer slipped comfortably into the circle of his arms. They didn't speak for a few moments as they concentrated on the music. The intimacy of their physical contact caught them off-guard. People were laughing, talking, dancing, picking at snacks on the table outside the canteen.

Tony broke the silence between them. 'Never thought I'd be leading a normal life again. Doing things like this. Though I suspect life on this island is rather unreal.'

'In a good or bad way? Or because of what everyone is doing? Either lusting and lazing in the sun or doing rather offbeat if important work,' said Jennifer. 'I guess it's not like the mundane mainland world.'

'I've changed since being here. Which was part of the reason I came. One, to do a story, and, two, to see if I could regain . . . myself. Some equilibrium. Memories of an ugly war are less sharp in sunshine on a beautiful tropical island.'

'I've noticed a difference in you,' said Jennifer carefully. 'I had you down as a loner, a reclusive, moody type. You've definitely come out of your shell.'

'Oh dear. Sorry if I was rude or anything. I hate moody types myself. My worry is I'll revert, be like one of your turtles and go into my shell when I leave here next week. Lovely as it is, this island is an excuse, a means to escape from reality.'

'Oh, don't say that!' exclaimed Jennifer. 'I've made some pretty dramatic decisions since being here. I hope I don't regret them when I go back to the mainland.'

'Like getting in the water, that was a big step.'

'And leaving my husband. That's been a major step.' She gave a small smile. 'Though, in talking it over with Isobel, it was a step following a lot of smaller steps going in the same direction to the same destination.'

'Oh. I don't know what to say.' Tony was flustered at her news.

'I wasn't going to tell you. It just slipped out. But I suppose everyone will know soon enough.'

'Are you sure you haven't been hit by island fever? That's a pretty drastic step to take . . . in your condition. And what about your studies? Does Mac know?'

'He knew before I did, I suspect,' said Jennifer with sudden insight. 'He's so supportive. Now you've got me worried. About life off the island. I keep assuming things will stay as they are.'

Tony tightened his fingers around hers. 'Nothing stays the same. We just have to hope they get better. And, I'm finding, they do.'

They moved slowly together to the undulating mood music. Tony drew her closer to him as he executed a turn, then missed a step and stopped, looking embarrassed and amused. 'I just got kicked.'

'Oh, did I? It's the sand underfoot.'

'No. I mean . . .' he pointed at her belly. 'Someone else is dancing.'

Jennifer blushed and laughed. 'Did you feel that? I'm getting used to all the bumps and rumbles and turns. The baby seems more active at night.'

'Don't worry about it. That was different.' He held her close again, mumbling in her hair. 'Are you okay about being on your own with a baby on the way? How does your husband cope with that idea?'

Jennifer wanted to blurt out the thoughts that came to her mind. *Blair never wanted a child. Well, not for some years. He'll be a provider but not a parent. Later on, when the child can communicate, then perhaps he'll take more interest. But no, this child is my responsibility and I'll wear the consequences.* Instead she said, 'We're still talking about the future. Blair will do the right thing. But he's ambitious and a baby and a wife veering off to do her own thing wasn't how he planned his life.'

'Oh. Why not? I would think that'd be quite an asset – an independent-minded wife.'

'Have you ever been married? Or thought about it?' asked Jennifer. She felt his arm and back go rigid and realised she'd touched a nerve.

'I've thought about it. Didn't happen.'

They danced for a moment and Jennifer decided not to probe further. Was Tony one of those men she'd read about in magazines with commitment phobia? Yet he seemed such a worldly man: well-travelled, experienced, sophisti-cated; he'd seen the underbelly of life, yet was sensitive, and also sentimental, she suspected.

But he seemed to want to talk. Holding Jen-nifer, talking into her hair, he couldn't see her expression, which made it easier for him. 'I've been emotionally wounded, which pales in com-parison to the wounded in war, but the final blow was trying to rescue a little girl and adopt her. I was prepared for the difficulties and red tape. I wasn't prepared for her to be killed. I came to the conclusion it was easier not to open your heart than to get it shattered.'

'Isobel says you have to trust. Believe there is something wonderful waiting for you. That you deserve it,' said Jennifer softly, adding, 'I'm work-ing on that concept.'

'You must be a strong woman,' said Tony. 'Not many would have the guts to do what you're doing. I admire you. You see a lot of bad relationships and marriages out there, and you think, Who'd want that? It all looks too hard.'

'Thanks for the vote of confidence,' she said wryly. 'I can't think past doing my degree, the book with you and Mac and, oh yes, having a baby.'

Tony gave a mock wince. 'Ouch. Makes my current lifestyle seem rather lazy. Another reason I like being on an island is I don't have to face a cranky editor, ageing parents, a sister with family problems and the decision about what to do with the rest of my life.'

'Oh dear. When does it get easy? Simple? I hoped I wouldn't have to struggle like my mother.' *Or be as unhappy.* She spoke lightly but he sensed something in her voice.

'What does your mother think about your big decision?' he asked gently.

'She doesn't know yet. I'm going over to see the doctor and have a mother–daughter talk in a few days' time. She'll probably be pleased.'

'Why would that be?' Tony was thinking of his own mother, how she longed for him to get married and how devastated she'd be if his pregnant wife left him. The enormity of Jennifer's step hit him even more.

'Oh, being a widow, the trauma of losing my father and brother . . . she's a bit possessive. Frankly, no man is ever going to be good enough for me. Blair never stood a chance. And because of her own baggage she dislikes all men. So there you have it.'

'Hmm. I suppose you can't blame her,' said Tony sympathetically. 'Though it must be hard on you.'

Jennifer felt a swift rush of annoyance and then immediately guilty. 'It is. If you met my mother you'd like her. And wonder what I'm going on about.'

'No, no, I know what you're saying,' he said comfortingly. 'My sister has problems with our parents and gets cross at me for not backing her up. Maybe that's the trouble. I'm too objective, I have to look at something from all sides, and that

annoys those close to you who want uncondi-
tional approval and support.'

'Maybe that's what makes you a balanced
journalist,' said Jennifer.

'Maybe it's what also holds me back in emotional relationships,' he said carefully. 'I'm not
prepared to dive in, throw caution to the wind and
be passionately committed, no matter what.'

'That's sad,' said Jennifer. 'I bet Gideon would
have something to say about that.'

'It's not easy to change, trust, relinquish your
hand on the controls.' He smiled at her.

'Look at me. It's easy!' She lifted both arms in
the air. 'I've taken the paddle out of the water and
I'm letting the current push my canoe along and I
have to hope I don't go over a waterfall.'

'God, you seem so fearless. Isobel is right. She
says women are stronger than men when it comes
to the heart stuff.'

'Don't beat yourself up, Tony. You've been
through more than most of us. I can't think how
I'd deal with a child I loved and wanted to protect
being killed.'

He drew her to him. 'Thanks, Jen.'

The baby seemed to resent the pressure of their
bodies pressed so close and did a small somersault.
They laughed and Jennifer lifted her head to see
what she could read in his sea-green eyes. Tony
was gazing at the shirt stretched across her
expanding tummy. Jennifer took his hand and
placed it on her belly so he could feel the rolling
movement of her baby.

'It's either a bum, a head, or a small soccer ball,' he grinned. 'Amazing. How do you sleep?'

The music revved up and they walked away. 'With difficulty,' admitted Jennifer. 'Speaking of which, I'm going to head to bed. I'll just check with Mac about the procedures and protocol for the big day – seeing there are so many VIPs around.'

'I'm going to be with Lloyd on the cruiser taking pictures. Could you tape some stuff?' asked Tony. 'Just chat to people. Everyone present will have something interesting to say, I suspect. It will be useful for my article and the book overview.'

'Sure. I gather people are going to be at the research station so I'll talk to them after the dive.'

'What these people are doing and learning is quite possibly going to have global implications,' said Tony, as they walked back to Mac's cottage. 'I mean, what started as looking at ways to save our Barrier Reef is turning into groundbreaking research into medical, energy, environmental and conservation issues on a massive scale.'

'I was talking to a scientist tonight – correction – I was listening to a scientist tonight, that fellow from Florida who was trying to explain the theory of interconnectedness in nature's network,' said Jennifer, shaking her head. 'Boggling stuff.'

'I'm still trying to grasp the finer points of the world wide web let alone the patterns and networking Mother Nature has created amongst planets, animals and the human sphere,' said Tony.

'It's hard enough just relating to other people. I think I'll stick to the written word.'

'I enjoyed the dance. And talking with you,' said Jennifer.

'Me too. You're easy to talk to, Jen. I've never been one to share personal stuff. I'm going to have a beer.'

'See you over at Gideon's in the morning,' said Jennifer. 'I'll bring my notebook.'

The next morning Jennifer was surprised at the crowd gathered by the lagoon outside Gideon's Shark Bar. Everyone from the research station was there, the documentary film crew, and standing on one of the resort's launches were Lloyd and Carmel with Tony, who had his camera out with a long lens attached. Doyley and Rosie were also watching. Blair, Jennifer had heard, was over on Sooty Isle. With Susie, no doubt. Rudi joined her.

'It's going to be interesting to see the video footage,' Rudi said.

'I don't understand how it works,' said Jennifer. 'And who's the Japanese scientist?'

'Mr Ikigawa. They've put up a lot of money for some of Isobel's experiments over the years. Japan is really the leader in deep-ocean technology.'

'Nice to see they're collaborating,' commented Jennifer, jotting in her notebook.

Isobel had a small group around her for a final briefing. Jennifer watched her talking, her expressive hands fluttering as she made a point, her dark eyes intense and excited. Even though she was short, her dynamic personality commanded everyone's rapt attention. She spoke rapidly, and ended by saying, 'If, as has happened in the past, we find an unexpected occurrence or creature, we shall pursue it, within limits.'

'Do you expect to find anything particularly unusual?' asked the reporter with the film crew.

'We are in alien territory, we still don't know what exists in the deep ocean beyond the outer reef,' said Isobel simply. 'Sometimes things swim up to meet us, or we stumble into difficult or unusual natural phenomena.' She smiled disarmingly. 'It is an adventure – yes? Which is why we are drawn there. Some people ask, "Why climb mountains?" Because they are there. The bottom of the ocean is the last frontier. We go because it is there. And because it is the last hope for this planet.'

'Everything in order, Gideon?' asked Jennifer, walking to the edge of the lagoon.

'Ready as I'll ever be. Question is, are they ready for us?' He jabbed a finger downwards. 'We'll be the unexpected visitors. I always hope to find answers to what *is* down there. Isobel looks at water as molecules of hydrogen and oxygen that share their energy to create water – the hydrogen bond that fuses the world together.'

'And you look at it more poetically,' smiled Jennifer.

He nodded. 'Do you know "Kubla Khan"? Samuel Coleridge's poem: *Where Alph, the sacred river, ran through caverns measureless to man, down to a sunless sea . . .'*

'Do you get scared . . . down there?' Jennifer was remembering her own fears.

'Can't think about that. There have been some grand pioneers before us. What do you suppose Wilbur and Orville thought when they went flying? Mr Beebe dived in his bathysphere in the 1930s to more than three thousand feet. In 1960 the bathyscaphe *Trieste* went to the bottom of the deepest part of the Mariana Trench, thirty-six thousand, one hundred and ninety-seven feet down. It's time we followed in their footsteps. Forget the moon, the sea is the last great frontier.' He raised his arm. 'And one day I will meet that mysterious fish. Then we'll know if we indeed walked from the sea.'

Jennifer took his arm, sensing the old man was looking for something other than the creature he believed existed somewhere in the depths of the ocean.

'I hope you find it,' she said softly.

'It's there. It'll make its presence felt when the time is right.'

'What are you talking about, Gideon?' Rosie appeared beside Jennifer. 'I couldn't miss this.'

'Ah, an old fisherman's tale, is all. I have to get Isobel, don't go away, Miss Jennifer.'

They watched him walk towards the cluster around Isobel.

'Gideon told me he once saw a wonderful unknown creature, a fish like our lung fish, with protuberances like legs. A bit like the coelacanth –

the last living fossil linking humans to amphibians,' Jennifer explained to Rosie.

'Is that why he keeps devising ways to go deeper into the sea?' mused Rosie.

'It does sound intriguing. A place where maybe anything is possible, where you can start again, do it right.' Jennifer stared thoughtfully at the shining surface of the sea and Rosie glanced at her curiously, then walked back to the Shark Bar where the group waited the hours until the sharkmobile returned.

After the celebration of the big dive came the sobering conclusion that the threat to the reef was real, continuing, and climate change was only part of the problem. It wasn't until the video footage was set up and played in the canteen, which was converted to a viewing room with a big TV screen, that Jennifer truly understood Isobel's world and her addiction. Gideon's too.

The lights dimmed. From Lloyd and Carmel's boat the camera crew caught the sharkmobile's bow wave as the submersible bounced slightly in the resort boat's wake. The knot of people on the beach outside the Shark Bar began to dissipate. Gideon's instructions could be heard above the engine as Isobel flipped through a clipboard covered in calculations and graphs.

'The island looks so lost, fragile, lonely out on its own,' Jennifer whispered to Mac beside her. 'I wonder how it's anchored there, what massive eruptions thrust that tiny dot out into the world of sunlight. No wonder I felt so isolated, so impermanent when I first arrived.'

'Each island is unique in its creation and development of its nature and fauna. An island has few enemies, perhaps the sea and wind,' he answered softly.

'It makes me feel that we're interlopers in a living museum. And wherever humanity goes, we destroy what is beautiful and special. And it makes me wonder, should we go down into that last frontier? I rather like the idea of it being unknown, undisturbed.'

When the boat and the submersible reached the outer reef it looked to Jennifer as if Isobel and Gideon had landed on some marine moon. The camera panned over the atlas of light and richly coloured reef channels and outcrops where the shallower water was pale and clear, to the inky indigo of the depths beyond the continental shelf. Jennifer imagined chasms deeper than the Grand Canyon, into which you could drop Mount Everest and never see its peak.

The camera zoomed in, shortening the distance between the boat and a spurt of seawater from a whale blow. In the next few seconds the dark back of the whale rose from the water to slide back into the sea with a silent gush of white water and shake of its tail flukes. There were three in the stray pod heading to their annual breeding grounds in the warm northern waters of the reef.

On screen Gideon, in the sharkmobile, and

Lloyd, on the resort boat, were studying the GPS sonar depth finder. Lloyd slowed the engines, then turned and called to Isobel, 'Anywhere in the next few metres will take you down to Plateau One.'

'Great. Let's do it.'

The acoustics were strange, not just from the sound-recording. Jennifer knew sound penetrated water more readily than air, some frequencies travelling hundreds or thousands of kilometres. No wonder whales could sing to each other across long distances. She glanced at Mac beside her, recalling his telling her that acoustic technology used for mapping the sea floor, and locating objects, animals and natural resources was also used for military purposes and for studies beneath the polar cap. It could detect if the ocean was cooling or warming. Or discover ancient undersea rivers.

There were three cameras, underwater and internal, which captured from various angles the sharkmobile's descent past brilliant coral hills, dazzling, jewelled fish and an occasional bombora pillar of ancient dead coral where shadowy large fish lurked. Jennifer had the sense that the submersible was swathed in soft blue velvet that had creased as if it had been slept upon. Shafts of sunlight sliced through the blue, making fishscales shimmer. Diaphanous jellyfish pulsed past and small creatures like spangled shrimp shot in jerky leaps, then froze, waving enormous tendril antennae before shooting off again.

Even viewing the footage, Jennifer lost her sense of vertical and horizontal. There was no horizon, just the rainbow sea all around. It was crystal bright and brilliant, the visibility strikingly clear. Occasionally the camera zoomed in on the brightly coloured soft corals, like incandescent organs, pulsing and throbbing in their quest for food particles. In the cockpit, Isobel and Gideon spoke quietly, respectfully, making notes, recording data, watching instruments and the small screens below the wraparound, clear nose cone. They hovered over a shelf of dead coral where a few remaining spiky crown of thorns starfish clung, sucking the last of the living polyps. While these periodic infestations of the predatory creature were blamed for destroying the Great Barrier Reef, Mac and other scientists believed that the blame really belonged to humans on the mainland. Jennifer felt and heard Mac's intake of breath as he watched.

The sunlight began to fade as the submersible descended and the water became inky. It looked cold. From the video, and she imagined it would be the same if she were in the submersible, Jennifer had no sense of speed, of motion in a particular direction. The shadowy shape of the reef slope rippled in the distance and disappeared in nothingness. Jennifer found she was holding her breath, expectant. But nothing happened. The screen became darker than dark. And then pinpoints of light. Flashing, luminous colours that spun and darted. Signals?

Gideon switched on the searchlight and for a moment nothing could be seen. Then the ugliest fish imaginable cruised into the beam of light. A giant head, enormous turned-down mouth slackly open with jagged teeth, sharp sticks and hooks, like fishing rods, sticking out from its head. A spiny, knobbly body. It looked prehistoric, evil.

It was the first of an extraordinary parade. Creatures so beautiful, from a purple bat-winged flying trapeze artist, a fat fish of glowing red with sparkling lights along its side like a party boat, to a slithering silver serpent with deadly jaws and mean, pewter eyes. And, slowly watchful, lazily cruising, a huge shark the only thing that looked familiar. Jennifer recalled one of Mac's graduate ichthyologists describing how sharks have changed little over their four-hundred-million-year evolution. And that, in addition to taste, touch, hearing, smell and good eyesight, sharks have a sixth sense, the ability to sense minute electrical fields that are generated by all living organisms.

Gideon turned off the light and even though the sharkmobile was moving and the hum of the thrusters was steady, the darkness, even on the TV screen, appeared liquid. When Gideon turned the light back on, a school of fish, thousands of odd-shaped striped ones, moved in a frenzied cloud that rippled in electric pulsing colours radiating fear. Isobel spoke to Gideon and the craft rose above the endless stream of running fish.

And then Jennifer saw the tip of the first long waving tendril, probing. Involuntarily she reached out, grasping Mac's arm. More pale fleshy but bigger streamers followed and as the camera shot up through the startled fish, it caught in its viewfinder a blank, bulbous eye, the size of a football, the gaping cavern at the tip of a giant squid so massive the sharkmobile could be vacuumed into its jelly-like, transparent body.

The camera charted the little craft's ascent, and by the time the first of the reef plateaus came into view the foundations of the ancient crater looked familiar even to Jennifer. The return to the surface, to sunshine, to friends, to a known world, was an odd transition. The lights went on and there was a scattering of applause.

Mac nudged her, 'So, what do you think?'

'It's like a dream, a movie! Just incredible.'

'They went to six hundred metres. I love the camera that's mounted inside the dome above the nose cone. Like they did for those dolphin movies.'

'I can't believe Isobel has been scuba diving so deep down. She's fearless,' said Jennifer.

'She's determined, for sure,' agreed Mac. 'I suspect Isobel has always got what she wants from life.'

'I doubt we're supposed to get everything we want in life. She tells me to opt for the best compromise in difficult situations,' said Jennifer, thinking of Blair.

'And Gideon tells us to reach for the stars,' added Mac.

'And Gideon thinks the stars are at the bottom of the sea,' Jennifer said, laughing.

It was hot in the middle of the day and the sandy paths were blindingly white. Mac and Sandy and Mick, the coral researchers, were intently studying two of the tanks outside the lab.

'Hi Jennifer, got a minute? Come and look,' called Mac.

'I'm stretching my legs, been sitting at the laptop too long. What's happening?' She couldn't see anything special in the tanks.

'The corals have been busy making sex cells, so they're going to spawn soon. It's an amazing phenomenon you and Tony mustn't miss.'

'Their one night of the year right on cue, eh? What exactly triggers the polyps?' asked Jennifer.

'It's triggered when the correct conditions of darkness, water temperature, moon and tide come together after the full moon. I reckon we're two nights away.'

Even though the coral spawning was a major event for the coral researchers, everyone at the station was anxious to see how big the mass spawning would be. They gathered after dinner to watch the tanks outside, while Sandy and Mick were monitoring the reef flats covered by the full tide. Mac handed around torches covered in red cellophane so as not to disturb the corals with bright light. Tony had his camera ready and several people were videotaping the scene as people hung over the tanks shining their torches into the water. Isobel and Gideon had a film crew in the sharkmobile filming the spawning at its source on the outer reef.

It wasn't until eleven p.m. that Mac gave a signal. 'Look, this one is going.'

Everyone crowded around and at first Jennifer couldn't see anything.

'Here, look through the camera, where Mac's shining the light,' said Tony, taking his eye away from the viewfinder.

From one of the living coral polyps she saw a tiny pink bundle of eggs and sperm released. It was swiftly followed by others, which became a stream floating towards the surface.

'It's like pink caviar,' she exclaimed as she handed Tony his camera.

'Over here, look at this one,' called Kirsty. A pink snowstorm was erupting in the large tank.

'Amazing. Imagine that multiplied a million times or more in the reef out there. It'd be fantastic to see it from inside the submersible,' said Tony.

'Even more amazing to scuba dive in it,' said Mac. 'Let's hope the larvae develop. We'll know later tomorrow morning how it's going.'

Tony and Jennifer walked down to the sea but even in the bright moonlight they couldn't make out much until they shone their torches into rock pools and saw the pink foam bundles on the surface. Further out, Sandy and Mick's dim red lights bobbed in the rubber duckie.

'I bet you never thought you'd be doing this,' said Tony.

'Never. I just find this whole reef experience fascinating,' agreed Jennifer.

In the morning Tony tapped on her door. 'Hey, come for a walk and look at the sea. I'm taking some photos.'

They walked around the beach and waded through the shallows for a closer look at the dusty pink slick spread like a cloud across the ocean.

'Synchronised sex in a soup,' said Tony. 'Let's hope all those baby coral larvae start building a new reef. The fish must be pigging out. Do they just settle on top of each other on another bit of reef?'

'It's the coral skeletons and cementing algae – the reef mortar – that Mac says is the key to holding all the limestone structures together,' said Jennifer.

'Apparently you can see the Great Barrier Reef from space,' said Tony. 'And all because of tiny coral polyps only a few millimetres long.'

'I'd like to come back and see this again next year,' Jennifer said.

'Maybe we could do a night dive with them.'

'Maybe,' said Jennifer. She was doubtful she'd ever do that, but she liked Tony suggesting the idea.

Most of the students had left. Rudi had flown to Canberra at the invitation of the Department of Defence. Isobel was packed up and Jennifer had taken over Tony's downstairs apartment with the bigger kitchen and closer access to the bathroom. She kept her upstairs space as a work area, but she was finding running up and down the stairs a chore now. She was feeling heavy and cumbersome, being over six months pregnant. As she packed a small bag for her visit to Headland to see her mother and the doctor, Isobel called in.

'Can I have a coffee, my darling? I want to explain something to you.' She sat at the small table as Jennifer poured the milky coffee. 'Now, this is how you must handle the matter of your future and your baby. I don't mean how you and Blair arrange visiting and such. I'm talking about practical things, Jenny. Money. You must do this now and finish it quickly.'

'Oh Isobel, it'll be all right. Blair will sort things out and look after us.'

'Do it now, darling. I have seen people draw these things out and then you get nothing. Or little. Say what you want and stick to it. Now – while he's feeling guilty.' She smiled.

'Isobel, I'm shocked. I can't be like that.'

'Be like it. Be fair but be firm. Ask him, "Now, what are you going to do, financially, for me and our baby?" And when he says he hasn't thought about it yet, then you say, "I have." And give it to him in writing. You see a solicitor this trip.'

'I hate that sort of stuff.'

'Shall I do it with you? I spend two days in Headland before I go to Brisbane and fly out.'

'Would you? I mean, really? I don't know that my mother would be very good at that kind of thing.'

509

'Then I shall be your watchdog. It's done. It is good to have things tidy and then you can enjoy the baby with no worries.'

'My mother says she doesn't believe in taking money from men. Though she did want Blair to put his house in both our names. I'm sure she'll be happy to know I'll be looked after. It's just till I get on my feet. Though it seems a long way off.' Jennifer sighed, thinking of the pile of work she had to read and analyse for Mac.

'You will get there. Things will happen that will surprise you,' said Isobel confidently. 'I am off to say goodbye to Rosie. I am flying on the chopper to the mainland. I'll call you from my hotel when you are at your mother's.'

They hugged, and Jennifer tried to thank her, but Isobel put a finger on her lips. 'I should be thanking *you*. You make me proud and happy.'

Saying goodbye to Mac as he headed home was difficult. 'You've changed my life, Mac,' said Jennifer tearfully.

'No, *you've* changed your life. And for the better. It'll be hard for a bit, but worth it in the end. I know you can do this.'

'Thank you, Mac. I'll try my best.'

'I know you will. You're stronger than you think, Jenny. Call me any time, email me as often as you like.'

'You have so many students, your family, the problems at uni, and here. I'll try not to take up your time unless I really need to,' she said.

'Don't be lonely. See Gideon. I know Rosie

will keep tabs on you. But use this time for yourself.'

'Thanks, Mac. Blair will be around, Rosie and I will see each other every day or so, I'm sure. I'm rather looking forward to the space to do my work and write.'

'Keep in touch with Tony. The work you do together on the island book will help the words flow for your honours writing. Good luck.'

She watched him cram a hat on, his pony tail tied back, a sleeveless vest over his plaid shirt tucked into his khaki shorts. He was wearing hiking boots and she laughed to herself thinking he looked like a naturalist about to strike out into unknown territory. And perhaps he was – a visit to Sydney and Canberra was on his agenda, places where he was not at home. Back home in the lush hinterland of Queensland he had a family who at times took second place to the sea, the island and the reef.

There was a small group waiting at the wharf in Headland Bay, tourists waiting to board the cat for its return trip to the island resort. Jennifer saw her mother waiting and Tony carried Jennifer's bag as she introduced them.

'Nice to meet you. Thank you so much for helping Jennifer,' said Christina formally. 'My goodness, you have blown up, Jennifer,' she added.

'That's what happens when you're pregnant,

Mum.' She laughed. 'Now wait here while I get the car; Vera let me leave it here.'

Tony held the door open for Christina and smiled warmly towards Jennifer. 'I'll be in touch. Good luck, with everything.' He closed the door, giving her a wink.

'Who is that man?' commented Christina as they drove off. 'What does he mean he'll keep in touch? Is he a friend of Blair's?'

'No, he's my friend. Tony is an investigative journalist. We're collaborating on a writing project.'

'Doesn't sound right for a married woman – a *pregnant* married woman – to be quite so friendly with a stranger,' said Christina briskly.

'He's not a stranger, he's a friend. I have a lot of friends on the island. And, Mum, you might as well know right off the bat, I'm not staying a married woman. Blair and I are separating.' *Oh God, it just fell out of my mouth! Oh well, it's done now.*

Christina grabbed Jennifer's arm as she stopped the car at the carpark exit. 'You're *what*? In your condition? Are you mad, Jennifer?'

'No. I thought you'd be pleased. You never seemed to like Blair much.'

'Don't try to blame me. He's your husband. What about the baby?'

'It's coming. I'll raise it and love it and Blair will be around as much as he can.'

'Oh, this is wicked. Just terrible. I can't stand it.' Tears trickled down Christina's cheeks, stunning Jennifer.

She reached out and squeezed her mother's shoulder. 'Mum, I'm sorry to shock you. I guess I've got used to the idea. Everything is going to be fine. I've thought it through and Blair is fine too. We were never right for each other.'

'It's history repeating itself. It's your father's fault,' she blubbered.

A car tooted behind them.

'Mum, that's silly. Come on, let's go and have a coffee somewhere and I'll explain things.'

Christina shook her head, brushed her cheek. 'I will not be seen in public like this and, besides, we don't want anyone listening to this. Oh dear, poor Vi and Don, they'll be so upset. And they'll worry. Really, couldn't you have waited, or just tried? Marriage isn't a bed of roses. You have to take the bad times with the good.'

'Mum, nothing would have changed. Why hang on and be unhappy?'

'I did,' said Christina quietly. Then, 'I hope that man doesn't have anything to do with all this.'

'What man? Oh, Tony? Good heavens, no.'

'What about that other man? The professor person I met. What was his name again?'

'Mac? No, Mum, this is between Blair and me. No one else.' Jennifer decided to edit Susie out of the story. Her mother would take up 'the other woman' scenario like a terrier and twist it so that Jennifer lost her husband for all manner of reasons. 'Mum, it's my decision, my choice, and I'm organising my life to suit myself.'

'And how are you going to support yourself and a child? It's not easy, I can tell you.'

'I know that. Isobel is helping me. She's a very clever lady. Don't worry, I'm in good hands.'

'Nice you have clever lady friends to help you. You might ask your mother for some advice or help from time to time, you know,' she sniffed.

'Of course, Mum. I just don't want you to worry. Let's just look forward to the baby, shall we?'

'Poor thing. Coming into the world without a proper father.' Christina gave a tut-tut then squared her shoulders. 'Well, it looks like it's just you and me, Jennifer. As it used to be. A good thing I moved up here then, isn't it?' She sounded quite cheered and didn't notice Jennifer's shoulders sag and her body slide down in her seat.

19

Ebb Tide

THE WEEKS PASSED. EACH day dawned, was filled, the sun set and then Jennifer rested. It was a rhythmic, methodical, calm sequence of minutes, hours, days. Jennifer had a routine and it was productive. The pile of papers and research material sent to her by Mac was diminishing. She wrote and rewrote. And when she felt her writing was becoming dry and academic with too many statistics, she went back to work on what she called Tony's book, even though it was being done for Mac and his university.

She walked along the beach at sunrise, did her stretching exercises, made herself breakfast and settled at her desk. She wrote and answered emails from Mac, Tony, Isobel and Trisha, her friend from Sydney, before settling to work. Late in the morning she walked through the pisonia forest to the resort for coffee with Rosie. Once she saw Blair crossing the freshly swept and raked sandy square in front of reception. He was hurrying, a folder under his arm, wearing long white pants, the turquoise and white resort shirt, and dark glasses. He was joined by Gordon, the English staffie, and they chatted for a few moments, then walked on together in deep discussion.

She watched Blair as if he were someone she knew once, long ago. He was familiar to her, she knew what his body looked like beneath the clothes, the sound of his voice, the way he walked, yet she remained strangely unemotional. Her hands went to her tightly swollen belly and she hoped their child would love and know its father and not feel this estrangement. How she had wanted a father in her life, and Jennifer promised herself that she would work hard to keep Blair involved with their child no matter that she no longer loved him. She continued walking, aware that in those moments something had gone from her life and she was free to begin again.

Blair had initially baulked at the swiftness of her presenting him with solicitor's papers beginning separation and settlement proceedings. Isobel had been so strong, so sweetly insistent to the solicitor they'd found in Headland. Christina had felt 'that woman' was forcing Jennifer to rush into things, but could not come up with any good reason to delay, so had reluctantly agreed Jennifer was doing the only and best thing under the circumstances. They'd all met for a coffee to read through the documents yet again, and Christina had sat there with tight lips looking disapproving. Jennifer saw her studying Isobel carefully, as a woman who saw a rival. And she knew her mother would never warm to her passionate, hot-blooded but clear-headed Brazilian friend.

She'd been surprised that Blair had caved in to her requests after his initial squawks. He had agreed to provide for the future of his child and to support Jennifer financially. Isobel felt Jennifer deserved a bigger settlement for her own future but Jennifer did not want to see Blair lose everything he'd worked for. He'd brought the house into the marriage, he could keep it. Nevertheless, to her surprise, he said he would sell it and split the proceeds. She suspected Blair had other plans, though he'd stopped hinting about becoming wealthy through the big deal his slick mates Holding and Fanzio were making with Reef Resorts. Probably so he wouldn't have to share any future profits with her.

Jennifer tapped at Rosie's door. 'Ready for a break?'

'Am I what. Been chaotic. I'm out of here. Blow having coffee in the restaurant, look there.' She pointed to a small basket on the floor. 'Fresh muffins, thermos of coffee, fruit. Let's go down to a quiet bit of beach.'

'Great.'

They settled themselves under a pandanus tree. The sea was iridescent aqua, the air balmy. They both wore hats and sunblock.

'I saw Blair with that English boy this morning. I'm surprised he's lasted this long. Connected to the resort owners, isn't he?'

Rosie rolled her eyes. 'He disappears for chunks of time, but he's Blair's responsibility. And Blair has promoted him to help manage Sooty Isle with Susie. They all spend a lot of time over there. Gordon is keen on boats, it seems.'

The reference to Susie and Blair on Sooty together registered, but Jennifer let it slide. 'Have the slick boys been back at all?' she asked. 'They seemed a cosy bunch. I hope Blair isn't involved with them. Do you think their super sports club idea is ever going to eventuate?'

'What do you care? Not your life any more.'

'I guess not. But I'd hate to see Blair get into financial trouble. That affects me, and the baby.'

'You're too soft. And we'll know what they're all up to after the London board meeting. Blair is going, with Gordon, who's going to see Daddy and Mummy.'

'Why Blair and not you? He's not on the board! I didn't really think he'd go.'

'Blair wants a job in Europe. Through Gordon and the slick boys he's getting a hearing from head office. Good luck to him. I'm happy in Australia. I've done the overseas thing. Frankly, Beverly and I don't want to leave Queensland. She loves her job at the hospital and as soon as I can I'll take early retirement and make ceramics,' said Rosie.

'It will be hard for Blair to see the baby regularly if he's overseas,' said Jennifer thoughtfully.

'Did you get enough money to go and see him twice a year?' asked Rosie.

'It's so hard thinking about all these things when the baby isn't even here yet!'

'Won't be long by the look of you,' laughed Rosie. 'What, two months or so?'

'I have another check-up next week. I have to go more often now. I don't mind the trip over on the cat. I can have lunch with Mum, come back at four. It's a nice day out.'

'I recall you were terrified of the catamaran when you first arrived,' smiled Rosie.

'I was a total wimp all round. Isobel and you, this whole island, have changed my life.'

'You've found your feet, a direction, and have supportive friends. What more could you want.'

'At the moment, that's great. I can't help wondering about the future, long term. Will I stay a struggling single mum? Will I find the great love of my life?' Jennifer flung out her arms in a joking gesture, but these were questions that hovered in her heart.

'You know what they say – stop looking and it drops into your lap.'

'I haven't *been* looking. I couldn't possibly manage a relationship in my condition! And who'd want to know? Never mind, I want a healthy, happy baby and first-class honours. That's enough on my plate for the minute.'

'I'd say so,' agreed Rosie. She poured the last of the coffee into their mugs. 'How well do you know Tony? I've always had a lot of respect for him as a journo. Hard to get to know personally, but you've spent a lot more time with him. Would you trust him?'

'God yes! Absolutely,' said Jennifer instantly. 'Why?'

'I think there's something going on here. I'm worried about Patch, for a start.'

'Where is the old boy? Haven't seen him around,' said Jennifer. 'I know he's talked to Tony. I never have anything to do with him. I still think he's a bit . . . off,' she said, unsure how to express the feelings she had for the old man.

'He is a strange old bugger,' agreed Rosie, 'but he's got all his marbles, have no fear. He's reclusive, but he's not like Gideon, who is more selective in the company he keeps, the way he leads his life. Poor old Patch has always been a victim, I suspect. A POW, not that he'll talk about the war. And like a lot of them, he never adjusted. Walked out of his marriage and left his kids, something he regrets as he's lost touch with all of them. He's a loner, and, while he might be a bit of a harmless peeping Tom, I think he hovers on the edge of other people's lives, living his life vicariously.'

'It's still creepy. Anyway, why are you worried about him? His health?'

'He's in his late seventies and quite fit, despite losing his eye in the war. He works on a contract basis and he's a whiz with mechanical things, so we keep him on. But I saw him the other week and he mentioned that if anything happened to him I should talk to Mr Tony.'

'"Happen", like if he keels over with a heart attack or something?'

Rosie was thoughtful. 'You'd think that's what he meant. But the way he said it, I don't know. He seemed scared, sort of. Oh, never mind. It's just that Patch doesn't volunteer information without a reason.'

'What else has he told you?'

'Oh, I wouldn't say he gossips, but if pressed he's been useful in flushing out information on some of the staff, who's been up who or whatever, when I've needed to know. He's been pretty accurate in picking out the troublemakers. We had one kid stealing stuff. Patch knew who it was.'

'So what's he told you, Rosie?' Jennifer had the feeling she was holding something back.

She shook her head. 'He has his hit list of people "up to no good" – Fanzio and Holding, Gordon, Blair, maybe, and he can't stand the glamour-boy Willsy, that TV guy. Willsy is a big fan of the resort and keeps coming back. Gordon will have him over on Sooty while Susie and Blair are away in London.'

Jennifer let the reference to Susie pass, and wondered if she should tell Rosie about the attack on Rhonda – what seemed an age ago. She would have handled that situation differently now. 'Why maybe Blair?'

'I think Patch thought Blair was being stupid, impressed with people's positions. Look, I'm not going to worry about some lonely old bloke's fixations. Got to go. Hey, want to have a meal with Bev and me next week in Headland? Bring your mother?'

'Thanks, Rosie, I'd love to see you guys. But you don't always have to include Mum. I'm sure Beverly sees enough of her at tennis, and the hospital.'

'Your mother seems to enjoy playing Florence Nightingale, bringing succour and smiles to the prisoners in bed,' laughed Rosie.

'You mean magazines, sweets and her life story. God, those poor people who have to listen to Mum go on about her days on the farm and so on. From what Bev's told me she's invented a whole new family history,' said Jennifer. 'Anyway, I'm glad she's busy and feeling useful.'

Occasionally Jennifer went around to Gideon's to watch the sunset or share a meal. He always walked back with her to the research station for his 'evening constitutional'. She was grateful, for although the island was familiar and the dark night in the pisonia forest didn't scare her, the empty cottages and labs at the research station looked forlorn. Where there had been music, chatter, laughter and activities, pumps and machinery operating, lights blazing, now there was the one light in the cottage shared by Mick and Sandy, the couple doing the coral research.

Without the presence of the others in the group, Gideon allowed his philosophical and poetic ramblings full rein. Jennifer loved the old man's company, she told him about her childhood, growing up on the farm, and asked him endless questions about his days sailing, travelling and what the island was like when he first arrived. He talked about the wildlife, the incredible fishing, the great love affair he had with a bohemian Polynesian artist. 'A female Gauguin, she was. Could have sold her work for a fortune to big galleries. I arranged an exhibition for her in London. She hated the greyness. She went back to her family. Our children were raised in her big extended family. Very loving, but when I was away one time my father sent my uncle to rescue the "poor, barefoot illiterates living with natives". They had a terrible time at boarding school till I kidnapped them back.' He chuckled. 'They spoke and read in three languages, could dance, sing, play instruments, sail a boat, knew astronomy, loved nature, swam like fish, climbed coconut trees, I mean, what more do you need to know?'

'I hope my baby learns all those kinds of things,' sighed Jennifer.

'We'll make sure of that,' said Gideon. 'This is your baby's home turf now. There'll always be a place for you on this island.'

'I hope so. Do you miss where you grew up?

You never talk about England, your family,' prodded Jennifer.

'Ah, boring stuff. Anyway, I told Tony about it. Once is enough. It's on the record now.'

Jennifer hadn't had time to go through all Tony's notes and tapes. In the evenings she listened to the radio after dinner and worked before going to bed with her reading material from Mac and books sent from the university library. She made a note to attack some of Tony's tapes. If her book was about the island and the work being done by the research team, she needed all the background that Gideon could provide. Most of all, Gideon talked of the mysteries of the deep sea and the bizarre fish he had seen one night: 'As big as a child, glowing luminous blue with fins like fingers and stubby legs.'

'Like a four-hundred-million-year-old fishy water-baby,' said Jennifer.

'Maybe some souls go into the sea rather than the sky. I rather like to imagine the bowl that is the Planet Earth being tipped upside down so the sky and stars are below us and the ocean above so we'd look up to see clouds of coral and rainbows of fish.'

'But the sea would rain down on us . . . fish and sharks and clumps of coral and storms of seaweed,' laughed Jennifer, enjoying teasing him.

'Mmm, then we'll leave the ocean where it is. But who's to say whether the land will be covered by oceans once again, or the seas will sink and shrivel. And we can't blame God for that.'

'I couldn't bear to live in a sealess land,' said Jennifer. Strange how attached she felt to the ocean now.

'We'd die. We're all made of water. We can't exist without the sun, air, or water. So, how's your work progressing? Is Professor Mac pleased? When do you go and sit in a classroom?'

'Not till after the baby is born. Four weeks of lectures and then back to wrap up and hopefully finish my paper.'

'You'll have the full team back on deck and not just a silly old codger like me to keep you company. But I'll be off in a few days to visit some of the offspring. In the Cook Islands. I'll be back before that baby arrives though. Want to be here to wet its head.'

'Great. I suppose the big event's going to hit me in a rush. At the moment I'm concerned about getting through my uni work.'

'You'll do it, kiddo. No stopping you now. Isobel is counting on you to follow in her footsteps.'

'Oh, I doubt that! But if I could work in this field – and be paid – well, that would be just perfect!'

To: *j.towse@branch.com.au*
From: *mac@q.uni.com.au*

Jenny, luv . . . the last paper was brilliant, really good. Maybe a touch 'flowery', meaning too descriptive in places for academic purposes, and if you draw a conclusion, back it up with

*references, footnotes and other examples, the
more the better. Think like a marker. If your
research gives you two roads to travel down,
then quickly explain why you did not choose
the other (just to show you have considered it)
before explaining why you chose the path you
did. Impresses the markers. I'm amazed with
what you've got through. You're on target. Finish reading through this next lot I'm attaching
and if you can keep close tabs on the nests
you're monitoring that's great, but don't sit up
at night and catch a chill. Look after yourself.
We'll all be back in time for the baby's arrival.
Glad to know things are sorted with Blair.
Move on, girl. Have the usual dramas here but
my missus is taking me away for a break to visit
the rellies. Some break! Miss the island, miss
you. I'm very proud of what you're doing, as is
Isobel. You're more than a special student,
you're 'family'. Lotsa luv, Mac.*

*To: j.towse@branch.com.au
From: isobel@oceandeep.com*

*My darling girl . . . how is our little girl coming
along? Dancing a lot?? Conference has been
enormous! I think I made an impression.
(Impassioned, the press said.) Hope the government bodies will act. El Presidente was
charming, hosted a reception for me to do some
private lobbying for funding for the work of
our foundation. Ah, so much talking, talking. I*

long to come back to your little island and sit
at Gideon's feet and watch the sea and listen to
Mac strum his guitar, and hear your news. Con-
gratulations on your hard work, it will pay off
for you. Be strong. Soon you'll hold your little
baby and your world will never be the same
again – even more wonderful! I am going to
change my schedule to get back to Australia a
few weeks early. A bientôt, bella bella. Is. xxx

Distant shrieks and calls of birds woke Jennifer early
one morning. Half awake, she listened to the unfamiliar calls, then they faded and she heard the usual
sounds. The mutton birds were rustling, grumping,
shuffling, gradually rising from sleep to swoop out
to sea for a day's fishing. Seeing the birds over the
ocean, graceful diving boomerangs skimming
waves, shooting skywards, quick and graceful, Jennifer could never equate them with the shrieking
moaning lumps of feathers and sharp beaks she
stumbled over on the night paths.

She stepped outside. The dawn air was balmy
soft, after a cold night it hinted at a hot day. She
decided to walk along the beach at Coral Point to
check the nests she was monitoring. She thought
back to the stranded mother turtle and wondered
yet again at the powerful instinct that drove the
female turtles to return to the spot of their own
birth. Would her baby feel the pull of this island,
this dot in the ocean attached to the iconic reef?

Jennifer began to worry about the birth of her

child. Supportive as her island friends were, it was scary to contemplate going through childbirth alone. Blair hadn't been keen on the idea of participating in the process but had agreed to go along to classes as the time approached. Jennifer was concerned about preparing for this event. What to do? The idea of staying on the mainland in order to do the birthing classes on her own didn't appeal. As she did so often these days she decided to seek Isobel's advice. She'd email her later. Having made that decision, she dressed and headed briskly for the beach.

The high tide had left a waving fingermark at its peak, the exposed sand smooth, damp, unmarked, shining palely in the first light of day. As Jennifer walked she saw in the distance the rumpled fresh sand leading to the water's edge.

She hurried to the turtle nest, but it took her a few shocked moments to fully grasp what had happened. The nest had been crudely dug open and all that remained were several dozen eggs, broken, trampled, with the crushed bodies of small, baby turtles. It was horrible. And where were the hundred other eggs, or had they hatched and escaped?

She searched quickly around the dune and sadly realised from the footprints and spade marks that someone had raided the nest and it was impossible to find any light trail marks from hatchlings in the sand. But why? And who would do such a thing? She raced along the beach and saw several guests from the resort crouching down. She saw a camera flash and a torch focused on the sand. Further up towards the dune slight movement caught her eye and with relief she saw tiny dark shapes spilling from a nest mound. Minuscule hatchlings, the size of her palm, were racing sure and true towards the water. The lead ones angled off towards the torch-light, their flippers propelling them in a swimming motion through the sand.

'Turn off the light,' called Jennifer. 'They're programmed to head towards the moon.' The tourists switched off the torch and for a moment the little turtles stopped, confused. 'On an island the moon is always over water, that's their guiding light,' said Jennifer.

'Point them to the sea then,' said one of the visitors.

'No, you're not allowed to help them.'

The little turtles could smell the water and redirected their energy to making a dash for the ocean.

'Oh my God, look out there,' said one of the women. 'Sharks.'

'They're reef sharks. Harmless to us, but they're just waiting to feed on the hatchlings,' said Jennifer despairingly. 'And once the sun is up the birds will be after them. Go on, hurry, hurry,' she urged the stream of miniature turtles as they now poured down the sand from the nest.

'How awful,' said the woman to Jennifer. 'It's hard to let nature take its course. How many will survive?'

'Sometimes less than one per cent. You didn't see anyone disturbing their nests, did you?'

'Goodness no, we've been walking along the water's edge. Who'd want to hurt such delicate little things? Hard to believe they're going to grow into those huge turtles.'

'Let's hope they do,' said Jennifer sadly as she continued on her way to where she knew the nests were. Around the island other nests had been roughly, hastily disturbed and the eggs and hatchlings taken. Many eggs about to hatch had been crushed underfoot.

She was shaken and upset. She went back along the beach as the sun rose and saw Sandy and Mick out on the reef returning coral and seaweed samples to their original sites.

She longed to talk to Mac but knew he was on holiday with his family. The fate of the baby turtles disturbed her and made her fearful about her own child. Would her baby be all right? What would the birth be like? She looked down at her engorged belly, wondering how the hell the baby was going to get out. It seemed a physical impossibility.

She returned home to make breakfast and was surprised to find Rosie looking for her.

'Can I grab a coffee with you?'

'What's up?' asked Jennifer. 'Come inside.'

'It's nothing too serious but we felt we'd better tell you. Bev rang me to say your mother isn't too well. Been off colour and she's had some blood tests done. She didn't want to worry you but Bev called me and we decided you should know.'

'Oh God. What kind of tests? For what?'

'Bev isn't sure. She reckons your mother has the

martyr act down pretty good but, just in case she isn't crying wolf, we couldn't forgive ourselves if we knew and didn't tell you.'

'Thanks, Rosie. And thank Beverly. I'd better go over and see Mum.'

'Bev said wait till she can find out what's happening. You don't want to be exposed to anything, and there's not a lot you can do anyway. She's resting at home.'

'But who's looking after her? Mum wouldn't like strangers trooping into the flat unless it was spotless. She's the type who'll drag herself out of a sickbed to wash the floors before the doctor visits,' said Jennifer.

'There's a seat on the chopper this afternoon, but Blair is the other passenger. How do you feel about that?'

'It'll be all right. I'll throw a few things together. Trouble is, I hate leaving my nests. I'm so upset, several of them have been looted. Looking at the marks I'd say they've been stolen. I can't believe it.'

'God, that's dreadful. Years back before the resort was built people used to come in and take the eggs. And before that there was the damned turtle-soup cannery. I'll get Patch and Doyley to keep an eye out for you.'

'Do you think they'd come back?'

'Probably not. Whoever it was would know we'd be watching,' said Rosie. 'The turtles are a big tourist attraction.'

'They probably thought there was no one at

the research station and it wouldn't be noticed.' Jennifer began to wonder if there was some sinister plan behind this raid. 'Who'd do this?'

'Kids, a collector, a pet shop, who knows. Don't worry. The majority of nests are intact, aren't they? We'll get a roster going amongst the staffies for a few nights. Till you get back.'

'Thanks, Rosie. I'll go throw a few things in a bag. Oh, do you know what Blair is doing, when he's coming back?'

Rosie hesitated. 'I gather he's packed up for London. He's also moved his gear out of your cabin. I didn't want to dump too much on you at once. He'll be gone a month on leave.'

'Oh well, he'll be back for baby's arrival anyway. Look, I'll move out my stuff from the cabin, not that there's much there. I've taken the few personal things I brought from Sydney. I'll take some baby stuff over to my mother's and put the rest at the research station. Then you can let someone else have our cabin.'

'Would be handy, thanks for that. So what are your plans for the birth and afterwards?' asked Rosie. Jennifer hadn't really thought that far ahead, wrapped up as she was in her studies and research. And the baby was due in less than two months.

'I hadn't thought much about those details until this morning. The eggs being stolen really threw me. I guess I'll move to Headland and stay with Mum – heaven help me – for the last two weeks or so. I'm supposed to do the pre-natal classes . . . next check-up maybe I'll start. I doubt Blair will do those, although he said he would. And then as soon as I can after the birth I plan to come back over here to finish my uni work. The gang will be back then. I reckon I can manage a baby and my final paper.'

Rosie shrugged. 'I wouldn't know. Seems hard on you. Are you comfortable here?' She looked around. 'It's cosy enough. I just worry about baby problems. The hospital isn't just down the road.'

'I'm not going to have a crying, sickly baby and that's that,' said Jennifer firmly. 'Mac and Isobel have kids. And look at all the babysitters around the place. I even have a grandfather in Gideon lined up.'

Rosie thought she saw a pain in Jennifer's eyes, despite her cheerful words. 'You don't have a lot of family around, do you?'

'Mum, Vi and Don are it really. But Mum won't come over here so I'll make a weekly visit to her. That's the plan anyway.' Jennifer smiled.

On the chopper she didn't ask Blair where he had moved his belongings, where the luggage for his trip was or if Susie was going with him. Jennifer and Blair got out of the chopper at the resort reception at Headland Bay wharf.

'As you've parked the car at your mother's I'll drop you off, if you like,' said Blair. 'I'm here for a day or so before flying out of Brisbane.'

'Thanks.' She waved to Bob. 'I'll let you know when I'm going back in case there's a seat.'

The pilot gave her a thumbs-up, watching the couple walk to the car. Man, they had certainly gone their separate ways. But it must be tough on Jennifer, he thought. Still, good on her for not hanging on to a miserable marriage and for doing her own thing. From what he'd heard there was no other bloke on the scene. Though Blair had that Susie in the wings. She was a go-getter and ambitious. At least they were in the same industry. Jennifer and Blair seemed an odd match.

'Sorry to hear about Christina. How crook is she?' asked Blair in the car.

'I don't know. Do you think you could see her?' said Jennifer.

'Oh for God's sake, Jennifer. And say what? She hates my guts.'

'There's no need to make it worse. Walking out without so much as a word to her . . . I can just hear her.'

'You're leaving *me*, remember. And, besides, I'm not dropping off the planet. I'm not handing over the upbringing of my kid to your mother,' snapped Blair.

'She is the grandmother. And your parents have rights too. I just don't want to hear her bad-mouthing you when you could easily pop in, see how she is.'

'Okay. I'll do it. But I don't really want you there. I'll go upstairs, take your bag and then leave. I hope you know what you're doing, Jenny.' His previous coolness and awkwardness on the flight from the island melted for a moment.

'I don't have a lot of choice, do I?' said Jennifer. 'But you're right. It's my decision.'

She never knew what transpired between Blair and Christina and for all any of them knew it could well be the last time they'd see each other. Blair came downstairs wearing a grim expression.

'How was it? How is she?' asked Jennifer.

'Well, she's not as sick as you think. That's one tough old bird. Gave me a few home truths, and I doubt there'll be any more get togethers. Don't let her take over your life, Jennifer. I was never good enough for you anyway and I've apparently confirmed all the dreadful things husbands do to their wives. You'd better choose carefully and warn the next poor bugger that comes into your life that he'll always be taking second place to you and your mum.' He got into the car and pulled the door shut.

'That's a long way off, and I can handle Mum,' said Jennifer. 'Well, this is it then.' She stood sadly by the car with the realisation that when Blair drove away the marriage was over. She was on her own, he was going to a new life too. 'I hope things work out for you, Blair, I really do.' She reached in and touched his shoulder, tears in her eyes.

'You did this, Jennifer. And I'm moving on. I hope you do the same. But no matter what, we have that baby. So . . . I'll try to be a decent dad . . . under the circumstances.' He briefly touched her hand resting on his shoulder. 'Good luck, Jenny.'

She watched the car disappear, and, sighing, picked up her small bag and trudged to her mother's bedside.

Christina looked pale and wan, though her eyes were sharp and alert. They darted to Jennifer's belly.

'It looks like you're the one who should be in hospital, not me. You poor girl. What that man has put you through. Let me make you a cup of tea.' Christina feebly threw back the bedcover.

'No, no, Mum. I've come over to look after you.'

'You didn't come over specially. Just for me. Oh dear.'

'What does the doctor say? And the tests, what were they for?'

'Oh, nothing really. 'Course it could be anything. Heart, kidney, liver, diabetes, who knows,' she sighed, falling back on the pillow.

Jennifer was going to ask about her symptoms but changed her mind. 'I'll make us some tea.'

She was almost out of the room when Christina said, 'Probably a good thing about you and Blair. We'll be all right, the three of us.'

Jennifer stopped, did not look back and continued into the kitchen.

'Look in your room, Jen-Jen,' called Christina.

There was a bassinet with frilled netting and a crocheted coverlet in bright yellow acrylic wool. Jennifer hated it. She'd planned to get a carry cot that she could move around easily. Still, while she was here this would be useful. She opened the cupboard and found a baby bath and a pile of baby items.

'Mum, you shouldn't be spending your money. I'll go round and find things I need.' *And that I like.*

'Oh, I've been picking them up at the stalls on a Saturday morning. The CWA ladies do nice handi-work. And there are so many clever things out for babies now. Not like when you were little. I barely had the basics,' she said. 'When I think of how I had to wash your nappies . . .'

'Well, that was then. Today's different.' Jennifer was brisk. *I am not being held responsible for your suffering.*

The following morning Christina looked and sounded brighter, and insisted on getting up and having breakfast with Jennifer.

'So what are we doing today, dear?'

'You're staying in bed and resting. I've made an appointment with my doctor and yours. And I'll stock up on groceries.'

'I'm sorry to be a nuisance. I suppose I should learn to drive, but things are close and the local taxi man is very nice.'

'I wouldn't worry about it now, Mum. When do Vi and Don get here?'

'In a few weeks, I think. Won't that be lovely, all being together for a visit with the new baby. They seemed quite disappointed not to get to that island, for some reason.'

It's a resort where people go on holiday, to relax, to have a good time in one of the most beautiful spots in the world. 'I'll make a list and see you round lunchtime.'

Jennifer rang Beverly and arranged to meet for a coffee after doing the shopping.

'Hi Beverly. Glad you're not on duty. Now, you're a nurse, what's going on with my mother?'

'I checked for you. Doesn't seem to be anything serious. She still sneaks a cigarette or two but I don't think she eats properly. You know how it is with people who live alone. She's very thin. The tan makes her look fitter than she is. She's low in iron and zinc.'

'I thought that was old people. Mum's only in her early sixties.'

'She says she's lonely. She's looking forward to having you at home with the baby. And I think she's actually pleased you've broken up with Blair.'

'I know that. But, Bev, I'm not moving back in with my mother. For a start, a little baby will probably drive her nuts. Crying, up in the night for feeds, all that stuff. She's forgotten that part of it. I'm heading back to the island as soon as I can. I'll have to come over for post-natal checks.'

'Mmm, maybe something can be arranged. I could be the assigned nurse and visit you on the island. Be nice to stay over a night with Rosie. The doctor prefers the nurse to go to the mother and baby. I'll see what I can do.'

'Oh, that would be so great. In the meantime, I'll have to get Mum back on her feet.'

'Jennifer, your mother isn't as lonely as you think. She has a lot of friends at the tennis club and there's a bloke who's a bit keen on her. He drives her places, takes her out, but she won't take him seriously for some reason.'

'I wish she had a boyfriend,' said Jennifer. 'It'd make my life easier. She's always put me first and then complains at having no life and makes me feel guilty.'

Beverly laughed. 'Good ol' Christina, she can be a lot of fun, but she's a feisty devil and likes to be the centre of attention despite being the martyr. You get on with your life. Though it sounds as if you're doing just that. I have to admire you.'

'Thanks. I've learned a lot from Isobel.'

Jennifer paid for their coffee and they parted, with Beverly promising to talk to Jennifer's doctor and the head of nursing to set up her post-natal visit on the island.

Jennifer loaded the groceries into the car and decided to walk to the Italian greengrocer for fresh fruit and vegetables. Her mother bought too much tinned stuff. The greengrocery was in a strip with a delicatessen, a bakery, a cafe and a coffee shop with sidewalk tables. It was crowded, as it was lunchtime. Jennifer glanced casually at the outdoor tables and pulled up as she spotted one group.

In a corner, under an umbrella, she recognised Tony, even though he had his back to her. He was in an intense conversation with Fanzio and Holding. The last email she had from Tony he was at his house at the beach up north. So why was he here? Why hadn't he contacted her, and why was he with these men? Of course he didn't know she was on the mainland, but, even so, Jennifer's dislike of these two smooth-talking executives put Tony in a bad light in her mind.

She hurried past with her head averted, hoping they didn't see her.

Christina was making a rapid recovery, even insisting on taking Jennifer down to meet her pals at the tennis club. Jennifer acquiesced, hoping she might meet the man keen on her mother. Christina, while showing off Jennifer, was inflating the importance of her research, and her brave and adventurous spirit – 'living on an almost deserted island and pregnant too! You should hear her adventures. There's some big secret submarine undersea spy thing happening too, isn't that right, dear?'

'Not quite, it's an oceanographic survey with one of the world's top marine biologists.'

'Oh, that woman,' Christina said dismissively. 'Goodness me, people do that sort of thing all the time.' Christina was always instantly an expert on any subject touched upon. And always wrong.

'I thought there was some fabulous resort on Branch Island,' said one of the men.

'There is,' smiled Jennifer. 'My husband, well, soon-to-be-ex-husband, is working there. I live far more humbly in the research station facilities.' She stopped, aware of the shocked faces around her, including her mother's furious expression.

'Ex-husband? You and Blair . . . ?' The question from one of the women hung in the air, as everyone listened with great interest. Christina, always boasting about her daughter, hadn't shared this bit of news. Her mother busied herself around the tea urn, her back to the rest of them.

Jennifer gave a nonchalant shrug as best she could. 'It's sad and difficult, but we thought it best as our careers and lives are going in such different directions. We're friends, and Blair will be involved in the baby's life. These things happen . . . I guess.' Her sentence tapered away as the expressions of her mother's friends didn't alter. After an awkward pause everyone began talking at once and tea was served.

Twenty-four hours later Jennifer drove down to the waterfront and sat in her car and looked at the boats. She was upset and hoped the scene might calm her before she went back to her mother's apartment.

Christina had made a rapid recovery and, despite being prescribed a few supplements, she'd been pronounced fit and well. She was making lists of baby needs, what Jennifer should take to the hospital and food supplies for her confinement. The thought of forty days and nights with a newborn in her mother's unit did not sound attractive and Jennifer thought she'd put off telling Christina she planned to return to the island after the birth until she was ready to leave.

But now things had changed. The visit to the doctor this time had not gone so well and she'd had a nasty surprise.

'Jennifer, it's nothing to panic about, but given there are three issues that concern me, I want to have you close by so you can be monitored in case there *is* an emergency. I'm afraid I can't have you over there on that island with elevated blood pressure, high blood sugar and a slight amniotic leak. One wouldn't be so bad, but taken overall . . . we don't want to take any chances, do we?'

Jennifer was miserable. The thought of spending these last weeks cooped up in the unit with Christina, instead of on the sunny, fresh and peaceful island, was anathema to her. But she knew she couldn't risk it. She'd talked it over with Beverly, who, being the responsible nurse she was, agreed that she must be close to medical care.

As she sat there feeling teary and alone, her mobile rang, making her jump. She'd become so used to not having it with her. What did Christina want now?

'Oh Tony! This is a surprise.' Jennifer kept her voice neutral. She was still wondering about his secret meeting with the slick boys.

'Listen, I'm in Headland, been here a couple of days. I just rang Rosie to get a message to you and she said you're here too. Where are you?'

'Down by the wharf. I'd love to see you.' Relief washed over her that he hadn't been hiding anything. 'What are you doing here?'

'That's what I wanted to talk to you about. I

think I'm closing in on something. I'll come down there. See you in the coffee shop by Vera's reception area.'

She gave him a big hug when she arrived and Tony gave her a long look.

'What's up?' he asked, sounding concerned. 'You look upset.'

'Oh, do I? Well . . .' She spilled the news, letting out some of her fears and frustration.

He took her hand. 'Jen, it's not so bad, and you can't take a chance. I'm sure everything will be fine, and as soon as possible you can take the baby to the island. Everyone will be there to help out. What's a baby in the middle of all that chaos. Be no problems. You'll zip through your final work. And get fit and healthy in no time. Swimming is great exercise.'

She smiled gratefully. 'You make it sound so simple. Even the swimming part. I do want to get slim as soon as I can.' She patted her tummy.

'I think you look gorgeous. Brown and healthy and glowing, as they say. And you know what I've learned now? Life is as simple or as complicated as you want, or make it.'

'Thanks, Tony. So, what've you dug up?'

'Ah. Now, at present there's bits of a puzzle. I fronted Fanzio and Holding about their plans for these upmarket sports clubs as there's no way they can make it happen. On Branch anyway. But they have formed a company off-shore and they do have a lot of capital. Oddly, they haven't produced anything too concrete in the way of a prospectus,

543

plans, whatever. So it's a front, but for what. I'm thinking possibly gambling, a casino or something. There are a few floating casinos around.'

'Why are you so interested in the slick boys? And why *can't* they set up a private club on Branch? If it's not going to conflict with the Branch Resort?' asked Jennifer.

'For a start, the last thing the reef needs is more development out on the islands. And I've had some very productive talks with Patch. He's given me information on tape and in writing that's . . . useful.' Tony didn't seem to want to elaborate. 'You haven't had time to read all the material or listen to the tapes I gave you – for God's sake don't lose them. I have copies but I don't want anyone else to know what we know.'

'All sounds very mysterious,' said Jennifer. 'Are Reef Resorts International on the up and up? Does Rosie know about this?'

'The main company is legit. These two slick characters are using their position with the resort and through Lloyd's dad I've found they have a close connection with a certain customs officer with a shady reputation. But what they're up to swanning around on *Kicking Back*, I'm not sure.'

Jennifer was trying to take all this in and one aspect worried her. 'I can't help thinking about Blair. He's convinced they're going to cut him in and give him some job in one of these flash sports clubs. Branch would be the start of it.'

'Jen. Not Reef Resorts, nor the slick boys, nor anyone else can do anything on Branch Island. It's privately owned, the resort leases their land with strict guidelines attached.'

'Nature rules, keep it eco friendly, I know,' said Jennifer. 'So maybe the owners have changed their mind and have agreed to Fanzio and Holding's ideas.'

He studied her for a moment, a faintly amused expression in his eyes. 'Never. Gideon would never agree to such a thing.'

'Gideon?'

'He owns Branch Island. He comes from a very wealthy old British family. He's spent his inheritance on building prototypes of the sharkmobile. The island cost him peanuts all those years ago. And he's bequeathed it to the university. Nah, Fanzio and Holding with a few pals like Willsy and that Gordon kid are involved in something else. And I'm going to find out what.'

Jennifer was digesting this news and then a thought struck her. 'Oh no. Poor Blair. I'd better let him know the club looks like a pipe dream. Or is he in on all this too?'

20

Storm at Sea

JENNIFER STOOD IN THE doorway of what she called
her treehouse – the upper floor of the shambling
cottage where she'd nested these past months at
the near-deserted research station. She'd tidied,
packed things in boxes and was now locking the
flimsy door. She found it hard to believe when she
next came back here she'd be carrying her baby.
That they would be two separate entities.

She trudged down the stairs to where Doyley
was waiting in the electric cart with her bag to
take her over to the wharf to get the cat. She
checked that the downstairs section was locked
and for a moment she smelled the aroma of Tony's

favourite coffee and imagined she heard the music he loved to play. It was merely a thrown-together piecemeal dwelling, not cyclone proof or in any way attractive compared to the architectural niceties of the resort. Nestled in the trees with a sandy, leaf-scattered front 'lawn', it was part of the village of the research station where no more than twenty-five people could stay at one time – though she'd never seen more than fifteen people in residence in the months she'd been here. The cluttered living quarters, labs, cottages, canteen, outdoor specimen tanks and equipment shed had felt more like a home than anything she'd known since life was safe and simple as a small girl on a faraway farm.

Rosie hugged her as she got on the boat. 'Don't worry, we'll be watching those nests for you. And I'll see you and Bev next Sunday. I'll miss you though. Blair is away, Gideon's gone on his trip, Lloyd and Carmel are still in Venezuela. Just as well it's a quiet season.'

The catamaran slid away from the wharf, the new arrivals wandering down its length, hanging over the railing to marvel at the huge and graceful eagle rays, the fish and the clearness of the water. The resort, hidden in the trees, looked tranquil and a place removed from the workaday world. The sunlight glittered over the submerged necklace of coral, the tiny band of sand gleamed white, all surrounded by the dancing blues and greens of the reef waters.

As the cat turned into the channel off Coral

Point Jennifer saw a lone figure on the empty beach and knew it was Patch. Watching, watching, and waiting – for what? In the lapis lazuli of the outer reef she could make out a distant yacht and the unmistakable opulence of the big cruiser *Kicking Back* cutting a slash of white foam as it cleaved through the water heading towards Sooty Isle.

Branch Island disappeared from sight. Jennifer went inside to chat to Vera and have a cup of tea. For the time being she would have to turn her back on the island and these pristine waters, which were now so familiar to her. In Headland Bay Jennifer would have to be patient with her mother, and concentrate on looking after herself and preparing for the actual birth. Thank heavens she had the distraction – and the excuse – of her work. She hoped Tony would be true to his word of driving down to Headland regularly to review things with her. Besides, she was anxious to hear what else he had uncovered.

Christina's flat was cramped, with a working space for Jennifer in the living room, plus the baby paraphernalia she had stashed everywhere – she'd even set up a playpen. But Jennifer made admiring and grateful noises. Suddenly she was tired and felt vaguely depressed. She missed the island already.

Her mother was full of energy and plans for chunks of the day but periodically became reflective, melancholy and negative. These moods were triggered by the sudden recall of an item missing from her life.

'I used to have a picture of you with your grandfather on the farm before he died. It was in a little silver curlicue frame. Who do you suppose would take such a thing?'

Or,

'Well, dear, I'm sorry I don't have any precious heirlooms to hand down to your baby. I had things put away, I'm positive. I sometimes wonder what happened to things at Vi and Don's. Those silly birds of his took up so much space.

'Where is this child going to grow up and think of as home? I wonder, Jennifer. I know this place isn't much. Really, just a holiday place. I haven't had a proper home myself since my parents' nice little house in Sydney. Oh that farm! I was never a country woman, I have to say. We'll just have to make do and hope we win the lottery, won't we? Then we can buy something really nice.' And with that idea in her head Christina became an ardent purchaser of Art Union lottery tickets in the hope of winning a luxurious five-bedroom brick glamour home in the middle of nowhere surrounded by cane fields.

To Jennifer's immense relief Tony phoned and they met for lunch at the growing marina.

He hugged her. 'You look a bit tired. These last weeks drag, I suppose.'

'Now they do. Being with my mother in a cooped-up unit is a strain.'

'I got us some lunch – a picnic. Let's go up the

hill to the park.' In the car he added, 'I read that last chapter you sent, and love it. You really captured the character of Gideon and Isobel, their passion for that world beneath the sea.'

'Watching the video footage from their dive helped a lot.'

'Where's your writing talent come from?'

'No idea. I like to think my father taught me to be an observer. Particularly of nature.'

'Your mother got any artistic talents?'

'If she has she never explored them. She always puts herself down. If you admire anyone's ability at something she'll say, "Well, of course I never had an opportunity to do something like that."'

'Oh dear.'

'She wrote me a beautiful letter once. She was away, I don't know why now, and I was with Vi and Don, and she sent me this really descriptive and interesting letter. I was so thrilled I read it over and over.' Jennifer was shocked at how painful the memory was still.

'And?' he asked gently.

'She rang up and asked if I got the letter and I said, "Oh yes." And then she said, "Did you show it to Vi and Don?" And I said, "No." Then she got quite cross and said, "But I went to a lot of trouble over that letter. I expected you to show them."'

'Oh shit, you poor kid.'

'Yeah. I was so thrilled she'd written me such a grown-up, special letter, and then I realised she'd written it to show off to them. Ah well.'

They were silent for a moment, Tony wished

he could find the words to say how much her story had touched him. So different from his own down-to-earth and affectionate mother.

Jennifer changed the subject. 'So what else have you found out?'

'The slick boys are heading to London. Willsy is on Sooty palling around with Gordon, who has been given the use of *Kicking Back*. Needless to say, they have a bevy of women in tow. If I were Rosie I'd be interviewing new assistant managers.'

'Blair and Gordon moving on, are they? Or up?'

'Don't know what's in store for Blair. He does seem to have legitimate ambitions in the hotel industry. Gordon is a playboy. Beats me why he's bothering to work at Branch.'

'His daddy is some bigwig in Reef Resorts, isn't he?'

'Chairman, no less. Though Sir Giles Blake doesn't soil his hands in the actual business. Too busy with his home county pursuits. According to my journo mate in the news bureau over there he has some huge country estate – lakes, woods, private zoo, fabulous art collection.'

'The usual.'

'If you're landed gentry, I guess,' laughed Tony.

'Maybe Gordon is being toughened up out in the colony, or picking up the resort business before going back to be put in charge of the poor old boys on the board,' said Jennifer.

'Quite possibly. Anyway, he's ripping up and down the coast in that monstrous cruiser. I've been spending a bit of time with Lloyd's dad and he's given me some interesting leads,' said Tony with a slight frown.

'Really? About ship building?'

'No, that's not my forte. Heath has mates in the coastguard and customs. There's so much unpatrolled coastline, all kinds of stuff goes on. And I thought sailing in Asia was a worry.'

'You really love sailing, don't you.'

'Yeah, wanted to sail around the world before I ended up covering hot spots. Take pictures, write stories. I still might one day. In the meantime, I'm content to potter around Queensland.'

'Sailing?'

'I've got Lloyd's sloop in my care. In fact, I'm living on it. I'm moored at the marina so I have a base here. Beats a motel. Though Isobel offered me a room at the house she's rented.'

'She's rented a house? Where?'

'Up in Headland Heights, overlooking the bay. Sounds nice. She's got it for six months, apparently. Said she needs a shore base as well as the island. But I'm happy on the boat. She's due any day.'

Jennifer looked at him, thinking Tony was still a private person even though he was tanned and looked more relaxed than when she'd first met him. The pain had faded in his green eyes and he smiled easily and often. His demeanour had softened and he was warm and funny. Jennifer was grateful for his comfortable, easy companionship.

He glanced at her. 'What are you thinking? That I'm a bit of a drifter?'

'Now why do you say that? I was thinking you're a free spirit. And that I'm glad I have you as a friend.' She was thoughtful. 'In fact, I've never had friends like I've made on the island. Mac, Gideon, Isobel, Rosie. You. I wonder if we'd have bonded so much in a normal setting.'

'Maybe not. People have intense relationships under extreme conditions. Not that a luxury resort on an idyllic island is extreme. Well, maybe it is . . . too much unreality.'

'I feel I've come down to earth, that's for sure,' sighed Jennifer.

Tony helped her from the car. 'And you're doing very well. You've changed too. You were so insecure when I first met you. Remember our first meeting and you told me how scared you were, how you'd landed in your worst nightmare?'

'Funny we told each other such intimate stuff when we were strangers on the shore, so to speak.' She tilted her head and studied him.

'Maybe we thought we'd never see each other again.'

'I'm glad that didn't happen.'

'Me too.' Tony seemed about to say something, but picked up the lunch instead. 'Come on, there's a seat over this way. I don't think you're the right shape to sit on the grass.'

'It's getting up that's the problem,' said Jennifer.

Two hours flew by.

'I'd better go. Have to pick Mum up from tennis.'

'How does she manage when you're not

around?' asked Tony as they packed up their picnic.

'Friends. Beverly thinks there's a fellow who's keen on her, but now I'm here she'd rather have me running her around.'

'How come your mother hasn't ever remarried? She's attractive, energetic.'

Jennifer shrugged. 'I wish she had. She dislikes men because of my father, I suppose. I wish she'd get a friend, at least. It makes me feel so guilty and responsible all the time. God, I hope I don't lay trips on my child.'

'We can only do what we think right, with good intentions in our heart. Do you know *The Prophet* by Kahlil Gibran?' said Tony quietly. 'There's a poem in there about children. It talks of you being the bow from which children are sent forth. *Your children are not your children but life's longing for itself. You may house their bodies but not their souls* . . . It's beautiful.'

Jennifer drew a long breath and leaned over and kissed his cheek. 'That's made me feel so much better. Some kind of release. Deep down I already know that while I'm going to love and protect this baby with all my heart, I'll one day have to let it go, with love. Because my mother has never let me go and it's a terrible burden. So, thank you.'

Tony put the basket in the back seat and took out a flat parcel. 'I brought you a sort of present. Just for now.'

'Oh, how sweet of you . . .' Jennifer unwrapped the package and found a framed photograph of

Branch Island looking towards Gideon's shore with the lagoon and the Shark Bar set between the pandanus trees along the beach. 'Wow. This is perfect! Oh, thanks so much, Tony. I can hang it on the wall and lie in bed and imagine I'm back there.'

'You really love that island, don't you?' He smiled.

'I do. And I love the reef, the idea of it. That it's so beautiful and protective and home to such magical life, and it's wrapped around the little island stopping the big seas, the predators.'

'We all need a reef between us and the wide open seas of life.' He laughed. 'Use that in your book. Hey, would you like to go for a sail some time? Just a doddle out of the harbour. A break away from Mum and work?'

'I'd love that! And I love the picture.'

Days later Jennifer was feeling more than 'draggy'. Instinct told her she needed to rest, and she lay in her room, grateful that Christina had to work at the hospital. She had hung Tony's photo of Branch Island – 'Doesn't look like much to me,' said Christina – on her wall so she could see it from her bed. If she closed her eyes she could see blue, feel warmth on her face, hear the birds. Jennifer missed the bird calls. They'd been so loud and active just before she left.

The phone rang and she debated picking up the extension, but was glad she did.

'Darling girl, I am here!'

'Isobel. Wonderful, wonderful. How are you?' Jennifer sat up, feeling better.

'More importantly, how are *you* and the little one? I was worried when I heard you had to stay close to the doctor.'

Jennifer smiled at the musical accent of her friend. 'We're hanging in there, but I'm ready to get this over with.'

'The last month is always a long one. So, what news? You are working? I am renting a big house, ordinary house, but with a lovely garden and fabulous views over the harbour. Do you want to stay with me? I suppose your mother would not like me to take you out of her nest, no.'

'You said it. But thanks for the offer. If I can see you that would be wonderful. Are you going to be around all the time?' Jennifer's heart leapt and her spirits lifted at the thought of being able to see Isobel.

'Of course, my bella. And you have seen Tony? He is being very mysterious. He loves that boat. So, we see each other very soon. I'll tell you all about the conference. Kisses.'

Jennifer smiled, glanced at the photo of the island, curled up in her bed and slept solidly until dinner. She allowed her mother to fuss over the meal which they ate on their laps in front of the TV.

By the following morning Jennifer was out of the house at daylight, walking briskly down to the waterfront, feeling terrific. She hadn't intended to do so but found she was walking past the crowded wharf where the tied-up boats, fuel and food supplies passed for a marina. Most of the boats were battened down and deserted, except for a fishing boat setting out, and Tony sitting on the deck reading the newspaper with a mug of coffee. Jennifer walked along the jetty finger and gave him a hoy.

'Any coffee going?'

'Hey Jen, what a lovely surprise! Come aboard.'

While Tony made fresh coffee Jennifer explored the boat, marvelling at how compact and comfortable it was.

'I don't think I'd squeeze into that small loo up forward in my condition, but I see why you like being here,' she said as they sat in the well of the cockpit watching the sun glint on the buoys, boats and glassy water.

'It forces me to be tidy, everything has its place,' he said. 'I'm afraid my study at home is overrun with books and paperwork.'

'What's your place like?' she asked curiously. 'I've never considered you having a permanent home. I figured you were like me living at the research station, on a boat, wherever, ready to go anywhere in the world at a moment's notice.'

'I've lived on the run for too long. You get tired of hotels. I don't mind it in short bursts, but when I came back from covering wars and seeing damaged and devastated lives and countries, I decided home was the most important thing. So I bought a rambling kind of a joint up the coast, near a beach. For once in my life I did something smart with my money. It's nice to spread out my things, know it's there to go back to and it's a good working base.'

'Who looks after it while you're away? No lady companion? Am I being rude?' asked Jennifer, suddenly thinking she was invading the very private wall he kept around himself.

'No, of course not. I had a relationship or two. They didn't survive my being posted away for such long periods. And I'm still a bit fragile.' He smiled. 'Like you said, having friends who are there but don't make demands has been helpful for me to start to trust again.' He took her cup. 'What about breakfast?'

'I'd better go. Mum will worry if she gets up and finds me gone. I might take some croissants home.'

'Let me drive you back up the hill, walking down is easier. We can go past the bakery.'

Christina was making tea. 'Oh, you've been out. You must be feeling better.'

'Yep. Here's breakfast. I've had coffee with Tony. He's taking me for a sail later today.'

'Do you think that's wise, dear? Don't you get seasick? How big a boat . . . does he know what he's doing?'

'Mum, Tony is the most responsible man I know. I feel totally safe with him. Anyway, what are you doing today?'

Jennifer loved the sail out of the harbour, tacking up the coast for two hours. She tried not to show her initial nerves as they picked up speed and the hull tilted as the sails billowed and the mast leaned towards the sea. Tony gave her a sheet to hold, slacken, and showed her how to fasten it over the cleat. The sound of the sail, the rushing water, made her feel exhilarated, light and free, not cumbersome and eight months pregnant. Sometimes they chatted, sometimes she sat and dreamed as Tony adjusted the sails, and for a while when she stretched out on the padded seat in the stern she fell asleep in the sun.

A day later Jennifer spent a morning with Isobel as she unpacked and spread photos, folders, papers and videos around. They went out for lunch and barely paused for breath as they laughed and talked non-stop.

'Now, what does the doctor say? What is the hospital like and what about baby classes?' demanded Isobel.

Jennifer shrugged. 'I don't know. Guess I'll find out.'

'Jenny, not good enough. Let's go up there and look at the facilities. And you must do some classes so you know exactly what to expect.'

'I'll find out when the times comes.'

'Nonsense. We will go this afternoon. You must get into training. You should have been doing this for weeks and weeks.'

Jennifer rang Beverly and they arranged to meet her on the third floor. Isobel toured the maternity ward like a royal visitor, and they peeped into the delivery room.

'Oh God, it looks like you're going to have limbs cut off,' shuddered Jennifer. 'I don't want such a sterile setting. I wish I could just give birth on the beach.'

'That's not an unusual reaction,' said Beverly. 'Maybe I shouldn't be recommending this, but a lot of women choose home births. If you have an experienced midwife and there aren't complications, it's much nicer.'

'I don't have a home. I mean I couldn't have it in Mum's unit. She'd freak, for a start. She'd never cope with me in pain or anything mucky and medical.'

'A lot of girls use a friend's house –' and before Beverly could say any more Isobel was hugging Jennifer.

'My house . . . it's perfect! There's a big bedroom with a spa and a deck that looks to the ocean. Oh please, please, have your baby there.'

Jennifer looked at Beverly, who grinned and shrugged. 'I know a brilliant midwife. And the hospital is close by. It's up to you to convince your doctor.'

Isobel clapped her hands. 'Wonderful! Let's call him and get everything ready, now. Just in case. I knew there was a reason I came ahead of time.'

The following week she told Tony of her plan.

'Isobel is so generous and her place is fantastic. I've rung mothers who've done home births and I really like Lizzie the midwife. Isobel and I went to a birthing class and I feel really focused now.'

'Well, if you're comfortable with the idea and there are medical emergency facilities on hand or close by . . . What's your mother think? And Blair?' asked Tony.

'I haven't been able to reach Blair, he's in London. I got a message that he'll call me next week. He'll say it's up to me. As for my mother, I haven't dared tell her yet. She'll think it's crazy.'

'More of Isobel's mad influence, I suppose,' said Tony.

'Mum wasn't happy Isobel is coming with me to the childbirth classes. I think Mum feels Isobel is stealing her grandchild from her. But Isobel's been so supportive.'

'Good. So long as you're happy. And your doctor. Well, come on, sailor, let's get on with the sailing lesson.' Tony had started explaining the principles of sailing to Jennifer to put her more at ease in handling the boat.

'I won't tell Mac I'm taking on another project just yet,' she laughed.

Just as Christina was getting more and more tight-lipped over the time Jennifer was spending with Isobel and Tony, Vi and Don arrived. Jennifer was thrilled.

'We went inland and over to Cairns and worked our way down the coast, and here we are.' Vi couldn't get over how healthy and fit Jennifer looked. 'We're booked into the caravan park for two months, so we'll be here for the big day. I'm really excited.'

Vi and Christina were busy in the kitchen. Jennifer and Don stood on the balcony while Don had a quick cigarette.

'I'm so glad you're here. It will be company for Mum and take a bit of pressure off me. I haven't told her I want to go back to the island as soon as I can.'

'You sure she won't come over with us? Vi is dead keen to go,' said Don.

'She has a thing about the island, crossing the water. Like I did,' said Jennifer slowly. 'I can't tell you how I've changed since being here, Don.'

'I can see that, luv. We're sorry to hear about Blair. You sure you two can't get back together, what with the baby and all . . . ?'

'It's fine, Don, really it is. I have such a great group of supportive friends.'

'Christina's talked to Vi. You know how your mum gets a bit jealous. Don't exclude her, pet. This baby means such a lot to her.'

Jennifer sighed. 'I know, and I want her to be the doting granny, but I don't want her smothering us – you know what I mean.'

'I do indeed. We'll try to keep her occupied, showing us around and so on. Though she says her job keeps her busy.'

'It's part time. And she has a man keen on her but she downplays that.'

'To you maybe – she's mentioned him to Vi, but insists she's not getting involved, which is a pity.' They both laughed.

'So what's so funny? Come inside and sit down,' said Christina to Don. 'You can't smoke around my grandchild, you know. I'm not.'

'Our great niece too. My goodness, to think you'll be a grandmother,' said Vi.

Christina fluffed her hair. 'Well, I hope I don't look like one. My friends at the tennis club tell me I seem far too young.'

In an aside to Vi, Jennifer asked, 'Do you miss home? You've been away a long time.'

'I worry, but the neighbours are so good. Don couldn't wait to get away after losing all his birds like that,' said Vi.

'They weren't pets exactly, but I knew every feather on every bird,' said Don with a trace of bitterness.

'No news or any idea where they went?' asked Jennifer.

'Not really. It's not uncommon for private breeders to get raided. There've been some scandals over the years with raids from statutory official bodies taking birds as well as thieves striking. I suppose there are bad eggs in every organisation.' He tried to smile at his pun.

'Don reckons he saw one of his birds in a petshop in Cairns. Never mind, darl, you can start again one day,' said Vi sympathetically.

Don shook his head. 'Nah, wouldn't be the same. Have to do something different. I wouldn't mind getting into tropical fish. My goodness, did we see some wonderful fish in Cairns. Fellow at the pub had an aquarium out the back. Amazing things in it.'

'I think it's better to see them swimming in their natural setting. You wait till you come over to the island,' said Jennifer, glancing at her mother.

Vi continued chatting. 'That man was quite a character, wasn't he, Don? Told us he could get anything we wanted. Heavens, how could we carry tropical fish back to Sydney?'

'What sort of a man?' asked Jennifer, suddenly curious.

'A one-time abalone diver. Said it was too cold, too rough down south and too many big men in grey suits so he went north,' said Don.

'He meant big man-eating sharks,' explained Vi.

Christina shuddered. 'I hate the ocean.'

'Mac loathes the aquarium trade, they're depleting the reef waters too. You guys best come and see the reef while you can.'

Jennifer was asleep when her mobile phone rang late one night.

'It's me. Sorry if I woke you up, I've been busy. How're things?' said Blair.

'Ah, okay. Been a few little problems, but I'm all right. Blair, I wanted to tell you something about Fanzio and Holding. Are you still planning on going into that deal with them? For the clubs?'

'Why?'

'Did you know Branch Island is owned by Gideon, and that he's bequeathed it to the university? There's no way they'd agree to that sports club idea in an environmentally sensitive area. Tony reckons it's a front, a cover for some other scheme.'

There was an intake of breath and she could tell she'd surprised him with this news.

'What kind of scheme? How does he know? Gordon's father runs Reef Resorts International. They know what they're doing. Are you sure about this? Why wouldn't they know about the private ownership? Maybe they've done a separate deal with Gideon. Ask him, let me know asap.' Blair sounded panicky.

'I can't. Gideon is visiting family overseas. Didn't they do their due diligence, or whatever they're supposed to do? Anyway, Tony is on the case, digging around.'

'Where's he getting his info, and why are you telling me this?' He sounded annoyed.

'Blair, despite what's happened between us, I don't want to see you get caught up in some stupid deal. Apparently old Patch has been watching everyone and everything on the island for years. So be careful. When will you be back? I'm going to have a home birth.'

'At your mother's? God, don't expect me to be there.'

'Isobel has rented a lovely house here, and the hospital is just a few minutes away if I need it. I had a bit of an argument with the doctor as I've had a few problems, but it's my decision.' She waited for his input but he brushed it aside.

'Whatever you want. I don't know what my plans are. I'm juggling a job in Switzerland in case Fanzio's clubs don't come off. They have other places round the world they say they're doing business with. Gordon's flying back soon, and Fanzio and Holding are already here for a meeting with the money men. I'll know more after that.'

'I heard Gordon's out on the boat with Willsy and some friends. How can you be involved with people like Willsy? After what he did, remember?'

'Ah, he was probably pissed. People do stupid things. He's all right. He's bringing in high-profile investors.'

'Blair! He nearly killed that girl Rhonda. What if she went to the media? His credibility would get blown out of the water. Leave them alone.'

'She's not going to, she's been paid off. And don't you ever say anything. Be careful, Jennifer, these boys don't mess around,' he cautioned.

This is not the man I married. 'Blair, what's going on? Listen, I'm more concerned about having this baby.'

After Jennifer hung up she got up and found Christina in the kitchen, boiling milk. Christina looked upset. Annoyed.

'That was Blair. He sounded like a stranger. He's changed,' said Jennifer.

'So have you. That woman is having too much say in your life. I couldn't help but hear what you said.' She banged the saucepan and swore under her breath as the milk boiled over.

'No chocolate for me, thanks Mum. And what now?'

'I hope you didn't mean what you said to Blair. About having the baby at that woman's house. You're mad, Jennifer.'

'It's how I want it. And the hospital is five minutes away. Even my doctor says the midwife is excellent.'

'So I've gone to all this trouble and expense setting up a little nursery here for you – I know it's not much – but I thought it would be nice . . .' To Jennifer's horror her mother burst into tears. She put her arms around her.

'Mum, it's lovely. I appreciate all you've done, I really do. I just thought for the actual home birth Isobel's place would be more comfortable, practical. I'll be right back here within a day.' This seemed to placate Christina, or was it the fact that Jennifer had her arms about her in a rare embrace?

Tony had been away for ten days and Jennifer had missed her sailing lesson. When he called her she was anxious to get out on the boat.

'I've been working very hard writing and studying. Plus, I have all the baby stuff done. My mother is not happy about the home birth. Isobel has been down in Sydney. I need an outing.'

'Terrific. I've made quite a lot of headway. When did you want to head out to sea?'

'Tomorrow? Can we make it an all-day thing. I'm feeling so housebound I need fresh air and easy company. The floor here is covered with eggshells.'

He laughed. 'I'll check the weather and lay in stores.'

Tony was running late and apologised as he stowed the supplies on board and readied the boat. As they motored out of the harbour Jennifer went below to put things away. The tiny galley wasn't designed for a pregnant woman, she decided.

When she seemed to be below a long time, Tony stuck his head through the hatch. 'What are you doing?' he called. 'You've been down there for ages. Come on up, we've got dolphins keeping us company on the bow wave.'

Jennifer settled into her favourite seat, cross-legged, nursing the bulk of her belly, lifting her face to the breeze and salt spray. The gentle rocking of the yacht was now familiar and comfortable.

'You all right? Want lunch soon?' called Tony. He glanced at the sky. 'Few clouds building up. Might swing around to a strong nor'easterly for the run home.'

'What's the weather report say?'

'Forgot to check, too busy in the bakery. But

we have all the high-tech gear on board, no worries.'

'I'm not worried. I never imagined I would feel so good on a slip of wood skimming the surface of the sea,' said Jennifer.

They ate lunch. Tony had a cold beer and with the boat hove to they wallowed slightly, the rocking lulling them to sleep as they stretched out in the sun.

Tony woke first, leapt up, glanced at the sky and shook Jennifer. 'Wake up, sailor, we might get wet. Squall on the horizon.' He spoke lightly but he went and checked the instruments and, seeing the rapidly falling barometer, cursed under his breath. 'Pack as much gear away as you can and make sure all hatches are closed tight. In the forward locker there's wet weather gear. Pull it out, just in case. Also, put on the safety vest.'

In minutes the sunny day turned sour and defiant. Jennifer couldn't believe the speed at which the day had deteriorated. She watched Tony's calm, efficient handling of the boat and was determined not to panic.

Wrapped in the plastic gear she heard Tony talking on the radio and her stomach contracted as she saw his face. 'What's up? Is it a storm?'

'Afraid so. Happens in the tropics. Trouble is, we're past the point of no return. Decision time.'

'What's that mean?'

'We're halfway to anywhere . . . it's virtually the same distance back to Headland or to get to the lee of one of the islands. There are a couple this side of Sooty. We can head into the storm, which will slow us down, or keep it behind us and run with it.'

'Whichever is quicker. The island, I suppose. You decide.' She hugged the plastic to her clammy skin.

He gave a quick grin. 'You said you wanted an outing. While we're in radio contact I'll tell the coastguard in Headland what we're doing.'

The sea was no longer benign. The waves blocked sea, sky and horizon in a heaving grey wall of water. The rain lashed sideways in sharp arrows, the boat climbed one wave to be almost airborne before crashing on the other side. Only the tiny storm sail was up, which gave them some steerage and control. Jennifer felt sick and frightened. Tony tried to insist she stay below deck, but he kept the engine running so the bilge pumps would remove the water they were taking on board, and the diesel fumes and bilge smells made her nauseous. She also wanted to watch that he was all right. He clipped a safety harness around her and to the rail, trying to be cheerful.

'With that built-in Mae West you'll float if you go overboard.'

'I hope Lloyd's father renovated this well.'

'We'll be able to give Heath a full report.'

Time was waterlogged. Minutes were measured by getting through and over each wave, avoiding the shifting wind and ignoring the water that streamed across the hull, soaking the deck. At one point there was a crack and Jennifer feared the mast had snapped, but it remained intact, though some rigging had broken. The boat strained but surged forward. Each time Jennifer lifted her head, through blurred wet vision she saw the silhouette of Tony moving, standing, holding the ropes and wheel, heading into a blanket of rain and water. She huddled, hugging her belly, protective and knowing all she could do was trust Tony, the boat and that the elements would not be too savage.

Tony was shouting at her, his voice whipped in the wind, but his arm was pointing. He kept glancing at the small luminous screen charting the bottom banks of coral. Jennifer moved closer to him, inching around in the well, holding on to the railing, cupping her hand behind her ear and signalling.

Tony leaned towards her. 'Look to starboard, there's a line of foam. We're coming in through a channel. The island is through that chunk of white water. I just hope we can navigate our way through without being whipped off course and onto the coral.'

'What island is it?' she shouted.

'It's just a rocky island. Cookshead. Shaped like Captain Cook's hat.'

'Well, at least he didn't leave his head here,' Jennifer tried to joke. 'No hostile natives then.'

'There's nothing here. No water, no trees. Birds, I guess. We'll find shelter and anchor.'

'The wind is dropping. Look, there it is!'

The rain was easing and they saw the thin wedge of paler light between the water and the sky and the dark smudge of the tiny cay. There was a slight bang and crunch and the boat lurched. They were over the rough water and although there was a swell the waves decreased, the mad open sea was behind and they were in a choppy channel.

'We're through, keep a lookout just in case.' Tony dropped the storm sail and engaged the prop, easing the boat slowly forward.

Why did she feel like they'd ridden through a wild night when it was probably only four in the afternoon? 'There, look, a kind of cover under that cliff.'

The small white boat and its weary crew of two eased into the comforting curve of a small cove cut into the coral rock that rose sharp and sheer around them.

'It's deep water here. I'll put out two anchors and extra chain. No wading ashore, I'm afraid.'

'What shore? Captain, that was well done. I salute you.'

Tony touched her wet hair. 'Go below and see if you can find something dry to put on. I have T-shirts and stuff below the main bunk. Don't get sick.'

'I'm not sick, I'm pregnant. But thanks, I will try to dry off. You too.'

'I'll make us a hot toddy. See if I can raise the mainland and let them know we're safe.'

Jennifer, wearing Tony's T-shirt, a pair of his cotton drawstring pants tied under her belly, and a large shirt, sat and sipped the hot coffee with a dash of rum. Tony was on deck and she could hear him trying different radio frequencies.

'No luck,' he said, swinging inside. 'The aerial on the mast has snapped. If I could get on top of the hillside I might be all right with the sat phone.'

'You can't climb up there. What's around the other side? Are we staying here till the storm stops, or what?' Jennifer didn't welcome the idea of going anywhere. She just wanted sunshine and smooth seas.

'I had a close look through the binoculars. There's a bit of a goat's track in the cleft between the two hillsides, above that rocky beach. I reckon I can get ashore in the dinghy and race up and give it a go before it gets dark.'

Jennifer was dubious. 'You told the coastguard we were coming out to an island. They won't be sending search planes or anything, will they?'

'If they don't hear from us by tomorrow's sked the alarms might go off. But with no distress flares or maydays they'll probably figure we made it.'

The realisation of how dangerous the trip had been, and how well Tony had done to get them to this tiny dot, hit Jennifer. 'Did you ever think we weren't going to get in here?'

'Often! Just joking,' said Tony, but she knew he wasn't.

Tony gave her a swift lesson in the communications and how to set off a flare should he not come back from his 'excursion'.

'Are you sure?' she asked for the fifth time.

'Back in a flash, Jen. It's stopped raining. Though it might come in again. Don't move around and trip or topple overboard. The water looks calm but sometimes movement can be unexpected.'

Jennifer had a flash as he spoke. The seventh wave, the unexpected water sweeping all and everyone before it. She shuddered and closed her eyes.

'Are you cold?' asked Tony. 'I won't be long.'

Grabbing the satellite phone, a torch, a knife, binoculars and a length of rope, he unlashed the small rubber dinghy and dropped it over the side as Jennifer held the rope. He clambered onto the transom, into the dinghy, and when the oars were fitted, nodded as she threw him the rope.

'Be careful!'

'Stay below,' he called.

As she waited in the empty boat swinging at anchor, a bruised sunset struggled behind leaden clouds. Jennifer wondered about this speck of rock. Who else had ever been here? Had the intrepid Cook passed in sight of this island as he charted the islands and cays of the Great Barrier Reef? Why was there a track on it? Had some sailor been shipwrecked and gone ashore? Had some animal survived and lived alone? Suddenly wild stories she'd heard in Mac's cottage of wrecks and pirates and outlandish deaths came back to her. The husband and wife washed ashore, he was sitting on a hill on the island believing his wife dead but heard her cries for help only to find she'd been washed into a cave below. The ship's captain beheaded in the rigging as his ship was crushed into a coral outcrop. People who mysteriously disappeared from their boats at sea. The threat of pirates further north. *Oh my God, why am I thinking of all this stuff now?* She peered through the porthole, unable to see Tony or the grey dinghy on the dark shore. The light was fading fast. No romantic sunset this evening.

Was that a flash of light on the hillside? She jumped to her feet, then gasped and froze. Her hands went to her belly. A stabbing, quick spasm. She'd moved awkwardly, she got these muscle cramps every now and then. Cautiously, she moved out of the galley, when it hit again. A rolling, muscular ripple from one side to the other.

It couldn't be.

She waited. Nothing happened. *Thank God. That's all I need.* There was a bang on the side of the hull that made her jump. And again. Jennifer scrambled out onto the deck and found Tony holding the dinghy to the side.

'Quick, take this line.' He flung it up at her and as she fastened it around a cleat, he leapt onto the transom, pulling the dinghy up. 'Get below.' He was curt, concerned.

'What's up?'

'In a minute. Go below.'

Silently she turned and went down the short ladder, but stopped halfway, clutching the handrails as the rippling spasm ran through her again. She sat on the seat bench, holding her belly, looking pale and worried.

'Unbelievable. Never thought I'd want that storm back.' He ran his hands through his hair.

'Why, what's happened? What did you find?'

'Well, the first thing is I was almost knocked over by some creature. Thought it was a man. Turned out to be a flaming emu!'

'What? You're joking!'

'It's been abandoned and so it's looking for a mate. I heard of a couple on Percy Island too. Bloody thing swam out after me. But listen, more seriously, we're not the only boat here. I got to the crest and found there's a bit of a beach on the other side. There're two boats moored.'

'They came in from the storm too?'

'Nah, it's the weather side of the island. They've been busy all day, I'd say. Now all the pieces fit together. Jesus.' He rubbed a hand over his brow.

'What? Who's there? What's happening?' demanded Jennifer.

He reached for the bottle of rum, sloshing a bit into his mug. 'One of the boats is *Kicking Back*. Our dear friends are on the beach transferring cargo to a large sort of inflatable boat.'

'What sort of cargo? Who, the slick boys?'

'No, they wouldn't do any of the hard work, though I bet they're on board. Two fellows I didn't recognise, the other two are Willsy and Gordon.'

'What's in the crates?'

'Animals, I'd say.' He sat down heavily. 'I've been doing some digging based on what Patch told me and a lead Heath gave me. When I was in Cairns I started to fit it together. I just didn't know who was involved or how it worked. I do now.'

He didn't notice Jennifer wince.

'Shouldn't we stop them? Report them? Did the phone work?'

'Badly. Then the battery went flat. I left a message with the coastguard that we were sheltering at an island. I didn't want to shout and alert those turkeys. They're armed for sure. That's big money in those crates and cartons.'

'What kind of animals? What's going on?'

'Wildlife smuggling. Exotic pets. The customs pal of Heath's explained it to me – birds, reptiles, tropical fish, marine samples. They fetch exorbitant prices overseas. They've probably collected them from everywhere and this is the distribution point.'

'My God, my turtle eggs! Is that what they're doing? But who wants them?'

'Collectors mainly. Private zoos, some pet-shops trade illegally. This guy in Cairns told me he could fill any order I wanted. The wildlife we take for granted can fetch thousands of dollars. It's mega business.'

'Why would the slick boys and the rest of them bother? It seems risky, a bit tricky to do even if it *is* big money,' said Jennifer, trying to absorb this information. 'Is this what Patch told you?'

'He told me what he saw, including some rather nasty events. He agreed to put all his stuff on tape – stutter and all.' Tony looked at Jennifer. 'I didn't want you to know about this until I was sure. I didn't know if Blair was implicated and I don't think he is. The boys needed access to the island and this area. They probably had some animals stowed on Branch. No one would have paid attention to extra bird calls.'

'So the club was a front?'

'Yeah. Gordon was on the ground and Willsy worked with him under the guise of hanging out on holiday charters. The animals are drugged and someone hands them over at sea.'

'At sea?' Jennifer was trying not to react to the grabbing pincers in her womb.

'Heath's customs mate said it's generally a freighter registered in China that hooks up with them just outside territorial waters. This is a bigger operation than smuggling some dozy birds or snakes through the post. They have boats that can outrun the coastal patrol. If they're ever spotted.'

'So what can we do?'

'Listen, Jen, this is dangerous. We have to sit tight and hope like hell they don't find out we're here. They'd have no compunction in sinking us, shooting us. I've turned off all the riding lights and the anchor light. We don't want them seeing us if they wander up the hill.'

Jennifer had a flashback of Willsy's temper. She shuddered and gripped her belly. 'My God. So what's going to happen to us?'

'Hope they go and don't see us. Hopefully we can alert the water police and customs before they get too far.' He looked at her face. 'Don't be scared. We'll just wait out the night. Er, are you okay? I know it's a scary business.'

She shook her head No, then nodded Yes.

'What's wrong, Jen?'

'I think I'm going into labour. It's early.' Seeing the horrified expression on Tony's face, she added, 'It might just be a false alarm.'

'We can't wait to find out. Damn this weather.' He slammed his hand down. 'I didn't want to alarm you but there's another front coming in. Could be a rough night.'

'I can't stay here! Can't we sail back?' Jennifer was now sure this was no false alarm, every instinct and fibre in her body was readying her for birth.

'No. It's too dangerous. Are you sure? I mean, it could be a day away, couldn't it?' he asked hopefully.

She shook her head. 'I don't think so. I'm sorry, Tony,' she said tearfully.

Tony raised his eyes. 'I don't believe any of this is happening.'

'So what are we going to do?' asked Jennifer, in a small, frightened voice. 'You ever delivered a baby?'

'No. And I'm not about to start. Can you walk?'

'Of course. Not on water though.'

He gave a brief smile. 'Right then. Here's the plan.'

21

Still Waters

IT WAS ALMOST DARK and the small dinghy was dragged sideways as Tony pulled at the oars. Jennifer watched for a few moments to see him scramble ashore and pull the little rubber boat high on the rocky beach. There was movement and for a moment as she strained in the fading light she was fearful a figure had lunged at him. But it was the wretched emu again, thrilled its new mate had returned. If this wasn't so dangerous it would be funny.

She went below, pushing the items they needed into a canvas bag – the handheld GPS, compass, bottle of water, torch, extra clothing, bucket and a blanket. She left the lifeless sat phone but put Tony's mobile in for when they got back in range. She dumped the bag next to the spare drum of fuel and looked around the comfortable small saloon, wishing she could stay here. The whole idea of taking a small boat to Headland was crazy. But as a firmer contraction hit her, she was reminded that they had little choice. She tightened the stays of her lifejacket.

'Piss off, get away!' hissed Tony, as the emu arched and craned, shoving its beaky head into his chest. There was no way he could creep down to the beach on the other side of the cay accompanied by this leggy companion. With a sudden flash of insight Tony stood on tiptoe and raised his arm straight above his head, his hand cupped like a beak, and waved it. Because he was taller than the emu, the creature crouched submissively, and as Tony made aggressive stabs it hunched away and watched him from a distance.

When he crested the hill he could see a flashlight moving along the beach. There were lights and activity on *Kicking Back* and it appeared all but two of the cartons had been loaded. There was only one man on the beach with the inflatable. Tony had to get to him before he went out to the cruiser. Tony's foot slipped and a small rock rolled down the hillside, but the man on the beach took no notice. He carried one of the cartons to the boat. Tony stood at the edge of the beach, his back to the dark hill. The man, intent on what he was doing, didn't look back. Tony began walking behind him, glad he had a black sweater on, holding the heavy metal torch at his side.

The man heaved the large carton into the boat and then spun around, his back still to Tony, who froze in his tracks. The emu had come over the hill from a different direction from Tony and was loping towards the man at the boat. He'd obviously had a run-in with the bird before as he flung his arms about, shouting at the emu.

'Bugger off! Go on, git the hell . . .' He didn't finish the sentence as the torch slammed into the side of his head with Tony's best forehand.

For an instant Tony and the emu gazed in shock at the man slumped on the sand. Then, adrenalin pumping, Tony stood on his toes and waved his arm above his head once more, this time adding the torch for extra height, and the emu slunk away.

Tony pushed the inflatable into the water and, looking anxiously at the big cruiser, leapt in, fumbling with the motors. The engines roared and the boat jumped forward. Tony steered towards the cruiser, then spun the wheel to one side and the boat swerved, heading across the shallows. Until the tide came in, *Kicking Back* wouldn't be able to get back out to sea. He hoped it would take a few minutes for it to register with the men on board that the inflatable was heading away from them.

He'd cleared the channel, skimming over the breaking waves on the reef, when he heard the crack of a rifle. He hoped they didn't have another power boat on board *Kicking Back* to chase him. Hopefully, they'd head out to sea and not think to go around the island to the cove, but they could get ashore and climb the hill and see Lloyd's boat. In the confusion he just needed enough time to collect Jennifer.

They didn't speak as she handed over the canvas bag and blanket and dragged the small fuel drum to the side as he held the boat. It was dark and she fumbled slightly, feeling sick to her stomach as she backed onto the transom and felt Tony's arms help her into the inflatable.

'My God, it's open. Will we get there in this?'

'It's got big engines. We'll shoot across the top of the waves. Sit in the centre in the middle, wrap that blanket over you, and the plastic tarp there, and hang on to that rope.' He hit the starter motor, gunned the engines, and they shot out of the cove, leaving the silent white sloop bobbing in the dark sea.

In minutes the rain started. 'It'll act as a screen, be hard for them to spot us,' he said.

'What about radar?'

'They won't have the gear on a little boat.'

'Will they catch up with us when they get across the reef?'

'I'd say they'd be too busy heading in the other direction. They'd want to unload that cargo as arranged. Pass me the GPS and compass so I can set our course.'

Jennifer handed him the small devices that

would guide them to Headland. As Tony adjusted direction, a wave sloshed into the boat.

'That's what the bucket is for,' he said.

Jennifer didn't answer as her breath was taken away by a spasm.

At first she kept glancing over her shoulder to reassure herself that Tony was still hunched by the engines, bulky in his lifejacket with a plastic rain cape thrown over his shoulders. Then she just hugged her knees, trying to find a comfortable position to help her get through the contractions. She tried to breathe steadily and deeply as Lizzie had shown her, thinking that each time the pain came it was just a wave to ride over, then she tried to relax in the space between them.

The rain was sheeting across them in gusts and downpours, blocking visibility across the water. Through it all Tony watched her, his heart aching for her, worried they'd not make it in time, praying that no mishap would befall them. He saw her body tense and shrink into itself every time she had a contraction, and he wished he could help her. Damn the sat battery not working.

When the engines ran dry, they wallowed in the troughs of waves, Jennifer gamely bailing out the water from the rain and sea. The rain came in lashing bursts, but the wind wasn't as strong as on their trip over, for which they were grateful. This time they were in a much smaller boat, without protection.

The engines sputtered and Jennifer looked up in alarm.

'The fuel is just running through. Bit of a clog in the line. It'll be right.' He reached over and caressed her cheek. The engines roared back to life, and Tony checked their position and sped into the waves again.

Jennifer was reminded of the surf boats she'd seen taking off from wave to wave, but this had been hours and her body was aching from the hard metal bottom of the boat banging down after each wave. At this rate the baby was going to be shaken out of her.

'How much longer?' she called.

'Not sure. Hang in there. Not long.'

'Are we going in the right direction?' She had a nightmare thought of them going round in circles in the middle of the ocean.

'You bet. Trust me.'

At one point, uncaring and tired, she felt like just lying back, giving herself up to whatever happened. But with the next jolt she sat up, feeling a hit of energy and adrenalin surge through her. Some preservation instinct, a desire to see her child safe, raced through her. This is what drives those mother turtles, she thought. If she fell overboard she'd start swimming for shore too.

Jennifer's eyes were closed, her hand twisted around the rope, her body hunkered down, when Tony touched her shoulder. 'Look.'

Through the streaming rain Jennifer could see a blur of lights. 'Is it Headland?'

'You bet. The main wharf. I'll see if the mobile works.' He dialled Isobel.

'My God, darling! Where are you both? We're all so worried.'

Tony kept it short. 'We're coming into the wharf soon. Can you meet us? She's having the baby, Isobel.'

'Oh God!' Isobel gulped, then was instantly practical. 'Lizzie and I will be waiting. Tell her to keep deep-breathing. It'll be all right. Kisses.'

'Isobel is meeting us. She sends kisses.'

Jennifer grunted and doubled over again.

'What's your mother's number?'

He dialled as Jennifer gave him the numbers. 'Hello, Christina, this is Tony Adams . . . yes, yes, we're fine. We're heading back into Headland. No, it's not really silly at this time of night, Jen is in labour, we're being met at the dock. She's doing fine. Yes, goodbye.'

'Is she in a flap?'

'I didn't give her time to chat. I have to call the coastguard.'

Tony was brief but to the point as he filled in his coastguard contact. 'Well, they'll get the police and customs on to it. Be a circus out there by daybreak.'

Jennifer didn't answer, she was focused on the world inside her.

The tiny figure of Isobel was at the end of the wharf waving a torch, Lizzie had a blanket and was holding an umbrella over them both.

Tony helped Jennifer onto the broad steps, supporting her as her legs wobbled. 'She's still got her sea legs. She's done brilliantly.'

'Why are you in that bathtub and not the yacht?' demanded Isobel.

'It's a long story. I'm dealing with it. Just take care of Jen.'

In Isobel's car Lizzie took Jennifer's pulse and temperature. Her hand rested on Jennifer's belly as a contraction rippled over it.

'Pretty intense. How far apart are they?'

'I wasn't timing them,' gasped Jennifer.

'Well, we'll see how far you're dilated when we get you home. You've done well.'

'Will the baby be all right? It's early,' she asked worriedly.

'Of course it will be,' Lizzie assured her, exchanging a glance with Isobel, who'd been concerned. 'As soon as I can check you both we'll decide if you have to go to the hospital.'

'I hope not. I thought I might be delivering at sea.'

Vi and Don arrived at Christina's, both looking slightly thrown together and excited.

'Come on, Tina, let's go,' said Don.

'We've got plenty of time. Don't rush me. I can't step out the door in my nightgown,' said Christina, who was wandering around, unable to locate her glasses, or clothes.

'Luv, just throw anything on. We have to get up to the hospital. I've been so worried,' said Vi.

'They say first babies take ages,' said Christina.

'Well, if that nice Tony risked coming over in

this storm it must be getting close,' said Vi. 'And it is early. I'm worried. If, God forbid, anything goes wrong, Jenny needs her family there.'

Christina glared at her. 'And what makes you think anything is going to go wrong?' she asked coldly.

Don could see behind the imperious voice that his sister was scared.

'It is early, you know. But she's in good hands now, everything will be fine. It mightn't even come tonight,' he said.

'Now, what do you want to wear, Tina? Let me help you,' Vi threw a look at Don.

'You don't have to treat me like a child, Vi. I can manage, thank you.'

'I'd hate to miss it all,' said Vi.

'Well, you're not going to be *in* there, just in the waiting room,' said Christina, making no effort to hurry.

Warm and dry, with Lizzie monitoring her and the baby's heartbeat, Jennifer began to relax, despite the fierce determination of the infant within her to push into the world.

'Where on earth are Mum and Vi?' she panted, as Isobel wiped a cool facecloth over her forehead.

'On their way. Lizzie has spoken to the doctor and he will stop by soon. You concentrate on helping your beautiful baby.'

Vi and Don hovered by the reception desk in the maternity wing as Christina marched through the hospital looking for a nurse she knew.

'Don, this doesn't seem right. I bet Jenny's gone to Isobel's house as she planned,' said Vi.

'Where's that?'

'Up the hill. I've been there once. I could find it again. Why don't we just go?'

'Wait till Tina comes back. She won't like it if Jenny has done that. And she won't like it if we leave her here.'

By the time the doctor arrived at Isobel's Lizzie had delivered the baby with Isobel supporting Jennifer.

'A girl! Bella, bella, I knew it was!' cried Isobel, hugging Jennifer, who couldn't believe the exquisite infant Lizzie placed at her breast.

'A little light, but sound. Well done, ladies,' commented the doctor, after examining the baby and Jennifer.

'What are you going to call her?' asked Lizzie, making a notation on her file.

Jennifer smiled at Isobel. 'Why, Bella, of course.'

The doctor was leaving the big white bungalow as Don, Vi and Christina hurried up the steps to the verandah.

'Ah, family. Hello, Mrs Campbell. Congratulations.'

'You mean it's *here*? It's all over?'

'Mother and child doing splendidly.'

'So what did she have?' squealed Vi.

'A little girl. She was lucky she got back to dry land when she did. Good evening.'

Jennifer was sleeping as Isobel settled Christina, Vi and Don in the sitting room.

'I'm making Lizzie a pot of coffee. Would you like some, or tea? Or champagne?' asked Isobel.

'Can't we see the baby?' asked Vi.

'Of course. Jennifer is exhausted. More from the trip than the labour. I'll bring Bella out so we don't wake her.'

'Bella? Bella? She's not naming the child that!' exclaimed Christina.

'You mean like Isabella? I think it's pretty,' said Vi.

'It means beautiful in Italian. I think it suits her. She's beautiful,' Isobel said over her shoulder.

She reappeared, holding a small bundle in a pink shawl, and Christina bit back tears. Part of her was angry at Isobel being there and holding her granddaughter before her, but, as Isobel placed Bella in Christina's arms, she could only stare at the sleeping baby in wonder.

Vi cooed and touched the downy head, and Don couldn't stop grinning.

'Careful, Vi, don't wake her up. Hmm, Jennifer did well,' announced Christina.

'She's a jewel,' said Isobel.

'Can I have a hold?' asked Vi as the phone rang.

'That might be Blair. I've been trying to reach him.' Isobel hurried away.

'Shall we just run out the door and steal this precious little thing?' laughed Vi. 'Oh my, oh my.' She planted a kiss on the baby's cheek.

'Now, Vi, be careful. Germs. Give her back to me.' Christina took command. 'The sooner we can get her and Jennifer back home, the sooner we can all look her over.'

'Ooh, she's going to be cuddled and cuddled,' sighed Vi, wishing she'd had children and could luxuriate in being a grandmother.

'Vi, we will not be spoiling this baby,' said Christina firmly. 'And I certainly hope Blair doesn't go along with this Bella business.'

Isobel came back into the room. 'That was Tony, he is very happy and relieved. Seems they had a bit of an adventure out there.' Isobel decided not to spoil the moment with Tony's news about what had happened.

When everyone had left, Isobel tiptoed into Jennifer's room and looked down at the sleeping child in the carry cot next to the bed.

'She's beautiful, isn't she?' Jennifer rolled over, leaning her head on the side of the bed.

'She is, of course,' said Isobel. 'Your family were here. Your mama does not like the name Isabella.'

'It's Bella. She'll have to get used to it,' smiled Jennifer. 'Did you speak to Blair?'

'Not yet. Tony rang. He is very, very happy. And proud of you.'

'Is there any news of *Kicking Back*? Have they caught them?'

'He said they wouldn't know for a few hours. He was very brave doing what he did.'

'Was a bit drastic. I'll have a story to tell Bella about the night she was born.' Jennifer paused. 'Isobel, it was strange. That trip over. I suppose I was hallucinating or out of it a bit, but I kept imagining I was in the water again . . . I kept seeing all these sea creatures, imagining Gideon's fish was there in the boat with me, talking to me. Now what the hell does that mean?' She laughed, but her eyes held questions.

'Who am I to say? Perhaps at times, emotional times, we see things . . . that fish is Gideon, the wise old man. The grandpapa you wish for Bella. Your past is linked to the sea, and so is your future, Jenny. We shall talk about this more. Another time. You still have unanswered questions in your heart.' She reached down as the baby stirred and whimpered and lifted her to Jennifer's arms. 'She is hungry.'

'So am I. My last meal was the picnic on the boat . . . God, how long ago does that seem!'

Finally, scraping over the reef, the *Kicking Back* had made its rendezvous at sea with the rusting, stained old freighter. The transfer of the cartons in a rope sling had been swift if precarious. Gordon had been the one to make the perilous climb up the metal ladder to negotiate payment. Holding, Fanzio and Willsy watched anxiously.

The two crew, one with a sore head, held the

cruiser in position as the two craft wallowed in the swell. Gordon appeared on the deck and gave a thumbs-up.

'Did you check the stuff? Make sure it's pure,' yelled Willsy.

The sling was lowered with large cartons wrapped in plastic.

Gordon climbed back down and jumped onto the deck. 'It's good stuff. No worries, mate,' he mimicked Willsy.

The painter rope was disentangled from the oily freighter and the engines got under way. *Kicking Back* revved up and sped through the dark water the way it had come. The crew were told to remain on deck in the flying bridge. Even with the rush of wind and water they could hear the raised voices. Holding was shouting. Especially at Fanzio.

'Listen, you're in this! All the way. You can't be half bloody pregnant,' yelled Fanzio.

'When we started in on this it was a straight sale of collectible species. Not bloody drug-running and money laundering,' Holding said.

'You weren't knocking back your share of the profits. So you share the risks too.'

'It's too risky. I want my money and out. No more.'

Fanzio stepped away. 'Gordon, get over here.'

'He won't talk, don't worry,' said Gordon in a low voice to Fanzio.

'I'll give him what cash we've got on board as a down-payment. We keep the stuff. But I don't want him to know where it goes. We have to keep him quiet, frighten him a bit so he won't talk,' Fanzio said.

'Get Willsy to rough him up,' said Gordon.

'No, too obvious. Where's that poison stuff you got? Jab him with that. It knocked out that other bloke in the lab, didn't it?'

'Shit, we don't know how strong it is. I thought it'd be worth experimenting with it on animals as a knock-out drug. Untraceable too, as no one knows what it is. Rudi conked out just breathing fumes of it.'

'So, experiment. Shut the bastard up. He's running shit-scared. We don't need this right now.'

'What's happening?' Willsy joined them. 'I don't trust Holding. Is this an act he's bunging on, or is he for real? If he doesn't get his share he'll talk to someone, believe me.'

'Pour drinks, keep him quiet and occupied. Gordon will handle it, won't you?'

The young man shrugged. 'Whatever you say.'

Holding sat cradling his drink, watching Willsy and Fanzio as they opened a box and unwrapped a small parcel of white powder wrapped in thick plastic. Willsy tipped a scoop of the powder into a metal dish over the small flame of a gas bottle.

'Just testing the strength. This will cut down real nice.'

As Holding watched intently, Gordon sat at the table next to him. Holding didn't see the syringe in Gordon's hand until it was too late.

His Scotch went flying as he leapt up, rubbing his arm. 'What the fuck! You're not injecting me with that stuff . . .' His eyes rolled as a wave of nausea hit him and his knees went.

Gordon caught him and laid him on the seat bench. 'Out like a light.'

'For how long? What's in that thing?' asked Willsy.

'Damned if I know. When I heard what happened to that guy at the research station I figured it might be useful,' grinned Gordon. 'So what's the plan now? What do we tell the boys upstairs?'

'Those pricks on Cookshead must've come in by boat. They'll be in Headland by now if they had any kind of navigation gear with them,' said Fanzio. 'We go back to Cookshead, find their boat, put the stuff in it, and you and Willsy take the boat to Branch. If they've notified the cops they'll be looking for this boat. We'll be clean.'

'What about him?' Willsy pointed at the slumped Holding.

'Too much grog, sleeping it off. Or heart attack, or something. See how he goes.'

'I'll tell the boys,' said Willsy.

'You sure you can trust your blokes?' asked Fanzio.

Willsy grinned. 'This isn't their first deal going down. They're greedy. They'll want more. They're sweet.'

Tony hadn't been to bed. His eyes were bloodshot and he was tired as he sat in the small office in the customs shed at the waterfront, listening to the crackling conversation between the patrol boat and the police search and rescue plane.

'There's only one boat in the vicinity they could have made a rendezvous with . . . a freighter. Got Chinese characters on her stern.'

'That'd be the one,' said Tony. 'Where's the cruiser *Kicking Back*?'

'Making for Headland Bay or thereabouts by the look.'

'Get a search warrant. She'll have illegal cargo for sure.'

The customs official looked at Tony. 'That's not easy.'

Very early the next morning Tony rang Rosie and told her about the baby, and all that had happened. 'Sorry to wake you but thought you'd like to know the whole story.'

'Bloody hell,' said Rosie when he'd finished. 'What do I do if any of them lob back in here?'

'Nothing. You know nothing. But I'd tell Patch to keep his head down. They know he's been talking to me. And what he's told me is crucial evidence now.'

When *Kicking Back* made it back to the Headland marina the ambulance Fanzio had called was waiting. Everyone assumed Holding had had a heart attack.

Then lawyers in suits appeared and Fanzio made outraged comments to the media about the 'wild' rumours and 'illegal' search of the company boat during which nothing untoward had been found.

As the weather cleared Tony caught the chopper over to Branch later that morning.

'You look dreadful,' said Rosie.

'No sleep. I'm still chasing loose ends.'

'Listen, grab a room and have a kip. When you're ready we'll have a meal. No one is going anywhere.'

'I have to get Lloyd's boat back. I just hope those bastards didn't sink it.'

'Later. Come on, I'll get my new assistant manager to show you to an empty suite.'

Tony raised an eyebrow. 'Blair has been replaced?'

'Let's say I think he's going on to bigger things. Apparently he made a swift move to distance himself from the slick boys. He must have had a tip-off.'

'Not me. Jen doing the right thing. She'll always have a tie to him.'

When he woke up and pulled back the curtains, Tony saw a brilliant sunset. The storm had passed totally and the lingering clouds made a spectacular show. He showered, borrowed a staff shirt from Doyley and joined Rosie in the bar.

'All my gear is on the boat. Well, here's to Miss Bella. And Jen.'

Rosie clinked glasses. 'Here's to you for a mighty job. By the way, Lloyd's boat is back. Willsy and Gordon sailed her.'

'What? I thought they were on *Kicking Back*?'

'Their story is they were sheltering from the storm at Cookshead. Their launch was stolen, they found the yacht and knew it belonged to Lloyd, so kindly sailed it back over.'

'Oh shit. When did they get here?' Tony leapt to his feet.

'Hours ago. They've moored it round at Gideon's. Why? What's the drama? I thought it was decent of them to bring Lloyd's boat back.'

'I'm not sure, but it doesn't sound kosher to me. I don't trust that Willsy bloke.'

'Willsy is here to unwind, he says. He and Gordon are taking a fishing charter out tomorrow. Business as usual.'

'Where's Patch?'

'Up round his area, I'd say. What's up? You haven't finished your drink.'

Rosie stared in astonishment as Tony bolted from the terrace bar.

He couldn't find Patch and a knot of fear began to tighten in his belly as he raced to the deserted research station. When he couldn't find anyone, he cut through the pisonia trees to Gideon's.

At the Shark Bar, neatly moored in the lagoon, was Lloyd's sloop. On board nothing was out of place. Tony searched the boat, puzzling over the reason Willsy and Gordon had sailed it back.

Obviously they didn't want to be caught on *Kicking Back*, even though by the time the police launch had located it there was no illicit cargo on board. The poor birds and whatever else had probably been dumped overboard or transferred to the freighter.

Tony grabbed his shaving kit and a change of clothes and went back to the resort. He and Rosie had a quiet dinner and when they left the dining room they heard Willsy in the bar, laughing, surrounded by people, ordering more champagne. Gordon was nowhere to be seen. With Blair away he seemed to have no boss and went his own way.

'I wish the gang were back here,' said Tony. 'I wish I could figure out what the hell went down over at Cookshead. I don't want to push Patch but he has given me some damning evidence. Now if I use it, his life could be in danger.'

Tony couldn't sleep. He lay in bed thinking back to this time the previous evening as he and Jennifer had made their dangerous trip back to Headland. What a trooper she'd been. When he thought how scared she'd been of the sea, even a little trip in the resort launch with Lloyd around the island from Gideon's had been such a big deal for her. After last night nothing would daunt Jen.

He began to ponder his feelings for her. He'd been so vulnerable when they'd met, sworn off relationships and needing to heal his heart and psyche. But she'd slipped under his radar. It had been easy to develop their friendship, given the circumstances and the group of people and the fact she was married and off-limits. She was safe. But as her marriage to Blair had disintegrated, their lives and careers had become interwoven, and now they had reached a different plateau.

He had played a small part in a significant moment in her life and he felt even more connected to her. But he was afraid to step forward, make any move or approach, for fear of damaging a friendship that had become precious to him. If this was as good as it got, that would be enough. He was not going to do anything to spoil the easy bond they shared.

Tony was dozing when he heard the tap on his window. He leapt up, pulling back the curtain, and recognised Patch. He slid open the glass door and brought him into the room, but didn't turn on the light.

They spoke in low voices, the old man's stutter worse with nerves.

'Patch, you go and get Rosie. Tell her what you told me. She'll know what to do.'

There was a cool edge to the night air. The moon hadn't risen to its highest point and was obscured by trees. Tony cursed as he stumbled over a sleeping mutton bird.

He slowed as he reached Gideon's compound. The goat was penned, everything looked in its place. Doyley was in charge of the goat, the garden and general maintenance while Gideon was away.

Tony stopped and looked at the sandy garden.

Even in the poor light he could see the scuffed marks in the sand. He had the key from Rosie but he went to the shed where the sharkmobile was neatly wrapped and covered. He stared at it in the light from the dim lightbulb, and saw one end of the cover had a loose tie. He pulled back the canvas and opened the small hatch. Inside the submersible were half a dozen large cartons.

He ripped open the top one and found it filled with plastic bags. He didn't need to open it to know what it held. The white powder was unmistakeable. In exchange for the animals, payment came in this form, Tony surmised. He stepped back, trying to calculate, and gave up. Over a million dollars or more depending on the purity of the powder. How many shipments of innocent creatures had been sold for this? he wondered. There was probably a huge money-laundering scam involved as well.

Who would have thought of searching the premises of the grand old man of the island? Fishing charter be blowed. This was going out tomorrow and would be on the streets of Sydney, Melbourne, Brisbane, in days.

Back at the resort Tony called Bob in Headland, who agreed to pick him up in the chopper at first light. After a few more phone calls he had everything in place to implicate Willsy, Gordon and the slick boys. And he had a hell of a story to write for the paper.

After two days Jennifer couldn't imagine her life without this small child beside her. Already she and Isobel agreed Bella was her own person, wilful, cute, dependent and kissable.

'I want to take her back to the island right now. But I promised Mum . . .'

'Jenny, she is still so tiny, you must keep in touch with the medical people, and you must get strong. Enjoy a couple of weeks' bonding and being with your mother. Make it a healing time. She is a woman in great pain,' said Isobel.

'Yes. But I'm so glad Vi and Don are here as well,' said Jennifer.

Later Jennifer realised how lucky she was those first few days alone with her baby to have Isobel calmly supportive in the background. When Bella refused to breastfeed, Isobel placed her on a pillow and gave Jennifer a small cocktail to relax her, sat and chatted and, before any of them knew it, Bella's rosebud mouth was clamped firmly on her nipple and Jennifer's let-down reflex allowed her milk to flow.

Christina seethed at being a 'visitor' to her daughter but Jennifer insisted she'd been advised not to upset her baby by moving straightaway.

When she did move to Christina's unit, Jennifer was confident and secure. She and Bella had a pact.

Blair rang. He was flying back to Australia. Jennifer assumed it was for the baby till Tony came to make his first visit and filled her in on the news. He arrived with flowers and stood staring at Bella in Jennifer's arms, deeply touched.

'So? What do you think of her?'

'She's just perfect. I'm trying to imagine what she thought about our boat trip.'

'I hope we can take her out sailing when she's bigger, and it's a calm and sunny day,' laughed Jennifer.

'She'll be swimming, sailing and diving before she can walk probably.' He grinned at her. 'Can I take a photo of you both?' After he'd taken several pictures, he sat beside the bed. 'Are you ready for the latest developments?'

'I saw the TV news, what on earth went on?'

'It's been a hectic week. Willsy and Gordon found Lloyd's boat at Cookshead. *Kicking Back* cruised back to Headland to be met by customs, who found nothing on board. Seeming to do a good deed, Willsy and Gordon took Lloyd's boat to Branch and unloaded the drugs at Gideon's. Who'd search his place?'

'But Patch, as usual, stuck his nose in,' said Jennifer.

'It's starting to unravel. I gave the cops the transcripts of all my interviews with Patch.' Tony paused and stroked Bella's tiny, curved, shell-like hand. 'He told me about Willsy and the girl,' he said slowly.

Jennifer stared at him.

Tony went on in a steady voice. 'He saw him attack the red-headed girl from the resort staff and she went to you and Blair. She stayed at your unit, and you got her out the next morning.'

'Poor Rhonda. Oh my God, he saw that? Why didn't he come forward?'

'He was scared. Who'd believe him? And you seemed to have it under control. But it's pretty damaging evidence against Willsy.'

'Rhonda has been paid off so she won't talk,' said Jennifer.

'She will if you and Patch go public. If we need to add that to the case.'

'Well, I'll speak up if I'm needed. I felt terrible about covering it up. I thought maybe it was best for Rhonda, but I hated to see Willsy get away with it.' Jennifer remembered the arrogance of the TV personality. 'Blair is pretty shattered. He's taking the job in Switzerland. What was Gordon's connection with all this?'

'I don't think Daddy knew what he was up to, until late in the piece when Gordon got involved on the ground here with Willsy. Gordon's father has a private zoo and he wanted the wildlife. He was prepared to pay money and unwittingly became part of the network.' Tony stood up. 'Look, don't fret about this. You have more important things to think about. We've done our bit.'

'Well, *you* certainly have. We'll have a tale to tell the gang when they come back, won't we?' She smiled at him.

'Yep. That's a few weeks off. You enjoy Bella. I'm going back home to do some writing. I'm on the email and the phone. I still have work to do.'

'I'll get back to mine when I go back to the

island. Tony, I can't thank you enough . . .' Jennifer faltered.

'Hey, what are friends for?' He opened his arms and gestured towards Jennifer sitting up in bed with her baby sleeping contentedly in her arms. 'This is worth everything.' He leaned down, kissed her cheek and brushed his lips across the baby's head. 'Ciao, Bella. Say goodbye to Don and Vi, they're good people.' To his relief Christina had made herself absent, walking to the shops.

Three weeks passed and Jennifer was so grateful she had friends to break the obsessiveness of her mother. Vi and Don adored the baby, but they couldn't help noting that, while Christina loved showing Bella off at the tennis club and around the local shops, her attention was constantly on Jennifer.

Outings, lunches and breaks away from Christina with Rosie and Beverly, Isobel, and Vi and Don, gave Jennifer great relief. She had Bella in a routine where they'd adjusted to each other, Jennifer fitting in with the baby's sleeping and eating pattern. In between, she tackled her computer, emailing Mac pictures of Bella as well as her redrafted papers.

Sitting on the balcony of her mother's unit while Don had a cigarette downwind, Jennifer told him, 'I'm making arrangements to go back to the island. I have to attend some classes at uni eventually, but I'll move back there. I was thinking of having the baby-naming on Branch. I want you and Vi there. What do you think?'

'We've been looking forward to an island holiday. Bored with the caravan park. But I don't know how your mum will take to the idea. She's been talking about having a party at the RSL . . .'

'No way, Don. All my friends will be back there.'

Don carefully stubbed out his cigarette, waving the smoke away from Bella. 'You do what you think is best and what you want for your little girl. We'll fit in, luv.'

Jennifer waited till the last possible moment to tell Christina of her plans, even though Rosie and Isobel had been working on them for two weeks.

Christina was not impressed. 'I know Don and Vi want to go to that place for a holiday. It's certainly not my cup of tea.'

'Mum, there'll be plenty of people over there. Carmel and Lloyd are back and engaged. The party is for them too. Please come over.'

'We'll see,' said Christina, which meant she had no intention of considering the idea.

Jennifer was packed and, with her doctor's consent, was moving back to the island. Bella was a placid baby, loved people, and was happy to be passed around to strangers like a parcel. Isobel and Gideon were featuring in the media – prompted by a great write-up from Tony as their film had been nominated for a prize in a world documentary festival. Isobel was using the publicity as a means to promote awareness of the dangers facing the Great Barrier Reef.

Rosie had a suite set aside for Vi and Don, who left on the cat for their holiday. Jennifer was taking the chopper over with the baby. Blair had promised to be there for the naming ceremony and, at present, the only unconfirmed participant was Christina.

As Jennifer carried her bags and boxes down to Isobel's car, Christina watched sullenly. Bella was asleep in the carry cot. Jennifer came back and looked around the unit filled with cards, flowers and small toys.

'Well, I guess that's it. I've left the bassinet and some other gear. It's great that's here when we come back over.'

'Oh, and how often will that be?'

'Mum, we'll visit every ten days. At least. Now come on, why don't you come too? It's not a big deal. You'll like it once you're there.'

'I will never set foot on that place in the middle of nowhere. I have no love for the sea, Jennifer,' she said pointedly.

'Mum, I don't want to hurt your feelings, but I want to have Bella's naming ceremony over there.'

'Tosh. Such new-age rubbish. I would like my granddaughter to have a proper christening. In a church. Before Vi and Don go back to Sydney.'

'I guess we can do that too, if you insist. But the Minister who does the marriages is doing it. Rosie has everything arranged.'

Isobel quietly appeared in the doorway and edged into the room, not wanting to interrupt.

'What if Blair doesn't get back from Europe in time?' said Christina in a rush, grasping at reasons to stall Jennifer.

'Mum, that's too bad then. Blair and I are separated. I want him to be involved in Bella's life but we're not going to run things to suit Blair. If he doesn't get there that's his loss.'

Christina caught sight of Isobel waiting in the background to take her daughter and granddaughter away. She spun around and pointed a finger at her. 'This is all *your* doing. Ever since you came along Jennifer has been different! You're brainwashing her.'

Jennifer laughed. 'Mum, don't be ridiculous!'

Isobel took a step forward and said calmly, 'No, your mother is right. You have changed, Jenny. You're not intimidated any more. You're making a life for yourself, finding a passion and a career. You should be proud of her, Christina.'

'I'll decide what I think, thank you very much.'

'Mum, you're just worried about me, that's all.' *And you're jealous of Isobel, you poor, insecure woman.* 'Look, I'm going to be fine without Blair. Things are different than in your day.'

Isobel stepped closer, smiling, placating. 'And look what a good job you did. You raised Jenny on your own.'

At this Christina exploded. 'Because I *had* to! Her father was no good. He just abandoned us. After everything that had happened, he ran away and faked his death . . . and I'm the one who had to struggle on, pick up the pieces, and what credit do *I* get?'

'Wait, wait, stop. What do you mean, Dad faked his death? He drowned, out fishing . . .' Jennifer's face was white and she took a step closer to her mother.

Christina backed away, her face frightened.

Jennifer swung to Isobel. 'What's she saying, Isobel? Make her tell me.'

Christina turned her back, her shoulders shaking.

It was obvious to Isobel that this shocking family secret was a revelation to Jennifer. 'This is the moment to tell your daughter the truth, Christina. It will be better, for you and her, if you do. Jennifer loves you, no matter what,' said Isobel gently.

Christina spun around, her eyes fiery. 'What would you know about my daughter and me? What do you know about the pain and suffering, the struggle, I've had? All these years knowing . . .'

'Knowing what, Mum?' Jennifer's voice was cold. She couldn't forgive her mother for keeping from her this secret. 'What happened to my father?' she shouted.

Christina seemed to shrivel. She twisted her hands together. 'He ran away. Staged the whole drowning thing. Pretended he'd gone fishing and disappeared.'

'How do you know? Just because they never found his body.' Jennifer couldn't bear to think he was out there, living somewhere she could have found him. '*Where is he?*' she shouted.

'I have no idea.'

'Did he try to contact Jennifer?' asked Isobel quietly.

'After some years. After I'd been to hell and back trying to make ends meet. Feeling guilty that he'd killed himself. I lost a son, too, you know,' she snapped at Isobel.

'Mum, why didn't you tell me?' Jennifer was bewildered.

'That he had done such a terrible thing? Been such a coward? All very well saying he was sorry and he wasn't coming back, but tell her I'm all right and I'll see her one day. What good is that?'

'One day? When? Where did he go?' cried Jennifer. 'How come he let us suffer so much? How could he do it? Why? What did he say to you before he went? Did you have a fight? What?' *He was running away from you! Not me.*

'Don't you dare blame me, Jennifer. How do you think I felt losing darling Teddy? It was your father's fault. He should never have let you go on those rocks.'

'Mum, how do you think he must have felt? He blamed himself too!'

'So Christina, you had no support, no money and no life as long as he was out there somewhere. Did you know where he was? He didn't tell you how to reach him?' asked Isobel, incredulously. 'Did he have any money?'

'Of course not. I don't care how he managed.

We had a useless farm, he wasn't much good at anything. He just made my life miserable, but was I going to go to the police? No. The shame of it. They wouldn't find him and what was I going to do? Force him to come back and look after us? Make him love us?' Christina shook her head. 'No, it was better to think he was dead. To me, he was.'

'But what about me, Mum? All the years I wanted a father, needed him. He's Bella's grand-father, for God's sake!'

'He doesn't deserve to be.' Tears streamed down Christina's face. 'I was the one who raised you, looked after you, made a home and a life for you. I tried so hard . . .' She began weeping, her face in her hands.

Isobel signalled Jennifer to go to her. But for a moment Jennifer couldn't move. Anger, hurt, frus-tration welled in her at the overwhelming knowledge her father was probably still alive. All the years they'd lost.

Isobel's voice broke into her thoughts. 'Jenny, think if it had been you. Remember back to how it was for your mother . . . maybe you would do things differently. But she did what she thought was best . . . for you.'

Jennifer held her mother and they both cried. Then Bella whimpered and Jennifer broke away to take her baby in her arms. She looked down at the small child with trembling mouth and trusting eyes. There would never be secrets between them. Silently she pledged always to be honest with her daughter.

'I'm sorry, Jen-Jen,' whispered Christina as she found a tissue and dabbed at her eyes. 'You go now. I'll be all right.'

Jennifer heard the edge of self-pity in her mother's voice, it had always been there and always would be. *I'm not staying, Mum. I will love you and share my daughter and my life with you. But I'm leading my life my way.*

'I'm going to the island, Mum. It's your decision whether you come over or not. Whatever you decide, we won't love you any less. You call me tomorrow and let me know.' Jennifer fled.

Isobel pulled the car up at the wharf and they sat looking at the water and the activity as Jennifer fed the baby.

'What are you going to do? About your father.' asked Isobel quietly.

'I don't know. I'm in shock.'

'It was a foolish, awful thing to do. But think of the pain he's lived with all these years.'

Jennifer looked at Isobel. 'Do you think so? Or did he move on, have another family and never wonder about me. That's what's so hurtful. Did he ever remember my birthday, wonder how I did at school, what became of me?'

'I think if he did try to contact you early on Christina would have fobbed him off. She wanted you all to herself. She knew he was alive and perhaps that's a reason she's never thought of remarrying. It's her way of paying him back. To punish him. He sounds a weak, soft kind of man. He wouldn't have fought Christina,' said Isobel.

'He knows Mum would have poisoned me against him. She's never made me feel proud of him, ever. But I remember good times. I loved him, Isobel. He was my father. And now I feel like hating him for this. I wish he *was* dead.' The tears came again, splashing onto Bella's soft hair. 'He probably has another family and forgot Mum and me.'

'In your heart you never forget your child. Come on, Bob is waiting to fly you back.' Isobel started the car, her heart aching for Jennifer. At some stage Jennifer would need to address this issue. She might have half siblings, another family somewhere. A family who might not know this history. It was not fair to deny Bella the chance to know her paternal connections. Poor Jennifer. Poor Christina. For a moment Isobel felt guilty that it was she who'd inadvertently pushed Christina into spilling her secret. But she hoped that now it was out in the open Jennifer and Christina would come to a better understanding of each other. She was happy Jennifer had asked her to be Bella's godmother – it meant she would always be close to them and able to help and watch over Jennifer and her beautiful Bella.

Epilogue
Branch Island, Five Months Later

IT WAS DAWN. DOORWAY to the day. It was a time Jennifer cherished on her morning walk. It reminded her of a watercolour painting, all soft, runny colours. But now she shared it with Bella. Snug in her piccaninny pack on her mother's back she cooed and sucked her fingers.

This bright morning Jennifer went through the pisonia trees, scattering noddy terns and seagulls and a swooping grey heron that appeared to delight Bella. Past Coral Point she saw a figure sitting in the lee of the wind, looking to sea. Poor old Patch, he still kept his distance but he seemed to have recovered from the blaze of publicity he'd triggered over the revelations in the press about Willsy. Rhonda had bravely told what happened, including being paid not to speak out.

It was just one of the stories to come out of the exposure of the wildlife being smuggled out of the country and sold for drugs to an international syndicate with the help of various officials. Branch Island, described as the sleepy island with a small and exclusive resort, had been the focus of major media though implications that the owners of the resort in the UK were involved in the illegal operations had been hosed down. Nevertheless, Gordon and his father were no longer part of the company. The chairman's desire to add to his private zoo was a bit too hot for comfort. Investigations and charges were still pending as legal teams, police and officials circled.

The positive stories had dominated – Mac's team at the research station and their work to save the Great Barrier Reef. Isobel and Gideon's film had caught everyone's imagination as to what beauty and mystery there was in the deep ocean, and the need to research it responsibly. Rudi's work had expanded into medical and energy sources, and he had gained an adjunct position with the university as well as working for a large non-government corporation to advance his research.

But for Jennifer it was past history. She had her future to think about. And now so many options were open to her. She was undecided about tracing her father. She put the idea on the back burner.

She could smell the coffee as she passed the

goat tethered in its patch. 'You're the only goat allowed to live in a National Park, I reckon,' she said. 'Maybe we should go back to Cookshead and rescue that poor old emu to keep you company. What do you think, Bella?'

'Good morning, ladies. How is my god-daughter this fine morning?' Gideon lifted Bella up and hugged her.

'Morning, Gideon. Ah, we have company. Mac, you're up early.' Jennifer sat down and stretched her legs.

'Planning the day, taking time out before the invasion,' he smiled.

'It's going to be quite a celebration, isn't it? I still can't believe I've done it. First-class honours, a scholarship, two job offers.' Jennifer shook her head. 'Who says sitting on an island is a cop-out? I've never worked so hard in all my life.'

'You deserve it. You can work with Isobel, take up a position with our university, or continue to write and research. Now the whole world wants to read that book you and Tony did together.'

'Yeah, well, I hadn't quite anticipated the end turning into a thriller,' she laughed, then said softly, 'I couldn't have done it without you, Mac.'

'Yes, you could've. You just needed someone to crack the whip occasionally. I think Bella's fairy godmother helped too.'

'Isobel? She sure did. I can't wait to see her. She says she's bringing back a pile of presents from Brazil . . . she spoils Bella dreadfully.'

'Rosie is going overboard with the wedding for Lloyd and Carmel. Her family are all coming. We're being overrun by South Americans!'

'Tony offered to take photographs. He'll be busy. Did you see the gorgeous photos of Bella he took?'

'I did. That man has a sensitive eye, all right,' said Mac.

Gideon joined them, handing around mugs of coffee. 'And a good eye for boats. We've finally found one that suits him. A small schooner with a romantic South Seas history. He's sailing it over for the festivities.'

'Is that what you've been up to? I wondered where you went,' grinned Jennifer. 'How exciting. He misses using Lloyd's boat.'

'Well, Lloyd and Carmel are going off in it on their honeymoon. Not telling anyone where.'

'And will there be a toast to our successful new PhD candidate during all this partying?' Gideon lifted his mug. 'To you, Jennifer.'

They clinked mugs and looked at Bella on the rug at their feet, happily sucking a sandy finger. 'And to baby Bella.'

The last of the flowers, scattered over the water as the honeymooners sailed away, had drifted to other shores or fluttered onto drifts of seaweed and coral below. The wedding visitors had left. Families had come together and gone their separate ways. Blair had marvelled at his exquisite daughter and returned to Switzerland. Jennifer had agreed to bring Bella to see him.

Christina had never visited the island but with Vi and Don back in Sydney she was planning trips 'down south'. Still she couldn't be away too long from her adored granddaughter. Tourists were settling into the tranquil rhythm of Branch Island. The birds and turtles continued their cycle of life on this particular part of the reef.

Mac had new students gathered in his cottage to hear Isobel give an impassioned talk about her work. They listened transfixed, taking no notice of the baby, who played with a toy on the rug on the floor.

Tony ran his hands along the bow of the old white schooner. '*White Lady*, she's got quite a history. She's led a colourful life. I feel privileged to own her.'

'Treat her with respect and she'll give you years of pleasure and loyal service,' said Gideon. 'A coat of paint and a touch-up here and there is in order too.'

'I'm thinking of asking Jen to write the story of *White Lady* as a book. In between everything else she has going!' Tony laughed.

'And it's a reason to . . . what's the word . . . collaborate?' said Gideon, lifting a quizzical eyebrow.

'Indeed, wise man that you are. Jen and Bella are very special to me.'

'When you feel the time is right, tell her so,' said Gideon softly. 'You'll know when.'

'Your island has been good to us,' said Tony. 'It's changed us, given us all a new way forward.'

Gideon was thoughtful. 'Sometimes you need time to sit on an island and reflect on what is important, where your life is going. I made my choice a long time ago.'

Tony looked across the aqua lagoon, past the white curl of the breakers on the reef to the silken dark blue sea. 'It's just a matter of charting a way through the reef into calm waters, isn't it?'

'Ah,' sighed the old man. 'We need those reefs in our life. And this is the beginning of what we're finding.'

Deeper and deeper still she glided through the translucent water. Clouds of curious neon-coloured fish swarmed before her face. A rose and yellow coral wall slid down to greener depths. Lazily, an enormous yellow-spotted blue Maori wrasse cruised past, its massive mouth closed in a benign expression. Manta rays performing their own ballet sailed above her. In the underwater forest she was dwarfed, threading her way through the fleshy waving tangle of seaweed arms reaching to sunlight.

In a stretch of clear water she felt she was flying through the sky. A flick and a shark was there, and gone, minding its own business.

Across the seagrass meadows of waving gold, to a ledge where anemones clung with the soft corals protecting their beautiful but poisonous residents, a starry reef eel slithered and a fat red emperor held its mouth open for cleaner fish to dart in and clean its mouth and teeth. The tiny blue fish swimming in and out of the predatory jaws had read the signals: they were safe until their job was done.

And in the shimmery distant water, did she glimpse for a moment or two the soft human shapes of a boy and girl? Holding hands, swimming together, at home and at peace in the warm kind waters of the reef and its world. So different from the turbulent coastal seas and a rocky ledge where waves had snatched a family's joy, children's dreams and a mother's hope.

Upwards, bubbles hissing from a breath, she broke through the surface. A hand reached down and helped her swing onto the ladder, and she pulled herself up as water streamed off her red wetsuit and silver airtanks. Jennifer pushed her mask back on her head, took out her mouthpiece and snapped the straps as Tony lifted the tanks from her back.

'Was it bella, bella?' he asked gently.

'Very. I never believed I would be able to experience, to really feel part of that world . . . down there.' She dropped her flippers on the deck and gazed down into the water. 'I'll keep doing this. But right now, at this moment, I feel a chapter has come to an end.'

Tony leaned over and kissed her salty wet lips. 'There will be plenty of time to begin other stories.'

It lay dead and white in the palm of her hand. The ancient shell she'd found in her father's field one day. Jennifer picked her way across the reef flat to the rim of deep water. The tide would soon turn back towards the island. She drew a breath and fell forward into the startling blue, kicking down, her arms pulling her towards the rocky ledge she'd seen from the surface. She saw a clump of pink branching coral nestled in the arms of seagrass and so she placed the fossil between them. As she thrust her body back to the surface she liked to think the limestone that had frozen the small shell in time would re-form, that grains of coral sand would support the tiny creatures in rebuilding, continuing the reef's cycle of life.

Her head rose from the crystal water. The sun was shining.

THE END

Di Morrissey
Barra Creek

In the wild Gulf country of northwestern Queensland,
there's a cattle station – Barra Creek – on a tributary
of the crocodile-infested Norman River.

It's 1963 and Sally Mitchell, the well-bred daughter of
a wealthy New Zealand sheep farmer, is on her way
to England with her friend Pru. When the young
women stop over in Sydney their plans go awry. Sally
impulsively takes a job as a governess at Barra
Creek, and when the mail plane that flew her there
takes off she finds herself left in a different world.
One dominated by the overpowering John Monroe
and his strict and proper wife Lorna.

Here Sally's life changes forever. The challenges of
coping with her three young charges, wild stockmen,
the heat and the Wet, brumby musters and cattle
rushes all pale beside a great passion, a great loss
and a gruesome death.

Only Lorna knows the truth of the death and of a
terrible injustice. Now, in 2003, she searches for the
former governess to finally set things right and share
her horrific secret.

Di Morrissey
Kimberley Sun

The remote town of Broome, the desert and the
Kimberley coast – Australia's last frontier and a land
of ancient beauty – are the backdrop for *Kimberley
Sun*, the sequel to Di Morrissey's international best-
seller, *Tears of the Moon*.

Lily Barton, now 53, is beautiful, adventurous and
looking for a life change. Sami, her daughter, is
driving alone through the outback to finally,
reluctantly confront her family roots. Together they
are swept into a world where myths and reality
converge, as they find that everyone they meet has a
story to tell. From Farouz, the son of an Afghan
camel driver, Bobby, the Chinese-Aboriginal man
who is tangled up in the murder of a German tourist,
to Biddy, the survivor from Captain Tyndall and
Olivia's era . . . and who is the mysterious artist
hiding in the desert?

All have a secret and a story to share as each finds
their place under the Kimberley sun . . .

Di Morrissey
The Bay

The Bay is a peaceful town on the Australian east coast; a melting pot of city escapees, alternative lifestylers, lost souls, and men and women in search of a new sense of identity.

When Sydney corporate wife Holy Jamieson turns forty-five she shocks her husband by buying an old house in The Bay with plans to transform it into a B & B. This gesture of independence soon changes her life. The Bay was once a whaling town, then a sleepy resort that became trendy, and now developers are moving in for the kill. Holly, her family, and an unusual band of friends are in the battle lines – and not always on the same side.

The Bay captures the atmosphere of a unique place and its people so you can feel that you are there.

Di Morrissey
Blaze

BLAZE exposes the new order of women and power in the cutthroat arena of up-market magazines. The idealistic baby boomers have been pushed aside and it's every woman for herself.

Ali Gruber, 28, is slick, smart, ambitious. She is determined to be editor of the New York edition of BLAZE, the world's most popular magazine. But fate intervenes, taking her back to the secret of her Australian childhood.

Nina Jansous, 60, is the founder of BLAZE. Croatian-born and Australian-raised, the elegant Nina is haunted by memories of the past.

Larissa Kelly, 35, has everything – a prestigious career and a loving man. But can the relationship survive when he's a stockbroker in Greenwich Village and she's been posted to BLAZE's new magazine in Sydney.

Miche Bannister, 22, wants to be a journalist and follow in her late mother's footsteps. In Paris, Miche infiltrates the life of supermodel Jessica Shaw and finds a murky world of drugs and sexual abuse. Should she reveal what she uncovers when faced with her mother's nemesis?

BLAZE is an intimate look at four women coping with their private and public lives in the world of magazines.

Absorbing. Biting. Funny. Real.

Di Morrissey
Scatter the Stars

A mesmerising novel of the film industry and one man's life that charts a path for all of us.

Larrikin Australian actor Randy Storm had it all. Swept up by Hollywood in the 1950s he had the looks, charm and talent to take on the world. But by the 1990s he's forgotten, burned out after a life of movie star excess.

When producer Michael Matthews meets the once great Randy Storm, he is surprised to find a man who is at peace with himself. Both he and researcher Janie Callendar set out to discover the source of this inner peace. Meanwhile his agent Ariel Margoles finds out that Australia's world acclaimed film director Patricia Jordan is making the hottest Hollywood film of the year and she sees a chance for Randy to be a star once more.

But just as Randy is about to reach his pinnacle, a secret from his past threatens to bring down his greatest triumph . . .